A History of Facelifting

PRAISE FOR DUNCAN FALLOWELL'S WRITING:

Satyrday

'Mordant, energetic and outrageous' – Camille Paglia

'Something for the 21st century' – Graham Greene

The Underbelly

'The author's pose and prose is that of dandy as cosh-boy . . . the writing attains a sort of frenzied detachment found in the drawings of Steadman or Scarfe' – Chris Petit, *The Times*

'Dudley Dennis is the most repulsive and terrifying fictional creation I have come across for years . . . What redeems the book, and even its author's extremely unpleasant imagination, is the fierce honesty of it' – Bernard Levin, *Sunday Times*

To Noto

'Witty, wicked . . . this extraordinary marriage of super-refined aesthetics and ballsy carefree-cum-frenetic jumpy showing off somehow manages to work' – Adam Nicolson, *Sunday Times*

'In a class of its own. Completely honest, deadpan, funny and shrewdly intelligent . . . a journey you will never forget' – William Boyd

One Hot Summer in St Petersburg

'An absolute knockout. Brilliant, passionate and very alarming . . . as exhilarating on St Petersburg as Isherwood's writings on Berlin . . . candour of every kind . . . It has everything' – Michael Ratcliffe, Books of the Year, *Observer*

'The best book so far about the latest incarnation of this endlessly reinvented city' – Michael Dibdin, Books of the Year, *Independent on Sunday*

Twentieth Century Characters

'Vivid, reflective, haunting . . . and very funny . . . like Aubrey's *Brief Lives* in twentieth-century accents . . . a rich, energetic frivolity and passionate curiosity about human types' – Richard Davenport-Hines, *Times Literary Supplement*

'An irresistible collection by a master miniaturist' – Selina Hastings, Books of the Year, *Daily Telegraph*

A History of Facelifting

a novel
by

Duncan Fallowell

A

ARCADIA BOOKS
LONDON

Arcadia Books Ltd
15–16 Nassau Street
London W1W 7AB
www.arcadiabooks.co.uk

First published in the United Kingdom 2003
Copyright © Duncan Fallowell 2003

A catalogue record for this book is available from the British Library.

ISBN 1–900850–79–6

Typeset in Ehrhardt by Northern Phototypesetting Co. Ltd, Bolton
Printed in the United Kingdom by Bell & Bain, Glasgow

Arcadia Books distributors are as follows:

in the UK and elsewhere in Europe:
Turnaround Publishers Services
Unit 3, Olympia Trading Estate
Coburg Road
London N22 6TZ

in the USA and Canada:
Consortium Book Sales and Distribution
1045 Westgate Drive
St Paul, MN 55114-1065

in Australia:
Tower Books
PO Box 213
Brookvale, NSW 2100

in New Zealand:
Addenda
Box 78224
Grey Lynn
Auckland

in South Africa:
Quartet Sales and Marketing
PO Box 1218
Northcliffe
Johannesburg 2115

Arcadia Books: Sunday Times Small Publisher of the Year 2002/2003

Duncan Fallowell is the author of two previous novels, *Satyrday* and *The Underbelly*; two travel books, *To Noto* and *One Hot Summer in St Petersburg*; the biography of the transsexual April Ashley; and a collection of profiles, *Twentieth Century Characters*. He lives in London.

To Bunny

Part One
AUTUMN

1.

The city was very hot. She had to get out of it.

2.

It was a little after nine p.m. when she left. The heat and noise had abated somewhat and the late August dusk was spreading a cloak in which she could hide. At first she hugged the slow lane and every vehicle overtook her. Roadworks appeared. The traffic contracted. She contracted. The roadworks came to an end. The traffic expanded and her stomach relaxed and she picked up speed, moving into the middle lane, trying to think of nothing, shutting out everything except the road in front which led away from the centre, away from the prison of walls and streets and associations, away from the source of her pain. Tension sat across her hunched shoulders like a wooden yoke but, despite her awful posture and locked head, something fresh did intrude as she left the core of the city behind. For the first time in God knows how long she smelt – already, even in this untidy suburb – a whiff of vegetation cutting through the polluted atmosphere.

August had been exceptionally hot. So had July. In fact from the middle of June the sun had shone relentlessly and the heat had tightened a choking grip on the brick, cement and tarmac of London. As she loaded the car, an acquaintance several doors away had been dining with a new girlfriend on his balcony where between the trunks of plane trees the couple could view the flyover and be serenaded by the pulsing drone of its traffic. She'd paused and looked up at them in their eyrie of romance and said 'I'm disappearing'.

The couple nodded and smiled. 'Where to?' asked the male acquaintance.

'Far away.'

'You're not staying for the carnival then?'

'No.'

'Good luck.'

The hum of the car and the slowly falling temperature eased her anxiety. At ten p.m. she switched on the radio. Interest rates had come down. More race riots across the Midlands. The Foreign Secretary was being forthright in Europe. Thousands of people in East Africa were dying from an outbreak of the geekola virus. Followed by the cricket scores. A motorway slid gently upwards. Its central thread of anorexic standard lamps poured out a colourless light which rendered black every window in the buildings which still bordered the road on both sides. To the left, blue signs came and went, indicating various congested options in the Home Counties, but she was going much further on. Passing overhead, a pylon line sizzled the FM signal. She turned the radio off, driving on in a soft roar of rubber, hypnotised by the urgency of escape.

The lamps came to an end and there was darkness. A rush of light around a group of hypermarkets – but darkness fell again like a plush curtain. The car sped through a cut in upland chalk and beyond it the landscape could be sensed opening hugely ahead. It glimmered mysteriously rural under the last streaks of twilight in the west, and through it the motorway, which was surprisingly busy, stretched an enormous distance. On her side of the road warm red lights were moving with her. On the opposite side hard yellow lights moved against her. At the next blue sign she veered off the motorway and took a quiet road which turned into a by-pass skirting an ancient university town. The venerable accumulation of turrets and pediments, domes and spires, floated by on the left absorbed in its own magnificence, subtly aglow. Several roundabouts pulled her in and flung her out, followed by a period of steady driving.

When a twenty-four-hour petrol station came upon her in a scarlet glare, she pulled over. Petrol gurgled, its perfume flamboyant, and inside the shop the cashier tore off the credit card print-out and asked 'Do you want stamps?'

'No thanks.'
'Premier points?'
'No.'
'Are you on airmiles?'
'Nope. Have you got any eggs?'
'Down on the right. Next to the chocolate.'
'Free-range?'
'Does it say on the box?'
'No.'
'VAT receipt?'
'No thanks.'
'We're giving away free tennis balls this month.'
'I'll have some milk please.'

The road began to undulate between trees, between fields, by-passing stone villages. Locals returning from pubs overtook each other with madcap confidence. Cat's eyes sparkled away down the spine of the road and into a curling mist, drawing her car – a bubble of reality flying through voids – as on a wire. The mist grew worryingly thick as the road descended into a broad valley but the wire took her safely into a Regency spa town where wrought-iron balconies swagged the streets with a dandyish gaiety. Groups of young people hovered in lamplight at intersections, wondering where to go next. She wound up the window. By the time the countryside took over again she had been driving for almost three hours.

As the night deepened so did her spaciousness. The moon was cream in a surrounding slush of peach light above a slumbering realm of timbered farms and lanes. The tang of vegetation had acquired a shiver of wildness. Ever increasing was the number of creatures killed by traffic which showed up in the hurrying scoop of her headlights, things squashed or torn or flattened, images of death, strangely beautiful, one after another. On she sped with bloody tyres. No other traffic now. None.

She tried the radio again. The shipping forecast, followed by Big Ben at midnight: *This is John Hughes with the BBC News from London. Following the departure of the Foreign Secretary from the European Assembly, it was the Minister of Power in Brussels today who spoke of the need to –* her heart and skin contracted icily and she switched it off. Simultaneously an electric rhinoceros charged out of the inky night. It was massive and made a terrifying din. She swerved, braked, bumped along the side of the road, came to a halt, supported her ringing head on the steering-wheel. Moments later she was walking up and down the road cursing lorries. As her eyes adjusted to the darkness, the outline of capricious hills showed against a starry sky. The moon had gone. The landscape was alien and horned. A trembling came upon her. Back at the car she fumbled in the boot, found a bottle of Scotch and took a slug. As always, the taste nauseated her. A rustling sound in the hedge made her jump but nothing came of it and when the shaking did subside a dead feeling settled over her. For too long life had been a battle against the dead feeling or the terrified feeling. When the man had asked which kind of feeling she preferred, her thoughts had fluttered uncontrollably and she couldn't breathe.

She studied the map and took minor roads which twisted in numerous curves. At one a.m. she halted in the small square of an empty and silent village. The crackle was noisy as she unpeeled a Mars Bar, followed by mooselike motions of her jaw, followed by – which was something she had never before done in her life – a long messy drink from the box of milk. She dabbed her chin carefully with a tissue before getting out to stretch her legs. Lampposts, hung with baskets of red geraniums, blazed triumphantly but not a single light was to be seen anywhere else. Even the pub was dark and dead, and with a little lifeless laugh she noticed it was called The Basilisk. It was as though the village had been evacuated by a catastrophe.

'Come on, you,' she urged herself aloud.

It began to spot with rain, a few large slimy drops falling through the clammy air, the first rain in ages. The road would be slippery. She revved up and drove on. Her bare arm, out of the window, loved the chill collisions with raindrops. The sense of relief was delicious. Obscure taut threads gave way within. But as she moved into fifth gear, an animal must have shot across the road. She both felt and heard the impact, and some kind of liquid spurted onto the windscreen. She shouted 'Hell!' and drove on. Having killed, she felt less dead.

For a long time there was nothing but herself on the softly pitching swell of the black earth. And suddenly she was there, had glimpsed the sign. Not believing it, she reversed the car and checked the nameplate screwed to a pair of metal posts at the roadside. Stamped in plain black letters were two words: Milking Magna. No other particular indicated that she had reached a place for, as far as she could make out through the dark veil of rain, there were only more trees, more hedges, more fields. She took a hand-drawn map out of an envelope, scrutinised it, and drove on.

After a mile or so the road tipped into a steep decline which ended in smudges of light and a stone bridge over a muttering river. Crossing the bridge, the car proceeded up a graceful curve. This was Milking Magna's principal thoroughfare. Gables and porches stooped secretively together on either side of a broad cobbled way whose gradient was relatively shallow and veered leftwards. Here and there more substantial buildings spread their wings. A dog sat laconically in a shop doorway and watched her go by. Life at last, she thought.

Halfway up, the High Street opened into a small village-green spiked with what looked like a war memorial. The outlines of an inn called The Zodiac rambled along a terrace. At the top a towered church, amid several packs of gravestones, created a T-junction and a forum-like space with the green and street below. She referred to her instructions: *Turn right at the church – take the road out of the village for about three-quarters of a mile – the hedgerow on the left stops at a clump of oaks and a track – drive up the track as far as you can.* Which she did, eventually stopping at a wooden latch-gate. Through the transverse rain, she stared at her destination – which resembled not at all the picture she had formed of it. Neither better nor worse, it was simply in every respect otherwise.

The cottage stared back at her. Its steep roof was wonky and patched with moss and a chimney stack perched precariously at either end. Sash windows with small panes of glass were arranged round a low door but an arc of bricks above each lintel lifted the expression of the front. Some minutes passed while she tried and failed to comprehend that this was her new home. Subdued by

an awful wave of loneliness she groped for a torch in the glove
compartment and when at last she forced herself from the car,
stepped directly into a muddy puddle and said 'Shit'. An owl
hooted in response and clattered out of a nearby tree. Her
instructions stated: *Key under stone to right of porch* but she broke
a fingernail looking without finding among the various large
stones and swore again, tired, dry-throated, tearful. Some sort of
animal dung defiled the front step. Rain wetted her face. All life
was damp, smelly, vindictive, absurd. And no fucking key! But
the front door when she tried it was unlocked.

A warmth, surprising after the cold rain, exhaled gently
through the crinoline-wide doorway from the darkness inside.
She paused on the threshold, swinging the beam of the torch in
broad sweeps, and as she did so it was as though the musty maw
of the interior drew her forward with a sighing inhalation of welcome. She was troubled by the building's air of expectancy. The
light switch, when she managed to locate it, did not work. She
tried several more times. Nothing. She stood back in dismay. All
by itself the centre light came on and a mean yellowness filled the
stone-flagged room. She pondered this for more than a minute,
shifting her feet and gaze several times, until a soft tap on the
shoulder made her scream.

Spinning round she saw a pair of antlers reaching out to her.
They were screwed to the wall beside the door and hooked onto
them were a forlorn Inverness cape and a variety of sunhats, all
heavily powdered with dust. One of the hats, nudged by her
shoulder, had fallen off and rocked to a halt on the floor. Her
skin spasmed into goose-pimples. With her right hand she vigorously rubbed her left upper arm. Facing the black fireplace
was a sofa, fringed and buttoned but very decrepit, which
invited her to sit on it – so she did. A chain hung down inside the
fireplace. A cobweb streaked her lips and she spat. There were
cobwebs everywhere, thin wraithlike ones you could hardly see,
which caught you across the face unawares. Some mouldy rolls
of Christmas wrapping paper were propped dejectedly in a
corner. Generally baffled, she broke the pads of silence with
'Some people know nothing about lighting'. She heard her voice
crack towards the end of the sentence. After a couple of table

lamps had been switched on she attempted to switch off the centre light, without success. The room quietly awaited her next move. Spiders, beetles, woodlice, earwigs moved in the corners of her eyes.

'Tomorrow I'll shift things about,' she said in a tinny, artificial tone. Her attention was taken by the glare of headlights through the open front door. She blinked and was relieved to recognise them as her own and she went outside, skidding slightly on the dung – took in a bulky canvas bag, abandoning fouled shoes on the doorstep – found an electric fire which worked – discovered her bedroom up a creaky staircase scarcely wider than her hips – certainly not crinoline-wide – they must've undressed downstairs in days gone by – or perhaps those who slept in this house didn't wear crinolines – and you'd never get a coffin down it – or up it – or whatever they did with the dead then – a double bed filled the bedroom with venereal emphasis – plain oak wardrobe and dressing-table – clean linen sheets – radio (broken) – dead flies on windowsill and more cobwebs – long foxed mirror fixed to wall – she caught herself in it – the distortion of her face appalled her – like one of those squashed things on the road – or a refugee in a newsreel. Instinctively she'd turned away but a masochistic egotism pulled her back to the reflection. Eyes creased and sore. Deep vertical grooves either side of the mouth. The skin shrivelled. Had she died without realising it? The face had wholly succumbed to a dreadful, downward pull. And worst of all, it was definitely her.

Downstairs in the kitchen she took another slug of whisky and grimaced. It was not her sort of drink. It was a man's drink. She'd bought it for the man. For him. She brushed her teeth to get the taste out of her mouth and now she was in bed. The hands on her special bedside clock moved soundlessly. It was gone three a.m. The rain had stopped. Water dripped sweetly from the eaves. Where was she? Who was she? Why had she come here? The quiet and the anonymity grew succulent as a sleeping-pill bloomed from within.

Unconsciousness had almost been achieved when her toe, moving murkily into a cooler patch of cotton, grazed something. It took several seconds for this to register and when it did the 'something' felt moist but distinct at the bottom of the bed. In another instant the light was on and she was standing on the floor, observing the bed's lower far corner. Yes, something was there, surely it was. Glancing about, she pulled on her jeans but felt exceedingly anxious about her feet. The feet had to be protected. She opened the front door – shitty shoes on the doorstep, other shoes in the boot of the car. What to do? The owl hooted again. The moon flashed its teeth between clouds. She closed the door sharpish. Back in the bedroom she sought to steady herself by breathing deeply and slowly, as once she'd seen an Indian yogi do on breakfast television, but it didn't work. She was in a seizure of breathless urgency and threw aside the bedclothes with a groan. Not far enough. She yanked and groaned again. Still not enough. At the third attempt she pulled the top bedclothes altogether off and there it was, nestling in the skewed bottom sheet. Yellow, bloody, veined. A severed foot.

3.

Earlier that week in Whitehall a man in a suit received a call from Brussels.

'It is the turn of your country to have a huge grant in order to develop an undeveloped area of your choice,' said the Brussels man. 'Your Minister of Power arrives in a few days to negotiate the deal but I thought you would like to know in advance that it is all arranged.'

'Thank you,' replied the Whitehall man who thereupon summoned his underlings. They sat round a teak table surveying a gigantic map of England, sliding it this way and that. They ummed and ahhed and bit their lips and cocked their heads. But the whole country seemed to have been developed already.

'What about the Lake District, sir?' asked a young man with red cheeks, blue eyes and black hair.

The Superior slapped the young man's wrist. 'Tucker, that's a national park! We can't touch those. Mm, well, do you know what I'd like to spend this money on?' He waited until he had their full attention. 'I'd like to spend it on something *useful*.'

They nodded agreement. Useful was a good idea.

'And up-to-date.'

Up-to-date too, yes, of course.

'And in fact I've had this pet fantasy for a number of years now which is nothing less than the creation of the biggest centre in the world for – artificial intelligence!'

He waited for their reaction and they dutifully went 'Oooooo'.

'Which would be', he continued, 'at the heart of a biotechnology city. Of half a million souls. Served by an airport. And a state-of-the-art road network. And all slap bang down on a greenfield site. What do you think of that then?'

'Oh yes, sir!' they chorused. 'You're so clever, sir! How beautiful, sir!'

'Um, sir?'

'Yes, Tucker?'

'Where will you find these half a million souls?'

'Immigration! None of yer local underclass thank you. The Third World is full of willing hands who'd *kill* for a chance to come to a green and prosperous place like . . . like . . . '

'Yes, that's the next question, isn't it,' whined Arbuthnot who was neither young nor superior. 'Which is to say – where will you put this city of yours?'

'Of ours, Arbuthnot, of *ours*. Where oh where indeed.' The Superior's eyes were searchlights across their faces.

Silence and furrowed brows.

A second young man, whose straight tallow hair fell in a deep fringe, snapped forward over the map. His lipless mouth broke open. 'If I'm not mistaken, sir, the area to the left of . . . '

Everyone peered closer so that their noses were almost touching. The second young man's finger was hovering over a green patch of eccentric shape. The Superior's eyelids quivered a second before he exclaimed 'You're right, Finch!' Everyone else jumped back. 'My God, yes – it's clean. It's *extremely* clean.' He leered round the table. 'Perfect. Yes. Let's do it – *there*!' And on that last word the Superior's pen stabbed exultantly, making a filthy mess over Milking Magna.

4.

The last murder in Milking Magna had been in the fifteenth century. Even the Civil War had passed it by. There had never been a policeman stationed in the village and in consequence it took the law forty-five minutes to arrive from Appleminster. They found her sitting in the car with doors locked, listening to Nighthawk from Hilversum, knocking back the whisky.

'Miss – madam – is this Glade Cottage?'

She wound down the window and said in a squeaky voice 'I tried to get away but my car won't start.'

'Are you an AA member?' asked the other policeman. She nodded. 'Ring them in the morning,' he advised.

'It's in there. Bedroom,' she squeaked.

'Technically we should breathalise you.'

Two minutes later one of the policemen emerged from the cottage rubbing a lump on his brow but holding the severed foot aloft by its big toe. 'Bloody beams! Come here please, madam.'

She jumped out of the car but fled past him and huddled on the sofa with two pop eyes above a pair of clasped knees. As he followed her in, the policeman lobbed the foot across to his colleague who, dangling it over his head, bit into its ankle with an upward lunge and strong teeth. Afterwards he growled at her. She hid her face in her hands and made an indescribable noise.

'He's playful,' said the first policeman, adding slowly 'Madam – it is made from synthetic rubber.'

She looked at him like a lost girl and mumbled 'Actually I think the official name is not Glade Cottage but The Glade.'

'She's overwrought.'

'Did you hear? A carnival item. Synthetic.'

'Yes, rubber, I heard,' she said looking at the chain in the fireplace.

'People play *nasty* tricks,' said the second, unaware of his sadistic intonation. 'But we'll take it away for examination if you like.'

'That rain was welcome, werntit. May I have an apple, miss?'

She looked round and noticed for the first time a pile of red apples in a cream ceramic bowl on the sideboard. They were as bright as a Matisse painting. 'Where did they come from?' she asked. 'How could I have not seen them before?'

They made her a cup of tea. 'Detective Hoskins will visit you tomorrow. Goodnight, miss. You wanna go blackberrying, miss. Nothing like it for calming down. Season's just come along.'

After she'd double-checked all the doors and windows, sleep struck her suddenly.

5.

In the Monkshood Nursing Home they were turning out the lights and locking the wards on the sane and the insane, the recuperative and the vegetative. In a private room at the end of a white corridor a solitary man, adrift in the infinite spaces of his damaged brain, stared at the ceiling. He hadn't gone mad because he'd never known sanity and had resided in this place since soon after his birth, having no competence in any of the arts of realism. During the last few years he had been cared for by a nurse called Melody and a tender bond had arisen between them. He recognised her almost always and insofar as he was able he loved her. Lately their association had made a discreet advance and sometimes, after she'd done the ward with the pill trolley and extinguished the lights, Melody would enter the room with 'John Smith' on the door, lock it behind her and slip her slim body into his bed for ten minutes or so.

6.

Disturbed by cockcrow, she awoke too early and put her head out of the bedroom window, breathing deeply. Much of the garden to the rear was taken up by old fruit trees, their bark scaly and powdered green, their branches arthritic. Between and beyond them, cornfields and woods and the plump pillows of hills overlapped and diminished as they receded into the distance. The clarity of the view and the vividness of its colour sickened her and she flopped downstairs to make a pot of tea. In the kitchen she took one look at the Rayburn and thought – How the hell do I work that awful great thing? Luckily the kettle was electric and taking her tea into the garden she sipped it on a dewy seat beneath a tree laden with flushed apples, while the aroma of blackberries reached her from the already warming hedgerow. You wanna go blackberrying, miss. Oh God. The tears came . . . and went . . .

On a nearby stone a Red Admiral alighted and lowered its wings, like a tiny firework going off since it carried with it its own pool of night. She'd always thought of butterflies as agitated, elusive, but this one took a calm and confident pleasure in its own existence, moved certainly and was unafraid. By way of breakfast she ate a muesli bar. The sunshine pressed unpleasantly on her eyes. The telephone rang and she went indoors.

'Detective Inspector Hoskins here. Will you be at home this morning?'

'Yes, because I'm waiting for the AA man but if he comes I'll have to go out afterwards because there's no food. Is there a food shop somewhere?'

'I'll be with you in about 30 minutes. Isn't it a glorious morning?'

She hadn't yet rung the AA and now did so and began to feel tired again. Detective Hoskins turned up in shorts, T-shirt and a fashionable haircut and, surveying her slowly from head down to toe and back up again, he asked 'You believe it was aimed at you personally, the foot?'

'I don't know anyone in this part of the world,' she simpered, taken aback by his air of capable, indifferent youth. He wore a small gold hoop through one ear-lobe, which didn't instil confidence, and he was too good-looking for a policeman, with a bow-lipped mouth which one couldn't help be fascinated by. It was a horribly mobile and kissable mouth.

'I wouldn't get too het up. It was only a rubber toy,' he said.

She was about to respond with 'How would your mother feel?' but checked herself from identifying with his parent and said instead 'How would your girlfriend feel if she found an old foot in her bed?'

'I'm gay.'

'Oh, well, um, how would your boyf – would you like a cup of tea? It's made.'

'We hear from Kipling that, in India, a fallen woman would have her hand severed at the wrist. What might a severed foot imply?'

'We don't have fallen women anymore.'

'I'd love a cup thanks.'

There was a knock at the door. It was the AA man. He busied himself under her bonnet while she stood there aimlessly. A pull at her elbow brought her round. It was Hoskins again. 'Do you have a work number?' he asked.

'Hullo, Hosky,' said the AA man, emerging briefly.

'Hullo, Jim.'

'The phone number there is 123123. But it's a private house and I expect I'll have a different office number. I'm going to work for the Marquess of Heavenshire.' Hoskins gave her a funny look. 'Isn't that all right?' she asked.

'I'm sure it's very all right. I've checked your bed. It was freshly made up. Presumably by someone from Heaven Park.'

'Presumably. And the front door was open when I arrived.'

'Wide open?'

'No. Unlocked.'

'That doesn't mean much round here. Well, thanks for the cuppa. I'll be in touch.' He looked her over once again and left.

The AA man said 'Your headlight switch was on. The battery flat as a pancake. And your oojamaflick's buggered as well but you'll have to get a mechanic for that. The nearest one on our books is Justice Royal. Good chap. Here's his phone number.'

7.

Gypsy Castle was a small estate of council houses, arranged in a horseshoe and tucked away at the top of the village. One of the houses, in violent contrast to its neighbours, sported spanking new paintwork of bright scarlet and inside this house Justice Royal was holding a book of recipes as far away as possible with floury hands (his eyes weren't what they had been). In a stoneware bowl he folded together eggs, butter, sugar, flour, spices, sultanas, currants, the grated rind of a lemon and a little milk, and beat it well prior to testing it. Withdrawing his middle finger from the mire, he sucked and pondered and added more sugar. The telephone rang. Justice wiped his hands on a tea-towel.

'Is that Mr Royal?'

'Yes.'

'My car's broken.'

'What's the problem?'

'Flat battery and the oojamaflick's gone.'

'No problem.'

'I'm at the Glade Cottage. Do you know it?'

'I do.'

'When could you come?'

'I can come at noon if that's all right.'

'That's fine.'

Justice replaced the receiver and levelled the glop into the greased and lined baking tin, whispering 'Ooo, Mrs Bladder-Williams, I love yooo.'

8.

So at long last she unloaded her luggage from the car and unpacked a couple of the smaller bags and, instead of sitting there until the mechanic was due, she decided to walk down the lane to the shops. Upon reaching the church she noticed, about a quarter of a mile further on beyond the village, a bunch of gothic pinnacles emerging from the salad of a wooded bluff above the river. That'll be Heaven Park, she thought, and turned left down into the High Street where the fish & chip shop was already active. Outside the grocer's she was waylaid into giving lifeboat money to a canvasser who pressed a sticky label to her front while, inside, she purchased all her immediate necessities with one exception.

'I can't find any nightlights,' she complained to the checkout girl, a vivacious minx whose buck teeth gave her attractiveness a quality of surprise. The girl replied 'Really? Dunno then. We got most things. I'd leave the landing light on if I were you.'

A presence loomed against the counter and she looked up at a very tall, very thin, very creased man in a grubby beige suit whose hips were swaying as though he were slightly drunk. His image was fixed by a bow-tie and pair of dark glasses with round metal frames which fitted into the sockets of his eyes. 'May one suggest the ironmonger's, madam? On the other side of the street. Further down.' His voice was deep, and rich with rubato, and over one arm he held a wicker shopping-basket.

'Thank you,' she said.

'You're new, aren't you?'

'Yes thank you,' and she fled.

The tall man addressed the checkout girl. 'Funny people we're getting round here now. Daisy, do you have any of my favourite wine out the back? There's none on the shelves.'

Daisy forced her buck teeth into a smile but couldn't conceal her irritation. 'Really? I'll go and look then, Mr Lomax.'

While she was out the back, he popped a packet of biscuits into his shopping basket, covered them with his newspaper, and waited patiently for Daisy's return.

9.

Meanwhile over at Puckford Mill, a short fat furious redhead called Sylvia Wetmore was throwing glasses at her husband and shouting 'Bastard, bastard!' It happened about once a month but this time it was more serious because when she stopped she looked down at the carpet for almost half a minute, exhausted, and crossed over to him, laying her head against the centre of his shirt front, and said 'O lover of the Nile, I'm leaving you, darling.'

His brow crinkled. 'But why?'

'I've got to.'

'Please don't.'

'Yes, I've got to, darling. I can't stand living with an alcoholic anymore.'

He pulled one end of his moustache and said 'Excuse me. I think I'm going to crap myself.'

10.

She sat in the kitchen, perusing her letter of employment and picking at a lunch of sardines, gluey coleslaw from a plastic tub, and brown bread and sunflower butter-substitute..

Heaven Park,
Milking Magna,   *tel: Milking 123123*
Heavenshire   *station: Appleminster*

Dear Madam,
   We take great pleasure in confirming your appointment for one
year at the agreed salary. When you arrive at The Glade you'll
find the key under a stone to the left of the front door. More detailed
instructions to follow. Alas, I shall be away until some days after
your arrival but please do in the meantime come up to the house and
introduce yourself. Any problems can be dealt with by Malcolm
Gibbet or Sidney. On no account let my sister interfere.

                                              Yours faithfully,
                                              Julius Heavenshire

A fly buzzing in the window annoyed her and she successfully
swatted it with a tea towel. Where's that bloody car mechanic? I
seem to spend my life waiting for people! . . . *you'll find the key*
under a stone to the left of the front door. She went outside and
checked among the stones to the other side of the porch and
found the front-door key. Obviously the right hand doesn't know
what the left hand is doing at Heaven Park, she judged, but
almost at once realised that of course which side is left or right of
the porch depends on whether you are going out or coming in.
There was a knock at the door at five past one.
   Justice Royal apologised. 'M'cake didn't rise. Very disap-
pointin. Forgot the bakin powder and had to do it all over. Forgive
me.' Then he smiled and she was won over. Justice's huge African
hands worked vigorously on the engine and afterwards he
announced with another reassuring smile 'He's right as rain now.'
   'Who is?'
   He blinked at her a number of times.
   'How much do I owe you?' she asked, obliquely aware of having
committed a faux pas.
   'Tenner'll do.'
   'Are you quite sure?' She wasn't comfortable with a tenner.
London had not only accustomed her to much higher prices but

had also made her highly suspicious of anyone who had anything
to do with cars.

'Yeah, yeah, it were nothin.'

'You're the nicest person I've met so far.' He laughed aloud
and looked at her sideways on. 'Can I ask you something?' she
proceeded.

'Of course.'

'What is Lord Heavenshire like?'

'Very fat. And I don't believe half of what they say about im.'

'What do they say?'

'He has a beautiful car.'

'Is that what they say?'

'It's what I say.'

'Listen, I want to tell you something.' And she told him about
the severed foot in her bed.

He was enthralled and he asked her where the other foot might
be. 'Why should there be another foot?' she warbled. He said
because round here feet usually came in pairs and perhaps it was
in one of the cupboards. She wished she hadn't started the subject and wasn't sure that Justice was quite as nice as she'd first
thought.

II.

At two-thirty she went to take a look at Heaven Park in her freshly
humming car. Guided by the distant pinnacles above the trees,
she followed the lane and then a paling fence and came to a small
lodge beside an open wooden gate. 'Hullo, anybody there?' Peering in through one of the lodge's trefoiled windows she saw its
main chamber filled with old brooms and garden implements.
Gravel boiled beneath the car as she turned into the drive which
swung out of sight beyond a group of cypress but directly after
that the house was upon her.

It was a monstrosity of manageable size in grey and greenish
stone, a tribute to the Middle Ages that was both tempestuous
and melancholy. Yet despite the spectacle of it, her eye was immediately caught by a young man who stood motionlessly on the
lawn beneath a half-dead oak tree. Coming to life, he pushed back

his brown hair and shaded his eyes to look at her, but as she wound down the car window to speak he turned on his heel and disappeared into a bank of rhododendron bushes.

Though her neck tightened from the sense of rejection she approached the house and beneath the spiky porch lifted a gryphon-shaped knocker and let it drop. A muffled thud like a heavy drumbeat resonated within, suggesting a large stony space, but otherwise nothing happened and so she did it again with more force. After a while several complaining grunts were heard approaching from the other side. A latch rattled and the door was pulled open. A woman old and stooped looked out with black beady eyes. From her lower lip hung a hand-rolled cigarette. Instead of greeting the visitor she stepped beyond her and scanned the drive and garden as though looking for something more significant. The old woman was hunchbacked.

'How do you do. I'm Alice.'

'Come again?'

'Alice.'

'Aint nothin to brag about.'

'I meant that I'm the one who's coming to work here.'

'News to me,' said the hunchback, drying raw red hands on her apron.

'And you are, if I may ask?'

'Davis.'

'I see. Er – is Sidney about?' Alice hadn't much gumption for this. One of the symptoms of her unhappiness was that her voice went thin under pressure and now, in trying to be bright, it cracked.

Davis glared. 'Who?'

'Is there anyone here called Sidney – or Malcolm? I do hope there is.'

'Well, there aint.'

Panic mounted in Alice's throat and the smile slithered off her face onto her shoulder which started to twitch. 'I'm coming to work for the Marquess on his project.' Her voice flicked up at the end, turning what should have been an assertion into a frantic question.

The hunchback narrowed her eyes. 'Where you from?'

'London.'

'Sausages an lemons says the bells of Saint Clemons!'

Alice held on to a crocket of the stone arch. Her limbs had gone spongy. Everything was going wrong. Her whole survival plan was dissolving away. There'd been a ghastly mistake somewhere. 'May I ask who lives here?'

'Sir Timothy Craddock of The Crag. Which is all you'll get out of me!'

'This isn't Heaven Park?'

'Good God, this be The Crag itself! An you're trespassin.'

'What a relief. I do apologise. But where is Heaven Park then?'

'Miles away. On the other side of the valley. An if yer going to work there yer wants yer head examinin.'

'Why say that to me?'

'Because they're *orrible* people, that's why!' Hereafter the crone constrained herself and tilted her head from side to side with a series of ingratiating sniffs. 'An what project would that be then that yer goin to work on?'

But Alice was wary. 'Goodbye,' she said, 'very kind of you,' and left. The housekeeper shouted after her 'Haven't you ever heard the prodigal of the parable son?' and slammed shut the studded portal of The Crag, obviously not wanting an answer. What a curious thing to say, thought Alice as she whizzed down the drive. After she'd passed the rhododendron bushes, the fronds parted and the young man re-emerged and followed her departure with gooseberry-green eyes. He now had on his arm a peregrine falcon which restlessly fluttered its wings.

12.

'Turn it off,' said Big Lark.

'Leave im be,' said Princess.

'Don't cross me! Oi said turn it off!' Angry boils stood out on Big's neck. Little Lark, nearly twice his father's height but only half the width, morosely turned it off. 'D'ya wanna end up like me, unemployed?' pursued his father. Little looked out of the front window with a bitter face.

'I was quite enjoying it myself,' said Princess.

Daisy's key was heard in the front door. She entered the lounge and slumped into an armchair. 'My feet are killing me. I must find another job. 'There's someone new in the village,' said Daisy to her mother. 'She came in and bought funny stuff, olive oil, things like that.'

'Beans-on-toast-with-bacon-and-grated-cheese-on-top OK?' asked her mother.

Daisy pulled her top lip down over her buck teeth and nodded and Princess slipped her feet into pom-pom slippers and withdrew to the kitchen. Big jabbed a finger at Little and said 'You – homework!' The lad plucked at the back of a chair before trailing his legs out of the room. Silence thickened between father and daughter until Big blurted 'You still seeing im?'

'Whom?' asked Daisy, emphasising the final letter.

'Glorywhatsit.'

'Give over, Dad.'

Daisy looked out of the front window with a blank expression because whether or not she was 'seeing' Glory Boy was something she never exactly knew. Glory liked to go out with her and he liked to have it off with her, but it never quite felt like a relationship. In the roadway outside, Justice was polishing the round black buttocks of his old Riley with firm motions of a chamois, and Daisy became lost in her vague dream of getting away to a place with palm trees. When Princess returned with her daughter's supper tray she asked 'What someone new was that then? Who bought the olive oil.'

'I dunno. Never seen her before. I think she might be Australian. Not from round here anyway. I heard she was going to work for im up at the Park. Can we have the box on?'

Daisy poked at her beans without relish. Princess, who soon became tranfixed by the screen, said 'Oh, didn't she do that beautiful,' as an East European gymnast floated over a vault and somersaulted three times in the air before landing pefectly. She glanced at her husband and said 'Look at Big's tongue hanging out.'

13.

Her eyes felt as though she had recently finished crying but she hadn't been crying. After standing in the garden and staring at nothing for a while, during which time thoughts went through her mind on the general weirdness and awfulness of the human condition, and sensations went through her body broadly confirming this, she realised she was cold and, picking up an armful of logs, returned to the sitting-room and laid a fire. It was a task that was new to her. First she made long spills from an old newspaper by rolling the broadsheets cornerwise and tying them in knots. This she recalled her mother having done many years ago when the central heating packed up. Next she took assorted twigs from a large basket. And finally the logs. One match was all it took but the fire smoked badly to begin with on account of the late summer dews which had crept down the chimney. Something darted into the room and flickered so rapidly that it couldn't be identified, but she knew it wasn't something normal and the hair rose on the back of her neck. She grabbed a roll of Christmas paper from the corner and struck out wildly. What on earth was it? And where had it gone? For as abruptly as it had appeared the wraith had vanished into the ceiling. Alert on the edge of the sofa, she waited and sure enough in a minute the wraith darted out again, flickering hither and thither. And again she struck at it, and again it retreated. But this time, as it wrapped itself up and wriggled out of sight, it was momentarily visible. A bat. A nasty little bat. It had embraced itself with an angular, hooked membrane – yuk! – and disappeared into a crevice. Before vanishing it poked its tongue at her. Unrolling the Christmas paper she stuffed it into the gap between plaster and beam, blocking the creature out. She was in no mood for alarming visitations. As a child her Aunt Renée had told her that, while walking with her sweetheart one evening, a bat had become entangled in her aunt's beautiful red hair which had to be shaved off with the bat still thrashing and shitting inside it. Alice took the second roll of Christmas paper and stuffed more of it into the crevice. She was dreading Christmas. The telephone rang.

'Hullo?'

'Tim Craddock here.'

'Oh. How do you do.'

'Bit of a cough actually. I'm sorry my housekeeper was rude to you.'

'Did she say she was rude?'

'I'm afraid she's rude to everyone. But I wouldn't lose her for the world.'

'I called by mistake.'

'It's not necessarily a mistake to call.'

'I thought you were Heaven Park.'

'That *was* a mistake, yes. The Park is classical. We're gothic. Hang on a mo.' There were pspsps noises in the background. 'My wife asks can you come to lunch on Sunday? I ask it too.'

'Er, well, um . . . ' The prospect was frightful.

'Excellent!' he said. 'Be here about twelve-thirty for sherry.'

She went out into the lavender twilight for more logs and heard a noise beneath one of the apple trees. A crow was dragging a damaged wing in no particular direction and, as she approached, it squirmed backwards into immobility, attempting to cancel itself among the long grass at the base of the trunk. Wounded creatures try to hide but will attack if interfered with, she thought. Alice found some plain biscuits in the kitchen and lobbed a few towards the crow and waited but the bird also was waiting and didn't move at all.

14.

Milking Magna is a village of middle size situated on a bend in the River Puck whose valley rolls up on one side to Saint Wendy's Church and The Crag, and on the other to the estate and enormous house of Heaven Park. The bulk of the village is on the former side, as was Alice's cottage, and here traditionally the Craddocks held sway, but they no longer had land, whereas the holdings of the Popjoys encroached on Milking Magna from every direction and Heaven Park was by far the greatest single presence in the county after the cathedral city of Appleminster. The Glade was the Popjoy property closest to The Crag and frequently occupied by a 'spy', so that Sir Timothy was always very eager to acquaint himself with anyone who went to live there.

The Crag was – theoretically – medieval in origin but had been so done over in the nineteenth century as to have once been described in an issue of *Jackanapes* magazine (June 1881) as 'a sensible modern house'. The article explained that 'For example, the Middle Ages did not understand staircases. They made use of suffocating spirals tucked into corners. It took the present age to create at The Crag a staircase fit for a Plantagenet.' In fact it was put in for the visit of Queen Victoria and carved all over with chevron-backed vipers; oak gryphons, their wings outstretched, were placed upon the newel posts; and the tall staircase windows had their lancet tops coloured with blood-red Latin aphorisms. But alas the good queen was diverted eastward and never turned up. Nor did the Middle Ages understand central heating, whereas The Crag had a system of iron radiators in the form of large heraldic beasts which mewed, hissed, growled, and shook throughout the winter – as a design feature it was unique and had featured in a television programme.

On Sunday the front of The Glade was a blizzard of fluffy white seeds blowing hither and thither from a bank of willowherb and as she took herself off to meet the Craddocks her apprehensions behaved similarly. Loneliness was bloody awful, bloody painful, bloody pointless, but that was something she was more or less prepared to take on board, the mental or emotional anguish. It was the physical anguish that was so impossible to deal with. Going to a strange house for lunch all by herself. Being stabbed by a thousand needles. Slices of sheer terror.

When Alice was announced, Sir Timothy, Lady Craddock, their son Robin, and a bald man in crumpled grey clothes, faced her shoulder to shoulder beneath a contraption of brass and bone which was the drawing-room chandelier. Which didn't help matters.

'Here's the last,' grumbled Davis.

'Sorry I'm late,' said Alice.

'You're not late,' said Sir Timothy.

'Davis is early,' said Robin.

'So you'll have to miss the sherry.'

'I don't mind missing sherry.'

'I hope you're only saying that to be polite.' Sir Timothy smiled at the mortified guest.

'Come and eat, Alice,' said Lady Craddock with friendly encouragement of her arm. Helen Craddock was very thin and wearing a sleeveless dress of no certain colour.

They proceeded to the dining-room where a bay of pointed windows overlooked a recently mown lawn.

'That's a nice lawn,' said Alice.

'Isn't it,' said Sir Timothy. 'And much easier to look after than the front one with that blasted oak tree on it.'

'I like the oak tree,' said Lady Craddock.

Alice couldn't help detecting a frisson and wondered whether there had been a row before her arrival. The bald man in crumpled grey, who was introduced to her as a scientist called Oliver Knott, offered an appeasing smile, exposing a rectangle of dentures. His smile stayed where it was, sticking to him like a label.

Lady Craddock asked 'Is the cottage all right?'

'Yes, thank you.'

'If you need anything . . . '

'Thank you, yes.' Be more resolute, Alice reminded herself. 'Er – what sort of scientist are you in fact?' She'd met scientists in her previous job.

'Mainly artificial intelligence. But I'm on sick leave.'

Sir Timothy, who was busy carving the meat with great deliberation and vertically to the bone, chuckled 'He's been on sick leave for nearly five years!'

Knott grinned pathetically while the son Robin said 'The Notting Hill Carnival was on the news. Looked like fun. You didn't stay for it then?'

'No, I didn't fancy it this year.'

'Too many murders, I suppose.'

Alice found herself smiling a smile in response to this and when it was time for the smile to go it wouldn't. Hers stuck onto her like a label too. She really tried to get rid of it but the relevant muscles simply wouldn't work and as she glanced helplessly round the table she noticed that everyone else had irremovable smiles on them too, with various forms of panic behind their eyes.

'It's not a real carnival,' said Sir Timothy. 'Real carnivals are in February. Carnay varlay in Italian. Good bye meat. Beginning of Lent. Pour the wine, Robin.' And he began to fork slices of juicy flesh onto the plates.

'Or would you prefer elderflower cordial?' asked Helen from the window bay where she was fiddling with a curtain. 'I made it myself.'

'Wine would be nice.'

Lady Craddock returned to the table and said 'If you need anything for your garden, I can help.'

'Helen's latest kick is the wilderness in the dingle beyond the spinney.'

'It's not a kick, Tim. It's a garden.'

Alice found herself disturbed not only by their tone and their bared teeth but now also by the sideboard. It was huge and black, with claw-corners, and imposed itself from the opposite wall like the sarcophagus of a dead pharaoh, despite the decanters on top, and so she attempted to alter the direction of her mind with 'Do you know the Marquess of Heavenshire?'

'To whom is that question addressed?' asked Sir Tim.

Alice's head heated up as she answered 'I just wondered what he was like.'

Helen left the table and fiddled with the curtain again.

'For God's sake . . . ' he muttered at his wife.

'Everybody calls him JJ,' said Robin.

Lady Craddock, carefully sitting down once more, said 'I hope you don't mind my being a vegetarian, Alice. Some people get awfully annoyed. Do try the mint sauce. It's a Davis special.'

'I'm one of the ones who get annoyed by it. One day we came back from my cousin's farm and that was that, she'd gone right off animal,' said Sir Tim. '*Right* off.' The implication of his glare was that his conjugal rights had suffered accordingly.

'It was that still-born calf coming out in pieces before lunch,' said Lady Craddock, running a hand over her head which made it evident that the hair under her arms had not lately been shaved. Alice assumed that hairy female armpits were an aspect of vegetarianism. 'Have you met Dickon yet?'

'Who?' asked Alice.

'He's your neighbour.'

'You'll have heard his tractor,' nodded Robin. 'Pass the spuds, Mum.'

Lady Craddock sipped from her goblet and said 'I'm getting rather good at this elderflower stuff.'

When the lamb course had come to an end, Sir Timothy, who was not in the mood for silence, said 'Unless there are serious objections, I think I'd like to sing a song.' Lady Craddock looked irritably askance as her husband launched his tuneful tenor voice.

> *From London to Freetown,*
> *Port Harcourt and Cape Town,*
> *On to Mombassa from old Zanzibar*

> *To Aden, Bombay,*
> *And Colombo, Calcutta,*
> *Rangoon and Penang, for no port is too far*

> *The Straits of Malacca,*
> *Singapore, Sarawakka,*
> *Up to Hong Kong on the South China Sea*

> *Pop down to New Guinea,*
> *And Auckland from Sydney,*
> *Across the Pacific to friendly Feejee*

> *Landfall at Vancouver,*
> *Jamaica, Bermuda,*
> *No port of the Empire is ever forgot*

> *Via Suez or Malta,*
> *Or Cyprus, Gibraltar,*
> *It's back home to London, the best of the lot!*

Alice was thinking – I feel hot all over and I want to get out of this ghastly room and run away but I have already run away and here I am . . .

Robin joined in the last two verses and at the end Lady Craddock thought an explanation was called for and said 'Tim was in the Navy'.

'Aren't you still, Sir Timothy?'

'He took early retirement.'

'Don't start on that, Helen.' He was relieved to see Davis enter with a steamed pudding and jug of custard and pointedly said 'Yum yum'. Davis briefly bared her brown teeth and shuffled out, leaving the door wide open. Sir Tim turned to Alice and said as normally as he could 'You've not met him yet then? Your employer. I call him Heavenshire, not JJ. I'm not a friend.'

'He said he'd be away when I arrived.'

'I don't think he's away.'

'He isn't away,' said the scientist. 'I met Pimm at the grocer's and he said he and JJ were going for a bar meal at The Basilisk.'

Alice made a mental note. Her employer was untrustworthy. Oh, she hoped not.

'What actually are you going to *do* up there?' enquired Sir Timothy.

'We're turning it into a conference centre.'

'How awful,' said Lady Craddock.

'Why did you say he's not a friend, Sir Timothy?' Alice felt it was a plucky question.

'Nothing against him personally. Just can't stand the bugger. There were a few of his type in the Navy. No problem. They fitted in – the Navy's a family. I just couldn't get pally.'

The scientist said 'The main problem is, face it, Tim, the man's a Popjoy.'

Leaning sideways, Sir Timothy said 'The point is the Popjoys can't get the simple things right. Like carving a leg of lamb for example. They think it should be carved horizontally to the bone. Can you imagine anything more absurd, more self-defeating?'

'The Craddocks and the Popjoys have been at loggerheads over this question for at least a hundred years,' explained Lady Craddock, raising her eyebrows and shaking her head at the childishness of it . 'They've hardly spoken to each other in all that time. *We* must carve a leg of lamb vertically to the bone, *they* must carve it horizontally. It's set in concrete. Actually I'm sure the present Popjoys don't give a twopenny damn about anything whatsoever, but you, Tim, still seem to take it very seriously.'

Sir Timothy sat up straight and put his fists on his hips. 'Someone's got to keep up standards round here!'

'Well, *I'm* speaking to them,' said Robin.

'Oh *you*,' said his father. 'Now look, Alice, who else do you know in this part of the world? We must get you introduced, mustn't we, Helen?'

'People are slow round here,' said Lady Craddock. 'Don't be surprised if it takes time. Unfortunately our daughter lives in Zimbabwe.'

'Yes, that is unfortunate,' agreed Alice.

Robin sniggered and said 'We heard about your severed foot.'

'Bad luck,' said Sir Tim. He bent towards her sympathetically. 'I know it will surprise you but I'm afraid there are a number of weirdoes round here. Any leads?'

'Not yet. What sort of weirdoes?'

'Well, we've got piles of severed chicken feet where I work,' said Robin. 'They freeze them and send them off to the Chinese who eat them.'

'Where do you work?'

'Harry Pulp's chicken farm, but only part-time.'

Lady Craddock said 'I'm dead against it. But there's no work round here for a young man. Is it true, Robin, that Pulp is planning to breed four-teat sheep?'

'Haven't the foggiest. I think I'll take out the falcon,' and Robin left the table.

'Can't you say excuse me?' Sir Timothy called after him.

'He said excuse me,' said Lady Craddock.

'He bloody well didn't.'

'He did to me.'

15.

It was a muggy, enigmatic afternoon. Though the sun was obscured, she could still feel its strength on her back as she made her way across a harvested field to the far hedgerow with its sequence of oak trees, each as distinct as a planet. At lunchtime there had been a shower and the water, trapped in the tubes of cut stalk, splashed sweetly up her bare calves. Her first encounter was with the damaged crow. It was squawking on the ground, pushing head and shoulders forward in a vomitory movement, but when it saw her it froze.

'Are you going to haunt me?' she asked it.

The crow no doubt had the very same thought and it hopped fecklessly, looking at her with sidelong madness. She bent down to – she didn't know what she was going to do really, try to communicate perhaps, but upon reaching out to it she received a well-directed stab from its beak.

'Get on with it then, you miserable sod!' she said and was about to step over the stile into the next field when she saw that it was occupied by cows. Cows she loved – in pictures, in advertisements, on biscuit tins and chocolate boxes and cartons of milk. But the ones in the field were alive, were big, were smelly, were moving, and the rip of grass beneath the feeding herd suggested a remorseless power and weight. They sensed her and looked up collectively, fixing her with moronic brown eyes. 'Hullo,' she said, staying precisely where she was. The beasts stared for quite a long time without moving – it was a sort of stand-off – but they gradually grew bored and returned to the superior thrills of grass. All except one – there is always one – whose intelligence was pricked, who continued to stare, who raised its tail and let loose a ton of shit, and who began to approach with slow implacable steps. Alice didn't want to be approached. She hurriedly took to the adjacent field, tramping down one side of it over the waves of ploughed earth. A tractor dragging an apparatus of small wheels in rows was coming in the opposite direction, throwing into the air a cloud of fawn and lemon dust which flashed where the feeble sunshine caught it. Alice stopped to let the tractor pass but it stopped too. Its engine pattered into silence and a man opened the cabin door and looked down at her. He was in his thirties, blond and tanned but roses still showed in his cheeks, and his eyes were grape blue. They smiled at each other.

'Boring job this,' he said.

'What are you doing exactly?'

'Ploughing in the stubble. Round and round and round. Can't even listen to the radio.'

'You should get a Walkman,' she said, shielding her eyes as she looked up. The faint sun was behind him and he seemed to emanate from its muddy shimmer. 'Don't you have a dog to keep you company? I thought all farmers had dogs.'

'He was killed by a car.' The farmer jumped down from the cabin and extended a hand. His forearm was strongly developed. 'You must be Alice. Oh sorry.' And he withdrew his hand before she'd taken it.

'Good clean dirt,' she said gauchely.

'We're neighbours,' he said.

'In which case you're Dickon.'

'That's right. You comin to the conkers do then? It's at the village hall.'

'I don't know.'

'You ave to come or else they'll think you're stuck up.'

'And we don't want that, do we.'

He laughed and asked 'How's Lord Heavenshire?'

'I haven't met him yet.'

'Haven't you?'

'He said come up to the house but he'd be away and I went up there but it turned out to be the wrong house and now I'll have to ring and see if he's back.'

'Back from where?'

'I don't know, and somebody said he hasn't even gone.'

'He doesn't go away hardly ever. Bit of a playboy at one time but now never leaves the county. You think it'll work?'

People round here talk familiarly without explaining what they mean, Alice thought, but she said 'Will what work? Sorry, I'm a bit stupid today.'

'His conference centre idea.'

'Ask me again in six months' time.'

'He gets these fads. I hope it works. About time something worked for JJ. It's a nice cottage The Glade I always think.'

'Yes, it's very pretty but the main light switch has gone. Should I ask the marquess?'

'That'll take years – he won't remember your light switch. And he's got a factor called Malcolm – he won't remember your switch either. I'll come and look at it myself. Probably dead simple. Better get on. Nice meeting you. See you later then.'

He climbed back into the cabin and trundled away in his spangling typhoon of dust. While they'd been talking, she'd noticed with a queer jolt that his fly buttons were undone.

16.

As the bodkin rose and pulled tight and plunged, pushed through and rose again, a crimson woollen skin healed over the curve of the darning mushroom, although the sock itself was magenta. Every so often plump fingers stopped and twirled to clear any cramping or to scratch at some part of a grossly overweight body whose rolls were wrapped in a tracksuit which could've done with a wash. There was music in the air. The bodkin halted at a particularly juicy group of chords while the oval face, its chins varying in number with the angle and direction of the jaw, paused in contemplation by looking upwards into the dimness of a coved ceiling where Hope was being tortured by Chastity. The lips on the wistful head were thick, the eyes bagged, the hair wavy and long, its original gold streaked with grey, and as the man came out of his thoughts and bent forward to retrieve a glass of something from the floor, there was an almighty scream of pain from beneath his bum because, unlikely though it was, this spreading blancmange was propped up by a tiny gilt chair which looked incapable of surviving even the weight of a geisha. Luscious chords surged again and washed the gold and marble walls. It was the first movement of *Psyche* by Franck, and JJ was seated on the only piece of furniture in the ballroom at Heaven Park, having discovered by trial and error that it was quite the best place in the whole house to listen to his records.

Rat-a-tat in the distance. An old man, bent at the knees, hand to his forehead, entered from one of the inlaid mahogany doors over which reclined various porphyry gods and goddesses blowing trumpets. The old man wore carpet slippers and a thick jersey, and his announcement across the swirling parquet that 'Dinner is served, m'Lord' echoed plaintively in the dirty vault.

'Almost done your sock, Sidney.'

'Very kind, sir.'

The chair screamed again as JJ rose and embarked upon the four-minute walk to the Summer Dining-room, humming to himself and now and again skipping his step. His sister and another were already seated, their nostrils tantalised but dutifully waiting. His sister said 'It'll be stone cold'.

'I uncovered part of a leg today, JJ,' said the other, a swarthy midget who peered out at the world through pebble-lensed spectacles. His hair was in a ponytail which gave him a fraudulent look that was misleading because he was a distinguished archaeologist.

JJ took up a pair of implements and began to carve the lamb by slicing it horizontally to the bone. 'Not another leg, Pimm. Were the Romans nothing but legs walking all over Europe? The ball-room needs cleaning, Minnie. The resonance is not what it should be.'

'What am I supposed to do, get down on my knees with a mop?'

'Mops are used standing up,' said Pimm.

Lady Minerva Popjoy was an unusual looking woman. Her face was assembled from right-angles and had the proportions of a playing card. It was powdered to an exceptional whiteness. Her eyes were narrow and horizontal and above them were horizontal eyebrows and beneath them a thin horizontal mouth and down the middle sliced a narrow vertical nose. This evening she wore a tennis outfit.

The last to arrive was JJ's daughter, Crystal, who confessed that she wasn't hungry, but her father ignored it and placed a couple of slices of meat on her plate. Sidney appeared in the doorway dithering with his hands. He was going to bring in pud-ding and leave it on the hotplate because he wanted to go and soak his feet.

'And don't forget, sir, you have a caller after dinner.'

'Oh damn, that woman's coming up.'

'Is she American?' asked Minerva. She ate incredibly fast and had almost cleared her plate.

'Didn't sound it particularly. Why should she be?'

'Because they're good at organisation.'

'So are the Germans.'

'Maybe she's German. Quelle horreur.'

'She could read Rilke to us.'

'In the original.'

'In the original, yes. She's come from London and I've put her in The Glade.'

Crystal, who had shoved her plate aside and was rolling a joint, flashed her eyes angrily. 'Robin told me that's what you've done and I think it's stinky of you, Daddy, because you said I could have The Glade.'

'Well, you can't. She's got it.'

'Can I meet her?' asked Minerva, successfully dislodging with one of her fingernails a sinew of lamb from between her teeth.

'Not tonight. I need to wind her up a bit. Think of it, Minnie. Conferences. *Men.*'

They were interrupted by a loud banging at one of the windows. Flakes of plaster descended from the ceiling and the chandelier swung slightly, shifting rainbows over their surprised faces. The banging redoubled and a tiny fist shot through the glass with an explosion causing burglar alarms to go off and floodlights to soak the external flanks of the pile.

'What the devil are you playing at, Sylvia!' yelled JJ. He went to a boiserie panel and opened it and hit several buttons. The exterior of the house collapsed back into silence and darkness.

'I've finally left him,' wailed Sylvia from the terrace. 'I didn't know where else to go. Can I stay in the stables until I've sorted myself out?'

'She can't, Julius, can she,' said Minerva.

'If she's left him, Minnie . . . '

'She'll spoil the conferences and the men.'

'She can stay for a little while. In her hour of need. Pimm, go and help her in. Wrap your hand in this napkin, Sylvia, we don't want blood on the carpet. Yes, you can stay for a little while. But no funny business. Here, drink this. You're hysterical.' JJ had a soft spot for Sylvia. It was something to do with her non-judgemental soul and the fact that though she was half his height they were companions in obesity. 'You can have the new flat in the stables. *For a little while.* And you must pay for the window.'

'I could help with the horses.'

'You know perfectly well we don't have any.'

'Horses don't grow on trees,' chided Minerva.

'Fancy a puff of this?' Crystal asked Pimm.

'Oh yes please,' Sylvia sobbed, wiping red wine off her chest.

17.

Alongside the road ran a massive wall over which hoods of ivy flung themselves and every so often its ramparts of pinkish stone bulged precariously, as though longing to topple outwards. After a mile or so of this wall she came to the Great Gate which was certainly an achievement of architecture but useless as a gateway, so impacted with rust were its hinges. An arrow directed visitors to a more functional entrance half a mile further on where there was another sign: *Warning – Aggressive Animals Within*. Just as the Great Gate never opened, so this one never closed and she drove through. The road surface immediately degenerated into potholes and tufts of grass, with scarcely a stone of gravel left.

The park itself was generally planted with oaks from whose leafy spreadeagling terraces peered owls and nightjars, but these gave way eventually to a formal avenue of monkey puzzle trees which were silhouetted like black talons against a lilac, starry sky. The avenue led to various oblongs and triangles difficult to decipher in the twilight but as she approached, an alarming amount of carved stonework and decorative statuary and balustrading began to fill up the windscreen. The house was vast. And kept on getting vaster. Pavilioned wings, travelling outwards on long arcades, disappeared behind foliage to left and right. Corinthian capitals propped cornices in a multiplicity of layers and volumes. The windows were numberless. Lights shone at a few of them, revealing small squares of fantastic opulence within. The car bobbed to a halt beneath awesome masonry.

She waited awhile, trying to adjust. Well, she'd wanted a change and it was certainly that! There was a little door at ground level but something much more magnificent up a switchback of steps adorned with marble trophies. Taking a deep breath, she opted for magnificence and began the ascent of various external landings ornamented with clusters of forgotten symbolism. At the top she found herself beneath a giant order that soared upwards into the night. Dabs of illumination from inside the building filtered thinly out. A bronze tassel, four feet long hanging off the end of an iron pole, was a parody of a bell-pull but it worked, although no one came. She tried again and at long last an old man opened one half of the huge studded door. His hand hovered over wisps of white hair and he said pathetically 'I'd only just started soaking them'.

'Should I come another time?'

'No, miss. His lordship is expecting you.'

She passed from a vestibule into an echoing hall of incalculable size, lit for the moment by a single lamp. The hall was severe and occult and made her feel she was in the British Museum after hours and that beyond the gloomy fluted columns lay relics of Babylon and Egypt, Greece and Rome, and yet the atmosphere was not institutional and the hovering scents of a very private and antique decay enthralled her.

The old man switched on a string of huge chandeliers. Ornate plasterwork exploded in vistas. He hobbled down a curving corridor with arcaded windows and she, not knowing what else to do, followed. Curtains of tattered brocade, their rococo pelmets twenty-five feet above the floor, blotted his moans, while portrait after portrait gazed at each other over his head. A bang was heard from the far end and a man came into view, drying his hands on a tea-towel. Though corpulent he walked with a relaxed upright gait. 'How do you do,' he called while still some distance away.

'How do you do,' she replied, decidedly overwhelmed, having had no idea that she'd be coming to one of the biggest houses there has ever been.

'And how is dear old London? I'm afraid I've forgotten your name.'

'Alice.'

'And this is Sidney,' he said, dumping the tea-towel in the old man's hands. 'You can go to bed now, Sidney, and you can lie in in the morning. Good night.' Turning back to her he said 'I had a cousin called Alice – she was from Bohemia. Do you have Bohemian relations?'

'No.'

'Neither do I now. She was killed by a stone dropped from a tower. Death so sudden that no adrenaline was found in the blood. Mind the steps.' He flicked a group of brass switches, opened a pair of heavy golden doors and another corridor opened up ahead of a shallow flight of alabaster stairs. Here the ravages of time were much worse. The walls were discoloured, the paintwork in urgent need of renewal, and many mouldings had broken away. 'The state rooms are now behind us,' he said. 'We use them. Not always. But not rarely. What's it like outside? I've not been out today.'

'It was breezy. But now it's still.'

'For me autumn begins with those several very windy days which usually blow up around the middle of September. I hope the cottage is all right. No more chopped feet.'

'The wiring's a bit – '

'So is ours.' He paused and looked at her and for the first time she noticed how kind his face was and that like most kind faces it was touched with melancholy. 'I'm sorry you had such a nasty shock on arrival. It was probably some kid having a joke. The vibes are normally very good at The Glade. Its end wall, you know – the right hand side looking at it from the front – is a crutch wall of about 1350. Which is not bad going because the oldest cottage in England is only 1335 or something.'

Alice said 'Really' as she followed him through a screen of pillars and across another hall, more fascinated by the man's grace of movement despite his enormous weight.'My neighbour said he'd have a look at it,' she said.

'Did he now.'

'I mean the wiring, not the wall.'

'Yes, I know what you mean.'

'But he hasn't yet.'

'He will. Dickon is maddeningly reliable.'

They went through three doors in quick succession, JJ flicking switches like a matador, and passed into a top-lit rotunda. A double tier of ionic columns was capped by a painted dome and lantern, all suffering dreadfully from dilapidation. But Alice couldn't but stop and gasp 'Oh, it's lovely!'

Though greatly wanting repair, Heaven Park was of course a major masterpiece and JJ flushed with pleasure, for he never tired of people's first reactions to his domain. The marquess proudly flourished his hand aloft. *The Conquest of the Caribbean* by the Earl of Cowslipvale. We tried to get Verrio but he died and we ended up with a pupil of Thornhill and the result is much better than anything Verrio ever painted. Notice the mosaic of single-breasted Amazons on the floor, the point being that nearly a quarter of it is from the original Roman villa which stood on this site. My friend Pimm can tell you a lot more about that. We're now in the family wing. Come along.'

JJ opened a curved door, embossed with tropical birds, set into the curved wall. Another corridor. Another corner. Another corridor. Another door. He stood aside for her to enter a very warm room lit by the glow from a log fire. Her host switched on a lamp and for the first time since entering the building Alice saw carpet. 'Welcome to the cosy. Plonk yourself down. I believe there's some champagne in the fridge.'

The room was a chaos of books, bottles, half eaten packets of snackery, mugs, wineglasses, videos, CDs, magazines, newspapers, and items of clothing cast about willy-nilly. He caught her expression. 'Yes, I know. I tell Sidney to clean up only once a month. I like mess. I need mess. The rest of the house doesn't allow it. But here I insist. Oh, sorry.' He moved a pile of rubbish along a sofa and she settled at one end. JJ turned on another lamp and some pop music. 'A new nightclub has opened in Appleminster. You must come with us one evening.'

While shimmying to the rhythm and untwisting the wires of the cork, he examined the visitor more closely. She apparently had all the necessary skills but meeting her now for the first time he couldn't honestly say that she was inspirational. Oh dear, he should have conducted proper interviews, not rushed into the appointment after a couple of phonecalls and a letter. But maybe she was one of those quiet little beavers who build empires when you think they're just sewing in the corner. Anyway it was too late to change now. She was here. He'd committed himself.

'Now before we become too friendly let's get something straight. Your job is to make lots of money. You do understand that, don't you?' He popped the half bottle of champagne.

'Let's hope.'

'No. I'm sick of hope. Any more hope and I'll choke to death. I want something to *occur*. This is a wonderful place but it's falling apart and I'm at my wits' end. You may see what you imagine to be possessions but I can't sell a bloody thing. And all the really tip-top stuff is on loan to the Victoria & Albert Museum for another hundred years. The house will be dust in a hundred years. We built up quite a lot from the usual grand tours. The eleventh Earl of Cowslipvale, whose son became the first Marquess of Heavenshire in the year seventeen let me think – oh, I'm boring you.'

'No, you're not.'

'Yes, I am. I can see I am.'

'Honestly, no. It's a lot to take in, that's all.'

'Normally I don't subject people to all the historical family shit unless they ask, but it's because you are coming to work for us, and well, if it really isn't a trial for you, it's very interesting actually, because Lord Cowslipvale purchased something quite extraordinary in Ferrara. You'll never guess what.'

'A giraffe?'

'Cheeky. It was a manuscript. By the hand of Leonardo da Vinci and the master had written *Astronomical Poems* across the cover. And guess what: they've never been published. As you know, Leonardo himself could be very secretive and I think he was embarrassed by them, always describing himself as an engineer and treating even his pictures as a bit on the side. And afterwards one of his brothers hid the poems away and when they did turn up it was in this drawer in Ferrara with a load of crap. We continued the tradition of secrecy and would never allow them to be copied or even examined but despite all our precautions the manuscript disappeared around the time of the Napoleonic Wars, some turd obviously nicked it. There was a general outcry but no trace has ever been found, and it's no good crying over spilt milk, but sometimes I do dream of how a teeny-weeny book of poetry would transform our circumstances. I mean, the museums would slash each other's throats for it, wouldn't they? There are some things I *can* sell, a few pictures, a portion of the land, but it wouldn't be nearly enough and so we really do have to find an alternative source of income. And that, my love, is where you come in. Get us some big fat conferences.'

Alice had gone white and drained her glass but after his address, JJ took to dancing with more abandon on those nimble ankles, waving the tips of his fingers and making suggestive movements with his shoulders. She said 'You're a good dancer. What's this music?'

'I'll Keep On Holding On' by the Marvelettes. I chose it deliberately, so on yer feet.' Instead of rising Alice tenaciously gripped her empty glass with both hands, so JJ refilled it for her and rhumba-ed across the carpet and slapped the face of a stone head on a pedestal. 'This hideous creature is the second Marquess, by Nollekens. My friend Pimm – you'll meet him – can't decide if he really is a friend – we've certainly known each other for ages and we don't fight but I always feel that he and I should be closer than we are and that he's a bit aloof – he's uncovering the Temple of Mercury up the road – well, my friend Pimm – I've forgotten what I was going to say about him.' JJ dipped and rose with the music.

'Are you insured for conferences?'

He fell into an armchair. 'I think we're covered for third party liabilities. Ask Malcolm.'

'And theft?'

'Yes, I'm aware that the impulse to steal is deeply implanted in the species. We're wired up. We can hide the knick-knacks. No one can afford to insure everything, can they? I keep a pistol under my bed. Who else have you seen round here apart from Dickon?'

'I had lunch at The Crag on Sunday.'

'Did you? They're very posh up there. They only use three-prong forks. Did the Craddock sing to you?'

'He did as a matter of fact.'

'He does that. It's a power trip. Everything has to stop for his fucking song. I don't eat there myself.'

'He doesn't invite you?'

'He did once. But I was doing something else. He took it personally.'

'Does he eat here?'

'They're such bores, I mean, life's too short but . . . there's a sort of feud. I find the whole thing embarrassing quite frankly. And he regards the village side of the river as his personal fiefdom. Well, he's welcome to it. Their son's got something wrong with him.'

'I didn't notice.'

'No, you don't notice at first. Then you notice. Who else was there? Anyone else?'

'A scientist.'

'He's sponging off them again, is he? On Sundays our house is open. In the summer anyway. Last Sunday was our last day. But we've been blacklisted because we've got no wheelchair access. I told them I'm not wrecking a triumph of English Palladian architecture with a load of ruddy ramps and anyway I'm frightened of infirmity, aren't you? People in wheelchairs give me the collywobbles. I do think defective babies should be exposed on hillsides or at least given a discreet jab of something terminal. You know, if a little judicious suffocation had been done a long time ago in this very room . . . ' He checked himself and emptied the bottle of wine into his glass. 'I told them we've got sedan chair access. They didn't like that. But why *can't* paraplegics employ a couple of village boys to carry them round? The lads could do with the work. Oh, no, they've got to wreck the building instead. Anyway, now you're here, there will be no more openings for at least a twelvemonth. That'll simplify life for a start. Half a bottle's never enough, is it?' He popped a second and topped up both their glasses.

There was a click at the door. The handle was turning. The door opened a foot or two and a long white face edged hesitantly round it.

'No!' shouted JJ and the face promptly disappeared.

A voice implored from the other side 'I only want to look. Is she reading Rilke to you?'

'No she isn't! Go away!' Footsteps retreated into an unknown region and JJ attended to their fading. When they had quite gone he explained 'That was my sister.'

Alice nodded discreetly and asked 'When's the dustman?'

'Who?'

'At The Glade. When do they collect the rubbish?'

'It's on a weekday. I'm not sure which one.' JJ threw a couple of crotched logs onto the fire and Alice realised with some pleasure that she had become far more at ease in this house than she had at The Crag. JJ switched on a third table lamp which threw a fan of custard light up an oil-painting which occupied the wall between two windows.

'*The Massacre of the Innocents* by Polpotto. We bought it from the Vatican when they were strapped for cash.'

'When was that then?'

He laughed broadly. 'Oh, fuck knows. My mind's gone. I used to be pretty good but after the age of forty, rot becomes a way of life. Round here anyway. But there's a kind of relief in accepting one's merely a ratbag doing one's best. The Surveyor of the King's Pictures is always trying to get that picture. Because they've got the other one at Windsor. But he shan't have it!' JJ clenched his brow and pressed his temples.

'Are you all right?'

'I get tight head sometimes, a certain dizziness. It's nothing. I wish you hadn't mentioned insurance.'

'I do apologise.'

'Well, get off your arse and give me a hug.' She did her best but he replied 'Hugging's not really your thing, is it. Everything's changing so fast these days but, you know, life used to be very traditional round here when I was a boy. Until quite recently a goat with gilded horns and ribbons tied to it was flung from the top of the church tower on Saint James's Day.'

'Alive?'

'Of course. Do you imagine they'd *murder* it first? You have a bloodthirsty streak.'

'But what was the purpose of it?'

'Isn't it always fertility or the evil eye? Anyway they stopped it. Mrs Bladder-Williams and that lot did. The RSPCA crowd. By the way you have to be a bit careful what you say round here. The wretches pounce on everything. So little happens, you see.'

'I thought you said it's all changing.'

'Some things never change.'

JJ walked across the room and switched on a fourth table lamp. This time Alice saw – and it caused a tingle to rush over her skin – that at the far end of the sofa on which she sat, beyond the intervening debris, a young creature was curled up asleep among velvet cushions. His plump red mouth was puckered and slightly open, exposing a glint of teeth.

'Don't mind him,' said JJ softly. But the lamp, unlike the music or voices, disturbed the boy who stirred and stretched and yawned and blinked his round bluish eyes and pushed back his tousled curls. When he noticed Alice, his cheeks contracted into a sleepy smile. 'What time is it 'n' stuff?' he asked her with a purring rustic accent. He scratched himself absent-mindedly through grubby clothes.

'Not late,' said JJ.

Glory Boy swung his feet onto the floor, paused briefly staring at the carpet, before lacing them into boots which he'd tucked out of sight round the end of the sofa. 'I've missed team practice. I need a piss,' he said and his body ambled out of the room with a low-slung swing.

JJ watched him go – the boy left the door open and JJ went across to close it. 'He plays football for the village. But I expect he's on his way to the pub. Have you ever been in love?'

Thanks to the champagne, she said 'Yes' without a second thought.

'Are you in love now?'

'I hope not. Finished with it for the time being. That's one of the reasons I'm here.'

'Really? I didn't know you were on the run.'

'I'm not running away. I want a new life.'

'But it's hell, isn't it.'

'Yes . . .'

'Unrequited love is the worst but I think all love has something unrequited about it There is always one who loves more and who is therefore always at a disadvantage, and it's never as complete, wonderful and easy as it's supposed to be. He's a total shit of course? Yours, I mean.'

'Of course.'

'There should be a Lovers Anonymous,' he said. 'To help people get off people.'

'And yours?'

'He's mischievous but not bad. And wouldn't the world be a ghastly place without a bit of mischief?'

'The thing is . . .' Tears filled her eyes and he took her hand and rubbed the back of it and kissed it.

'Because something comes to an end, Alice, it doesn't mean it was in vain. Now let's open another half-bottle. Actually champagne's an English invention but the French, bless em, brought it to perfection. I reckon the only thing that works is to find a new obsession. You can fall in love with me if you like.' Pop!

She locked her ankles and rocked forward in the seat. 'I'm sure there are lots of people in love with you.'

'Nobody has ever been in love with me,' he said.

'Oh, I'm sure –'

'No. No one has. Not a soul. That's one of the crosses I bear.'

He put the Marvelettes on again and dragged her to her feet.

18.

The village hall occupied the main room of the Old Grammar
School, a late sixteenth-century flinted building adjacent to The
Zodiac inn. On the Saturday evening before Harvest Festival
Sunday it was customary for the village to gather in the hall for
an event which went back into prehistory and which was half
party, half rite. The drink was mostly ale, the food mostly sausage
rolls, and the music had for the last two years been supplied by
DJ Meat, better known as Jason, the butcher's son. Paralysed by
indecision, Alice had thrown a coin at the last minute and it fell
with the 'don't go' face upwards which Alice in a fit of perversity
decided to contradict. When she arrived, inquisitive but beset by
squalls of nerves, the place was horribly packed with noise,
smoke, bottoms, elbows and boobs.

'You came then,' said Dickon right off. Alice hardly recognised
him in his bright white shirt but he disappeared immediately and
she felt gormless. Crystal Popjoy, in green jeans and a green silk
blouse, tweaked her arm. 'Daddy won't come. Can you buy me a
drink? I've got no money.' Alice stood at the bar with growing
vexation while everyone else was served and when finally she
managed to extract a couple of shandies and return to Crystal, the
girl said 'What's this?'

'A shandy.'

'But I said a large vodka.'

Heavy beat music crashed in the air like plates and boulders.
Dickon reappeared, pushing and pulling Alice's elbows from
behind. 'Don't you know Buttered Pease? Everyone knows that!'
he said and she danced despite herself, while an unpleasant buzz
raked her mind, and she heard herself say 'Thanks for mending
the light'. He'd repaired it some days before while she was absent
from the cottage, leaving a note on the table, which instead of
seeming neighbourly had revived her sense of feeling vulnerable
to intruders. She was certain she'd locked the back door but
clearly she hadn't – unless Dickon also had a key. But – oh yes –
he'd told her that he found the back door was open and he
wouldn't have a reason to lie about that, would he. Would he?

Dickon stamped the floor, grabbing and releasing her in unexpected ways, while Crystal slithered round Glory Boy who

danced in a trancelike, self-absorbed manner looking downwards. Unable to find the rhythm, Alice's feet hopped like random frogs – would she never be released from this agony of self-consciousness? At the end of the track Glory looked up at her and bared his white gappy teeth, but kept a distance.

'What's she like?' Glory asked Crystal.

'A bore,' she whispered, wetting his ear.

The Tewkesbury Boys arrived in blasts of motorbike exhaust. They weren't really criminal but they could give rise to sudden, quickly forgotten events, and so added an edginess to the proceedings. A trio of girls from Gypsy Castle giggled coyly at them. It was early in the evening, angst and lasciviousness were uneasy partners, and things never really warmed up until after the ceremony known as Searching for the Conkers of Galadriel.

Crystal however was well ahead in bonhomie, throwing back her long chocolate hair and laughing immoderately. Earlier she'd had a blast of grass from the greenhouse, plus a line of cocaine left in a drawer, and she'd managed to screw a double vodka out of Hoggart by tickling him when his wife wasn't looking. Now she lolled against Dickon, making him dance, but he seemed bashful about touching her.

Why wasn't he bashful about touching me? wondered Alice, obliquely offended. Does he think I'm some pathetic old bag who needs help?

The Revd Sinus Simm gave Alice a wave but Crystal span across it in order to kiss Paul Crimsoncourt who had at that moment appeared with a girl nobody knew.

One of the Tewkesbury Boys asked Alice 'Are yearn?'

'Excuse me?'

'Are yearn?'

'I'm sorry, er . . .'

'Oi said *are* YEARN?'

'I don't believe I am.'

The Revd Simm interjected 'Oh, don't be so modest. I'm sure you are. Shall we be seeing you at Saint Wendy's tomorrow?' But further conversation was cut short by a man decked out in fruit, vegetables and sheaves of cereal, who raised his arms commandingly with the words 'Silence for the Corn King!'

They roared back as one 'Silence for the Corn King!' and laughed.

The cornucopian figure went on in his town-crier voice 'The Corn King enjoins you to search for the Conkers of Galadriel!'

'The Conkers of Galadriel!' responded the throng.

'Firstly we require – what?' asked the Corn King, adjusting his fruity cap.

'A young virgin from the village!' came the collective response.

'I knows an old un!' called out Selwyn Blagdon.

'Oooooooh!' hooted the rabble.

'There aint been no virgin yer fer forty years!' bawled a Tewkesbury Boy.

Alice bent her head to Dickon. 'What's it all about?'

'Shsh,' he responded.

The Corn King twitched and cocked an ear. 'Who is that whispering?' And the crowd parted as he strode inexorably towards Alice. She quaked. 'You!' he admonished. The eyes of the Corn King ravaged her.

'Me, no, I'm not a virgin, honestly I'm not, please, no, not me – '

The crowd cheered and brayed as with his leaf-covered mittens the Corn King buffeted her towards the centre of the floor where a lad with a white silk scarf waited to blindfold the victim.

Robin Craddock blew Crystal a kiss and she laughed out loud. The Corn King spun round glaring. 'Silence, everyone!' he commanded. Crystal spluttered. Robin thought how vulgar she became when enjoying herself and how often people one loves are a mortifying embarrassment to the nobility and tenderness of one's feelings. Oh, my love, please don't laugh with your mouth open in *that* way!

With eyes bound, Alice was rotated slowly by rough, warm hands until she'd lost her internal compass. Which didn't take long. Her internal compass had been fragile for some years. The crowd drew back as far as it could in those confines, the men forming an inner ring. The sweaty, breathing silence terrified her more than the banter. She was shoved gently from behind and ordered by the Corn King in a tone not at all self-parodic to 'Go yonder. Search. Galadriel's conkers.' She stumbled forward, arms outstretched. 'What must I do?' was her pitiful question.

'Feeeel your way! Feeeel your way!' they jeered.

Alice tottered, making a thin moan, until her fingertip touched denim. It was the Tewkesbury Boy who had earlier addressed her and who now, pelvis jutting forward, placed himself in her path. She probed, felt a soft mass, quickly moved her hand upwards to a belt, and drew back with a muted squeal. Everyone howled and the boy hopped coquettishly away.

'Keep on searching!' exhorted the Corn King.

A voice at the back of her skull replied to him 'Piss off, you pathetic twit' and this voice clearly wanted her to throw off the blindfold and walk out of there, but somehow she couldn't, she was hypnotised by the necessity of participation, and took more hazardous steps, tip-toeing along the edge of an imaginary cliff, and once again touched cloth . . . and bone . . . there was a sweet, sickly smell . . . 'My good woman, pray – ' The rich actorly voice skidded upwards into a whinny. It was that Lomax person, yuk, no, and she quickly trickled on. Like a dancing bear she was teased and cajoled round the circle of upright males and at one point she sensed the proximity of Dickon but passed on without contact. Eventually the alternating hoots and pindrop silences got to her – she found an enormous hand, held on to its comforting warmth, and her fragile nerve gave way. She fell against the massive chest of Justice Royal, the car mechanic, and helplessly put her arms round him.

'Well done!' laughed the Corn King, removing Alice's blindfold. He removed his own disguise. It was Detective Hoskins. Alice was disconcerted all over again – he had been transfigured, possessed, another. 'You two are now the Harvest Lovers!' said Hoskins. Justice chuckled modestly while Alice, exalted because it was over and she had come through, wondered what the implications might be. The answer forthcame. 'And if you refuse each other, the Corn King is by ancient custom permitted to debauch you both!' The room rang with more laughter. Crystal said in mock cockney 'Dickon sent this across. Say ta everso.' Alice sipped the presented brandy and said to Detective Hoskins 'You're rotten to do that to me. I'm new.'

'You're much less new now. Wasn't it fun?'

'Only afterwards.'

'Better fun after than no fun at all. You've got apples in your cheeks suddenly. It always happens that there comes a moment when the girl can't stand it any longer and clutches desperately at anyone.'

'Do you do it every year then?'

'Not me personally but they were stuck and I said I'd help – my mate does the disco.'

'What *are* the Conkers of Galadriel?'

'Depends.'

'Did I find them?'

'They've never been found,' scoffed Glory Boy who was nodding to the sound of a current hit, 'Insect' by Paedophilia, 'and anyway it's too early for conkers.'

Jason Hoggart increased the volume. The rhythms were complex and fast and on the other side of the assembly that Lomax person was keeping up with them in the centre of an appreciative group who clapped him on in time. 'Go it, Max!' they urged. Before leaving the caravan that evening Lomax had, as he always did for a dance, put on his old tap-shoes, and now his limbs clattered like crazy broom-handles, and sparks and smoke flew from his hysterical heels.

> *You tried to revile me*
> *By calling me an insect*
> *But let me remind you*
> *That insects deserve respect*
> *An insect has a heart*
> *He cannot live apart*
> *He loves to kiss and hug*
> *And dance the jitterbug*
> *But if you interrupt his thing*
> *He has a wicked sting*
>
> *Insect outsect insect outsect insect outsect*
> *If you can sing that*
> *You*
> *Deserve some respect*
> *Too*

Lomax skidded on a pool of beer and would have crashed but, before you could say Jack Robinson, Glory Boy had saved him. The dancer tapped on but was clearly discomfited and afterwards, out of breath and without smiling, walked through the gauntlet of pats to the bar where a number of complimentary drinks awaited him. DJ Meat began a new mix and the crowd took to the floor. For the unattached it was pick-up time.

'Let's dance,' Robin asked Crystal, trying to be casual but sounding negligent.

'We'd clash. I'm in green and you're in green but you're in the wrong green.'

'Oh, come on.'

'I'm going to dance with Paul.'

Robin gazed with dismal longing upon her receding back.

19.

JJ had his feet up in the cosy – he knew he was fat but was proud of his ankles and didn't want swollen ones – and he was flicking from the back forwards through a computer magazine. A dozen more were scattered over the carpet. He'd have to rig up Alice's office with some of these contraptions. Nowadays a telephone, a typewriter and a paper basket were no longer enough. A single rap on the door was followed by a skinny figure in jet jewellery and a lemon ball-gown drawn tightly in at the waist.

'My, you look good. So you're going down to the village after all?'

She screwed up her nose.

'But you've got changed, Minnie, and you were looking forward to it.'

'I know I was.'

'And you didn't go last year.'

'I know I didn't.'

'Perhaps you'll never go again.'

'I shall!'

'You used to love it so, especially when they picked you for virgin.'

She hummed introspectively, sinking with a scented rustle onto the sofa beside him. 'But if you won't go with me, Julius . . .'

'Really I can't bear it anymore.'

'So why should I endure hell in order to find no one to be sweet to me?'

'Crystal's there.'

'She'll be all over the place.'

'Well, she's twenty years old, she's allowed that. And Alice will be there. Probably.'

'I don't know her.'

'You could get to know her.'

'And what if she isn't there?' Minerva turned away, pushing her fist into her cheek. 'Oh – I feel such a fool the whole time, Julius.'

'Why is that?'

'Oh – because I am a fool probably. So I shan't go.'

'Of course you're not a fool, my sweet.'

'Let's play Scrabble instead.'

'And that beautiful frock will be wasted.'

'No, it won't. I'll pretend I'm dressing for dinner.'

'We've already had dinner.'

Brother and sister sat side by side on the sofa, both pairs of knees together, looking into the fire and remembering and dreaming and drifting and vaguely hoping as the flames fluttered over their warm faces.

20.

The Zodiac was a free house. It had existed as a hostelry even before the foundation of Saint Wendy's which itself took place in the middle of the ninth century (although the Venerable Bede implies in an ambiguous aside that there was a Christian church here in late Roman times). A verandah along the pub's front was railed off by a wooden bar running between four massive oak posts and polished to an adamantine shine by generations of drinkers' hands. The posts supported an overhanging gable where, written in a faded copperplate, *The Best of British Ales &*

Spirits – Wines & Brandies from Foreign Parts encouraged passers-by to take the broader view of life. The verandah was much sought after in warm weather but it did make the two ground floor bars dark: lamps with red shades always burned within, even at midday.

The hard bar and the soft bar were entered on opposite sides of the front entrance but linked by a broad archway at the rear where they effectively became one. There was a cigarette machine in a corner of the soft bar and a fruit machine in a corner of the hard, but otherwise the arrangements had hardly changed in a century. The soft bar possessed the same foxed Beardsley prints and stuffed animals, the same comfy chairs and carpet; and the hard bar, where a desultory darts match was taking place, was still papered with Victorian newspapers varnished over and browned with smoke, still furnished with stools and settles on a stone floor. Since the occasional room was let in the crooked corridors above, it was known as The Zodiac inn.

Hoggart the Butcher said 'There's nothin like avin someone at home to get you out o' the house'.

'Wouldn't know,' scowled Selwyn Blagdon who lived alone in a picturesque hovel on the edge of woodland.

Both turned as Sir Timothy Craddock came through to the back on the soft bar side and reciprocal noddings took place. The Craddock, though dapper in tweed and spotted neckerchief, did not look well. It was as though the green hues of his suit had seeped upwards. On his way down to the inn, for he nearly always made a point of coming on foot, the High Street had without warning pitched like the sea and his head had swum as though in shipwreck, and not for the first time this month.

'Are you all right, Sir Tim?' enquired the barmaid.

'Funny turn on the pavement, Lois. Must be the cold.'

'But it's been very warm.'

'In which case it must be the heat. Make it a double single malt please.'

'You sit down on them cushions an I'll bring it over.'

'Bless you, dear.'

The Craddock subsided into a moth-eaten armchair and suffered a delayed distress, because funny turns had played no part whatsoever in his life until the last few weeks. A cough was one thing, but losing one's marbles quite another. He knew he had to visit the bank manager in Appleminster at some point fairly soon to sort out finances and wondered if that might have something to do with it. The soporific thud of darts into the board soothed him and by the time his friend arrived he was capable of pretending to be his old self.

'What'll you have, Oliver?'

'Same as you.'

'You can't have the same. You can have similar.'

'You got that from Flannel Williams at school.'

'Do you want to buy some raffle tickets, you two?' asked Lois, resting her breasts softly on the bar.

'What's it for?'

'A new village hall.'

'We don't need a new village hall.'

'That's what I say. They're going to call it the Community Centre.'

'Your hand is shaking, Tim.'

'I'll be straight with you, Oliver. I had a funny turn. Out there. Just now.'

Oliver, for whom funny turns had been a way of life for many years, proposed a selection of pills and offered to escort the Craddock home but Sir Tim said 'Don't fuss. Clear as a bell now, clear as a bell. Look, why I asked you here is because . . . ' He leant closer and one eye throbbed conspiratorially. 'You see, I was talking to a friend of mine on the blower this morning and he let something slip. He used to be one of the high-ups in the Ministry of Power and he said – ' the Craddock edged even closer, relishing the thrill, as though after many a long year he was once again close to the centre of events – 'he said, and it sounds really awful, but apparently, and I stress apparently, as a matter of fact it beggars belief, but *apparently* there is a plan afoot to build some futuristic city right slap bang on this very spot where we are sitting!'

Oliver Knott was silent.

'You're silent.'

'Yes. That's because I did have a phone call on the subject.'

'I knew it! They still value your advice at the Ministry. Can you find out more?'

'I'll try.'

'Because it will have to be stopped, Oliver. We can't have things like that round here.'

'Computers aren't all bad, Tim.'

'That's not what I'm talking about as well you know. I'm talking about *desecration*. So be a good chap and make some further enquiries, will you?'

Later, when they'd gone, Hoggart said to Blagdon 'Did you hear what I heard?'

'I did that.'

'No good'll come of it.'

'No good at all.'

Hoggart stretched his body and looked out of the window at the sky. 'Nights drawing in. Same again, Selwyn?'

'Make that a similar.'

                                   21.

Max Lomax, in his dark glasses, was sitting in an awkward position on his front step as gusts of wind raked the Beowulf Caravan Park. He was polishing his tap-shoes to a beetle-bright shine as a kind of therapy because he'd had an awful night, disturbed by the thud of conkers from a nearby chestnut tree. Worse still, this morning had found himself unable to 'go' which was not typical. Max had the peculiarity of expelling every day around nine a.m. one large turd like a brown cucumber and for the first time in ages it had not happened. Furthermore he had a cold coming – he knew what that corrosive sting at the back of the nose portended – so that all in all his mood was distinctly gruff. The only good thing was that summer was over, the ghastly aren't-we-all-having-fun summer was – thank the Lord – *over*. He lifted a hand by way of greeting as Mrs Punch came by in her headscarf. She was the wife of a retired taxidermist – they lived four caravans along – and she was on her way to buy a number of nutritionless, tooth-rotting products from the village shop. Max sneezed.

'Take care of that, Mr Lomax.'

'Presently I shall concoct an inhalation.'

'Don't do yerself a mischief!'

Stupid cow. He shivered, clambered to his feet with a cracking of joints and stood for a while stretching out his full height beneath fast clouds, before going indoors to put on the kettle. Removing his dark glasses he scanned the shelves of the kitchenette: Marmite, Ovaltine, arrowroot biscuits, a bottle of horse-radish sauce, borax in a jam jar, Milk of Magnesia, Cellophane-wrapped crumpets spotted with blue mould, Camp coffee syrup, two tins of condensed milk, Maynard's wine gums, Bisto, friar's balsam, witch hazel – ah, his incomparable witch hazel! When life had overdone its demands and the poor bloody ogles had reddened and puffed, he would lie on his bunkette, knees bent to the right, head raised on a pillow, eyes padded with cotton-wool soaked in witch hazel, and the cooling pleasure would last for about ten minutes after which time he would become annoyed at being unable to stretch out his legs properly because if he did his feet would strike the end cupboard and his legs still not be straight and this would remind him that despite his talent and determination, he had never been in a position to buy a caravan of sufficient length and had been compelled always to rest or sleep with bent legs which was a chronic source of bit- terness for a tap-dancing man.

All Bran, Bird's Custard Powder, a tin of Golden Syrup very sticky round the lid, Elastoplast, Vick – yes, Vick – that's what he wanted and he took down the plastic mini-tub and was reminded as always that once upon a time Vick's Vapour Rub had been sold in small jars of Bristol blue glass and that as a little boy he had collected these beautiful jars, pestering neighbours during influenza epidemics, until he reached one thousand, whereupon his step-mother had thrown them all away, the shitty bitch. Yes, that was a bitter blow. A bitter bitter blow. Threw them all away she did without so much as mentioning it first. He'd punched his step-mother in the bottom but that didn't bring his jar collection back. He'd had a big problem with people in authority ever since.

Max unscrewed the top of the plastic mini-tub and stuck his conk in. Oh, the wonderful balmy aroma! That hadn't changed. He spooned some into a bowl, poured boiling water over it, sat down and put his head under a towel and inhaled . . . my goodness, how it stung the eyes, but he persisted and his thoughts turned back to the good old days, how he had loved the good old days, how he missed the good old days and I must wash my shirts and why have I never been invited to Heaven Park even though I've lived here for years and used to be the most debonair song & dance man on the coast and could fill the Pavilion Theatre at Puckermouth on any Friday or Saturday night in the season while my record of 'Moon River' outsold Kathy Kirby one week, but the world today has no time for a polished performance because everything is cheap and nasty and demolished and covered with concrete and stupid and slapdash and I don't even get a pension for the privilege of living in this hellhole, not for another five years anyway, and how I'm expected to survive until then I can't imagine –

There was a tap on his back. The towel flew into the air and the bowl onto the floor and through Vick-impaired vision Max made out a gouache of Detective Hoskins.

'Did I make you jump?' enquired Hoskins.

'Jump?'

'Yes. Jump.'

'No.'

'Expecting me were you?'

'Certainly not.' Max fumbled for spectacles.

'Sorry. I don't like to interrupt a man when he's ill.'

'I'm not ill.'

'Let's say – you look ill.'

'I often look ill. It's from my father's side. And I often get a cold at the change of season. Please, sit down.' Max cleared the bed. 'I'll put the kettle on.'

'I've never before seen you without dark glasses, Mr Lomax.'

Max's eyes were pale grey but nervously alert and in certain lights, such as the present one, they glinted silver. 'If you'll forgive me, Detective Inspector, I'll put them back on because I'm very light-sensitive. Thank heavens the autumn is here. Goodbye to all that dreadful holiday cheerfulness. Hullo to wind and rain on black nights and snuggling in front of the electric fire. Do you take sugar?'

'No thanks.' Hoskins had a carrier bag on his knees and he withdrew from it a large rubber article, hideously veined, and placed it on the bed. Max, who was sitting on a stool with his legs wound round each other several times, leant forward.

'Haven't seen one of those in yonks,' he said. 'Tommy Trot used to use that sort of thing in his act.' Max spooned five sugars into his own mug and stirred methodically.

'Have you seen this particular one before?'

Max stretched across and lifted the object between thumb and forefinger. 'Can't say I have, dearie. Bloody realistic though. Yes, I can safely say can't say I have.'

'You know where this one was found, don't you?'

'Of course. The whole village knows. Has the poor little mite recovered?'

'It was only a practical joke but one doesn't want this sort of thing to get out of hand.'

'I better show you something right away.'

Max squeezed past Hoskins and removed a cloisonné vase from the top of a wicker trunk. He opened the trunk and dived in. For a while his red-corduroy bottom dominated the corner as Punch & Judy glove puppets, a string of mock sausages, a rubber sword and a donkey's head flew out, but when Max stood up he was holding – a severed foot. 'Tommy left me his prop basket when he walked the gangplank. But as you can see this one is an inferior product. It lacks the ankle.'

Hoskins flexed his bow lips a couple of times and said 'So it does, Mr Lomax. You obviously know about these things. Well, I shan't keep you. Thanks for the tea.'

Closing the caravan door on the outside world, Max whispered to himself 'Silly little poof'. But the detective's visit had been a stimulus and, manoeuvring spindly limbs into the narrow water closet, he squatted and embarked upon his singular motion.

22.

A capacious black car purred down the High Street and stopped a few yards from the bridge. Four men in suits, two young and two middle-aged, climbed out and confabulated round the bonnet on which one of the young men opened an Ordnance Survey map. The bonnet was warm and arousing under the young man's hands. 'Looks like we go back up the hill and ask,' he said, shielding his eyes from the sun. It really was a beautiful October morning. The languorous haze of summer was only a memory now, for sharpness and purpose, space and time had returned to the world.

'You've got it upside down, Tucker,' sighed the Superior.

'Ahem, sir,' interposed the other young man, Finch, the tallowy one. 'If I'm not mistaken, we go over this bridge, bear round to the left and take the first right.'

'Precisely,' concurred the Superior with relief. He turned to the fourth man, his Chief Assistant, and said 'I hope you're noting this down, Arbuthnot. *No* marks to Tucker, *another* mark to Finch.' Arbuthnot tapped into a computer the size of a bar of soap in his palm. 'You can drive for a bit, Arbuthnot. Finch has earned a rest. Tucker, sit in the front with Arbuthnot.' The Superior beamed at Finch who had the good sense not to beam back.

Hedgerows swished metal flanks as the road narrowed to a single-track which passed between shaggy coppices turning various degrees of autumnal red. Finch was yawning at the tedious rusticity of it all when action manifested itself on the left. Half a dozen small cars splashed with mud were parked at random on an apron of waste land and beyond them assorted characters were toiling backwards and forwards with buckets of rubble. Part of the site was protected by a tented superstructure.

'Pull over, Arbuthnot. I smell trouble.'

The Superior jumped out of the car, waving his arms. 'Hallooo!' A pert maiden, breathing heavily, halted and said 'Hallooo!' back.

'What's all this?' he asked proprietorially, walking towards her. Acorns crunched under his feet.

'The Mercury dig.'

'And you are?'

'Veronica.'

'And who's in charge?'

'He's over there in the tented bit. Thick glasses and a ponytail.' And she continued walking with her bucket, eventually tipping its contents on a mound near the feet of Arbuthnot who said 'Steady on. These are new shoes.'

'Sorry,' said the girl, 'but you're standing on our mound'.

The Superior located the man in charge who was thoroughly absorbed and working away with a brush. He was one of seven or eight kneeling sacerdotal figures, with brushes busy, under the 250 square feet of tarpaulin. All about them a time-eaten foundation of stone, pockmarked like meringue, had been exposed and in certain spots small assemblages of mosaic floor, some a mere handful of pieces, others quite extensive, flaunted the colour schemes of Flavian Rome.

'It really looks awfully good,' said the Superior peevishly.

'Isn't this an unusual border. Rams' heads and oak leaves.'

'Who's sponsoring you?'

'The Department of Culture, the European Monument Fund, Unesco and Oxford University.'

'Oh,' responded the Superior with annoyance. How it made him want to chop off that cocky little ponytail. 'And you are who?'

'Pimm.'

'Anything to do with the Pimm who is number two in Anglo-Scottish Oil?'

'No. Definitely not.' Pimm always denied his cousinhood to that odious man.

'Mr Pimm, we are looking for a thing called the Heath. Can you direct us to such a place?'

'Keep on up and you'll come to it,' said Pimm, reapplying his brush with delicate fury. An ancient mosaic eye, glistening black, emerged from the dust. 'Look! The past is watching us!'

The Superior leant over with a nauseated interest. 'Likewise the future, Mr Pimm. Don't forget that.'

When the Superior returned to his colleagues Tucker asked 'What news, sir?'

'No news. Just some little nerd with a rat's tail down his back.'

'Shall I drive now?'

'No, Tucker. Arbuthnot wants to drive.'

With sullen face, Arbuthnot (too young to retire, too old to enjoy work) eased the limousine uphill. The landscape of woods and fields gave way to a tougher realm. Thorny bushes tore out of the expanses of coarse grass which ran ahead in great tilted planes to the line separating hill from sky. Here and there lakes of bracken quivered in the breeze. But behind everthing were the low, distant rises and falls of a prehistoric wind as though the creator of time itself were musing on his handiwork. This wind seemed all about the place yet was not insistent or fretful or close at hand but strung out in long faraway moans which drifted towards infinity. They got out and muttered round the map again.

Tucker, indicating their chart position correctly for once, observed 'Stones'.

'We can see that,' snapped Arbuthnot. He was thoroughly fed up.

'No – he means *standing* stones!' exclaimed Finch with unsuppressed excitement.

'Suppress your excitement, Finch, and explain.'

Finch's lipless mouth folded in on itself, since he was not often rebuked, and it was Tucker who responded with 'Megaliths, sir,' and a little hopeful nod.

The four heads turned in unison to the right where not far away, on a broad table of turf , battered rocks were arranged with a degree of forethought. The sun threw shadows which emphasised their erectness – or complete lack of it in some cases. The silence was intrusive. Even the wind had paused.

'Finch. Information.'

Finch whispered 'The Ring of the Moon it says here'.

'Why are you whispering, Finch?'

'Don't you find it spooky up here, sir?' asked Tucker and the pink tip of his tongue protruded nervously.

'Not in the least!'

'Masses of sheep shit,' said Arbuthnot.'But no sheep.'

'Is that your idea of a mystery, Arbuthnot?' sneered the Superior while at the same time he stared at the megaliths as at the enemy.

As for the megaliths themselves, which had stood for nearly 7,000 years in that high clean draughty place, they possessed the mind-numbing hauteur of an excruciating antiquity and were hardly aware of the Superior – though they were not altogether unaware. Suddenly the Superior ran towards them, his pinstripe jacket flapping wildly, and his rampage was marked by numbers of terrified grouse battling into the air. He dragged his way through fern and thorn, drew blood on the back of his hands, jumped a ditch and a gulley, picked up another footpath, stumbled, scrambled, carried on, and ran right into the ceremonial centre of the Ring where he flung his arms wide and span round, commanding the trans-county views through all points of the compass. An uncanny assurance swelled his bosom. He knew himself to be at the very heart of all things and at the top of his voice he proclaimed to the three bemused faces now several hundred feet away 'Yes! Here! We shall build it here! This very spot shall be the heart of the City of Cognitive Neuroscience! And from it shall radiate in every direction lines of infinite wisdom and power!' And the wind roared back in his ears.

He did a few more revolutions on the pivot of an Oxford brogue and returned to his underlings with a jaunty stride, one hand in pocket.

'Marvellous, sir,' simpered Finch.

'But isn't it a bit remote, sir?' wondered Tucker.

'Very remote. I thought that was the whole point, Tucker. We'll put a motorway there.' His arm slashed through a vista. 'And another one there.' He did it again in the opposite direction. 'Of course only the absolute core of things will be up here. The Ring of the Moon can be the main feature in the atrium of the central memory complex. Housing for the plebs and all that will be down in the valley and done in ultra modern architecture for once. None of this vernacular crap to appease the hillbillies.' The Superior was aglow. He looked twenty years younger. It would be his final grand project before retirement and the knighthood.

'But won't there be protests, sir?'

'Of course there'll be protests,' and a leer oozed about the Superior's mouth. 'I love a challenge. We'll have all the usual feasibility studies set in motion but, believe me, work will begin here' – he stamped – 'sooner than you could ever imagine'. There was a profound pleasure in his eyes, tantamount to tenderness, which they had never seen before. 'Remember, boys, politics is either complacency or panic. We in the Civil Service are interested in neither. We are interested in achievement.'

On the way down he asked Arbuthnot to pull over again at the Mercury dig. 'Stay here, you lot. Shan't be a sec.' The Superior trotted across to Pimm, ullulating again. Pimm looked up and wiped some soil from his spectacles.

'Mr Pimm, I'm sorry to trouble you further.' Pimm turned back to his work. 'But would you tell me who owns the land round here?'

'Various people.'

'Who owns where we are now for example? And that wonderful megalithic site up on the Heath?'

'The Ring itself belongs to the Earl of Moon by ancient title. But all this round here and some on the other side of the valley is the property of the Marquess of Heavenshire.'

'He must be a very rich man.'

'In fact he's desperately broke.'

'Is he now. Desperately broke you say. I am very sorry to hear that. Desperately broke. I see. Well, thanks for your time. Ciao.' And he trotted back in euphoric mood to the car, chanting 'Desperately broke desperately broke *desperately* – broke!'

But Pimm had ceased to be aware of him or of anyone else because with that fluttering fastidiousness of brush which as a boy had been the first sign of his calling, he had begun to uncover a mosaic Roman nose adjacent to the single eye and, since it wasn't another Roman leg, Pimm was fomented by delight.

23.

How she loved her surreptitious orgy of spraying, rubbing and shining! Of course once a week, on Wednesday morning, Mrs Lark popped in and cleaned for three hours, because it was an aspect of Mrs Bladder-Williams's self-esteem that she should have someone in to clean for her – but she so loved to give the place a good doing-over herself. At this moment she was polishing the silver which had the added advantage of reminding her that she had silver to polish. She always told Mrs Lark not to bother with the silver. To be honest, Mrs Lark wasn't very good at cleaning, always chipping ornaments and saying nothing, leaving rings of grease on surfaces which only became apparent in

afternoon light, and never to be trusted with cabinet figurines;
but she was cheap.

Mrs Bladder-Williams pouted when she came to the silver
cakestand, an heirloom, for upon it squatted a Victoria sponge.

Since I've known Mr Royal, she thought, my cakestand's
hardly had the weight off it. She frowned at a framed photograph
on the wall above the sideboard. It was of a plain, smiling man
wearing false teeth and a dog collar – the gloss of the one seemed
somehow linked to the gloss of the other – and clasping her hands
to her bosom she said aloud 'Eustace, forgive me!' The Revd
Eustace Bladder-Williams had left her childless and a widow
thirty years previously. His had been an awful death, by fire, since
when she had passed from hopeful young wife to pillar of the
community largely by way of compensation. But after that first
devastating year of widowhood, life had not been impossible.
There was the modest pension, plus a small annuity of her own
and, after she vacated the vicarage at the top of the village, the
Church generously allowed her to live for a peppercorn rent in
Church House, the eighteenth-century property it happened to
own down by the bridge. Church House had two bays either side
of a shell porch and stood behind a shallow railed garden. Its
staircase of barley-sugar banisters rose from a square panelled
hall and this gave a grandeur to one's first impression which was
not born out by a subsequent tour of the house, although it was
more than enough for a solitary woman now sixty years old.

But within her roomy heart, Mrs Bladder-Williams felt *unused*.
Not that anyone would have suspected it. To committees and
charities and worthy causes she had given herself with gusto –
many had been subjected to the flying pumice of her principles –
and in addition she also had her personal projects. This year for
example she was dragging her way through the tropical novels of
Henry de Vere Stacpoole. Only eight more to go and then perhaps
she'd have a crack at North African cuisine. But no, the yearnings
of her heart were not appeased by these exertions. As the years
dropped off the calendar she'd become more not less aware that
in a fundamental way she was unfulfilled, and as more years
dropped off she understood that what she wanted was love and
not any old love either but real love, *physical* love.

The constraints of her age and position had walled her off from physical love. She wasn't sure how it had come about, that she was no longer entitled to contact of that kind, but come about it had and it was to her credit that she recognised it also had something to do with her own general embarrassment vis à vis the erotic, that in her own mind to express a sexual need would render her both vulgar and vulnerable. Yet it would be misleading were any of this to suggest a creature small and shrivelled. Mrs Bladder-Williams was quite the opposite. Her figure went out at the bust and stayed out. From the bust it descended in a straight line. The overall weight threw her back at the shoulders, giving a belligerent quality to her stateliness. The whole was wrapped in a frock which stopped just below the knee to reveal Olympian calf muscles and sturdy shoes with a heel which though low was yet higher than one would have expected. Her hair was tightly marcelled.

Oh, go on, she said to herself.

She lifted the cake-slice and cut a wedge of sponge at whose centre a red line of jam shone alarmingly. The thin end of the wedge went into her mouth and, opening wide, she pushed until the limits of capacity had been attained, whereupon she bit downwards and waved the sawn-off remainder in the air. Her jaws worked slowly; eyes were closed. The telephone rang and she panicked, having been caught in an act of self-abuse.

'Mrs Bladder-Williams?'

'Yes.'

'Oliver Knott here.'

'Who?'

She hadn't meant to be slighting. Distracted by the necessity of emptying her mouth and finding somewhere to plant the remaining wedge, she hadn't paid attention to the voice down the line.

'Oliver Knott?' it repeated, but equivocally as though itself unsure of who it was.

'Mr Knott, how are you?'

'As well as can be expected.'

'I'm sorry to hear that.'

'I was wondering – '

'Were you? Yes, I'm sure you were. Well, stop wondering. Don't sit there. Do something. That's my advice.'

'Oh, um – thank you. What do you advise I do?'

'Anything. So long as you believe in it.'

Oliver sighed – what an amazing woman she was – she had gone straight to the heart of his problem. He was a scientist. Always he saw through the spirit to the underlying mechanism. His existence was surrounded not by people but by mechanisms and this was his private terror: he couldn't believe in *anything*, couldn't have faith or trust in *anything*, he had to mechanise *everything*.

'I was wondering, Mrs Bladder-Williams, if um . . . Are you still there?'

'Mmmmm.' She was licking a fringe of sugar from her lip.

'I was wondering if you would do me the honour of coming to dinner.'

'That is very kind of you, Mr Knott. But it depends.'

'Does it? On what?'

'Not on what but on when.'

'Whenever you wish.'

'In that case I gladly accept.'

'You do?'

'You can't imagine what a pleasure it is for a woman to be fed by a man.'

On replacing the receiver, she picked up the remaining portion of wedge and ate it, but as her mouth moved towards swallowing she realised that no date for dinner had been established, and she waited for the telephone to ring again, but it didn't.

24.

'Watch out!' yelled Alice as a hedge came at them like a plank.

Pimm was interrogating the wet road through his pebble lenses and through the smeared windscreen as well and, as a bonus, one of the car headlamps wasn't working. 'Would someone else like to drive?' he asked curtly. There were no takers. Robin Craddock was in a sulk because Crystal, who'd said she'd come, failed to appear, and he occupied a leathery corner of the battered Rolls Royce while an acidulous soup sat in his belly. Minerva was in a sulk because the presence of Sylvia Wetmore galled her no end. Alice would love to have been in a sulk, but at this period of her life sulking struck her as a gay and unattainable luxury. JJ, who was doing his best to maintain élan, didn't think he would be able to drive as well. And Sylvia was too short to see over the dashboard – which was very nearly Pimm's problem too.

They flew into Appleminster and were whirled round the city by the one-way system. The cathedral, floodlit until midnight, slid past the window like a purple ship.

'It's beautiful,' said Alice.

'I think it's ugly,' said Minerva, 'like a load of thorns'.

'The ghost of the Revd Eustace Bladder-Williams haunts the tea-room in the cloisters,' announced JJ. 'He was burnt to death there.'

A car of yobs briefly mobbed them, which was quite exciting, but when the cathedral slid past the window like a purple ship, or a load of thorns, for the third time, JJ complained 'Get it together, Pimm.'

' Where do I go?' floundered the archaeologist.

'Stop here and Minerva can ask.'

'I don't want to ask.'

'It's your turn to ask, Minnie.'

So Pimm pulled over and Minerva opened her door and tried the air. At least it had stopped raining. There was nobody about, apart from a young man in boots slouching against a mediaeval wall. She stepped cautiously onto the wet pavement in a picture hat and dress of turquoise lace flounced out by underskirts. Goose-pimples bubbled on her arms and she wished she'd brought a shawl. The young man regarded her with furtive anxiety.

'Where's the nightclub?' she asked him.

'Which one?'

She turned back and put her head into the car window, almost knocking off the picture hat which she retained with the flat of her hand. 'Julius, what's it called?'

'The Race Against Time.'

'It's over there,' said the young man, having heard the name, and pointed to a neon-framed doorway beside an estate agent's shop. 'Are you foreign?' he asked her.

'No. Are you?'

'A quarter. My gran was from . . . I forget.'

JJ leaned out of the window and said 'What a nice zombie you are – won't you join us?'

'No offence but I ave to get along.' And the young man walked briskly into the night, never to be seen again. (The window of opportunity, which had briefly opened to him, did not do so again and the young man, good-looking, good-natured, but fearful of the unknown and lacking any sort of enterprise, lived a life of growing despondency and beer and crisps and cigarettes and died of bowel cancer in early middle age.)

They abandoned the black hulk of the car where it was and filed into the club doorway where a bouncer asked 'Where're youze lot going?'

'It's me.'

'Oh, it's you, sir. I hope you'll pay this time.'

'I was only looking for a friend last time.'

'But you was in for an hour.'

'And I couldn't pick up *anyone.*'

JJ paid for the party. Alice alone proffered a crumpled bank-note but he nobly refused it.

The Race Against Time was surprisingly large and surprisingly empty. Aggressive beat music boomed and Sylvia pulled JJ at once onto the deserted dance-floor. This pair of rotundities, one great, the other tiny, swung weightlessly around each other like the sun and the moon, titivating the air with their hands. Another couple, thus encouraged, took to the floor but were poor in the comparison, dancing hard to little effect. Robin bought the first round of drinks and picked up a flyer on their table, angling it under the red light. 'It says there's going to be a singer on later. Stormy Weather, a Hong Kong gal fresh from triumphs in Tokyo and Manila, will sing some classic numbers live.'

'Live?'

'Live.'

'But nothing is live any more.'

JJ escorted Sylvia to the table and said 'The great thing about this place is one never knows anyone here'. He took a handful of peanuts from a bowl and Pimm said 'I wouldn't eat those, JJ. Tests have revealed that the average bowl of bar-snacks contains traces of twelve different sorts of urine.'

JJ took another handful and chewed them assiduously. 'I am afraid I can only detect three or four. Go on, Pimm, don't be dreary. Ask her.'

'Would you like to dance, Minerva?'

'If you insist,' she replied and swanned onto the illuminated dancing circle. Once there she turned in the manner of a dervish upon an undeviating point. In her long dress and Gainsborough hat, she was captivating to behold, leaning back slightly as she turned, hands at her neck in autostrangulation, quite unaware that she was supposed, however non-committally, to be dancing with Pimm. His compact frame meanwhile jumped up and down at tangents to her skirt in complete independence of the music's rhythm. A few more punters trickled in.

At midnight the music was shut off and a cheeky chappie, wearing a cream velvet suit, came onto the small stage with a microphone in his hand. 'Ladies and gentlemen, please return to your seats . . . Please come along now . . . Thank you . . . That's right. Many thanks. Because I'd like you to welcome with a warm round of applause the star of the evening. She's come all the way from dear old Hong Kong and I know you're going to love her – chanteuse extraordinaire and a great beauty to boot, none other than the frighteningly fabulous, the certainly sensational, the unique, the absolutely epileptic STORMY WEATHER!!!!!'

A few flabby claps percolated the hush as a slender creature, in a tight gold space-suit with upcurling epaulettes and gold sticks in her hair, walked onstage and stood stiffly at the microphone stand. The silence deepened uncomfortably. 'Hullo,' she said in a voice no larger than a thimble. No response. Someone coughed. 'Take it away – *Sam!*' said thimble-voice, jerking her hips. Silence spread like a cold sweat.

'Get on wiv it!' heckled someone.

'Take it away – '

The tape started abruptly. Big band music. It was torrentially loud. Stormy flapped at a sound controller in the wings and the sound dipped and she went into the opening number, 'Love

Me Do', which she pronounced 'Rub Me Do'. Delicate oriental features were disfigured by passion. Her voice, in song, remained thimble-sized but was an unexpectedly penetrating and well-pitched warble, cunningly attractive in its own way. The second number, 'Rubber Come Back To Me', passed without incident It was as she lifted a leg and stepped into the third, 'Cly Me A Liver', with a rehearsed routine of her tiny feet, that a burble from the direction of the audience began to make itself heard. It was pernicious and came from a most unlikely source. It was Alice letting go. Alice, of all people, letting go. In public.

Alice had been unable to have a proper cry for quite some time, despite a growing need. When at last the process of leakage began – tonight, here, now – perhaps triggered by a line in one of the songs – or probably by all the lines in all the songs – there was an accumulated pressure behind it. Soon she was weeping uncontrollably. Robin, Pimm and Minerva fixed each other with looks of consternation but Sylvia and JJ urged Alice on. 'Let it out, girl, let it out!' Their encouragement was hardly necessary because the loosened woman was bringing forth oceans. 'Cly Me A Liver' rolled to an end and Stormy introduced the next song, 'Miss Otis Leglets', which was no match for Alice whose sobs had now become aggressive.

Had Alice realised any of this she would have died from shame but she was beyond such feelings, had leapt all the fences of self-consciousness and was in that sublime state where one is governed purely by the promptings of the body. Fortunately for the singer the next routine was an up-tempo Beatles medley and by the time it ended – it did go on a bit, actually, with few of the songs recognisable – Alice had drained herself and was feeling much better: tears had enlarged her personal space. Stormy Weather received threadbare applause followed by a scramble for the bar. This seemingly didn't disappoint her. Indeed she maintained an uncanny sang-froid throughout. JJ buttonholed the cheeky chappie. 'Please ask Miss Weather to join our table.' And when Miss Weather did, she was in excellent spirits.

'I must apologise for the conduct of my party.'

'Ever so sorry,' said Alice who felt not in the least contrite.

'I fick skin,' said Stormy. 'You must in dis business.'

'You have an unusual voice,' said Sylvia.

'Have you thought of taking it up professionally?' asked Minerva.

Stormy did something oriental with her fingers and asked JJ 'Where you live?'

'He lives in a palace,' said Robin.

'I rub palaces!'

'Feeling all right now, darling?' asked Sylvia.

'Much better thank you,' replied Alice

'If I hadn't just left my husband, I think you might've started me crying too. What triggered it off?'

'Nobody asked me to dance with them – then everything else.'

'Oh lover of the Nile, I'd've danced with you, poor sweetheart! Let's have a bop now.'

'No, not now. It's passed. Sylvia – is Dickon married?' and Alice burped.

'Rather rapid change of subject.'

'But is he?'

'Oh God, and how.'

'I never see a wife or anyone about that farm of his.'

'You've been exploring!'

'No I haven't but he is my neighbour.'

'She's an invalid. Virtually bedridden. But she has him by the balls.'

'You'll have to drive back, Robin. Pimm's had too much.'

'But I can't drive that thing.'

'You drove it on my birthday.'

'Only on the lawn.'

'A road is no different from a lawn. Longer and thinner, that's all.'

'How long has she been an invalid? What do you mean by the balls?' asked Alice but Sylvia had to go for a pee.

'I can drive if you like,' said Stormy.

'You can?'

'I rub cars. What type?'

'Rolls Royce.'

'My favourite!'

And Stormy soon returned to them with her reticule at the ready and a feathered cape about her shoulders.

25.

'Here in the glass case we have my great-great-grandfather's collection of shrunken heads, especially prepared for him by the Jivaro Indians, including the head of his chum Colonel "Bandy" Pope-Alexander. And above them in that tortoiseshell box is an electrum ring containing a single gold hair from the head of Lucrezia Borgia. It came from my great-great-great-oh . . . something who was the mistress of Leigh Hunt who received it from Byron.'

Stormy was in bliss and asked 'How many lounge you got?'

'I don't know. The house is very big.'

'Yeah. Fings far apart.'

'Some things.'

'Most fings.'

Minerva entered in a full-length miniver and asked if anyone wished to go mushroom-picking. JJ buried his face in her shoulder and, turning it out of the mass, said to Stormy 'I adore the smell of furs, don't you?' But he wasn't going in search of mushrooms on any account. Glory Boy was expecting him at the hut and JJ felt himself to be in urgent need of such a rendezvous. It seemed ages since JJ had slipped his hand into that luxuriant crotch.

But Stormy went mushrooming and so did Crystal, bare-legged in her wellington boots and mini-kilt worn off the buttock. They crossed the fields with wicker panniers to Home Wood.

'Here's a good un,' said Crystal, bending over to pluck a large flat cap.

Stormy said 'You lubbly bum'.

Crystal was startled but walked on, not turning round until she was sure the blood had drained from her cheeks. When she did turn round she asked 'Where are you singing next?'

'Lussia. I been before. They like me lot. I like you lot.'

'Please don't. I go all gooey when people say things like that.'

'Gooey good,' said Stormy and on the way back she managed several times to scrape the outside of Crystal's thigh with her long fingernails, sending an electric tingle up into the girl's privates.

Despite a dinner of gold and silver pheasants roasted with Jerusalem artichokes and served on a bed of water cress, JJ was in low spirits – Glory Boy had not been at the hut as he'd promised and was doubtless having terrific fun somewhere with some slag. Minerva attempted to lift the atmosphere with a poem.

> *Yesternight – ah yesternight!*
> *Your mouth, full as a peony,*
> *Your mad, mute, mushy mouth,*
> *Wet wound, crimson rip – oh, you –*
> *Don't!*

JJ asked sluggishly 'Post-modern was it?' Minerva sucked in her cheeks and said nothing. Stormy sat on her hands wondering where Crystal was and why the girl wasn't eating with them.

The nightclub singer had been put in the Dowager Suite which was distinguished by having its walls set with green and lavender glass in diamond facets. After a soak in the bath, in which she could manage several breast-strokes before hitting the end, she cooled off and slid between linen. But Stormy could not sleep and selected a book from the compact group on top of a commode. It was Count Algarotti's *Il Newtonianismo per le Dame*.

'I'm bored!' she puffed. The enormous building clicked, boomed and purred amid profound silences of random duration. Depth, distance, noise, all were magnified by her restlessness. So she decided to go for a walk.

Outside her room Stormy unsuccessfully wiped the wall for a light switch. The corridor was spectral with starlight from the cold bare windows. Suddenly she caught her breath. There, in the window seat not far away, a long smudge of paleness undulated awfully.

Crikey, one of them English things, a ghost, thought the singer. Stormy, being one of the spunky types who must confront a horror in order to dispel it, went up and gave the ghost a prod.

'Ouch. Careful,' said Crystal.

'Aw. Sorry. It's you.'

'I can't sleep.'

'Snap,' said Stormy, embracing the girl round her cool white shoulders.

'Will you tell me a story?'

'Course, angel bum. But not here. I chilly.'

With the final click of the night they both crept into Crystal's bedroom.

26.

Sir Timothy angrily paced his study as outside a powerful gale blew from the west, churning the trees with its enormous lungs. The noise of it came and went, stopped and restarted, like the sound of battle. He sat down, pulled open a copy of *The Gun Room Guide*, slammed it shut, and marched into the hall where his wife was arranging in a vase three large twigs of dead leaves.

'Where's Robin? I asked him to see me in the study at three. It's now quarter past.'

'You'd better go and find him then.'

'Helen, I wish you wouldn't keep bringing that rubbish into the house.'

Robin was lying on his bed, the prisoner of a yearning which made his eyes sting. He had hardly slept. His heart with a will of its own had beaten loudly in his ears all night. He'd been full of Crystal. He'd been full of her throughout the day too and despite several masturbations his erection would not fade. Involuntarily and uselessly his hand sought out the swollen member as images of the girl shimmered in his head. Which is what he was doing when his father entered.

'Can't you knock?' growled the young man, sharply drawing up his knees.

Sir Timothy, who had once commanded a destroyer, noticed nothing strange. 'I thought we had an appointment at three.'

'It's only two-fifteen.'

'Typical. You forgot to put your clock forward last night.'

'Is that what you wanted to tell me?'

'I wanted to ask you – don't you think you're getting too involved with that Heaven Park shower?'

'Meaning?'

'They'll turn your head and drop you over a cliff. That's what they'll do. They're that sort.'

'Dad, you might as well know, I'm in love with Crystal.'

Sir Timothy winced. For him there was something obscene in unclad emotion. 'Is she in love with you?'

'I doubt it.'

'Then forget her.'

'I can't.'

'Confound it, Robin! Unrequited love is the cruellest poison in life. It's a mug's game. It's like . . . like trying to get a television picture by fiddling with a radio.'

'You know this from personal experience?'

'Yes, actually. And I'll tell you this man to man, it wasn't your mother.' Sir Timothy sat on the end of his son's bed in a movement which began in tenderness but ended in fear. The question uppermost in his mind suddenly became – was he going to have another funny turn? No, he wasn't. Of course he wasn't. But something in him was flickering from the sense that he felt a stranger in his own son's bedroom. So he sighed deeply. It was amazing how many loose ends, even for a naval man, a good sigh could tidy up. 'I do wish you'd choose another sort of girl from a different family. It's not the carving of the lamb.'

Robin was trying not to pay attention.

'I'm going to use an old-fashioned word. Probity. It's in very short supply these days but it was probity which made the British Empire possible. You see, Rob, the distances were so great, the entire globe in fact, that without probity, with every little pip-squeak taking the law into his own hands, the Empire could never have happened.'

'What has this to do with Crystal?' And he thought, please don't call me Rob, it really makes me squirm.

'Nothing. She and probity couldn't be further apart. Whenever one sees anybody from that house they're *stoned*, every one jackass of them. Are you on drugs?'

'Dad, I've got it bad.'

'Oh dear . . . '

'I'm afraid I'm mad about her. I've known her all my life, could take it or leave it, then a few months ago – wham.'

'Well, if you can't forget her, I suppose there's only one thing to do. Fire a shot across her bows. Stick it in and find out.'

'You mean sleep with her?'

'So long as it's not in this house. I won't have the floozie rogered in this house, is that clear? But if you're head over heels, there's no point in just playing with yourself for the next ten years.'

Robin rolled off the bed and went to the window. His father had shocked him. The gale blustered beyond the mullions and clouds romped across the sky. Yes, his father had really shocked him, so much so that it was a moment or two before he realised that a major event was taking place in the garden below.

'Dad, quick, look at this!'

Sir Tim reached the window in time to see the great oak on the front lawn, mercilessly buffeted all day, twist in an absurd caricature of anguish, all flailing arms and rushing foliage, and somehow turn around and upwards like a dancer onto her toes, before it shuddered its whole length, toppled sideways in slow motion, and fell to the ground with a crash. While this staggering prima donna performance took place, the oak communicated its agony by running the gamut of utterance from scream to bellow, culminating in an awful boom as the ground shook beneath the concussion of its weight, followed by the death rattle. A tremor passed through the stones of The Crag. The two men looked at each other in wonder, their first eyeball to eyeball contact in many months. The tree was a magnificent, a tragic sight, its limbs either smashed or reaching up pathetically like those of a stricken dinosaur. Where it had snapped at its half-rotted base the trunk was a mass of ugly teeth.

'Hurrah,' said Sir Timothy. 'I've been wanting to see the back of that horror all my life. Your mother wouldn't have it chopped down of course. Here's something to occupy you, Robin. Contact the Bonfire Committee and tell them that The Crag will this year donate a tree. An entire oak tree. You and Little Lark can saw it up. Now come downstairs and watch the football with me.'

But Sir Tim watched the football alone while overhead Robin, encouraged by his father's pep talk, ejaculated into a Kleenex for the fourth time that day.

27.

The black fangs of Hallowe'en devoured the light of day as Davis mixed into a bowl a bit of this, a bit of that, lots of the other. Into the mixture she poured a stream of shrivelled black insects, as she fancied, but actually they were currants. Concoctions, decoctions, infusions and potions were round about the kitchen, having already played their part, along with bags, boxes and jars. There was blood on the chopping board and vegetable shavings in the bin. A knock sounded at the front door. Davis sprang to the window, burning yet another hole in the curtains with her cigarette, to check who it was. 'Varlets,' she divined but opened the door nonetheless.

Tiny Colin Lark piped 'Penny for the Guy!'

Such is the force of even so modest a tradition that Davis obligingly withdrew to the parlour where her mother sat in a chair beside the fireplace (in which flames were never seen, Davis preferring the convenience of a big electric fire with illuminated logs). 'Mumsy, where's the purse?'

Mumsy, otherwise known as the Old Un, a knot of pure cadaverousness, lifted a pair of near-blank eyes and croaked like a dainty bullfrog. Familiarity enabled Davis to translate this as 'The purse is where it always is, you ninny, in the green fruit bowl on the red cocktail trolley, and could I have a cup of tea coz I'm parched.'

Davis extracted a coin and conveyed it to Colin who examined it huffily. 'What's this, lady?'

'What you asked for. A penny.'

'But you carnt get nothin for a penny.'

'No? I'll have it back then.'

Colin cogitated a moment before returning the penny to Davis's leathery palm. 'C'mon,' he said to two companions.

'Told you,' said one of them.

In the parlour she said 'They didn't want it.'

'Nobody wants it,' croaked the Old Un, making a gesture with one of her tiny withered hands, followed by 'Clean it up, clean it up!'

'OK, that's enough of that. You'll never guess what's happened, Mumsy. The great oak came down at The Crag. You remember, the big one at the front. In the gales. Made a right mess it did. They've taken it to Townside Field for the bonfire.'

Did something dimly glow in the cancelled spaces of her mother's eyes?

Yes!

'Nobody wants it, nobody wants it!' fluted the Old Un with rare animation, lifting up the skirt of her black bombasine frock in time with the phrases. 'Nobody wants it, nobody wants it!'

'Now, Mumsy, you know you mustn't do that. I'll have to give you a blast of gas if you keeps on.' It was Davis's custom to wheel in a drum of gas and put the hose up Mumsy's nose if she got out of hand. The remedy usually worked. As Davis flattened down the skirt again, the Old Un looked into her daughter's eyes and – it had a peculiar terror of its own – straight out the other side, as though her daughter were not there, as though no obstruction were there. It was eternity gazing into eternity.

'Was it something about that oak tree which got you wound up? Seemed right discombobulated you did.'

But this time there was no response. Eternity breathed quietly on.

'I'll get yer tea.'

After she'd thrown three cups of pellets to the bantams out back, Davis set about tying up an assortment of pots and covered dishes in cloths and placing them in a hamper. There were more footsteps outside. She shot to the curtains, burning more holes. The kitchen curtains, which were plastic and featured a design of oranges and lemons, had been reduced almost to lace by Davis's failure to take the fag out of her mouth before snooping from behind them. This time it was Mrs Bladder-Williams walking past, the robust heels of her steady stride tapping out clearly, thanks to a lull in the wind.

'Damn that bitch, always on the dot, an I'm late!' Davis dutifully prepared the Devil's Claw tea for her mother, wrote out a detailed bill and placed it in the hamper, and sat down. 'If I'm to be late, I might as well do it properly.' After an indulgent interval during which she had another fag, she followed Mrs Bladder-Williams up the road to Oliver Knott's cottage, carrying the dinner hamper breast-high with both hands.

And why was she going to all this trouble? Because Sir Timothy Craddock of The Crag had requested it. Oh, Sir Tim was just about all right. She'd worked for him ever since she could remember and it was the natural way of things. But she didn't see why she had to service all and sundry at the drop of a hat. Sir Tim had asked if she would be kind enough to prepare a dinner for Mr Knott who couldn't cook but who was entertaining a lady at his cottage, and although Sir Tim had adopted his most deferential manner, there was in his eye that effortless authority which said I am your employer and you will do as I bid, and as a result of which Davis had been slaving in the kitchen on her one evening off and I bet that Knott questions the bill but so what if it's a couple o' quid over what it cost, an if you ask me this is only the tip of the ice-bucket, but no it aint see, coz I'm sick to the back teeth of having to attend to the requirements of other people, be they Craddocks or Mumsy or any other, an if I had two farthings to rub together I'd be off bang into the wild blue yonder. In the hills around Milking Magna the wind raged like the long-accumulated fury in Davis's breast.

28.

The annual Guy Fawkes celebration was always held in the Townside Field of Lower Farm which permitted road access and parking and was far enough from habitations to be safe. This year the bonfire was the largest in living memory, thanks to the donation of the oak from The Crag. The main trunk, shorn of its limbs, had been dragged there with chains and placed at the bonfire's heart, and many strangers turned up to witness the end of what hearsay had suddenly declared to be the oldest, the tallest, the most historical oak in the county. Had not Merlin sat beneath it in a fit of melancholy and seen a vision of Avalon? Had not the Emperor Constantine diverted to it for spiritual guidance on his journey from York to Rome? Had not griddle scones, made from a pastry of its acorns mixed with milkwort juice, cured impotence if consumed during Rogationtide? Maybe something no less extraordinary would attend its immolation.

Sir Timothy's Land Rover, the first car to arrive, overtook a procession of women carrying banners. Mrs Bladder-Williams, Mrs Punch, two nuns and his wife Helen were among them.

Sir Tim stopped and wound down the window. 'Helen, I wish you'd remember that more children are injured annually by drinking household bleach than from fireworks.'

'Democracy in action, Tim dear. And you're blocking the lane.'

'And you're missing the point, Tim,' said Glyn Trossach, the local MP, who was seated in the back with his wife. 'Fireworks give pleasure. That's why they want to ban them. In politics you very quickly learn that, although individuals are always in favour of pleasure, the British public is always against it. Funny thing that and never worked out why.'

A jalopy behind the Land Rover sounded its horn several times in succession and Big Lark shouted 'Land ahoy, Admiral!' Behind Big Lark the whole village was building up, on foot, on bikes, in cars and small vans.

Sir Timothy leant out and shouted 'A little courtesy, if you don't mind!' and drove on but was stopped at the field-gate by a lad called Ragamuffin who said 'Four people and one vehicle is a fiver'.

'But I donated a whole tree and I'm lighting the bonfire!'

'No exceptions is me orders.'

'From whom?'

'The Bonfire Committee.'

Someone shouted 'Get a fucking move on, yer toffee-nosed git!'

Robin handed over the money in embarrassment and Ragamuffin said 'Thank you kindly – would you like a programme?' But Sir Timothy did not want a programme – doubtless they cost a fortune – and drove through in silence, pulling up under a hedge not far from where the vicar and his wife had set up their stall of parkin cakes and soft drinks. Further along was the open-sided mulled-wine tent where Alice was already holding her warm glass and stamping her boots. She'd come early by walking down the fields, deliberately alone, to prove to herself that she was unafraid, and as it turned out she'd been less afraid than she expected to be.

'I adore Guy Fawkes,' said a fruity voice in her ear. It was Lomax looking naked without his dark glasses. 'I'm a night person,' he went on. 'Daylight feels like exposure. My greatest moments in life have always been after dark. Did you see the anti-life brigade at the gate?'

'Apparently Mrs Bladder-Williams lost a husband by fire.'

'One can't blame the fire. One must blame the husband. I was reading today about a proposal for a new town in this part of the world. It was announced by the Minister of Power. That man deserves a whack. Tell me, young lady, what did you do before you came to live among us here?'

Coming at her so viciously in a damp, dark field of strangers where she had felt protected by her anonymity, the remark had a rapist's force. And anyway what business was it of this creep? He was prying. He was a snooper. He was repulsive.

'Boring office work, I'm afraid.'

'Is your office work less boring now?'

Jesus, the nerve of him. 'Have you seen Dickon, Mr Lomax?'

'He's with Oliver Jones and Harry Pulp, organising the display. You seem put out. Have I said something untoward? Do forgive me if I have.'

A group of village boys wheeled an effigy across the field in bobbing torchlight.

'Burn the bloody Pope!' roared Sir Tim jovially. It never took him long to get back into the saddle of his self-possession.

Sylvia Wetmore waddled by, already the worse for drink, with Hoggart the Butcher on one arm and Selwyn Blagdon on the other. They'd come from The Zodiac.

'Is Crystal with you?' Robin asked her.

'Peter Crimsoncourt turned up at the house with a convoy of people and loads of bangers. Tourbillion, roman candle, devil among the tailors, jack-in-the-box, goblin gun, mine of serpents, girandole, and I say it again, *girandole.*' She enunciated the names of fireworks with actressy accuracy in an attempt to clear her head.

Little Lark entered the mulled-wine tent. 'A drink for the fireworkers please.'

'Hullo, Little,' said Sir Timothy. 'When do they want me to light the bonfire?'

'Oh sir,' answered the six-and-a-half-foot stripling, 'Mr Pulp said my brother Colin's gonna light it, seeing how Colin worked so hard an all to make the Guy. Isn't that fair?'

'Nobody told me. But we mustn't cross Harry Pulp, must we,' said the Craddock with a tight grimace. That large industrial zone which went by the name of Pulp's Chicken Farm was the chief employer of the district. 'By the way, Little, how's school?'

'Excellent, sir.'

'That's the ticket. Study hard. Be a good lad.'

Sylvia pushed her face at Alice's. 'Had anyone in the village yet?' She was slurring her words but trying to be gay. The effect was somewhat tragic.

'Loads,' replied Alice.

'Really?' said Sylvia, looking sick. 'New face, bound to, beginner's luck, who, tell me, go on, was it Hoggart?'

As if by magic Sylvia was no longer there but Glory Boy was. 'Wassamatter?' he asked Alice quietly.

'People keep saying cutting things. Do you want to finish my wine?'

He took the white plastic cup from her hand. 'You've a couple of skins too few at the moment. Don't worry. You'll be all right. Come and meet Daisy.' His smile touched her and she suddenly, unexpectedly got the point of Glory Boy, his adorableness, his – Sylvia reappeared, her teeth wine-dark. A cigarette dropped out of her fingers onto the wet grass. 'Who was it you had then? Glory was it? Oh, Max, hullo. Have you two met? Max and I were in rep together, weren't we, darling. Max put the programme together. No, silly, the *firework* programme. Here, read it. It's awfully good. You're not appreciated, Max, really you aren't. I've got to have a pee. Be a poppet, Maxie, and stand guard for me over by that bush.'

Half a minute later a spectacular flame shot fifty feet into the air. The bonfire had been doused with petrol and very soon the entire field was illuminated. It happened so quickly that Tiny Colin Lark burst into tears of emotion. He ran to his father who kissed and cuddled him and held his hand, not far from where Sylvia was floodlit mid-pee against the hedge while Lomax cowered from the glare.

Rockets zipped into the air and exploded like giant hats. Roman candles spat stars in rapid succession. Ornamental sprays coloured the air with vivid smudges. The part of the programme which so impressed Sylvia were the sentences on the back, not written by Lomax in fact but stolen by him from a book, *In Praise of Fireworks*. Fireworks are beautiful, expensive, alarming, and vanish almost at once, it went. Transience is the secret of their allure. Fire is our friend in the eternal night of space. And the explosion of a firework is analogous to the mystery of life and of our individual lives too: incandescence out of a black medium, the theatre of life emerging from the darkness. Fireworks therefore remind one of death. Death is both the consuming power of fire and the black night to which all fire returns. So do not go home too suddenly after a firework display. Linger a little in life. Lovely is the animation of faces by bonfire light.

Indeed. After the display had shot itself to pieces the bonfire long continued to burn in Townside Field and happy groups roasted potatoes in its hot embers, talking spaciously. They had perhaps hoped for a phenomenon – something spooky – to take place on the destruction of the legendary oak tree but it hadn't happened and they were the more content for it. Suddenly there was a detonation high in the night sky way over to the right: golden rain hung in sheets, then shimmered white, and at the last throbbed with purple stars. It must have been above Heaven Park.

Another shell burst. Waves of white fire, like sea-horses bucking in foam, overarched the heavens. A third sent masses of silver snakes wriggling and screaming along the valley, their death throes attended by flares of acid green. The firework party of the Popjoys had begun. The youngsters said 'Cor' and gazed joyously at this bonus, but Robin with a suffocating sense of fatuity realised that he was in the wrong place, had been in the wrong place all evening, and would probably be in the wrong place for the rest of his life.

But the most interesting feature of the night did not become apparent until the following day. When Dickon arrived in the afternoon to check the bonfire, after everything else had been cleared away, he discovered a stump of the Craddock oak remaining unconsumed. He struck at it with an axe. Ash rose in a cloud and the embers revived. He struck again. There was a clang of metal on metal which was a very curious noise in the circumstances. He cooled the ground with splashes of water and after multiple hackings was able at last to pull from the disorder a rectangular metal box about one foot square. It must have been immured in the Craddock tree for many years, perhaps centuries. He rubbed the top of it with his glove. It was still warm. Engraved on the top of the box was one word. *Fireproof.*

29.

In the Monkshood Nursing Home, Melody was doing her rounds with a trolley which squealed when she moved and rattled when she halted. She loved night duty. Melody often suffered from insomnia and to be useful after dark came naturally to her. Her last call was at the room with 'John Smith' on the door. He was as awake as he ever got and in the softly flashing fog of his consciousness he saw her and his eyes brightened.

'Hullo,' he said.

'Hullo.'

As had become customary the imbecile made a space for Melody in his bed. She crept in and put an arm round his waist. A long curl of peace enwrapped their joined bodies.

She whispered in his ear 'John, I'm pregnant. I don't know how it happened. But I'm glad.'

He smiled from afar and said 'Good', or some palatal equivalent, not grasping the import of her words but charmed by their sound. The words were full and warm, were about kindness and babies and life. This he knew. That they were also about drama and disturbance, obligation and travail he did not know.

Melody was an old-fashioned girl at heart and did not want her child born out of wedlock, though she had no illusion that she'd be acquiring a husband in a more substantial sense. One week later the chaplain of the nursing home privately married the two parents, with two fellow nurses as witnesses.

30.

As the rain slid down the window of her office at Heaven Park, Alice rang, left messages, mailed letters and brochures, and nobody ever rang or wrote back. Despite abundant signalling to the outside world about the glories of having a conference in this great country house, she was unable to provoke any feedback whatsoever and this gave her a stressful feeling of non-existence. Sometimes it was as though the rain slid down her very eyeballs. Perhaps she should go to the doctor for a course of anti-depressants. Apparently lots of people did. Including people you'd never guess – so perhaps they occasionally worked . . .

Sidney brought in a pot of tea and two rock cakes on a plate. 'You need fattening, Miss Alice. Cook says you are to eat both, not only one like yesterday.'

'I think I'll take up smoking, Sidney.'

'What a good idea, miss. Keep busy.'

JJ popped in, going 'Money money money', and asked her if she'd had any luck.

'Not yet.'

'Perhaps soon.' He avoided her eyes. 'This used to be a boot-room. One of eleven boot-rooms. It's exactly four times as high as wide.'

'A computer would help. E-mail.'

'Yes, we can fail to receive e-mail as well as the other sort. It's like buying ski-clothes, Alice. They don't help you ski. Can't you chat them up more?'

'JJ, either they want a 200-room mansion or they don't.'

He took one of her rock cakes and ate it in two bites. 'Wear more colour. It doesn't have to be jeans and jumper every day.'

'By the way, the centre light switch has gone at The Glade.'

'I thought Dickon fixed it.'

'So did I.'

'I'll tell Malcolm.'

31.

Dickon returned to the farmhouse in the evening and kicked away the leaves which had gusted against the back door. The BBC News reported calamitous floods in China due to deforestation and soil erosion. He took a cup of tea upstairs to his wife who was sitting in bed fondling the single plait which fell over her shoulder in anticipation of seeing her husband come through the door. Dickon was the only thing in her life and his every move, his every remark was an event for her.

'Thanks, love,' said Meg. 'Your supper's in the oven. I had a good day. Got downstairs and made some congress tarts.'

'Yea, I had one.'

'You look tired, Dickon.'

She wept a little. He let her and afterwards dabbed her eyes with a corner of the sheet. The telephone rang. 'I'll take it downstairs,' he said.

It was Malcolm. 'The electrician's been to The Glade and said the wiring was a right mess. What did you do to it?'

'Improved it.'

'I wish you hadn't. It only costs more in the end.'

'That wiring's over fifty years old, Malcolm. You blaming me?'

'Please don't interfere with other properties on the estate, Dickon, that's all.'

Meg edged her way carefully downstairs to watch him eat his beef stew.

'Who was it on the phone?'

'Malcolm.'

'Trouble?'

'No.'

'When are you going to open that thing?' she asked, pointing to the box in the corner. The metal fireproof box, large and ugly, had been sitting in the kitchen ever since Guy Fawkes Day.

'It won't budge. I've got to get a special tool. Don't want to damage it, do I. They don't make boxes like that these days.'

'I wish you'd put it somewhere else. It's spoiling the room. Will you be going out again?'

'To High Field.'

She took a quilted jacket off a peg on which also hung an otter hunting suit unused for two generations. 'Put this on. It's getting cold nights. Do you see her much up there?'

'Don't see anyone much.'

'What's her name again?'

'Alice.'

'We're running out of morning wood, Dickon.'

Dickon watched the end of the news – the King Mother was opening a homoeopathic hospital in the Midlands – and went out into the lonely, vegetable night.

32.

Crystal took the small yellow car from the stables and drove away with the radio blaring. It was Toxic Genitalia's single 'Jealousy' from their new album.

> *It's late*
> *But I wait*
> *While she talks in bars*
> *To boys with scars*
> *   Pain in my brain, dart in my heart*
>
> *I'm burning and afraid*
> *You love me like a razorblade*
> *I feel cold*
> *Nothing to hold*
>
> *I'm her bloke*
> *Her joke*

I hate it
But I can't sedate it
Pain in my brain, dart in my heart

She thought she might invite the band down to Heaven, impulsively, just like that. They might even accept – pop groups were the world's biggest snobs. The lead singer, Anal Mucus, had been associated with a number of fashionable figures. Crystal wanted to be a fashionable figure. A deep streak of shyness held her back. She didn't know why. Should she have analysis to find out? All her family had this deep streak of shyness. But they'd never had analysis. Perhaps everyone in the world was shy really, underneath, and civilisation was the attempt by humanity to overcome its shyness, its fundamental puzzlement at finding itself alone and stuck between earth and sky. Perhaps she'd write a book about it. She could be a writer. She could be a singer. It was a matter of doing something other than being a . . . breeeeeeeder. Generations of her family had devoted themselves to the idea that people like Crystal should do nothing except stand about in pillared halls flashing their tits, hoping to be chosen by someone higher up. It was with a start that Crystal realised she was in tit-flashing attire tonight. She should rebel against that and open an orphanage in Armenia. Or Bolivia. One of those getaway places. And with another start she recalled that several women in her family had rebelled thus and graced various outposts of the Empire with a Popjoy Foundling Institute or a Heaven Home. Was there no escape from the stricture of her genetic current? She longed to be Crystal, not some . . . type. Squealing on the sharp bend, she bounced over the bridge and bumped up the cobbles of the High Street and jerked to a halt outside The Zodiac.

Robin said 'You're late'.

'What shall I have?'

'Whatever you like.' Robin broke his gaze which had attempted to capture all of her. It was hopeless. He was never able to capture all of her. He could focus only on bits of her. Never the pulsating whole. Maybe one day he'd contemplate her in a devouring serenity, instead of always finding himself zooming in on this bit, zooming in on that bit.

'What are *you* having?' she asked.

'Beer.'

'I don't want beer. You choose for me.'

'I don't know what you want.'

'Then give me a surprise, for God's sake! What's on in Appleminster?'

He bought her a double vodka and tonic with ice and lemon.

'*Destroversion* at the Regal,' said Lois.

'I saw it with Cook.'

Lois shook the local paper some more. '*Spermaid* at the Flea Pit.'

'OK, I'll surprise you,' said Robin.

He was sapient with lust, his mind of a jumpy but phosphorescent clarity. Goaded by her sneering moodiness, he knew precisely where he would take her.

'Drink up. Get in my car.'

Veering down a lane he startled two sheep who capered ahead flicking up their behinds until his fierce honking catapaulted them through a gap in the hedge. He was soon on the main Appleminster road. The speedometer moved smoothly over seventy, eighty, ninety miles per hour. Crystal was breathless, giggling nervously, and wound down the window. The night whistled in like a banshee.

'Where are we going?' she yelled.

'You'll see!'

He turned off the main road, revved up a hill, crunching the gears, and put his foot down again as the road levelled. Her forbearance had held over the last fifteen minutes but now she said it: 'Not so fast, Robin.'

'This isn't fast. I'll show you fast.'

The tin box rattled round the bends. Crystal gripped the seat, her feet pressed forward, but she said nothing more. He let out an alien cackle as the wheel hit a large stone. The car shook, skidded on wet leaves, rocked as brakes were applied. Turned. Skidded again. Rubber burned and screeched. Another bump. She was thrown forward; his hip and shoulder hit the door. A headlamp burst. Crash and tinkle of glass. Stop. Silence. For some reason the interior light had come on. Her chocolate hair was spread over the dashboard in front of him.

He was sweating. The sharp smell of his own sweat or oil maybe or was it petrol . . . Eventually he began to rub his shoulder. The chocolate hair stirred and turning round she asked 'Are you OK?'

'Yes.'

'Don't ask if I am, you little shit.' Her grey eyes drenched him with contempt. They got out of the car. A breeze ran along the lane and sycamore propellers descended round them. They didn't speak.

When he tried the car it started without difficulty and he drove on for a further twenty minutes until they came to some kind of concentration-camp gateway closed with a chain. A broken-down sentry box stood at one side. Robin unwound the chain. To the loamy smell of rotting leaves was now added the smell of rotting allsorts as a row of derelict Nissen huts floated phantomly into the single headlamp. The huts exuded visions of torture, decomposing violence, an extreme wretchedness. At the last hut he stopped and took a torch from the glove compartment and a woollen blanket from the back seat. Crystal slouched after him through a smashed doorway, scuffing on broken glass. Boxes of canvas straps and metal water bottles and piles of slimy shoelaces and a couple of old mattresses tossed askew, all rotting, rotting, rotting, their mongrel perfumes singing of a ferocious, desperate, yet banal past. Among various obscene graffiti someone had written 'The great thing about war is that it replaces the private terror with a public terror'.

Robin propped the torch upright in one corner and it illuminated a leprous patch of ceiling. Carefully, like a nurse, he spread the blanket over one of the mattresses. Crystal was already taking off her clothes. Naked, they slithered around each other, attempting to make their insides outside and their outsides inside in order to annihilate their separateness, which they achieved for whole chains of moments at a time. Though it was the first time they had made love together, it was as though this were an amazing routine which they both thoroughly understood, an automatic knowledge of each other which had only masqueraded as ignorance. He came almost at once, and later once again, while her deliquescences rolled continuously. For only one moment did she break the surface of that ecstatic sea, when she felt bubbles in her fundament and thought she must fart, but Crystal held it in for the sake of romance. An hour passed outside time. Afterwards they drew the blanket round themselves and looked into the beautifully shattered room.

'I'm sorry but I love you,' he said.

'Thanks a million.'

'But it's more than love.'

'More than love?'

'I love you and when I'm with you I feel more than love. Do you understand?'

'Not really, no. Where are we? What is this place?'

'The old aerodrome. The RAF flew bombing raids out of here. Last time I found a pre-war map of Berlin.'

'Who were you with the last time?'

'Myself. I often come here by myself. Can you hear the planes?'

They were quiet for a while. They heard aeroplane propellers, the taking off, the fading drone. They heard clipped incomprehensible voices over crackly loudspeakers. They heard big band dance music, laughter, camaraderie, and death. Yes, even death had a noise, a kind of slushy, echoey human murmuring repeatedly fading away. They strained to catch seductive, poignant echoes down the tunnel leading to the past and she hummed the song 'Stormy Weather'.

'Why are you humming that song?' he asked.

'I can hear it. Can't you?'

'No.'

'You're not sensitive.'

'Are you on the pill?'

'I stopped taking it. Are you?'

'No. Anyway I want to get you pregnant. Ouch.'

'What is it?'

'My shoulder.'

'Give me the torch. Let me look.'

He was badly bruised down his side. She covered the bruises with kisses, making him wince. She wanted more. It was the best sex she'd ever had – or ever would have.

33.

Melody knocked on the door.

'Come in,' said a voice.

She entered Dr X's secretary's office. 'Good morning, Melody. Dr X will see you now.'

Dr X, a wise man with shaggy white hair and gold-framed spectacles, was the director of the nursing home. He knew of her curious marriage to one of his patients but she had told no one of her pregnancy except John Smith and from this perspective, as from so many others, John Smith meant nobody. Dr X said 'Good morning, Melody. Please sit down. I hear you want to leave us.'

'My father is unwell. He needs me.'

'But will you come back to us?'

'Yes, I'll come back to see John. Look after him while I'm away.'

'I hope your father recovers soon. Good luck, Melody. You've been popular here.'

She shook his hand and left and that afternoon waited at the chilly roadside for a bus which when it came was full. So she had to wait for another and when that came she had to stand. This took her to a busy bus station where she awaited another bus which, when it came, was almost empty and she was able to place her suitcase on the adjacent seat. All at once she was weary of the whole business. She had never lied to her colleagues before. She had never had to escape before. But she couldn't possibly go through her pregnancy at the nursing home, not with all the attention, all the explanations. In her mind, yes, without a doubt she wanted the baby and would keep it and love it and be proud of it, but her soul did not exult. Something which was not her was growing within, something very complicated which in due course would have to be expelled. She was its vehicle. Let it do what it must then.

A hand touched her shoulder. 'This is it, miss.'

'Thank you.'

Melody gathered up her bags and stepped off. Appleminster Omnibus Station. It was cold. She took a woollen scarf from one of the bags and wound it several times round her neck.

'Excuse me, where's the bus for Milking Magna?'

She was fortunate because there were only two such buses daily, one at nine a.m. and the other at nine p.m. She sat down in the waiting bus and rummaged in her bag for a round of sandwiches wrapped in foil while a picture developed in her head: the girls at the nurses' hostel saying goodbye. She held back tears and became more solid when the sandwiches were inside her. The bus shook as the driver climbed into the cabin. The engine fired and ticked over soothingly and before long friendly warm air seeped among the few passengers and the bus pulled away. The driver moved through the angled streets and past windows giving a view into cosily lit rooms. The next time she looked out all was blackness. A boy and girl were talking with animation several rows ahead and she caught scraps of adventure from another world, though could not work out whether they were a couple or just good friends or brother and sister. A surprisingly large portion of her journey was occupied by trying to solve this question.

It took over an hour to reach Milking Magna. The boy and girl disembarked too and strode off springily arm in arm. Cloud streaked across a cruelly white moon. Half way up the High Street she took a lane to the right which ran between old terraced cottages. At the top of the rise the lane opened out to a bedraggled plot with trees and parked cars and on the far side of it, in a murderous wash of sodium light, was the horseshoe enclosure of Gypsy Castle. The boy and girl came into view again, swinging round the corner. The boy quickly kissed the girl and disappeared in another direction. The girl knocked on one of the doors and a man opened it.

'Where the ell've you bin?'

'*Destroversion* at the Regal. Forgot my key.' Daisy pushed past her father into the house.

'Wiv im?' And the door closed.

When all was quiet again, Melody approached the house next door and pressed the buzzer. A tuneful ding-dong was heard within. The door had changed colour since her last visit and was now a vehement red. She was very anxious. She hadn't telephoned to say she was coming but she knew he would be there.

He was always there. Justice opened the door, chewing a mouthful of supper and stared at her face, at her suffering expression trying to be bright, not quite grasping it.

'I think I'll be staying for quite a while, Dad,' said Melody, 'if that's OK'.

Part Two
WINTER

34.

'Have you seen his Twombly?'

'What?'

'He has an amazing Twombly. Have you seen it?'

'I don't believe I've seen it,' said Alice.

'You'd know if you had.'

'I suppose I would, yes. In that case – I haven't seen it. *You* have presumably.'

'Yes, I saw it this morning,' said Pimm. 'He's put it up in the Long Library. Not the best place for it if you ask me.'

'Nobody *is* asking you,' said JJ, coming across with bottle poised. He was wearing a frayed candlewick dressing-gown and brown suede shoes, and said to Alice 'That's all my wife ever gave me. A Twombly.'

'And a daughter,' said Alice.

'No. I gave *her* that. And she didn't want it, it turned out.'

Pimm sucked in his breath but the conversation was prevented from turning sour by Sidney who announced Sylvia Wetmore and Max Lomax. From the moment that Sylvia had moved into the stables Max plagued her with requests for an invitation to the great house and she'd prevailed on JJ to get it over with so that they might all have some peace. Minerva entered behind Sylvia and Max, and negligently overtook them, her green satin train hissing like a reptile over Lomax's highly polished shoes. Sidney told the company not to hang about because the food was already set in the Winter Dining-room.

'We're having an arty farty evening, Mr Lomax,' said JJ as he sat down at the head of the table. He wore a piggish expression and his dressing-gown gaped, exposing saggy teats.

'An arty farty? Why, yes, of course, Marquess, that is to say, um, well, er, if I heard correctly, that would seem to be . . . '

His discomfiture was palpable and continued throughout the dinner which was rent by long harrowing intervals when no one spoke. Everyone, even Sylvia who was normally so voluble, even that Alice person who was normally so gauche, seemed to accept these silences without difficulty. It was as if their conversation had been stretched by the size of the house until large holes appeared in it. Living in a caravan, Lomax preferred more concentrated activity. These conversational holes made him panicky and he plugged one of them by saying 'When I was in rep with Sylvia we lived in terror of forgetting our words but neither of us ever did.'

Pimm toyed with his ponytail. 'It should be remembered that the logos *is* the phallus. The word is by its very nature a rational creation, that precise thing piercing the primeval fog of fancy and emotion. The very existence of language is penile.'

JJ was helping himself to vegetables from the hotplate on the sideboard and replied 'Yes, Pimm, I can see that the logos is the phallus, but is the phallus the logos? I think not. Cock is greater than word, contains word.'

The language these people use in public, thought Max. No better than sluts!

Minerva, not to be outdone, threw her arms wide and exclaimed 'But what *are* hermeneutics?'

After this outburst of chat there was another colossal lull and Lomax was mightily relieved when they decamped to the Long Library where the two fireplaces were in an affable uproar of blazing logs. The flames reflected gorgeously on the golden grilles which protected the books. More books were scattered over tables and chairs, with a few out-of-date journals and last month's newspapers.

Lomax put on a pair of clear glass spectacles and his eyes darted everywhere. 'It is essential for man to make things of the mind,' he said with professional zest. At least he was trying. The others weren't even trying. He was very disapopinted in Sylvia. She'd simply cast him adrift on deep waters. 'Mind that is not connected to things', he persisted gamely, 'cannot exist in time and therefore cannot communicate'.

Minerva perked up at this. It was a rather sharp thing to say. She was almost certain she'd never heard it said before. 'D'accord, Monsieur. Le silence de profondeur est très egoïste, n'est-ce pas?' proposed the lady. Lomax mumbled something, clueless, and she asked him 'Were you ever married, Mr Lomax?'

'I was divorced, madam.'

'That's not the same thing at all.'

She led him off to a round table inlaid with ivory vine leaves and picked up a book, rubbing the dust off it with her taffeta sleeve. '*Orchestra* by Sir John Davies, Mr Lomax. A poem of dancing in rhyme royal. I know you love to dance.'

Lomax caressed the volume's cover stamped with silver strawberries, but his eyes were continuously sliding over the shelves and tabletops, looking, looking, looking. 'Dancing was only *part* of my act, Lady Minerva,' he replied, in order to dispel any implication that he was akin to a chorus boy.

Minerva sighed and glanced about with a sentimental expression. 'I used to have harp lessons up this end. Plink plonk, plink plonk, year after year.'

'It is said that only spinning at the wheel rivals harp playing in gracefulness.'

'I do have a straight back, don't I. But I didn't want to be a harpist, Mr Lomax. Nor a spinster.'

'Lady Minerva, who could ever imagine you as a spinster?'

'That's right. My condition is merely temporary. Are you a *close* friend of Madam Wetmore?'

'A good friend, Lady Minerva, that is all.'

'Do you two want any?' called out JJ. He was leaning forward on a sofa by one of the fires, pouring coffee into tiny cups, and the massive ham of his naked leg protruded through the front of the dressing-gown. Minerva rustled towards him and said 'But it will keep me awake.'

'So what. You don't have to get up for anything.'

'Black or white, Max?' called Sylvia.

'Black. And five sugars please. A-a-ah, very fine aroma of our pernoctation,' he declaimed from some old play, approaching the others and moving away from the scene of his crime. His eyes glinted like Sheffield plate and he was smiling unpleasantly.

His crime? Yes, indeed, his crime. To be more specific, his theft. He had only seconds ago *stolen* something. He simply couldn't help it. He *had* to. First visit to the great house and he was compelled to defile it, to make his mark perversely as it were by an act of subtraction. Voomph – in it went – just like that. And it wasn't *Orchestra* either, or John Dee's *Propaedeumata Aphoristica*, or Soderini's *Treatise on Orchards*, or any of the other gold-tooled morocco-bound poncy volumes lying around ever so casually just to make Maxie feel like a penniless illiterate peasant, no siree, it was something far, far more interesting.

JJ, when not working on his affairs in the cosy, liked to pursue them at one of the desks in the Long Library, and Lomax's roving attention had of course fallen on the one and only item in the room which should have been carefully locked away from prying eyes. It was in fact *partially* hidden. Peacham's *Compleat Gentleman* lay on top of it. But partially hidden wasn't enough. The words 'The Monkshood Nursing Home' could be seen clearly printed. It was a bill. Written on it was 'Annual Extras' followed by an account. Lomax with unerring instinct, as well as a sleight of hand acquired under the tutelage of Tommy Trot, deftly invaginated the document when backs were turned. All innocence and with one leg ever so casually bent at the knee, he stood scrutinising a large picture, an abstract arrangement of rusty nails, which hung on the chimney breast above the nearer fireplace.

'What on earth is that?' he asked brightly.

'My wife's Twombly,' said JJ, drawing across a flap of dressing-gown to conceal his naked leg.

'Is it a good likeness?'

'Very good.'

35.

Alice had yet to join the others for coffee in the Long Library. On the walk there, Sidney had drawn her aside and said 'The Lady Crystal said she would much appreciate it if you'd take her up some pudding. She's not been well.'

'Of course, Sidney.'

Crystal lay glumly on the bed as Alice entered with a bowl of trifle and cream. 'I'm starving,' she said.

'Sidney said you weren't well.'

'I was sick this morning.'

'You seem fine now.'

'Yeah, I'm fine. Until, I expect, tomorrow morning.'

'What's that supposed to mean?'

'I'll give you one guess.'

'Oh my God, Crystal!'

The daughter of the house pouted inanely.

'Are you sure?'

Crystal nodded.

'How long have you known?'

'I don't actually know. But it obviously is. I'm going to Boots tomorrow to get one of those pregnancy kits. I had to tell someone but don't tell anyone else, don't tell Dad, not yet.'

'Oh God, Crystal.'

'Don't bring me down, Alice. I feel like a silly kid. Aren't you supposed to congratulate me or something?'

'Congratulations.'

'Do you know anything about babies?'

36.

The drizzle outside and the coal fire within charmed Alice into a mood which connected her to life and her gratitude drove her to gather some strands of the blue speedwell blossoming beside the front gate and put them in a tumbler of water. A few tears. Followed by her morning yoga. She'd found a beginner's text at Waterstone's in Appleminster whose manager, Martin, had been very helpful. He was himself of a beautiful shape and had said to her 'I go to the yoga class at the leisure centre. Why don't you come?'

Shoulders to the left, head to the right, arms over the back, clutch ankles firmly, and pull. She did her best. There should have been a loud crack, accompanied by an apparition of Ma Durga, the Many-Armed Indian goddess of strength. Neither happened. She presumed it was because the more she tried to empty her mind the more it filled up with envy of Crystal's pregnancy.

It was time to change and go to work at Heaven Park. Must push on. Every day had to be pushed. But as she took a fresh jumper from the wardrobe, something tumbled out with it, something parcelled in newspaper. Alice stood for a moment nonplussed before gingerly undoing the twine, opening the bundle, and dropping it like a hot brick. Oh no. Oh God. Oh hell. It was another bit of, another chunk of – pushing back her hair, she unlatched the bedroom window and gave herself by the bedside clock a full minute of yogic breathing. At the end of the minute her heart was still thumping away like a steam hammer but she was determined to examine the object.

It was an elbow, hinged, with half an upper arm and half a forearm, and made from the same material as the foot had been, a type of foam rubber. When she pressed her thumbs into it the substance succumbed like muscular flesh. It was very convincingly made. But why these tricks? Why this persecution? Why her? Why here? It was like voodoo. She was being targeted. Secretly. It was awful, nasty, wicked. Come out, come out, whoever you are! It was *unfair*.

She left a message for Hoskins at the County Constabulary and almost half an hour later he rang back.

'So it's happened again.'

'Yes.'

'Have you any enemies?'

'Apparently I do.'

'Any other clues?'

'It was wrapped in the local newspaper. Nothing was disturbed in the house.'

'Then it must be someone with a key.'

'Anyone could've made a key. The key was probably left in the door for months before I moved in.'

'These cases are troublesome but usually harmless. Some pathetic freak. Do you know any freakish people?'

'Not really . . . '

'I'll pop over.'

The elbow occupied the kitchen table. She went hot and cold – then hot again – then cold – then hot – she stayed hot and was still decidedly warm when Hoskins arrived.

'Calm down and take it from the beginning,' he said.

'There isn't a beginning.'

'What were you doing when you found it?'

'I was trying to get a vision of Ma Durga,' she began. He raised an eyebrow but didn't interrupt. During her discourse Alice was reminded of how Hoskins always seemed to have just had a haircut whenever she met him, to be excessively spruce about the ears and neck. And the ear-ring, bit louche for a copper – he was fiddling with it as she spoke. Not to mention that bow-lipped mouth of his squirming away – it was on permanent snog. Talking to him was a constant reminder of oral sex. Stop it. This isn't the right moment. Alice finished up with 'So you can imagine what an awful shock it was'.

He turned the elbow between steady hands. 'Nice piece of work.'

'Do they make them like that or will it have been chopped from a whole, you know, body?'

'It looks hacked off. But you can buy anything these days. Maybe it's a sex toy.'

'I didn't know elbows were particularly – '

'You'd be astonished what people get off on. Don't you remember those lines from *The Mikado*? I have a left shoulder-blade that is a miracle of loveliness. People come miles to see it. My right elbow has a fascination that few can resist.'

When she was alone again, she slumped aimlessly. The next thing Alice remembered was being handed a cup of tea by Dickon. 'Hoskins told me,' he said.

'I must've nodded off,' she said, only vaguely alarmed by her neighbour's intrusion.

'There aren't enough people around, are there. One can feel a bit isolated. It would be better if there were more people around, just a few more. When I was a kid there were people working in the fields, walking down the lanes. Now the land is empty and I work alone.'

'Can't Meg help you at all?'

'Only indoors. In the summer we get a lad from the Agricultural College to help out or a contract driver for a bit of mowing. But basically I work by myself and if there's anything on my

mind it can be hell, up and down, up and down, alone in a tractor all day.'

He sipped his tea.

Isn't *he* supposed to be comforting *me*? she thought. 'I assumed
you loved the farming life.'

'It's what I do and I get this feeling I'll do it year after year after
year and nothing else. What's the word? Unremitting. Shouldn't
think Hosky was much comfort.'

'He thinks it's all just a practical joke.'

'Well, it is, isn't it? What else could it be?'

She shrugged.

'If you're all right now, I'll be getting back.'

'Can I walk with you? I need some air.'

'Come across and have a spot of lunch. Meg won't mind.'

They walked across the fields to the farmhouse with the great
tithe barn beside it dwarfing the other outbuildings. Meg, smit-
ten by a streaming cold, was preparing a meal of frozen Chicken
Kievs, peas and potatoes. Alice found the combination of Meg's
invalidism, her cold and her food quite repellent, and she also
thought – A microwave is not very farmhousy.

'Another mouth,' said Dickon.

'I wish you'd warned me. I'm not dressed or anything.'

'Please don't bother, Meg. I can eat at home.'

'Alice had a shock.'

'Severed elbow in wardrobe I'm afraid,' said Alice goofily.

Meg tutted and invited her to sit in the easy chair by the hob.
'They should never've cut down that rowan tree as was always by
The Glade.'

'Don't talk daft, Meg,' said her husband.

'It aint daft. The rowan is a protection against witchcraft.'

'Don't mind Meg. She's too much indoors. It makes her fanci-
ful.'

'Don't you talk about me as if I weren't ere.'

Mid-Kiev the telephone rang and Dickon answered it.

'Hi . . . ' he said dully. A man on the other end spoke for quite
a while. 'What . . . ' mumbled Dickon. 'But that's crazy . . . Of
course we should put em back . . . This is absurd. Look, I'm
eating my lunch. I'll discuss it in the morning . . . Yes, there *is*
something to discuss.'

He banged down the phone. Meg hankied her nose and asked 'Who was that?'

'Malcolm Gibbet. The bastard won't let me put the hedges back.'

'What's it to do with him? Isn't this your farm?' asked Alice.

'Is it fuck!'

'Dickon,' upbraided Meg. 'Please.'

'I'm the *tenant*. Didn't you know? This is part of the Heaven Park Estate. Please excuse me.' He slammed the door on the way out.

Meg stood up and moved flimsily in no particular direction, hankying her nose. Alice couldn't swallow any more food. The clock ticked loudly.

'He tries to do it all himself,' said Meg. ' Dickon needs an extra hand here. It's me, you see. I can't even do the shopping. I'm an albatross. I know I am. And I tell you what else is an albatross too, that bloody box in the corner which Dickon found. It's been givin me the willies.'

'Where did he find it?'

'He says I'm not to say. He's got a thing about it. For some reason he don't want to open it. But what if it contains a million quid?'

'If it were me I'd open it like a shot.'

Meg must have misinterpreted Alice's movement because she said 'No, you mustn't touch it. That's Dickon's box, that is.'

37·

An imprecise tingle had lately accompanied Alice wherever she went. Plus a sense of impending headache. Several Christmas cards had already been forwarded to her from her London address, flying in from her old life like skewers. She had not intended to begin a new life so completely, merely to get away for a year while she got over . . . *it*. But there now existed a sharp angle between her past and her future, and though she was living in the future she had not yet managed to catch up with it. Christmas cards? No, this year she wouldn't send any and that would solve a lot of problems about whom she knew or whom she wished to know. Sometimes people did that. Stopped sending.

And as for Christmas shopping, who was there to buy for? No one she could think of. A vertigo hit her. She fell through space. It was with relief that in a day or two Alice came down with Meg's cold which gave her a straightforward reason for feeling how she'd been feeling.

Helen Craddock rang and said 'I hear you're poorly'.

'The flu.'

'There's one going round that feels like flu but it's a cold. And there's another going round that feels like a cold but it's actually flu – with a nasty sting in the tail. Leaves you very drained.'

'Yea, that's the one.'

'You mean you're on the mend?'

'No.'

'Don't resort to antibiotics. Mrs Punch's sister from the dairy died from antibiotics. She had too many and when she got pneumonia and really needed them they didn't work. Have you noticed how just before coming down with a cold one feels fantastically well?'

'I missed that bit. Probably because it's flu.'

'I'll bring over a spot of lunch.'

Helen arrived at one o'clock and dumped various provisions along the kitchen dresser: tins of rice pudding, bananas, Lucozade, Vick, a loaf, four perfect lemons, a bag of apples, a bag of tangerines, frozen soup in plastic boxes with handwritten labels. Coming back into the sitting-room she said 'I've left the bill on the kitchen table. Is vegetable soup all right for lunch? This cottage looks much nicer than when the previous occupant had it.'

'Wasn't that Gibbon Tuft?'

'That's right.'

'Who *was* he?'

'He was what Tim calls a weirdo. And don't ask me why he left because I don't know. He upped and went. It was he who cut down the rowan tree, to give more light he said but Lord Heavenshire was furious. Deliberately cutting down a tree is a jolly big thing to do, isn't it. Whereas if one just happens to fall down, like ours did, that's different. That's nature taking its course. How is Meg? I should visit her. She's a sort of cousin but Tim doesn't like her, says she's a malingerer. She had a miscarriage and hasn't been right since.'

'How long have they been married?'

'Ooo – it must be over ten years. Despite everything, Dickon is devoted to her. It's very touching to see them together. I hope we'll see you over Christmas.'

'I've been invited up to the Park.'

'Why don't you come to lunch with us on Boxing Day? It will be quiet. No one's staying this year.'

Alice's head thickened. 'Christmas, I um haven't yet . . .'

'You don't *have* to come,' said Helen with a jocular twist of her mouth.

'Sorry, Helen, it's this flu and I've got my period as well and I'm still upset about opening cupboards in case things jump out at me.'

The pan hissed as it boiled over in the kitchen. When Lady Craddock returned she was carrying on a tray two steaming bowls of broth with bread and butter. Alice beamed. How lovely to be cared for. Helen also got a buzz from it. In fact she was at her best when people were ill. All year round Lady Craddock tried to connect with people and failed but when they were ill she clicked with them immediately. Yet almost the moment they were better, they clicked out again; it was quite precise; Helen actually felt them disengage.

'Delicious soup.'

'Davis's recipe. It was my idea to add the tarragon. It can't be nice, dear, bits of rubber being left about the place. Tim thinks you should rent a flat in the village. You'd be less remote.'

There was a kerfuffle at the front door as Crystal barged in. 'Poor Alice. I've brought some mince pies from Cook. Hullo, Lady Craddock.'

'Hullo, Crystal. Would you like some soup? There's some left in the pan.'

'No thanks. Do you mind if I smoke?'

'Please – Alice's cold.'

Alice sneezed mournfully.

Crystal lit her cigarette with a purple plastic lighter. 'I'll keep the smoke away. Any more manifestations? Bits of corpse? It's obviously Daddy playing rotten tricks.'

'Oh, Crystal, he wouldn't!'

'He can be absolutely dreadful, Alice. You hardly know us yet.'

Helen looked out of the window and said 'Your garden's a bit of a mess.' The sky was low and drear as though it too had a mucus-laden virus.

Alice suddenly wanted them both to leave and said 'Dickon never caught the cold. It passed from her to me, by-passing him. He's strong. Why is it always the women who are sitting and waiting, having miscarriages and getting the flu?'

'You're just under the weather, dear,' said Helen.

Time hung heavy like an unmilked udder. Later she had a hot bath and rubbed Vick over her breasts, savouring the chill glow. Outside, the air turned brittle and the first severe frost of winter descended, sugaring the earth. Carol singers called. She gave them a pound. In bed, between hesitant sips of scalding Ovaltine, she read a page or two of *She Knew What She Wanted* by Mimsy Quagga, the Nobel Prizewinner from New Zealand, but couldn't work up an interest: one minute she found it too pretentious, the next not pretentious enough. Alice's head lolled over on the pillow.

Surely JJ wouldn't do a thing like that? Surely Crystal was a lying little beast? For all his faults there was nothing mean about JJ. A dead, silvery moth was floating on the surface of her drink under the lamplight. Fresh anxieties nagged. She was getting old. She didn't throw things off the way she used to. Should she start a pension plan for her old age? Wasn't it time to visit a dentist? Would the crow with the broken wing be killed by the frost? Were the people she'd let her London flat to making a wreck of it? And finally the image of her one-time lover and boss, the Minister of Power, leered out of the gloom, only his head leering at her and the mouth of it moving, and lies, only lies pouring from the mouth like minestrone. Lies lies lies! He'd lied to her about everything and she'd come to this country spot to find a life that wasn't built on lies. But it wasn't turning out to be so easy. She emerged from bed and stood at the window cooling her ankles. The moon, effulgent over hill and dale, slowly changed from green to blue to red to purple to white. Must be the virus, thought Alice.

38.

It was Christmas Eve and very still. At six o'clock she drove over to Heaven Park where she was welcomed by Sidney who explained that tonight a buffet would be laid in the State Dining-room and that if she wanted to go to church afterwards she should be in the Great Hall by eleven-thirty p.m. She went up to her allotted bedroom, the Silver Bedroom in the Cameron Suite, where sprigs of mistletoe had been twisted into the silver wall sconces and into the silver mirror hanging above a narrow fire-place of white marble. Orange coals filled the grate and the room was warm. She opened a window onto vertically falling snow.

A white plastic radio beside the bed kept her company while she bathed and changed, and with a coat over her bare shoulders she descended to the State Dining-room. One of JJ's antecedents had decided that yellow and gold convolvulus scaling the walls and clashing in plastered tumult across a ceiling whereon, in large painted roundels, gorged the Olympian gods, and all reflected many times over in the fogged glass of Mr Whittle's wriggle-framed mirrors, was an effect conducive to digestion. And fun-nily enough, it was. Festive streamers and candlelight had been added for the occasion.

But what had happened to everyone else? Alice sat at one corner of the giant table and picked thoughtfully at her gammon. As she collected some pears in brandy she decided to prick her-self on one of the sprigs of holly in order to assert a sense of real-ism. The small berry of blood, like one of the holly's own, grew dreamily on her fingertip and seemed no more real than anything else.

At eleven-thirty she waited patiently in the Great Hall, over-coat buttoned with collar turned up, feet together, gloved hands at her sides. Lit with starry lights, a very tall Christmas tree dwarfed her, but the stone columns dwarfed it. Her small cache of presents had been placed tidily at the tree's base but there were no others. For some reason a broken egg was lying on the marble floor not far away, its yolk intact. The hall was bitterly cold and Alice wondered why the hell she was going to midnight mass at Saint Wendy's if nobody else were going except that, yes, she cer-tainly would go, otherwise it would only be food and drink and awful presents and not Christmas at all. When Sidney hobbled forth, Cook was on his arm reeking of sherry.

'Shall I drive?' asked Alice.

'That would be kind.'

The world was silent, soundproofed with snow. They purred down snow-filled lanes and snowflakes rushed at the windscreen. All three were absorbed in their bitter-sweet memories of Christmases past. On the very first Christmas morning she could remember, Alice had run down the stairs to her father. Father Christmas had terrified her, a huge threatening presence at the end of her bed. Daddy comforted her: 'No, no, my little darling, it is only the pillowcase of presents which he left for you' . . .

On Christmas morning it turned out that JJ had taken the others to a party in a neighbouring county the night before and Alice felt rejected. At noon she met Minerva and JJ in the Red Drawing-room for champagne and the exchange of presents. Alice had never seen this room before except in a coffee-table book called *Private Palaces of the World*. Beneath a ceiling of red, gold and lemon lozenges, hung the famous twelve Leaping Portraits of the family by Gainsborough. The carpet matched the ceiling but was much obscured by the mountains of puffy gold furniture designed for the room by . . . by . . . oh terribly famous, JJ had told her, a terribly famous name, you *know*, her mind was going, couldn't recall simple facts any more, she was great on scenes, whole scenes came winging back, but simple facts and her mind was a sieve – as for her French, only the other day she'd thought of mass-mailing France, but her French . . .

Through the arcaded windows, the sun shone from a blue sky upon a glittering landscape. Near to the house a flock of buntings danced above the box hedges, looking for a break in the snow-cover where they might peck for seeds.

JJ handed Alice an odd-shaped parcel tied with string. At the best of times it was an embarrassment opening presents under other people's eyes but to this, because of Alice's recent trials, were added visions of rubber hands, rubber faces, artificial hair, glass eyeballs. What gruesome trick might this parcel be? It took her a while and every so often she pulled a silly face. Then it was done. Wrapping off. And she gasped.

'Oh! They're wonderful!'

JJ and Minerva beamed.

'But surely it's too much,' said Alice.

'We found them in one of the lumber rooms and immediately thought of you,' said JJ, 'so accept them with our love. You're lucky to have the pair.'

'They're *fabulous*. I adore them *totally*.'

Alice no longer felt rejected, such is the power of presents. Her eyes moistened and she kissed sister and brother. As she gave them their gifts, she said 'I'm sorry, I can't compete'.

But Minerva and JJ tore greedily and were overjoyed. People hardly ever gave them presents.

'Here you are,' said Minerva to her brother. She handed him a plastic carrier bag from Marks & Spencer.

He lifted out a garment and held it despairingly against his cheek. 'It's lovely, Minnie, but you know I can't wear manmade fibre.'

'Give it back then,' snapped his sister.

JJ twirled his fingers through his hair and looked tragically at Alice. 'Brings me out in prickly heat. She knows that.'

'What did you get me?' Minerva asked.

He handed over a square parcel.

'Just what I've always wanted!' exclaimed Minerva. Her happiness exited through the narrow gape of a horizontal smile.

'Don't you think you ought to open it first?'

They sipped more champagne and chatted, waiting for Crystal and the only other guest, Archie Popjoy – who was a cousin and JJ's heir – but neither of them materialised and Sidney said that Cook couldn't delay any longer and would they please take their places under the convolvulus.

'I don't know what's got into Crystal lately,' said her father. 'She's being very odd. I can hardly forgive her for trying to stir it up between you and me, Alice.'

'I never believed it was you playing those tricks, JJ.'

'I shouldn't be surprised if it were *her*. Trying to get you out of The Glade so that she can move in. Pull my cracker with me.'

'I think she's annoyed, Julius, because Miss Weather wouldn't come for Christmas.' And Minerva shouted across the table to

Alice 'Do you know where Leicestershire is? Pimm's gone there for the week. Is it near Cornwallshire?'

It was as they engaged with the might of Cook's Christmas pudding that there was a series of raps on the window. JJ adjusted his orange paper hat and blew a toy cornet in the direction of the noise. It was Sylvia. Alice let her in. She was in furs and her face pink-tipped. 'I'm dying of cold. The heating's gone off in the stables.'

'That's because we turned it up in here.'

'But Wetmore and I were having our Christmas dinner.'

Minerva said 'I thought you'd separated'.

'It's Christmas, and the poor bugger suffers terribly from anal pruritis, especially at this time of year. He's gone to bed with a bottle of whisky.'

'Aliquid in recessu,' quipped JJ.

Sidney re-entered and asked 'Where would you like the coffee, liqueurs, meringues, candied fruit, chocolate Yule log, and Heaven pineapple in kirsch?'

'Stick to the Red Drawing-room. It's already heated. Any sign of Glory?'

'I'm afraid not, your lordship. And thank you for my present, Miss Alice, and Cook thanks you for hers. She's says it'll come in very handy.'

Alice thought it was fun having Sylvia join them, but in the drawing-room Minerva was huffy about it and played patience at a card table a little way off from the others. Alice saw out of the window that it was snowing again and JJ said they should all go for a walk. Sylvia said that walking in quiet snowfall was one of her most favourite things in the whole world but by the time they'd got ready, it was getting dark and so they didn't go. Instead, assisted by liqueurs, Sylvia, Alice and JJ had a conversation on the nature of love.

SYLVIA: As far as love is concerned, there are two sorts of people.

JJ: The haves and the have-nots.

SYLVIA: I was going to say the straight and the bent, by which I mean those who are not open to possibilities and those who are.

JJ: But I may be straight in one respect and bent in another. Even in love, we are many things. I don't think people should even *try* to be one thing.

ALICE: You don't believe in integrity?

JJ: Only of the individual, not of the type. People who are all male or all female are not interesting.

SYLVIA: Do such people exist, JJ?

JJ: No. But they imagine they exist.

SYLVIA: Oh yes, the mono men. Wetmore for example.

JJ: If you prefer stereo types, why did you marry him?

SYLVIA: Because stupidly I fell in love with him.

ALICE: Did he fall in love with you?

SYLVIA: Yes – but more.

JJ: Because you were good in bed.

SYLVIA: Yes.

JJ: There is no satisfaction in sexual love. It's about the thrill of need. That is, of dissatisfaction.

SYLVIA: That's me. It's not Wetmore. He wants peace of mind. A bonk on Saturday after he's turned off the races.

JJ: In my own life I have discovered an appalling fact – that unreliability is arousing. As soon as one is absolutely sure of another person they lose their magnetism.

ALICE: Aren't you mixing up love with sex?

JJ: Constantly. I think it's inevitable.

SYLVIA: Do you believe it possible for love to become marriage without it also becoming banal?

JJ: Anything is possible but it's not very likely.

ALICE: I yearn for the banal but I can't achieve it.

SYLVIA: You wouldn't be so keen if you had achieved it.

JJ: Alice loves being the mystery girl.

ALICE: That's not true, JJ. And I think it's childish to sneer at reliability.

JJ: It certainly isn't childish! The one who is loved can never be possessed by the lover – except in death. Which is a great tragic theme. That is the challenge of sex. One returns again and again, trying for ever greater possession, but it always eludes one.

SYLVIA: Men are so weird with their talk of possession.

ALICE: The woman's form of possession is called marriage.

JJ: Is impotence allowed, Sylvia?

SYLVIA: Of course. I'd go further and say that a man who's never experienced impotence doesn't know how to make love. But it mustn't become a habit.

ALICE: A weak man is easier to possess than a strong man.

JJ: My goodness, it's clear that you women want to *devour* your men. Possession is not nearly enough. *Devour* them you must. Only then do you feel safe, with your man inside you. But that's death for a man because a man must be mobile. Only then can he do his other job.

SYLVIA: Which is?

JJ: Bringing home the bacon.

SYLVIA: I brought home the bacon in our house.

ALICE: I bring home my own bacon.

JJ: Wetmore did all right by you, Sylvia.

SYLVIA: You call that all right?

JJ: My father always admired his achievements on the Turf.

SYLVIA: Your father didn't live to see the outcome, did he. The humiliation. The only way to live with an alcoholic is to become one yourself. Well, sorry, but no thanks, I just like getting plastered occasionally. It's been a rotten marriage and I can't pretend otherwise. He's sozzled now in your stables.

JJ: From the outside it didn't look so bad.

SYLVIA: That's because we didn't want to lose all bloody dignity.

ALICE: All relationships have these two aspects, the sharing and the battle.

JJ: For men there is a third aspect. All men require a degree of loneliness. A man is drawn to other men through this loneliness he shares with them.

SYLVIA: Is that why you're gay?

JJ: I'm not talking about homosexuality. Oh, yes – I read the other day – on the subject of what makes men happy – the Greek poet Theognis. 'Whoever does not love horses and boys and hounds, his spirit shall never know peace.'

SYLVIA: You hate horses, darling.

JJ: I don't hate them – I simply don't ride them. Oh, perhaps I do hate them. I hate those silly long yellow teeth when they laugh. Reminds me of that Lomax of yours. I must be honest, Sylvia,

I can't stand Monsieur Lomax. I made the effort but it's no good. The trouble is that I got the feeling that the Lomax who was talking to me was not the same as the person who was actually there.

SYLVIA: That's show business, JJ.

JJ: In which case I quite understand its seedy reputation.

SYLVIA: Have you ever made love with another woman, Alice? I have.

ALICE: Er . . . no.

JJ: You don't seem quite sure.

ALICE: That's because I've thought about it.

SYLVIA: Thought about it generally or with someone in particular?

ALICE: Both actually.

JJ: Thinking doesn't count because almost every possibility, including murder and God knows what else, passes through our minds at some time. It's getting it from the inside to the outside that makes the difference, going from the hypothetical to the actual.

ALICE: If I'd had a bit more going for me in the straight line I might've given it a try but –

SYLVIA: Oh, it doesn't work like that, no, no. Like everything else in life, it's about curiosity. Everyone has a million opportunities every day but only the curious follow them up.

ALICE: And what makes a person curious?

JJ: That's easy. A mixture of courage and imagination. One's no good without the other. Courage without imagination is pigheadedness. Imagination without courage is whimsy. A person acquires curiosity when the two combine.

SYLVIA: Which brings me back to my original point. Some people are open to possibilities, others are not.

JJ: That's the passive version. Some people create their opportunities.

ALICE: Either way you're saying I'm a limited person.

SYLVIA: Yes.

ALICE: But I do know from my own experience that there are avenues of the unknown which only come into view under a measure of constraint.

JJ: I've never gone in for bondage myself.

ALICE: Oh, JJ! What I mean is – if I focus on someone I can't do
it with anyone else.
SYLVIA: Yes, falling in love is a form of constraint, JJ, but it cer-
tainly does makes things happen too.
JJ: Things happening can be very uncomfortable.
SYLVIA: Isn't that the whole point?
JJ: What, discomfort?

His question ended the conversation there, as behind them a door
swung open and Archie Popjoy appeared, honking in a repulsive
manner. Goofy-toothed and bony-faced, with long tapering fingers which opened and closed rapidly when he was the least bit
excited – and he was very easily excited – Archie took the look of
inbred refinement beyond all decency. He was aggressively het-
erosexual besides and jabbed his little horn into any doxy he
could find, shrieking and dribbling and wagging his head as passion mounted. Though hideous, he was without shame and
therefore had enormous success and a number of children dotted
about the world. Archie swayed a moment in shabby tweeds and
unbuttoned shirt, probing the room with needle eyes. He caught
sight of a new face, Alice's, shrieked and pranced across, holding
a wishbone of mistletoe over her head. 'Who's zis zen?' A strand
of his saliva fell into her lap.
    'She's Alice. Leave her alone.'
    'Hu-hu-hullo, Alice. Don't mistletoe berries remind you of
honk honk s-s-s-pe-r-m?'
    Minerva looked briefly up from her card game. 'You pinched
that from one of my poems. *Hommage Fantasie – Among sloe the
gin-berried, Neath mistletoe the jissom-berried, Auntie Flo is dead
and buried.*'
    'Archie, have you seen Crystal?'
    'We had a line of coke. She's on the-er *roof* somewhere. The
Heaven pineapple!' honked the drooling, prancing, goofy creature with a dive to the bowl.
    'We've been talking about love,' said Sylvia. She'd had Archie
years ago and wouldn't be having him again.
    'The word "cunt",' said Archie, biting down on a slice of
pineapple at the same time, with splashes out the sides of his

mouth, 'though not very descriptive of of honk honk of a wet and yielding orifice, is evidence of sex language being a a a a *male* creation!'

'Archie, please, we've got guests.'

'The word derives onomatopoeically from the-er the-er the-er honk honk sex g-r-u-n-t of males. Say it, Alice. C-c-c-c-u-n-t honk honk! And you'll get what I mean.'

Alice moved aside with a slur in her expression as juice and spittle came her way.

Archie reached across her for another slice of pineapple and proceeded to worry it with his mouth. His shirt was undone nearly to the waist and his ribcage showed corrugations in the lamplight. He now picked up a glass, stood on tiptoe and threw it furiously into the fireplace with a short scream. 'Merry merry!'

Minerva slammed down the cards. It was Archie who had done the kindness of relieving her of her virginity on her twenty-first birthday. And at the same time she'd relieved him of his – he was eleven at the time. And they had remained distantly attached. But she was angry and yelled 'You damned clot, those glasses were given to Daddy by Marilyn Monroe!' and punched him on the face. Archie ran into a corner, rolled himself into the smallest possible ball, and whimpered 'Don't hurt me, don't hurt me!'

'Forgive me, Julius,' said Minerva. 'But I was fond of her.'

'You knew Marilyn Monroe?' asked Alice.

'That was Minnie's nickname for the Old Un.'

Minerva snuffled 'She used to work here when I was small'.

'The Old Un did?'

'Yes, and she was very pretty.'

'The Old Un was?'

'Yes, and she was very nice to me,' said Minerva.

'You never visit her now,' mused JJ.

'Of course not.'

'The bungalow's not very far away.'

'Her daughter runs The Crag.'

JJ flicked back his hair and said 'Excuses excuses'.

39.

The Larks were watching the King-Emperor's Christmas Day speech from Windsor, the first from the castle since the sale of Sandringham to the Chinese.

'I can't stand im.'

'Oh, he's sweet.'

'Can't stand the other one neither.'

'I like the King-Mother best.'

'Where was is crown then?'

'Don't talk daft.'

'Don't e ave a crown?'

'Not on telly.'

'Are we going next door?'

'I don't wanna.'

'You wanna date, Daisy?'

'She wants a different sort of date.'

'I don't like dates.'

'Big, she don't like dates now.'

'You gettin veggie . . torian ideas?'

'Dates aren't meat.'

'If they aren't meat what are they, clever clogs?'

'Dates are like eating cockroaches without arms and legs. They look like the bodies of cockroaches, dates do.'

'Is this your latest thing dates aren't meat but cockroaches?'

'She's trying to spoil our Christmas.'

'She'll get a clip round the ear.'

'I bought a load of dates special. Big, stop pickin them boils.'

'Sorry.'

'And puttin yer fingers in the dates afterwards.'

'Oi said oi'm sorry.'

'It's not nice.'

'All right, all right, just don't put me down in front of the kids, OK?'

'Then don't do it in front of the kids.'

'You askin for a clout?'

'Where you goin, Little?'

'If you're gonna ave a row . . . '

'Sit down, it's Christmas.'

Next door Melody and Justice were dozing in front of the fire. Through half-closed eyes Melody surveyed her swollen belly. Seven months gone. She'd be glad to get it over with. Justice yawned deeply, lifting powerful arms over his head. Shouting came through the party wall from the Larks next door, followed by a smashing of glass or of pottery perhaps, followed by crying.

'Didn't you ask them round, Dad?'

'I did.'

'Wish you hadn't.'

'It's Christmas. You've got to be neighbourly.'

'I like it the two of us.'

'Shouldn't always be the two of us, Melody.'

'Soon it will be the three of us.'

'What about him?'

'Yes, that's right, it will be a he, I feel it too.'

'No, I mean the father, Melody. The baby's father. Still won't talk about it?'

'The father is . . . isn't well.'

'That's no reason to deprive a man of his child.'

'Perhaps they won't come round.'

'Perhaps they won't, my beautiful.'

'You haven't touched those dates, Dad.'

40.

Max's caravan rose out of the thick snow like an igloo. As the King-Emperor's speech came on the televisionette, Max turned it off – he was a republican – and turned on the radio. A church choir was singing *In Dulce Jubilo*. He turned that off too – he was an atheist – and mindlessly pressed the tip of his nose against the window which was wet from condensation caused by the gas-heater. He was like a caged specimen trying to get out. On a formica ledge the turkey roll, shoplifted on Christmas Eve, sweated a grey steam. He sawed off a couple of slices. Mashed potato, made from powder in a cardboard drum, and a portion of overcooked brussels sprouts completed the main course.

Max chewed slowly for want of anything quicker to do, his attention wandering through the swirls of his eyes to an ink-standish at the far end of the caravan, a thirteenth birthday present from Aunt Fred in Burnley. Long dead she was. All of em, the whole Lomax pack, long dead. Burnley long dead too no doubt . He'd heard it was full of black foreign shit these days. Did anything survive there? Any street one might recognise, any building with a past? For all he knew maybe the centre of Burnley was a miracle of preservation but somehow he doubted it. If it were anything like Barnsley – the last place he had tried to recapture a boyhood memory – there would be nothing left whatsoever. Never again would he revisit the past. The past had been destroyed and it hurt, like one's own hands and feet being hacked off, and to avoid that hurt he had decided twenty-five years ago to inhabit the beautiful eternal present of unspoilt Milking Magna. But now unbelievably there was a threat to that too! It beggared belief and he had finally decided that enough was enough and he'd contacted Joyce through an intermediary and beseeched her to allow him to so something, anything for the cause, and finally word had come back that she'd said no, that he was too old, and that was the end of it because Joyce the Leader had spoken. He was too old. Too bloody old to be of use.

Christmas pudding was a slice of Dundee cake with a pouring of cold ready-made custard from a tin. His eyes had gone wuzzy and so had his brain. Too long inside the caravan did this to him. He hated Christmas and New Year and all the days between like an everlasting string of Sundays. Sundays of course he hated too, and anything resembling Sunday such as Good Friday or a Bank Holiday. He popped on his specs and examined a group of novels, colourfully jacketed, which he'd presented to himself this very Christmas morn . . . *Tender Is The Meat, Jayne Mansfield Park, Warm and Peaceful, Wootherin Gites, Death by Pudding*. He selected *Warm and Peaceful*. It opened with a crack and the cardboard cover came away from the rest of it. On page one a ball was taking place, attended by people whose lives had consequence, who were involved – the print went sharply out of focus and he began to cry. He despised this weakness in himself, his Sunday tears as he called them. Being a man of the theatre he pretended to be someone else who was crying and this made it easier.

'Bloody life!' he blubbed. 'What is it for? Too old she said!
Joyce the Leader says I'm too old! How can I be too old? Nothing's happened to me yet! I'm nothing more than two eyes staring out of a head which moves around on two legs. Nothing but a
mobile lighthouse! I wasn't a mobile lighthouse when I was
young. I don't want to be a mobile lighthouse! Well, they won't
bloody get away with it, not any of em they won't! I've seen that
bill from the nursing home and I'll get to the bottom of it and I'll
show em all right I will!'

With a snapping of joints he stood up and rummaged in the
vitals of the prop basket until he found Tommy Trot's ocarina.
Max was once a bit of a dab at the ocarina himself and blowing
into the instrument and fingering the holes he forced out a
melancholy tune and heard in his mind's ear Tommy's roughcast
tenor coming up the warm tunnel from the past.

> *Who was that*
> *In my bed?*
> *Was it a hat*
> *Or was it a head?*
> *Funny weather for the time of year*

> *Sought an answer*
> *Got a question*
> *Wanted love*
> *Got indigestion*
> *Funny weather for the time of year*

> *Dreamboat*
> *You've gone*
> *Were you here*
> *Or was I always alone?*
> *Funny weather for the time of year*

41.

Boxing Day dawned ice-cold, pink and clear. By ten a.m. Sir
Timothy was sweeping snow from the front porch of The Crag,
sending up powdery fluffs which flashed in the sunlight. He felt

150 per cent. Not a cough, not even a sciatica twinge. Funny how these things came and went. Helen on the other hand had caught Alice's cold and was spluttering through the festivities as best she could.

'So you won't be seeing off the hunt then?' queried her husband in the drawing-room. 'You didn't last year. The village will think you're disowning me.'

'Poor little fox.' She blew her nose.

'Why don't you take antibiotics?' he asked.

'Because I don't believe in antiobiotics, Tim. I've told you a dozen times.'

'You prefer to be ill. Hand me one of those, pet.'

Helen was eating dried figs, soft as scrotums, from Fortnum & Mason, and Sir Timothy's paw foraged in the box. He must have been in a terrific humour because he didn't often call her pet. When Alice arrived, the knight and his lady were sitting among the strident chords of Beethoven's *Victory of Wellington* from the radiogram. As he turned it down, Sir Timothy informed Alice that 'Our history is glorious and our people free,' in case she might not have known. 'But the English are embarrassed by their triumphant past. Others may exercise national pride but the English must forever be apologetic.'

'But a gentleman never boasts,' said Alice.

'My dear girl, it's not boastful to mention the truth occasionally. We may live in a cynical age but I will *not* be told that the freedom, honesty and justice for which my own country has striven are no better than the torturings and extortions of some tin-pot dictator. Remember – and how few people do! – that we abolished the slave trade. The Americans, the Arabs, the black slavers themselves wanted to continue it but the English said no, it's wrong, it must stop, and stop it did.'

'Don't tell me there's no racial prejudice in this country, James.'

'Yes, there is, Helen, but it's nothing compared to the prejudice between tribes in Africa. They chop each other up on a regular basis. And while we're on the subject, show me a black country that's a success. There you are. Silence. I'm not anti-anyone but we should face facts.'

'Maybe they are successful at different things,' proposed Alice with a caring frown.

'Damn right. They're terrifically successful at embezzlement and pauperisation and thuggery and running. Especially running away from their responsibilities. The white man's burden – we've been trying to give it up for generations but the negroes won't let us. We're still bailing out the buggers! It obviously has something to do with the fact that of all the major races, the negroes never taught themselves to write. No intellectual life, you see, none at all. And yet there's hope. Why? Because they have open minds. Unlike the Islamics. *They've* gone round the bend and thrown away the key. Well, I'm all in favour of suicide bombers so long as they don't kill anybody else. But too many Islamics have been let into this country. Over the centuries we've managed to purge England of religious mania. I don't think we want it in by the back door thank you.'

'How did we get on to all this?' asked Helen.

'It's Christmas,' he replied, 'so one's thoughts ascend. How was your Christmas at the Park? Was the Bowsprit there?'

'The heir. Archie,' explained Helen with a dismissive flourish of lawn hanky.

'Yes, he was there. Highly strung I thought.'

'It's difficult to believe,' said Sir Timothy, 'but they'll make that prat a Knight of the Garter when he inherits the title. Not that one could ever imagine that the *present* incumbent was a Garter knight but he is, and goes along to the gatherings too, the rituals, the pageants, but keeps it quiet, *slinks* off, and then you see him flapping about in a cloak on television. I think he takes lots of tranquillisers to get through it. Judging by his appearance. There was a close-up once – he was talking to thin air. It's the oldest order of chivalry in Europe, you know.'

'Are you sure, Tim? I was always told that the Yeomen Warders at the Tower of London were the oldest.'

Sir Timothy sighed. 'Helen, the Yeomen Warders are not an order of chivalry. What they are is the oldest military corps in the world. I wish we shared more interests.'

'So are you saying there's an older order of chivalry outside Europe?'

'No, I'm not saying that, because orders of chivalry only exist in Europe.'

'What about the samurai?'

'What about them?' echoed Sir Timothy. 'Bunch of cut-throats, and queer to boot. Now look, Alice, Helen's not bothering but will you be seeing off the hunt today?'

'Is it today?'

'Of course it is. And it's for everyone. People get it all wrong, Alice. Hunting is about dissolving divisions in the countryside and reconnecting with the instincts and the elements. You will observe for example our disregard for hedges, ditches, roads, and what have you. The idea is to gallop freely across the landscape. To integrate.'

'In pursuit,' said Helen with a curt toss of the head.

'Of course. There has to be a focus. Activity without an objective is a queenless hive – lots of faffing but no life. But what goes deep, Alice, is that riding with the hunt is the nearest you can come to flying *without actually taking to the air*.'

'Sounds lovely,' said Alice.

Sir Tim lifted his eyebrows. 'Do you ride?'

'Only donkeys at the seaside.'

His eyebrows dropped. 'I ride because this is not a sailing county. Landlocked, we are. I think that's what made me go to sea. Had to get away for a bit.'

Davis appeared in the doorway. She stared long and hard at Alice who, becoming uncomfortable, asked 'Have I done something?'

Helen said 'I think she's going to tell your fortune. Davis tells fortunes at Christmas. She told me I'm going to live in a big black wood.'

'Obviously a metaphor,' said Sir Tim. 'She wouldn't tell me mine this year, and she wouldn't tell me why she wouldn't tell me mine, would you, you stubborn old bat. So I fear the worst.' But he laughed.

Davis said 'It's because yer don't know which side yer head is battered, Sir Tim. Now look, there's lunch. Master Robin's already in there scoffin.'

Cold meats, mashed potatoes, green vegetables, beetroots, pickles. Followed by Lemon Meringue Tart and a Double Cottenham cheese.

ROBIN: How was Christmas at the Park *really*?

ALICE: Honestly, it was very nice.

ROBIN: Why don't you move up there? Live above the shop. It would be safer.

ALICE: I'm not going to be driven out of my home thank you.

ROBIN: You feel The Glade is home, do you?

ALICE: I can close the door on the world.

ROBIN: But it's a shame for Crystal. She was all ready to move in there.

HELEN: Her-hum – you must stay here tonight, Alice. We've made you up a bed.

ALICE: I'll go back if that's all right.

HELEN: But if you change your mind . . .

SIR TIM: Did Lady Minerva say whether she'd be joining the hunt this year?

ALICE: Does she ride? JJ said they weren't horsy.

SIR TIM: He isn't. She rides occasionally. Borrows a mount from Harry Pulp. And the marquess's wife certainly rode.

ALICE: Who was JJ married to?

SIR TIM: To whom was JJ married? A rabid vixen is putting it mildly. The title went to her head.

HELEN: Don't start all that, Tim.

DAVIS: I'm off now. You'll have to put the pots in the washing machine yerself.

HELEN: Thank you so much, Davis. It was good of you to come on Boxing Day.

DAVIS: Don't I come on Boxing Day every year?

SIR TIM: And we want you to know it's appreciated.

HELEN: How is your mother, Davis?

DAVIS: A bit intercontinental, sir.

HELEN: Eggs and bananas are very binding. Please take her present – and yours – they're on the side in the scullery. She'll be missing you.

DAVIS: The Old Un don't mind being left. She'll be watching that Spanish flamingo dancing on the telly. Before I leave I want to say this to you, Miss Alice: Thy teeth are far apart – far apart they are – which is a sign thou wilt travel far and grow rich. You mark my words, Miss Gapteeth. You mark em. Well, ta-ra, everyone, and don't do anything I wouldn't do.

42.

Buttoned up in their pinks, Sir Tim and his son trotted to the green which fronted The Zodiac. Hot mince pies with punch were passed around on trays. While the riders sat above in a loftier realm, occasionally bending in the saddle to greet a friend, a good portion of the village mingled with the horses, blowing out their cheeks and bashing mittens together.

'The going is harder than I'd like but it should be fun,' said Sir Tim who turned out to be Master of foxhounds – he'd not said. The Revd Sinus Simm, roseate with sherry, rode up in the company of Dickon and several other farmers. Mrs Bladder-Williams, fronting a group who held a banner across their fronts which read YOU'RE VILE, shouted to the vicar 'Aren't you ashamed of yourself?' The Revd, who had a very correct seat, replied 'God moves in mysterious ways'. Hoggart the Butcher, astride a motionless nag which resembled something stuffed on the pantomime stage, hollered 'Loose the dogs on er! Fight fire with fire!'

Alice had never seen Dickon so grand and remote and thought he looked stupid, especially in the black riding cap which emphasised his ears. He touched the peak of it to her but spoke soothingly to his nervous skewbald, and when he raised his eyes again it was to look over Alice's head to where Lady Minerva Popjoy was clip-clopping up the High Street, side-saddle, a black top hat athwart her coiffure and a very curious costume below, which combined a short embroidered gown with thermal long johns and a tatty jacket. She was seemingly talking to herself as she progressed. None there knew that she was intoning *The Hymn to Artemis* by Callimachus, done into English by herself with the help of her brother (but she'd retained artistic control).

Lo! Artemis the Bringer of Light be I!
Hi! Give me the Moon's pale fire
And sixty daughters of Oceanus for my choir
All nine years old, all maidens yet ungirdled.
I bring gold, prosperity, mother's milk uncurdled.
So why do you frown?
Ah, yea, for seldom it is that Artemis goes down to the town
In a short embroidered gown.

The hounds arrived from Cowslipvale, tails up, bottoms clean. Little Lark, with yellow fuzz showing on his cheek in the sharp light, saluted 'Good luck, Sir Tim!'

'You must join us next year, Little. Come up to The Crag in the New Year and let's have a talk about it. You're still a stalky boy. I expect you'll fill out soon.'

'Maybe I won't fill out, Sir Tim,' said Little. 'There's got to be some stalky folk around.'

'Ah, I see you're a philosopher too, young man. Hullo, Malcolm. Where's Jack Farrier?'

'Sprained his ankle playing ping-pong.'

The hunt jangled down the High Street. The horses' hooves struck sparks off the cobbles. Alice and others were to follow in cars as best they could but the hunt early on struck across fields away from any road (with the exception of Minerva's steed who took it into his head to nibble grass from a verge and there was nothing she could do about it). Then, for the first time in eight years, a fox was sighted. The riders were astonished, unsure what to do next.

'Blow your horn, man!' ordered Sir Tim.

The horn blew. Uproar broke out, horses' necks going this way and that, but they were soon galvanised into a single organism which swarmed up the white side of the valley to the left of Heaven Park.

From the roof of the great house, Crystal, enfolded in her grandmother's sables, followed Robin with a telescope until he and the rest of the scarlet dots disappeared into a wood. When can I tell him I am pregnant? she was thinking. I don't want to tell him. He'll pester me to marry him again. Typical Robin to go for the most boring solution, two little biddies with a babby, yuk yuk yuk. Oh dear oh dear oh dear. A life with someone like Robin doesn't resemble any kind of life I've ever dreamed of, no matter how well he makes love to me. I'm a wild person. Yes, I am. Really I am. Dad knows I'm a wild person, so does Aunt Minnie, even Sidney and Glory know it, and they love me for what I am, but Robin will want to change me, yes he will want me this shape and that shape, he'll want me to be a . . . to be a . . . wife or something. Christ, being a mother's going to be tough enough without having to be a wife as well! Perhaps I shall tell him it's not his. Or perhaps I'll have an abortion. That would be the easiest, to have it removed like a winkle on a pin.

A minute later the hunt emerged from the wood into open country and against the sounding-board of the hillside, the horn brayed unnaturally loud. They reached the Ring of the Moon and galloped over the brow of the Heath, jackets still vivid against a pewter sky, and out of sight. Crystal felt a stab, like a waif abandoned, and took herself back into the building beneath her feet. Since she was a wild person she both wanted to be alone and didn't want to be alone . . .

It was well after dark when Sir Tim and his son returned to The Crag, flushed, tousled, large in heart. Alice for the first time saw these men as sexual beings. Sir Tim leant confidingly towards her and she caught the whiff of his singing flesh as he murmured with a wink 'The fox got away'.

'Good,' said his wife with a flirtatious twitch of her face (for the sexuality of the hunt had touched even her).

'And Malcolm Gibbet was thrown. He really is hopeless. Can't ride for toffee. Mum, I could eat a horse,' laughed Robin as he cast a couple of split logs into the dying fire.

That night, after Alice had gone home and Helen and Robin had gone to bed, Sir Tim sat alone with a final glass of claret in front of the embers. 'Why are those bloody things shaking?' he wondered and scrutinised the pair of gryphon radiators for almost a minute before rousing himself to walk across and touch them. 'Very odd,' he divined. 'They aren't shaking at all. In which case it must be I who am shaking. Humph. Presumably muscular fatigue after the ride. Better get some rest.' Whereupon he sneezed sixteen times in a row. It really had become very cold in the room all of a sudden. And he sneezed yet again.

43.

Kevin, half Old English Sheepdog, half Jack Russell, padding from spot to spot, periodically paused to look round at Glory Boy who walked along behind with a sprightly step, hands in pockets, boots breasting the dry uneven snow. The ice-cream light of lunchtime had given way to the pearl grey light of afternoon and the woods were all hushed in an atmosphere of clandestine repose. Where the snow had not penetrated, the roots of trees were wrapped in pelts of green moss, while above, the branching tops stood out starkly like river maps against the blank page of the sky. A buzzard was being mobbed by crows.

Everywhere white carpets invited the footprint and over one of them Glory peed a thick cable of urine, drawing yellow lines like a Miró, before following Kevin out of the wood and down the slope towards the Puck and level ground. Glory sat on a boll of roots beside the giggling water and rolled himself a cigarette while Kevin lifted a paw, took several steps forward, and pranced upon a molehill. Soil sprayed between the dog's hind legs and he wedged his teeth deep in the earth, the snout bent backwards, attempting to extract the living mole. The frenzy of his assault implied that there had been successes in the past but there was none today. The lethargic, vanilla-scented smoke wreathed Glory's curly head. The lad felt complete. Life could offer no more.

Of course perfection is a very vulnerable state, and he hadn't even finished his cigarette when he became aware of unusal noises – squeals and rushing. Down the steep track out of the wood and onto the level bank shot a figure on a toboggan. It slithered to a halt and a woman laughed. It was Lady Minerva Popjoy. Almost at once a second figure, in colourful scarves and bobble cap and acres of overcoat, shot down the track and it slammed harmlessly into her, sprawling and laughing without restraint. Kevin trotted over and licked their faces. JJ righted himself but as he spotted Glory his expression altered dramatically. He clambered clumsily to his feet, shook the snow from his coat, and was on the point of speaking to the boy, who all unconcern had amiably waved his cigarette in recognition, when an animal shot across the space between them. It was a fox. Kevin sat down with a bump of astonishment. A great hullabaloo swelled in the woods above, burst, and avalanched down. Kevin, held by the collar, added his manic bark to the din as hound – horn – harness of the Milking Magna Boxing Day hunt crashed in from one side and was immediately sucked out at the other. For several seconds the entire universe had smudged. The horn faded round a bend in the landscape.

On the return of equilibrium, which took a little while to re-establish itself, Glory said 'Phew' and smiled brilliantly.

But JJ walked across to Glory and stood in front of him with an exceedingly doleful expression. The boy grew perplexed. He didn't understand. At last JJ said 'Why didn't you come yesterday? I had a present for you. It was Christmas Day and it felt like nothing. Why didn't you come? You promised you would. Why didn't you? Why are you doing this to me? '

44.

Alice, mulling over the absurdity of Davis's fortune-telling, examined herself in the mirror. Her teeth were *not* far apart. There was a tiny gap between the front two, that was all. Glory Boy was much more gappy – and *he* hadn't travelled far, *he* wasn't rich. All her life she'd been told that this tiny gap between her front two teeth gave her face character. Her father had had a similar gap. It gave his face character too. She went out of the back door and crumbled the remains of a crusty loaf over a heap of logs. The damaged crow stirred in the hedge. Catching sight of it made her feel sick. She switched on Radio Four *News at One*, pillar of BBC security, feeling sicker, and by the time she turned on the other pillar of BBC security, *The Six O'clock News*, she was feeling sicker still. Eventually she went to bed. At four a.m. she awoke, feeling dreadfully sick. She brought a plastic bucket upstairs and lay on her bed with a towel over her pillow and a cold flannel on her brow. Perhaps it would pass. But the poison con-

tinued to gather in her guts. Around eight in the morning she
started to bring up bile in muscle-wrenching, throat-stinging,
eye-bleeding bouts of vomiting. Between the bouts she felt easier
and prayed it might all be over but the pressure would rebuild
and the vomiting recur. It went on well into the afternoon until
she had nothing left inside. Hereafter the body calmed. When she
arose at five p.m. to make herself a cup of weak tea she knew the
attack was over. In retrospect Alice saw this twenty-four hours of
physical hell as a crisis of cleansing, a turning point of sorts.

45.

Ward hated this time of year. Once Christmas had dissipated int-
self in the longueurs of Boxing Day, he was hungry for a return
to work, though the rest of London seemingly preferred to
slouch on well into the New Year. Except for red-nosed faces outside the foyers of cinemas and theatres, their breath burning in
the frosty air, the streets of the West End were empty and quiet.
Even the post-Christmas sales produced only a very localised
turbulence.

Ward's burgundy-coloured Bentley slid into the basement car
park of the building in Berkeley Square whose top two floors
were occupied by his 'firm'. What was this agglomeration of
imprecise but profitable activities? Part advertising agency, part
media production, part computer software, part digital commu-
nications – he knew very little about these things in particular but
a great deal about them in general.

His was the only car down there. 'The only one! No wonder
the country is going to the dogs, he said to himself.' Except of
course that it wasn't going to the dogs because there were people
like Ward dotted all over London making sure that it wasn't. At
least not in the sense he meant which was economically. It was in
quite different senses that the country was going to the dogs,
senses which would have a bearing on his life much sooner than
he realised.

Removing a Smarties tube from the back seat, he locked the car
and took the silver lift aloft, relieved to be away from the family.
No matter how judiciously he and Larissa organised the twins'

presents there was always contention. This year the problem was
the kinkaringo. They'd been given one each but Jocasta decided
that she preferred the colour of Fortinbras's. By Christmas Day
afternoon the kids were squabbling like chip fat. And how fast
they were growing! Pressing against the walls and ceilings of the
flat with strong young hands. This very morning his wife had said
'It's no good, Ward, I been thinking. They can't be stuck in
London all the time. We should find country place to grow them
up in. Only one childhood will they have.'

46.

JJ had a difficult duty to perform. Malcolm Gibbet, JJ's factor, in
being thrown from his horse during the hunt, had subsequently
accused Dickon of deliberately riding across him and JJ felt
obliged to call on the Master of foxhounds and ask him what he
knew. But he had not expected to find the Craddock ill in bed and
wheezing horribly.

'None too spry, Marquess.'

'Shouldn't you see a doctor?'

'Can't call em out for a bit of a cough. I'm very sorry about
Malcolm's fall.'

'He said Dickon rode across him.'

'So I've heard and it wasn't true and the man's a cad to say it
and I'm afraid he cannot ride with the hunt again.'

'Malcolm may not accept that.'

The Craddock went into a spiral of coughing which left him
weak and with a large mucus-filled handkerchief on his hands. 'In
which case he can sue me or challenge Dickon to pistols. The fact
is your man's no good on a horse and there's an end to it. But I'm
pleased you called because I've got more important things on my
mind, in particular my son who seems to be nuts about your
daughter and it's making our lives hell.'

'I don't interfere in other people's romances, Sir Tim.'

'But does your daughter return this feeling?'

'You must ask her.'

Alas the knight was unable to do that. On New Year's Day, with
rasping gullet and heaving gizzard, he was conveyed by ambulance to the Heavenshire County Hospital in Appleminster.

47.

'Hullo. Is that Heaven?'

'Yes.'

'Russia here. We saw your advertisement in the *Conference Gazette* and we like to book Heaven Park for a week in March.'

'What week?'

'Any week.'

'Excuse me for a second.'

Alice stared at page after spotless page in a ledger marked *Bookings*. 'You're lucky. We've had a cancellation for the third week.'

'We take it. How to pay?'

'In advance.'

'No problem. We send our requirements e-mail.'

'We don't have e-mail. Could you send a fax? And what's it for?'

'Paradjanov Festival of Incarcerated Genius.'

'Gosh. Marvellous.'

'You know his work?'

'No.'

'Great man. We have many other genius we put in prison and we celebrate their art with Western showcase, lots of films, big discussion.'

'And may I ask, why choose us?'

'It says you have Cameron Suite, his only work outside Russia, and I always want to sleep in bedroom by Cameron.'

'Yes, it's fabulous, you'll sleep very well. Should I hire a film projector?'

'We bring everything. Don't worry. Goodbye.'

'And could I have a name?'

'Piotr.'

'And a contact number please.'

Alice rubbed feathers of frost from the inside of the window-pane with her gloved hand – the heating system didn't extend to her office – Malcolm had been promising to supply a mobile gas-heater since before Christmas – and she was got up like a Siberian mammoth in a number of coats and scarves. But now scrolls of excitement arose from within because the impossible had occurred: there had been outside interest. *Outside interest* was the

most interesting interest in the world. In fact it was the only
interest. And a bag beneath each eye disappeared as she pirouet-
ted on her mammothly booted toe, knocking over a desk-lamp
which broke, and went in search of JJ. He wasn't in the cosy. She
skipped through a dozen rooms and in the thirteenth found Minerva. The poetess was examining a pair of Boningtons through a
lorgnette.

'Minerva, I've booked a Russian mad genius festival for
March!'

Not quite taking it in, Minerva carefully assumed the vertical.
She was swathed in plum velvet, thrown up and about her with
the brio of a figure in a Venetian altarpiece. 'There's something I
want to tell you, Alice. About my birthday.'

'Oh blast, did I forget it?'

'No. It's about my birthday *party*. I want to get one thing
straight – I'm not inviting you.'

'You're not inviting me.'

'Don't take it personally.'

'It sounds personal.'

'I'm only inviting men.'

'Is it soon then?'

'No, it's not for ages.'

Alice crossed the Great Hall. Sidney and Ben Thicknesse were
in the process of dismantling the Christmas tree. 'Sidney, this
broken egg is still here on the floor by the column.'

He came across. 'So it is, miss.'

'Nor is it twelfth night yet.'

'Sorry, miss, but his lordship wants it down now.'

'Have you seen him?'

'Upstairs, miss.'

JJ was sewing and listening to the radio news in his bedroom.
That very morning terrorists from the Green Kingdom had
blown up an aerial motorway junction near Birmingham. Alice
clapped her hands and said 'Listen, I've got a booking for
March!'

'Tell me another one.'

'Honestly! They wanted to e-mail me. It was so embarrassing.'
She read from her jotting on a slip of paper: 'The Paradjanov

Festival of Incarcerated Genius. It's to celebrate the work of people who were put in prison because they were amazing.'

JJ's eyes dilated into saucers and she saw that their blue was warm with a hint of violet, like the blue of hyacinths.

'How did you do it?'

'Quite a hustle actually.'

'Liar. You're as surprised as anyone.'

48.

It was the evening of January the fifth: Old Christmas Day. A few vagrant snowflakes blew about the gothic spikes of The Crag. In the kitchen Davis was boiling a pan of milk.

Sir Tim had developed Galloping Pneumonia and the administration of powerful antibiotics at the County Hospital had produced no effect. He insisted therefore on being returned home where he was nursed by Helen and Davis while Robin stood at the foot of the viper-carved staircase with three fingers at the side of his mouth or took the falcon up to the Heath.

On this evening Davis poured the hot milk into a pair of blue-striped porcelain mugs in which tablespoonsful of cocoa had been moistened to a dark paste. She stirred vigorously, added sugar, stirred again, and placed them on a tray beside a plate of fig-roll biscuits and took it upstairs. Helen and Robin were sitting exhausted in the sickroom. Davis said 'Here's something to keep you goin before I let meself out'. Helen nodded.

Mostly in delirium, Sir Tim's mind occasionally rallied. Earlier that day he had informed his son that 'During the Great War the first part of the dead soldier's body to be eaten by rats was the lips which caused the corpses to grin. Lips were the tastiest. Followed by the earlobes and cock.' It was difficult to make out what his father was saying, even during rational episodes, because his teeth occupied a tumbler of water beside the bed and his mouth had collapsed inwards. At the end the knight, who so rarely spoke of the sea with which he'd always seemed to have had an ambiguous relationship, who'd taken early retirement for reasons which never quite made sense, burbled snatches from a shanty . . .

Goodbye to the girl on the jetty
Hullo to the boys who are free
Goodbye to the land where I was born
Hullo to the swinging sea

He repeated them over and over again in a fading decelerando until there was barely a pulse, barely a breath. How many days would it go on for? Helen and Robin sat there for another hour. Robin said 'I'm going downstairs for a sandwich'. Helen nodded.

Her son had been out of the room scarcely a minute when there was unexpected movement in her husband's bed. Terrifyingly he sat bolt upright, face purple, mouth contorted. Helen froze, expecting some ghastly pronouncement. Instead Sir Tim fell back with an eerie slowness into the pillows. There was a deep flushing sound – whooosh – as his interior musculature relaxed entirely and the stomach and intestines emptied their contents into the bed. Vice-Commodore Sir Timothy Craddock of The Crag had crapped his last. The stench was appalling. As she left the room, hand over nose and mouth, she said quietly 'Thank God it's over. I hated him.'

49.

Mrs Bladder-Williams was buffing the silver cakestand with a yellow duster when the doorbell rang. She hid the duster before answering.

'Do come in, Mr Knott.'

He followed her into the drawing-room which was spiritually cold and reminded him of the room in Harley Street where he would wait to see his specialist. He expected to find copies of glossy magazines with *Do not remove* stickers on the covers.

'I've brought you these,' he said, presenting gladioli to her bottom. She was kneeling in the fireplace, trying to light the mock-coal gas fire. It lit with a bang, knocking her back in surprise.

'Are you all right?'

'Yes.' She staggered to her feet, pushing herself up on the arm of a chair, but she was missing an eyebrow. 'It's a bit early for tea but I'll get some anyway because I want you to tell me all about this dreadful computer city they're planning to dump on us.'

'It's only at the exploratory stage,' he said, exposing his dentures. How sometimes he so reminded her of dear Eustace.

'That's a stage too far, Mr Knott.'

When she returned with the tea his dentures were still exposed. He was charmed particularly by the missing eyebrow. 'You do look nice,' he said. Oliver was alarmed by his own daring. It had popped out while his self-consciousness wasn't looking. Just for a second his self-consciousness had wavered and there, he'd said it. What a tricksy thing is even the most watchful personality.

Blood flooded her upper bosom. Alone for so long – and now two courtiers! She shifted across to the window with what she knew was poise. It was a dull, cold afternoon, the sort she liked. That pretty girl Melody Royal was at that very moment walking down the High Street with a carrier bag of groceries either side of her enormous belly. Mrs Bladder-Williams wondered whether she should invite the girl in. Melody reached the bridge, stopped, and looked over the parapet. The coiling waters, boosted by snowmelt, were rushing beneath. Melody was mesmerised but from behind the glass, Mrs Bladder-Williams got her funny feeling, a twinge in the thighs – surely the girl wasn't considering suicide? Life could be hard for a single mother but even so . . . She opened the front door and called 'Melody!'

The girl looked across.

'Please, come in for a cup of tea.'

Melody entered Church House for the first time, scanning it with large careful eyes.

'Come through, dear. Leave your bags there.'

She followed Mrs Bladder-Williams's heroic calf muscles.

'Sit there by the fire. This is Mr Knott. Will you have some cake?'

'Don't move. Let me get it for you,' said Oliver. He had never spoken to a black woman before, not even when he taught at Cambridge.

'Can't be long now,' said Mrs Bladder-Williams.

'Next month.'

'What will you call it?'

'John.'

'And if it's a girl?'

'It won't be.'

'You've had a scan?'

'No. But I'm convinced.'

'I think you're very brave,' said Mrs Bladder-Williams.

'Lots of women have babies.'

'I mean without a – ' Mrs Bladder-Williams decided it was better to stop there.

'A couple of months ago I had doubts but now I'm looking forward to it. Children stop you getting stuck in the past.' She blew on her tea and sipped.

'Only when they're young,' said Mrs Bladder-Williams. 'When they grow up and leave it's very ageing. My son lives in Algeciras but it might as well be on the moon.'

50.

On a morning so cold that no steam issued from the mouth, Lady Craddock and her son Robin, and Emily Postlethwaite (Sir Tim's younger sister), and Frobisher Craddock (Sir Tim's remote cousin) assembled at the offices of Dewdrop & Danvers in Appleminster for a reading of the Will. Young Lawrence Dewdrop entered. He shook hands, opened a file and said 'Normally this would happen after the funeral but I gather there's a delay because the vicar is on holiday in West Africa. So let's get on with it.' He read: *I leave everything to my dear wife Helen, with the exception of sufficient funds for a horse and its upkeep to Mr Little Lark, the necessary sum to be determined by the executors.*

Frobisher shrugged philosophically – he had enough betting money to see himself out. Emily declared it outrageous and that she'd be contacting her own solicitor – Papa would never have wanted her to be passed over for an *outsider*.

Young Dewdrop raised a white, cold hand. He hadn't finished. 'Everything,' it turned out, was nothing. Actually, it was minus nothing. There were debts. Considerable debts, for Sir James had presumed to live in the style appropriate to his station. The Crag and its contents would have to be sold and when the debts had been settled there might be enough for Lady Craddock to rent a couple of rooms above a shop. Sometimes young Dewdrop experienced an impudent pleasure in his work. 'So you see there will be no question of jigging about on horses or anything like that. Mr Lark appears not to be present.'

Helen, catapaulted without warning into an absurd world, muttered 'I forgot to pass your message on to him'.

'Well, time is money,' said Dewdrop. 'So I'll set the sale in motion if you like. No point in hanging about.'

Frobisher laughed drily and said 'The old sod!', while Robin's interior was blasted by a polar wind, though his exterior remained impassive. Not so Emily's, whose anger, tears and bewilderment fought each other fatuously beneath the brim of her hat. But nothing could change the facts. The Craddocks were destitute.

Robin took Lady Craddock's arm: 'Mummy, you need a good steak. Let's go to The Green Dragon for lunch.'

51.

The world was back to work and Ward, taking his stroll after a pie at The Princess of Teck, saw that the Mayfair traffic had seized up in gridlock. He scrutinised the drivers' faces which were variously apoplectic, spaced-out, anxious. Very few were good-humoured or philosophical and none looked wholesome. Yes, a country place was definitely the next step in the evolution of the Dashman family. Larissa and the twins should be there full-time and if the local schools weren't up to scratch the twins could board somewhere. It would do them no harm to be separated for a while. The twins, that is. And himself and Larissa, come to that. He would join her in the country at week-ends but have a pied-à-terre in town during the week and could take a mistress. He'd been feeling the pressure of that particular requirement for a year or two. He was passing the offices of estate-agent Rutley Wood Ltd at the time and, since there is no motive like the sexual motive, he stepped inside. An assistant of supercilious decorum registered his particulars and showed him brochures of properties in the Home Counties: Georgian, neo-Georgian, Tudor, mock-Tudor, ivy-clad or tile-hung, on the river, on the downs, on the coast, all of them under-designed and over-improved. None caught his imagination. At forty-one years of age, Ward required a taking-out of himself.

'They're all very nice but haven't you anything more . . . far out?'

'Literally or figuratively?' asked the assistant who'd been sent to an expensive school and gone on to take a degree in Media Studies from the University of the North Sea and had never imagined he'd find himself working as an estate agent. It was only temporary, if you can call temporary what had already lasted three years, but this year the assistant really was determined to find something which was more . . .

'Both,' replied Ward.

'This came in yesterday. It needs modernisation.'

'Much modernisation?'

'Quite a lot, yes.'

Ward beheld a flourish of steeples and machicolations in a sylvan setting. After half a minute had slipped by, the assistant said 'It's rather outré, isn't it.'

'What?'

'Outré.'

Ward smiled.

Thus it was that on a sleety Saturday afternoon Ward Dashman, his wife Larissa, the twins Jocasta and Fortinbras, and Hendrix (a black yapping poodle) nudged the burgundy Bentley towards the west and found themselves rolling up a drive between pools of snowdrops.

They'd come to view The Crag. Davis with crooked finger beckoned the visitors into Sir Tim's old study, one of the few uncleared rooms, since the bulk of the furniture had already gone to the auction house. Ward, who was good-looking, with all his hair and all its colour, stood in front of the stone-cold fireplace with thumbs in his armpits. He had taken psychological possession and was feeling manly.

'Will we go to the village school?' asked Jocasta.

'We don't want to be with common children,' said Fortinbras.

'I expect they cover their books with *brown paper*,' said his sister.

Fortinbras blew a raspberry.

Davis returned unsteadily with a laden tea-tray. These events had greatly put her out. The tray and her hump appeared to be jockeying for the same position and she walked with a deeply dipping motion which set everyone on edge. Hendrix bared his teeth. Davis attempted a smile. She was hoping to come with the house.

'You're the worst thing I've ever seen,' said Fortinbras.

Davis lifted a lip and snarled but corrected herself and turned to the parents with an unctuous simper, saying 'Clever children, pretty children – orange juice?'

'I hate orange juice, you grotty witch,' said Jocasta.

'We like wine,' said Fortinbras.

'What's that funny hump on your back?' asked Jocasta.

'They're a right couple of characters,' said Ward.

Davis gave up the struggle and said 'Those kids should be gassed'.

Larissa, Ward's wife, generously put the remark down to a faithful servant's sense of bereavement and went to practise on the viper staircase, adopting the various attitudes she associated with Bette Davis, Greta Garbo and Vivien Leigh. Robin caught her unawares.

'Sorry, but I'm afraid my mother's not well.'

'The loss . . . ' sympathised Larissa with a torch-song gesture from the half-landing.

'Actually it was some steak she ate, and being a vegetarian it's sort of gone on and on. She apologises. But I can show you round.'

'I like it,' said Larissa. 'Only problem is my husband's mother is dying of Alzheimer's in a nursing home about an hour's drive from here.'

'And you'd like to be nearer.'

'No. Further away.'

As they entered the study Hendrix growled and Robin said 'I'll have to kick your dog if it goes for me'.

'Who's the funny old woman?' asked Larissa.

'Our housekeeper.'

'Absolutely terrified my children.'

'I'm not afraid of *her*,' said Jocasta.

'We'll give her an arsenic sandwich,' said Fortinbras.

'Do you know what an erection is ?' Jocasta asked Robin.
'Yes,' replied Robin. ' Do you know what a broken neck is?'
The ever-faithful Hendrix struck.

52.

It was a curious mix, as such events usually are. Much of the village was in attendance and all the shops were closed. Lord Moon,
pale and papery, Lord Lieutenant of the County, was there as
representative of the King-Emperor (neither of whom had ever
had any personal doings with Sir Timothy), along with sundry
dignitaries from the defence, diplomatic and field-sporting
worlds. There was a couple from Bermuda whom Lady Craddock
couldn't place, though they remembered Robin as a little boy.
Helen's daughter couldn't make it from Zimbabwe – she feared
that in her absence her ranch would be confiscated by the latest
dictator. Frobisher Craddock bobbed about making a video of the
proceedings.

So on a gusty afternoon, funeral cones with black crosses on
them were placed along the road outside Saint Wendy's to prevent car parking and, soon after, the official cars dropped off their
occupants. Last of all the hearse drew slowly to halt. An ensign-
draped coffin was carefully excreted from its rear on rollers.
Robin and Little Lark were pallbearers and both significantly
taller than the other four who were sailors from the Royal Navy.
Princess Lark was noticeable at the ceremony on account of her
proud carriage. She'd taken on the quality of a principal mourner
without in any way putting herself forward. Obviously she was
very gratified that her son had been chosen to be one of the pallbearers, people said. And she did indeed look with adoration
upon her lovely Little throughout the service which consisted
mostly of Sir Timothy's favourite hymns, beginning with 'Sound
the Tabor', 'Jesus is Without' and ending with 'The Vacuum
Sucks us to Another Realm'. Robin and Little never spoke a word
to each other – or ever again.

Alice had been in two minds about coming but in her conversations she realised that everyone assumed she would be going
and she was surprised to discover that possibly she belonged after

all. She always imagined that communities such as this resisted outsiders for many years but she was wrong. She would always be classified as a newcomer but she would always be expected to turn up. Newcomers too were an ancient and necessary class. And unknown to her, even those who had lived in the village for generations frequently felt like strangers in the world they inhabited and could readily understand and bond with outsiders on account of this.

After the service Lady Craddock gallantly received mourners in the empty drawing-room at The Crag. They were offered sherry and sweet biscuits but no one stayed for long since the atmosphere of the house was more deathly than the church and none of the hectic humours which often mark a wake had arisen here. As Alice departed she told Helen to pick up the phone if she needed anything but Alice, in trying to be thoughtful, was thoughtless because widows don't pick up the telephone and impose themselves, as Alice would discover in her own widowhood which lay far in the future. Lady Craddock, floating meaninglessly behind her veil in one of the few remaining chairs, looked up at the girl in disbelief and wondered whether or not they were of the same species. As the last guests were leaving, a new group bustled in.

'Have we missed the funeral? Sorry about that. Hope it went well,' said Ward Dashman genially.

Frobisher, who was listening to the three forty-five from Haydock Park on a mobile phone, put it down and picked up his video camera to record the late arrivals.

'Mummy, can my room be at the front?' whined Jocasta.

'Did someone die?' asked Fortinbras loudly.

Davis, exposing teeth the colour of autumn leaves, cringed in front of Larissa and asked 'What are me orders, madam?'

'Orders?'

'I'm the housekeeper.'

Larissa Dashman's short laugh cut like a snap of pruning-shears and she escorted an impeccably groomed Indian male the size of a doll across to Lady Craddock. 'This is our domestic manager, Bunjie Gunj.'

Helen lifted her veil, blinked, and dropped it again. She did not speak.

Bunjie bowed quickly from the waist, flashing very white teeth and cuffs. He asked somewhat lispingly 'As the previous owner, you may tell me, what are the main problems with the house?'

The voice behind the veil said 'The people who live in it'.

'Er – anything else?'

'It's haunted. Very haunted.'

Gunj, noticeably bothered by this, drew Larissa aside and said 'That woman is not knowing her arse from her elbow'.

53.

Crystal invited Robin up to Heaven Park for supper that evening but he said 'Don't be daft. I've got to be with Mum.'

'Walk with me then,' she said and ran along a tractor track, exploding the frozen surfaces of puddles with her boots. Smash! Smash! Smash! 'It's a lovely feeling. Like breaking glass. Have a go.' He smashed some too but without her vehemence. They kissed beside a black thorny hedge.

'Who *are* they?' she asked.

'Who are who?'

'The new people at your house.'

'From London.'

'Too many people coming here from London.'

'Don't you like London?'

'I love London,' she said. Smash! Smash! 'She looks *awful*. But he looks very nice.'

'He's in telecoms or something.'

'Poor, poor Robin, poor Lady Craddock. Where will you go? What will you do?'

'I don't know where we will go. But – oh please stop smashing those things and listen to me. I've thought about it. What I want to know is – will you marry me, Crystal?'

'What?'

'You heard.'

'You're not serious, Robin. It's too soon after your father's death.'

'I am serious. It's not too soon.'

'Did you love your dad?'

'I don't know . . . '

'I love mine.'

'I'm cold, Crystal. Help me a bit. Don't be cruel. Please.'

She held him and they made love standing up behind a tree. Afterwards she said 'There's something you ought to know . . . I'm pregnant'.

54.

In The Zodiac all heads turned. Oliver Knott was shouting at Justice Royal. 'You're trying to make her fat with your bloody cakes!'

'Calm down, little man,' said Justice, staring into his pint.

Knott jabbed but Royal cleverly deflected the blow.

'Trying to make her fat and ugly!'

Royal extended a fist which put Knott on the floor. A ring of stars revolved in Oliver's head.

'Stop it, boys!' commanded Lois.

''E just came up an hit me out the blue. Fuckin psycho,' blustered Justice.

'Are you all right, Mr Knott?' asked Daisy Lark, helping him into a chair.

'Am I who?' probed the scientist.

'I'm surprised at you, Justice,' rebuked Lois. 'You're such a big chap.'

''E came at me out of the blue,' Justice protested in amazement.

'You know he's upset at the death of Sir Tim. They were very close friends.'

A deep and corrosive contempt for the world in which he found himself began to rise through the subterranean passages of Justice's soul but he pushed it down again, as he always did, because embittered he had determined never to be. White men ruled the roost and you had to get on with it. But there were times when he'd've liked to slit every white throat in sight.

The problem had been that the newest pills prescribed for the improvement of Oliver's state of mind had backfired in what is known as the paradoxical effect, perhaps encouraged by the beer. When Oliver understood this, it didn't change anything, for he still wanted Mrs Bladder-Williams to cradle him in her arms and he still hated Justice Royal and he still found daily life a prickly cactus. The only thing to change was the pills. New pills came onto the market every week. What he liked about pills was they were mechanical. You didn't have to believe in them.

'Fuckin psycho,' reiterated Justice.

55.

Alice entered her office with a frown and thought she'd better ring the Russians. Already she'd sounded out the new woman at The Crag about helping possibly and Larissa Dashman had been delighted to be approached by a local so soon. Alice explained that the Crag and Heaven Park were neighbours. But time was short, there had been no communication from Russia itself, and JJ was getting worried. So she rang the Moscow contact number and asked for Piotr.

'He is not here.'

'When will he be there please?'

'Later.'

She rang later.

'Yes, Piotr here later.'

'How much later?'

'Midnight. Try midnight.'

'I'm not at work at midnight.'

'Yes, try midnight.'

She tried midnight from The Glade. The phone rang and rang at the other end and eventually a bleary voice answered 'Halloa'.

'Is Piotr there?' asked Alice.

'He sleep.'

'You said try at midnight.'

'It is not midnight.'

'It is here.'

'Here it is three a.m. Try tomorrow please.'

'What time?'

'Midnight.'

'Will he be asleep again?'

'Our midnight he will not sleep.'

'Thank you.'

She tried at their midnight the following day. 'Is Piotr there please?'

'Who is it?'

'Heaven Park in England.'

'One minute please.'

Strange words blistered angrily in the background and a man came on the line. 'Halloa.'

'Is that Piotr?'

'Yes.'

'This is Alice.'

'Who?'

'Alice from Heaven Park? It's about the Paradjanov Festival of Incarcerated Genius.'

'Ah, yes, you want the other Piotr. He will know.'

'Can I speak to him?'

'He is not here.'

'*When* . . . when will he be there?'

'Tomorrow.'

'What time?'

'Morning – or afternoon.'

'Am I calling a private flat or an ofice?'

'Both. We sleep here at night. Other Piotr has office here in day.'

'Can you leave a message?'

'Yes, I can leave message. Try in morning.'

She tried in the morning.

'Is Piotr there?'

'Yes.'

'Festival Piotr?'

He laughed and said 'Yes, me'.

'I'm calling from Heaven Park in England. You made a booking for the Paradjanov Festival – '

'Oh, Alice, how do you do. Did someone not call you?'

'No.'

'I told my secretary to call you.'

'She didn't.'

'The festival is cancelled.'

'Oh no.'

'Very sorry.'

'Why cancelled?'

'Money problems. Big pity. Maybe another time?'

'Oh dear.'

'You are disappointed. Please forgive us. Give my love to the King-Mother. We love her in Russia. And give my love to Trafalgar Square. Very sorry. Goodbye.'

He rang off. Alice was gutted – the two-faced bastards – what a shitty thing to do . . . A door was banging somewhere. She threaded corridors, traversed saloons and hallways in order to find it, but the gently banging door was always somewhere else. JJ was sitting in the kitchen with cook, doing a crossword.

'The Russians cancelled.'

'Oh no. Just like that?'

'Money problems.'

'That country was always a mess.'

Her face puckered but she held back the tears with a sharp inhalation and looked aside.

'I'll get you a computer,' he mollified.

'What good'll that do?'

'OK, we are all helpless jumping beans on the tablecloth of destiny.'

'No, you're right. One *can* make a difference. Where's that banging door?'

'I don't hear those things.'

'It's driving me mad.'

'I've never had a Russian. I was looking forward to it.'

The door banged fugitively in the distance.

56.

He stretched and yawned and revolved and looked at the bedside clock. It was eight twenty a.m. Time to get up and make tea. But his heavy muscular body was warm and reluctant to enter the chill day, and he turned over instead and pythoned his arm round Jason Hoggart who was in bed with him, who was usually in bed with him, in fact they lived together.

'I'm asleep,' said Jason.

Hoskins kissed the back of his friend's neck and said 'I had someone last night'.

Jason was caught on the raw but tried not to show it and waited five long seconds before asking 'Where did you find him?'

'The Bag & Whistle.'

'How old?'

'Your age.'

'Exactly my age?'

'Bit younger.'

'Nice looking?'

'Handsome.'

'Nice body?'

'Big cock.'

'What did you like best about him?'

'Great kisser.'

'Oh piss off.'

'I wanted to tell you.'

'We agreed not to tell.'

They'd discussed infidelity a while back. Two men together, there had to be a bit of freedom, otherwise it would put unreal pressure on their relationship. But they agreed never to play games in front of each other or bring any tricks home or tell each other about anything on the side.

'What do you like best about me?' asked Jason.

'I like all of you.'

'Tell me one thing you like.'

'Your eyes.'

'You always say that.'

'I love you, Jason, and I wanted to tell you.'

'I hope you didn't do anything silly.'

'Of course not. I'll make the tea.'

'What was the worst thing about him?'

'His name.'

'What was it?'

'Tony Tucker.'

'There's nothing wrong with that.'

'I had to find something.'

Hoskins was late for work. A colleague said 'There's a demonstration outside County Hall. The chief wants you to take a look. We've already sent a dozen men down.'

The County Hall in Appleminster was an Edwardian extravagance inspired by the Gates of Nineveh, but whereas the Nineveh Gates were relatively modest in their proportions and simple in decoration, the County Hall was very large, containing many offices, and its façades were dressed in eclectic devices and emblems from county history. Tourists to the town, drawn by the cathedral, stayed on to wonder at it.

The instigator of the demonstration was Mrs Bladder-Williams, Hoskins's aunt by marriage, and she had persuaded Alice, Dickon, Pimm, a group of nuns, thirty or forty students from the Agricultural College, and others, maybe one hundred in all, to stand about the base of County Hall's steps and wave placards on the occasion of a planning meeting with the men from Whitehall. The black car duly drew up and, despite a restraining police cordon, protesters surged across their path as four men got out and attempted to mount the steps. The Superior gave Mrs Bladder-Williams a nasty shove and spat 'Go to hell, you old cunt!' The pavement was slippery and she fell. Dickon saw it. He grabbed the Superior by the collar. The Superior wailed to his three assistants 'Don't stand there! Kill im!' The junior assistant Finch entered the affray by snatching Pimm's spectacles and stamping on them. More police tried to move in but the nuns, with deft use of their habits, made complications. By the time Hoskins arrived it was a right barney.

'I'm sorry, Dickon, but I've got to detain you,' he said. 'That's not fair!' shouted Alice and Pimm in unison. Alice imprudently yanked Hoskins's overcoat, saying 'Where's Mrs Bladder-Williams? She'll tell you who started it.' But Mrs B-W had been taken off to a local teashop by two solicitous nuns. Pimm, groping in fog, unintentionally manhandled the trousers of a policeman who thereupon detained the archaeologist by his ponytail. 'Tony!' exclaimed Hoskins as he saw the other junior assistant, Tucker, in the struggle. Despite all the distractions, Hoskins's cock stirred eagerly. 'Same place, same time,' Tucker shouted back. 'You're collaborating with them, Hoskins! And your own aunt knocked down!'

yelled Alice. 'Bastards!' exhorted Dickon. A mini-cab pulled up and Oliver Knott climbed out, his face tense and grey, and he tried to enter the County Hall. 'They're all collaborators!' shouted Pimm. The Superior, who'd wriggled his way inside, appeared on the balcony above the main entrance and harangued the mêlée. 'Industrialisation is the only hope of the poor!'he proclaimed. The lipless Finch stood to attention at his shoulder. Dickon, Alice and Pimm were arrested and the remainder ordered to disperse.

In the black maria, Hoskins apologised to his bag of three: 'I had to do something. There were reporters there. We'll put you up for the night in the county gaol and let you go in the morning. It's not so bad. The tea's good and so is the breakfast. Bacon sandwiches.'

'Why didn't you arrest the others?'

'Because they're government people doing their job. I'll have a word with Auntie.'

'You do that!'

Alice contemplated the pronged poetry of Appleminster Cathedral as it swam across the window of the black maria and thought, at last, life again!

57.

'I want it, I want it, I want it!'

The Old Un's bawling grew so bad that Davis went to the parlour doorway and wagged her finger. 'Gas, Mumsy, if you're not careful.' The Old Un quietened at once but added in a small croak 'I want it'.

'Yes, you'll get it all right. There's a piazza warming in the oven so shut yer gob.'

The Old Un's mouth pursed like an anus.

Davis, more miserable than for many a month, returned to her henbane tea in the kitchen and lit a fag. Her lungs exploded with phlegm but the fag hung on gamely to the lower lip. In addition to the loss of her position at The Crag Davis had to contend with Mumsy who had been behaving very oddly of late. Davis had been especially troubled by the addition of 'Innit romantic!' to Mumsy's limited repertoire of phrases. Innit romantic indeed.

I'll give er romantic. Propped on the dresser was a black metal tray which depicted Rio de Janeiro in garish colours.

Some folks has holidays but not me, no. Have a holiday, me? The whole village would kill emselves laughing. Old housekeepers with humpbacks don't ave holidays! I'd love to see Rio derwhatsit but all my life slaving for others and in the end what thanks do you get? None! Thrown out on yer ear! I polished that Crag age upon age and it coughs me out without so much as wiping its nose!

The rancour of a lifetime boiled round Davis's heart into a white-hot venom. Her eyes rotated inwards like corkscrews. Aye, corkscrews of self-pity, paranoia, victimhood! After a few more sips of henbane tea, she heard the voice of the Devil which came to her very sweetly and strongly like an actor trained in the classical manner. The Devil said:

Enough is enough. The clouds have haemorrhaged and like airborne hearts they pump it down, the bladed rain screaming redglitter revenge. The very birds stop in the sky and streak down in dead squadrons, thudding the earth. Of course you are flotsam heartache and all you ever wanted was nimbus afternoons where the water flows tangoes and buttercups and cornflowers, and to approach your destiny with saucy sidewind lidflutter and slouch together cheekdust soft. Instead from the ceiling hangs the cadaver quietly dripping into a bucket, birds plummeting all the while, striping the sky with blood, again the blood, and everywhere the rocks are splashed with organisms that failed. Cool cadaver, the memory of your beautiful face inspires epigrams of needlelust, spirals of pain. But enough is enough! The geometry is collapsing all around, the monster squats gibber at the fountain and alarmed goldfish pirouette on the surface, while chimneys along the roofline expectorate skeletons, packs of cards, canteens of cutlery. Your last words in the long watchtowered night were Whoa, the planet lurches! Ankles liquefy. Sores open hooded eyes and drip, everything drips, runs cold. Laughter jets over a tree and is gone. Flotsam. Heartache. Yes, enough is enough. Come, little lavender babies, disclose your entrails to the moon.

58.

A musty chart unrolled scattering dust. It was the old estate map in the back hall, from the days when The Crag had land. One large field remained and Ward had put in planning applications to build on it a wind farm, a supermarket and a multi-screen cinema, on the grounds that it would be good for his family life if he could develop some local interests and cut down on his commuting between town and country. The move to the country was, of course, turning out to be not quite what he'd envisaged. The expenditure on the house, in the hands of Larissa and Bunjie, was completely out of control. There was Mother dying in a nursing home not so far away and from that source came a hose of guilt. And after a life in the town he felt curiously exposed out here where there was nowhere to hide. He let go of the toggle and the map rolled up with a ping – it still worked perfectly. The house didn't need modernisation, only love, as he kept telling Larissa as she ordered a new kitchen, new bathrooms, new window frames, new doors . . .

Most of all there was Crystal Popjoy, the long-legged hair-tossing beauty who wandered along the littoral of his attention even when he thought he was thinking of something else. The last thing he wanted was a girl down here. Family were down here. The girl was supposed to be Little Miss Raunch asking no questions in London. But the moment he'd set eyes on Crystal he knew he wanted her with an awful shag-till-you-drop, prime-of-life, got-to-get-it-all-in-before-I-die yearning, the yearning which, contrary to what he'd read, grew more not less intense the older he became. In the corner a unicorn radiator gurgled painfully. The heating bill would be fun.

Jazz, the New Zealand nanny, called from the kitchen 'The twins want you to play football, Ward. They're out the front.'

He saw two balaclavas zip past the hall window. Apart from Fortinbras skidding on the dogshit of Hendrix and knocking his head on the trunk of a tree half an hour ago, happiness bubbled about the lawn. Only a trained ear could have detected that it was too highly strung and contained within itself black flecks. Fortinbras stopped playing as his father jogged towards him across the grass. The boy stood near the rhododendron bushes with a remote expression on his face and his little hands paddling at his sides. His breast began to palpitate, accompanied by a new sensation, that of hot ants scurrying about in his lungs, and after that his throat tightened. He clutched the air in alarm as the full paroxysm struck. It took some moments for Ward to realise that what was happening wasn't a game and by the time he had, Jocasta, not to be outdone by her brother, found herself swept away by a copycat attack. Ward shouted 'Larissa! Bunjie!'

Bunjie, whose upper teeth were set slightly behind his lower teeth, was discussing one of the bedrooms with Larissa and saying in his lisp 'What about eau-de-nil damask with apple-green fringes for the curtains and green and purple gingham for the tub chairs?' Hearing Ward's cry, they threw open the window and their heads looked down from a corbelled parapet as, on the lawn below, the twins went through the terror of their very first asthma attack.

59.

Her salubrious disposition filled her with confidence towards the coming birth but Melody was oppressed by being so much indoors and liked to go for a walk each day. Insulated by her Puffa jacket, she launched herself into the February afternoons and the tautness at her temples would be eased almost at once by the fresh air. 'Come along, John,' she said – John gave a kick of acknowledgement inside her – and the two of them took the lane up the opposite slope of the valley. After quarter of an hour she halted and looked down upon the rooftops of Milking Magna where threads of smoke rose vertically into the wintry sky. It was cold and still. A pair of red-collared ducks flapped up from the riverbank and sped into dark woodland.

In another quarter of an hour she reached the Temple of Mercury. A security guard had arrived and the diggers were leaving for the day because of the failing light. The last to leave was Pimm on his bicycle. 'Hullo,' he said.

'Hullo. Can I look?'

'I'm afraid the lasers have been switched on. But come another time and I'll show you round. Aren't you Justice's daughter?'

'Yes. I've not been this way before. Where does it lead?'

'To the Ring of the Moon.'

'All this old stuff around.'

'The Temple's a child compared to what's up there. When the Romans came, the Ring was already many thousands of years old. It's older than the Pyramids.'

'How much further is it?'

'About twenty minutes.'

'I'll give it a go.'

'Are you sure?'

'Of course I'm sure.'

'It's always further than people think.'

'I'm a nurse remember.'

'Then I'll come with you,' he said.

They sauntered uphill past trees nude and lanky.

'Is it true they're going to build over all this?'

'They'll protect the sites but the setting will be destroyed.'

'Why here?'

'Because it's classified as undeveloped. They don't like that. But we're fighting them all the way.'

'I saw it in the paper. It was brave of you to go to prison for it.'

'I'm afraid it was only for one night.'

'Perhaps there will be other opportunities.'

He smiled. 'I'm sure there will be.'

With every upward step it seemed to Melody that a slightly more satisfying state was attained, up here where the views had wings. There weren't many trees now, a few stumpy ones, wrenched by the weather, and outcrops of rock burst through the turf like bone through skin. Though it wasn't a blustery day, a wind moaned distantly without cease up here, as though mourning the tragedy of time's passing. His bicycle clicked cheerfully along beside her. Yes, it was nice walking with this man. She'd made no connections in the village but had been accustomed to her own company all her life. She recalled as a girl playing with her dolls because there was no one else to play with and on the whole that was all right, she and the dolls got along fine. But yes, it was very nice to be walking with this man. She hoped it wasn't too far now because she was feeling tired, suddenly, yes, she was feeling tired.

'Is this a mountain?' she asked.

'I don't know. It's more than a hill. We need a word between the two, don't we. Look, patches of snow up there. Climbing a mountain, yes, it's hard going up, but there comes a time when you are released from the pull of the lower world and are taken by the upper world.'

She replied 'That's like life too – there's a time when you know something has been left behind and you've entered a new period.'

'Is that what you feel? I just seem to add things.'

'It's what I'll feel after the baby is born. Is it much further?'

'We're here.'

'It's bloody freezing.'

With mittens joyfully extended, Melody tramped round the Ring, ooo-ing and aaa-ing at its radiating vistas. But she was exhausted and, after the initial uplift, pressed her damp brow against one of the mighty stones. He propped his bicycle against another one. She turned her face sideways as he came near and smiled at him. He wanted to say 'You are the prettiest woman I have ever seen' but what in fact he did say was 'These grooves in the stone were obviously used in transporting it from the Mountains Beyond the West, which is the nearest place for sarsen, but quite what system of transport they employed remains conjectural. Professor Gutteridge in his *Neolithic Enquiries* – a terrific little book by the way – more of a meditation on prehistory – it's in paperback – I can get it for you – he's come up with a suggestion which . . . hypoth . . . esises . . . '

Melody was walking away from him.

She's not interested in me, he concluded with a sinking heart.

She sat down on a stone in the centre of the Ring, the altar stone, and swayed rhythmically with her back to him.

He let her be for a while, and when he did approach it was not directly. He preferred to follow the arc of the circle. As she came into view in the frames between the upright stones, he saw that she was holding her belly and her face was contorted with pain.

'Melody!' He ran forward.

She said nothing.

'What is it?'

She opened her eyes with a curt laugh. 'I think it's starting.'

'You think it's starting?'

'Labour.'

'Labour?'

She chuckled beatifically. 'Men.'

'Tell me what to do.'

She groaned, winced, groaned, her sounds melting into the moaning of the wind, the long tilts of calming wind adrift towards the end of the world.

'Come to a more sheltered spot.'

'There isn't a more sheltered spot.'

He took off his coat and laid it beneath her on the altar stone.

'They say it's better squatting if you're – aaaaaaaagh – caught like this. Don't worry, I'll tell you what to do. But I feel very weak. I don't know why I feel so weak.'

'I expect you overdid the walk. But you'll be fine.'

He helped her to lie down, feet drawn up to raise the knees.

'Aaagh . . I'm sorry if this is embarrassing,' she said and tried to loosen her clothing. He did it for her, attempting to keep the rest of her warm.

'It's premature,' she said.

'I'll dash down and contact the security guard at the site.'

'Don't leave me please. It's coming.'

He held her hand, his mind blank, all attention on the moment. Many moments passed.

'John . . John . . John,' she murmured softly between groans and held his hand fast.

Her courageous spirit briefly deserted her and he saw fear flash in her eyes. This alarmed him. She was a nurse. She was going to tell him what to do. What would happen if she fainted? Would the contractions stop or were they automatic like breathing? Or did nature make it impossible for a woman in this state to faint? What if *he* fainted? He knew nothing about childbirth. Once he'd asked a woman friend what it had been like and she'd replied 'Like crapping a wardrobe'. The procedure began in earnest. A blade of pure pain cut downwards into Melody's very soul, stopping all thought, as the flesh split along her perineum. Water and blood splashed out. And a little scalp appeared.

'Aaaagh . . . '

After this major event nothing happened for a while. Then the slow pumping started and the scalp became a head. Then nothing.

'Push,' he heard himself say. How did he know that he should say that? 'Push, Melody.'

'Ugh.'

And it restarted. A pair of soft miniature shoulders appeared and edged down towards his coat.

'Aah . . . '

It was getting dark. At all points of the compass the world was shutting down. And now she thought what a very beautiful place this was in which to bring a child into the world, how a child born in such a place would be an exceptional being, with the world at his feet and the sky in his hair and a generous spirit. Oh yes, he was bound to be a fortunate child. Melody's face shone with sweat. Her eyes were closed, her breath heavy and short. Around them the silence was vast. Even the birds had fallen silent. Even the wind had drifted off beyond hearing. Not a shift of wind or rustle of grass or pumping of blood in the ears. Nothing. Nothing at all.

'Aah . . . '

'That's right. Nearly there.'

'Aa . . . '

The child slithered out. It was a boy.

For how long did Pimm look at it? Melody still held his hand. She clutched slightly and then let go.

'What should I do now?'

There was no reply.

'It's a beautiful boy, Melody.'

He mopped the child with his scarf.

'Melody?'

She was dead. He knew she was dead. There was an awful logic to it. He should have told her sooner that it was a boy. She never knew it, not for absolute certain, he thought. Apart from that thought Pimm was numb and acted automatically. He bit the umbilical with his teeth, wrapped the baby in a thick scarf and tucked it inside his coat, covered the mother as best he could, and bicycled rapidly downhill.

Part Three
SPRING

60.

The forthcoming ordeal had overwhelmed her with an obtuse fatigue, followed by an acute excitement, followed by a headache. She carefully washed off the peanut & deadly nightshade face-mask and examined the result in a heart-shaped mirror. 'I should be whiter than that,' she opined. How she could have been any whiter was a mystery, since Minerva was by far the whitest person in a very white district. Extending a long pink tongue to the right of her mouth, she retrieved a stray piece of face-mask and ate it and passed into her dressing-room to look for a paracetamol. Her apartment at Heaven Park had been last done up in what Sidney called the Jessie Mathews era. It featured waxed maple furniture, pink chenille chairs, and alabaster lamps with jade-green shades, and pretty though it was, patches of damp had broken out all over the walls and ceilings.

Minerva's fingertips fidgeted across a row of gowns in one of the wardrobes, back and forth, stop and go, until her tongue clicked against the roof of her mouth and she disengaged a cream tussore evening-dress embroidered with tiny red strawberries and their green leaves. It had belonged to her grandmother. Dear granny. Famous granny. She had taken the air in Hyde Park in a carriage drawn by zebras. Stupid granny. The thoughtless goat had gambled away their London house at a club called Crockford's. Minerva had not been to London since her girlhood and sometimes quizzed Alice about it, although Alice didn't like talking about her past and would say that London was dreadful these days – you couldn't go shopping without being trodden on or being mugged. So what – all it meant was that London was attracting more people than ever! Yes, Minerva would again visit London. One day. Somehow.

She squirmed to left and right before the looking-glass, her shoulder-blades jutting and writhing beneath the membrane of her skin like the featherless wings of a new-born bird. She was attempting to hook up the back of the dress. It was impossible. A maid, a maid! Dresses like this could not be worn without a maid. She'd never had a maid but she'd read about them in novels and seen them in films. To live in London. With a maid. Paradise.

Minerva gave up on the hooks and turned her attention to decorum. She fully extended her right arm, from which hung a hand like an empty glove, and essayed a few introductory 'How do you do's', while her face adopted expressions variously gracious, surprised, appreciative, intellectual, coquettish and, most off-putting of all, ingratiating. 'What a charming . . . *suit.*' She did hope the men would be in suits and not looking like her brother. She was sick of gatherings in which only the women made any *attempt.* Minerva of course would be the sole woman present on this occasion, apart from Crystal who, being her niece, could not be thought of as a woman.

Standing on a stool she took down from deep inside the wardrobe a leather box. It had dull gold clasps and was stamped with a coronet. She placed it lovingly on the counterpane and tentatively lifted the lid. This was always a magic moment, an occasion for thanking destiny. 'Happiness is a tiara,' she informed a chenille chair. It was with some difficulty that the thorny head-dress went into the mousy mousse of her hair whose curls had seemingly been piped out in rows by a pastry-cook one above the other to a considerable height. Yes, it had been a long afternoon spent behind locked doors with several sets of heated rollers. Her great idea in presenting herself on these occasions was to draw the eye as much as possible away from the chin. Minerva did not like her chin. It was responsible for turning what should have been a Gainsborough oval, like her brother's, into a Mondrian rectangle. On the other hand Julius had fat – was a fatso – wobble wobble –whereas she, well, she ran her palms slickly down her sides and felt with satisfaction the protrusion of hip-bones. 'And I no fatty like *her.*' This reference was to Sylvia Wetmore.

The chimneypiece clock, built from stripes of gold and mirrored glass, tinkled the half hour. It was seven thirty p.m. Minerva had thought about it: she would not receive her guests as they arrived but would make an entrance when they all had. The invitation read: *Lady Minerva Popjoy At Home in the Blue Saloon 7 p.m. sharp cocktails*. They'd all be there. In suits. She cast about for the scrap of paper on which she'd written tonight's conversation opener. It lay smudged on the cistern by the loo. 'Strange how seldom the coypu is eaten, even in East Anglia where it is endemic.' In front of the glass she rehearsed it, smoothing the dress against her body. Only half a dozen hooks had she managed to fasten and so of course it didn't look right, neither one thing nor t'other. What was to be done? Yes, she had beauty, she saw that. Apart from the chin. But what of allure? What of erotic magnetism?

In the family's collection of Inigo Jones drawings, currently held at the Victoria & Albert Museum, she had once seen that the ladies of the English Court in Renaissance times often went about bare-breasted, a fashion begun by Queen Elizabeth I herself. How often Minerva had cause to remark the similarities between herself and the Virgin Queen. Except of course that Minerva wasn't a virgin. Bloody hell, she wasn't *that* inept. So, yes, on this her birthday, Lady Minerva Popjoy would revive the fashion, whereupon she gave the bodice cups a yank and her breasts popped forth. They were small and separate, pale and amethyst-veined, and tapered towards the nipples like pears. Still not right. Too much blank space between chin and boob. She jerked open drawers and swirled among jewellery until her breastbone had been covered with a necklace of gold cupids wielding platinum machine-guns. Ready at last.

At the head of the Staircase to Eternity she tried to compose herself by making sure that neither heel was caught in the voluminous skirts of her dress. It looked an awfully long way down. Minerva surveyed the eddies of oval space and came over all weak. On pressing the sides of her hair she felt the garrotte of anxiety at her throat. 'It is curious that the coypu isn't seldom – no . . . Seldom is the coypu strange . . .'

Below meanwhile Sidney, in the tartan slippers which Alice had given him for Christmas, was announcing guests as they arrived. The Blue Saloon was dressed with narcissi whose scent gave the atmosphere a disturbing heaviness.

'Mr Malcolm Gibbet!'

JJ handed the factor a champagne cocktail and said 'Swallow one of these. They're killers.'

'Mr Ward Dashman!'

'So glad you could come,' said Crystal with as expressionless a tone as she could manage. The evening would've been fun without Ward Dashman. If only the bastard had gone to London as he'd promised. The *nerve* of him showing up and putting her on the spot. Of course Aunt Minnie had invited the new male at The Crag but he'd *promised* not to come. He was obviously one of those pushy males who do exactly what they like. Just a spiv after all like everyone was saying. What a fool she'd been. She'd nip it in the bud. No more secret assignations that was for sure. 'My aunt will be down soon.'

It was Ward's first visit to the house and it had taken him the best part of fifteen minutes to get from the front door to here. He slapped his thighs nervously.

'Mr Robert Wetmore!'

'Hi, Bob. Minnie will be down shortly.'

'The Superior! Accompanied by Mr Arbuthnot, Mr Finch and Mr Tucker!'

'The very people I want to see,' said Ward.

'Lord Crimsoncourt!'

'Here, have a puff of joint, Paul. This is Ward.'

'Where are the sharp cocktails?'

'It grows ever more fascinating,' responded the Superior as JJ led him behind a blue marble pillar. 'It has now been decided that the City of Cognitive Neuroscience will be devoted primarily to the development of laser computers working at the speed of light and biological computers even faster than that, so fast indeed that they give the answer *before* you ask the question – and then they give the question too!'

'Look, can I have a meeting with you in London? We could talk more clearly in London.'

'London is the least clear of the great cities. But you may call on me there at any time.'

Tucker asked 'Who did the plasterwork in here?'

'Fanghiglio,' said Finch. 'But his masterpiece is the Witch Chapel at Bloodwood Court.'

JJ turned to Finch and said 'You seem to know a lot about decoration. Do you like older women?'

Crimsoncourt kissed Crystal longly on the neck while she looked over his shoulder at Ward who turned away to Bob Wetmore and said 'Don't you think you ought to slow down, old boy?' Wetmore was swallowing champagne cocktails like oysters and a great amount of sugar had gathered in his moustache. 'Jesus was a drinker,' answered Wetmore.

Above meanwhile, Lady Minerva, almost one third of the way down the Staircase to Eternity, had a panic-attack. The stairwell swayed pitilessly. She sweated and snatched at the banister and one of its posts came away in her hands. She flung the post aside. It clattered hideously down the steps. In desperation she resorted to her mantra. 'Strange how coypu is the seldom . . . in Stanglia where . . . it is anaemic.' It was no good. And she pulled herself back upstairs for a quick lie-down.

Oh what an ordeal! And to think that Granny was an aviatrix! But Minerva knew what it was. Because every year it was the same. The mortal terror of her age! Not of the age itself. She knew what that was, as indeed did a number of governmental officials. But of her age *coming out*. It must never come out. Ever. Were she to be challenged as to why, she could not have answered because it wasn't quite rational, the degree to which she held this fear. It was probably what the newspapers called a phobia. Which didn't make it any easier! Age was prejudice and she didn't want to be stigmatised. She was stigmatised quite enough already. What a stigmatic obstacle her title was for a start. Of course she had to use it. Mummy would've been horrified if her daughter had gone into the world nude of title. But she could see the way other people cowered halfway between awe and revulsion in consequence of those four letters ablaze on her brow. Next she was stigmatised on account of her height – and her sex – and her artistic inclination – and her singularity – her singularity both general *and* particular – oh oh oh stop it, Minerva, stop torturing yourself! The Mackenzie's smelling salts passed back and forth beneath her palpitating nostrils. All right I'll stop torturing myself but I don't want my age coming out as well – *especially* as it's my birthday party. The thing about birthday parties is that they drew attention to one's age. She must be mad to let Julius give her a birthday party every year! Oh, but the poor darling would be so hurt if she protested, so very hurt. She couldn't possibly do that, she couldn't, and so now everybody would be downstairs wondering how old is the stigmatised one, how old, do tell. But they must never know. Never. And if that were a phobia, so be it. There were worse phobias. Fear of soup for example. To think that there were people who were terrified of drowning in their soup. That must be a simply awful phobia. You could never have dinner in case soup came along and terrified you out of your mind. No, as phobias went she was getting off quite lightly, really she was. She sniffed again at the Mackenzie's smelling salts, a little too keenly. Her head snapped back. Calm yourself, calm yourself. Nobody's going to ask. Nobody's going to. And strange to tell, they never did ask. Somehow Minerva gave off a vapour which cauterised such enquiries at source. No one ever had the temerity to ask. And those that knew, such as JJ, Paul Crimsoncourt or Archie, they never mentioned it. They were gentlemen. Quite ghastly a lot of the time but still, they instinctively knew about things like age. Paul however she was worried about. He was the weak point in the gathering always, the one who might go beyond the beyond, who might *let it out*. Gentleman yes but he was once voted the rudest man in England in *Tatler*.

The party below was edgy. Sidney's bunions were playing up and he shuffled from foot to painful foot between announcements.

'Mr Oliver Knott!'

'Don't we want to speak to him?' Arbuthnot asked the Superior.

'Relax and have a drink for God's sake, Arbuthnot, he's already in the bag. Have you ever met a scientist who wouldn't bend over for the slightest hint of a grant?'

'And above the fireplace is Popham Popjoy stroking a blue leopard. They made him Earl of Knockledandy when he became Viceroy of Ireland. That one over there is his younger brother who, though not an able man, became Viceroy of North America and some people do say that it was because ... ' JJ was expatiating with an oleaginous half-smile. Tucker sucked his finger, trying to look interested. JJ thought Tucker was *gorgeous*.

Crimsoncourt said to Malcolm 'Jolly decent of JJ to have these fuck parties for her every year. Do you know how old she is?'

'No.'

'Sixty-two. It's in Burke's. Ever screwed her?'

'Once. When I was eleven.'

'Same here. Archie put me onto it. Where is the old bag anyway?'

The Superior said to JJ 'Do watch your step, Lord Heavenshire. I hardly have to remind you that your secretary has become notorious as one of the Puck Valley Three.'

'I ticked her off. I really did. We can't have members of the staff in prison, even for a night. We're down to the absolute minimum as it is. The place would go to pieces.'

'The Ministry wants as little trouble as possible.'

'She's influenced by one of our farmers. He's not a bad man really. But he is a depressive. Try one of Cook's puffs.'

'Who are you?' Crimsoncourt enquired of Ward Dashman.

'I live at The Crag.'

'An ugly house. Are they lining you up for Minerva?'

'I don't think so.'

'If they rope you in, remember she likes a banana up her bum. Unpeeled of course. It'll save you a lot of work.'

'I thought that was her brother.'

'No, no, with JJ it's everything except the anal.'

'Do you happen to know anything about asthma as well?'

Crimsoncourt laughed with the freshness of a teenager. 'Crystal can still take my breath away.'

Ward lurched in with 'Have you had her?' and couldn't prevent his nose from crinkling up as he put the question.

'Not since I was eleven.'

'I see.'

'I've had Crystal though. One *memorable* afternoon.'

Minerva, above it all, made another reluctant sally at the stairs. There was a spasm of spiralling nausea as she toppled and took the first step down but she managed to do the whole lot – half-landings, landing, double-loop back, and final sweep – by the simple expedient of looking everywhere except where she was going, so that it was with a jolt which ran up through all her joints that she discovered there were no more steps to descend, and with a sense of amiable surprise that she found herself standing on the marble floor of the Middle Hall. Sidney, in the doorway of the Blue Saloon, saw her coming and his mouth fell open and did not close until she was upon him and due to be announced.

'Go on, Sid. Do your thing.'

He coughed twice. 'Pray silence for the Lady Minerva Popjoy!'

Nothing resembling silence manifested itself until Minerva halted a few feet into the room, looking to left and right, bowing slightly, tiara flashing, whereupon silence fell like a guillotine. It congealed into a rubbery resilience which only extreme nerve could pierce and this was supplied by Paul Crimsoncourt. 'Is she on drugs?' he asked in a general way.

JJ waddled up and whispered furiously 'You didn't mention you'd be hanging yer tits out!'

She flinched as though struck. It was her party, her outfit, her hopes, her decision – 'I'm reviving the custom of the Elizabethan Court.'

'Would you kindly make an announcement to that effect?'

'Mes amis,' began Minerva, making a curtsey so deep that her breasts swung freely, 'and niece . . . Please do not be alarmed. My ancestors at the Courts of the First Elizabeth and the First James appeared thus on gay occasions. The custom was revived at the Court of Charles II. And is here again revived tonight. But please do not take advantage of my interest in history. I am to be touched only upon request and the request may not be granted.'

'Seen worse,' said Malcolm to Wetmore who was pulling at his trouser-seat with a sucking-lemons expression.

Minerva sought to capitalise on the impetus of her arrival by asking 'Sidney, where are all my birthday presents?'

'As the guests arrived, m'lady, Mr Boy took possession of them in the Great Hall.'

She seemed satisfied with this and advanced elliptically upon Ward. 'Strange how seldom the coypu is anaemic . . ' He gamely stood his ground which flustered her and forced her to change the subject. 'Do you know the Whore of Babylon?' she asked him.

'No, but I'd love to.'

'Bad luck! She's not coming. I've forbidden it.' A dab of red burned on each of Minerva's chalky cheeks. Ward was staring intensely into her eyes as though nothing existed below them and she lost her nerve. 'I can show you the Long Library later. For the present I must circulate,' and she careened off to someone less challenging, Oliver Knott, and interrogated him against a cabinet. 'You are not wearing a suit, Mr Knott. They are all wearing suits except you.'

Knott jabbered 'JJ isn't. The invitations didn't say.'

'Most unsuitably dressed you are. But – my fault! All my fault!' Minerva remembered, yes, could hear the voice, she had to be gracious. Mummy always said before a party 'This time, Minnie dear, do try and be gracious.' She could be. She could be gracious if she wanted to. Why, she could kill with graciousness. Oliver's heart stopped as she bent close. 'I forgive you, Mr Knott. And if anyone says anything about your disgusting jumper, send them to me!' Minerva straightened up with a crimson smile already smeared by the first cocktail. Her chin passed with predatory concern along the line of nervous males. It stopped at Tucker. 'You've got a nice suit.'

Tucker stammered 'T-t-terrible pity about the Himalayas . . . '

'Isn't it a pity about the Himalayas,' she acquiesced and thought – I like a man with a concern for nature.

'Pray silence for Cook!' commanded Sidney.

All heads turned, relieved to have some other distraction. Cook pushed a cake through the door on a trolley, a round sponge sandwich with buttercream in the middle and topped with pale pink icing. Whorls of silver dragees glittered beneath the flames of many candles. Cook swayed but Sidney was there and he steered the drunken creature out, though she managed to blow a kiss to the assembly before disappearing.

'That was a nice gesture.'

'Wasn't it nice.'

'But there won't be enough to go round,' pouted Minerva.

'I don't want any,' said Knott.

'Neither do I,' added Crystal.

Lady Minerva impaled them with tearful eyes. 'But it's my birthday. You've got to have some.' She remembered to be gracious. 'If there's a shortage, I shall go without.' At which point Minerva saw her brother approaching with a decisive step and she backed away. 'No, Julius.'

'Yes, Minnie.'

'Julius, no, please, I beg you!'

'Yes, yes, yes!'

JJ, Crimsoncourt, Crystal and Malcolm Gibbet each took a stick-like arm or leg of Minerva's and began a bumps-a-daisy in the centre of the carpet. Minerva, as light as dried twigs, was soon flying high. She sailed upward with a screech like a thousand fingernails on as many blackboards and descended with a howl to give wart hogs migraine. Up, down, several times, during which her tiara flew off and chipped a dolphin comport, and it might have continued thus through her innumerable years had not Malcolm disclosed 'She's not wearing knickers!' On learning this JJ simply let go of the arm he was in charge of and walked away.

Minerva was sailing upwards at the time, so that it was less risky than it might have been, and she used her spare arm to wave jubilantly at the guests. The descent however was another matter. They slowed her up as best they could so that she might extend a saving hand towards the floor. This part worked quite well. But in order to achieve it, her legs had remained much higher than the rest of her, with Malcolm and Crimsoncourt pushing up hard on each ankle to avert a tragedy. Crystal quickly placed in position the support of Minerva's other arm. At the end of this operation, Minerva was upside-down, with her skirts hanging towards the floor and all her private parts tensely displayed.

'Anyone for shove ha'penny?' asked JJ, salting the wound.

The ankles were carefully lowered and in a trice Minerva was on her feet, smoothing down her dress, and saying 'No damage. Everything fine. Drink up.'

Ward said to Crystal 'Let's make a date'.

Crystal glanced at him through a chiffon of cigarette smoke and whispered 'Another one?'

'Yes.'

'You're keen.'

'Yes, yes, yes. But our secret. Promise me – our secret.'

'Oh God yes.'

'Don't worry about the Dickon bloke,' said Malcolm Gibbet to the Superior. 'He's a trouble-maker. But his tenancy comes up for renewal soon. We'll have him out like that!'

'When all the planning permits have gone through, Mr Gibbet, Lower Farm will be *extremely* valuable. Please remind the marquess of that, won't you. We don't want any waverers.' The Superior's face narrowed effectively. 'We thought the leisure centre would sit nicely there, in the curve of the river, with plenty of flat for a car park.'

'Mr Wetmore, there's something I've always meant to ask you,' said Minerva, combining expressions coquettish and ingraciating. 'And that is – why did you marry the Whore of Babylon?'

'Because I loved her, your ladyship. Possibly I was a bit whiskied up when I proposed.'

'Do you love her still?' Minerva waved the tiara in her hand with what she hoped was a gesture of intellectual detachment.

'One never really knows what love is after marriage. Marriage replaces love. You sort of relax into it and don't have to worry about love any more.'

'Until the marriage stops.'

JJ tilted backwards on a twist – at times his agility was astonishing – and laid a boneless arm on Bob's sleeve. 'I'm going to persuade Sylvia to return to you.'

'Do you think you could?'

'She's been in the stables long enough.'

'Julius,' said Minerva, reinserting the tiara into the mayhem of her coiffure, 'Sylvia is very happy in the stables.'

'It was you who said you wanted her out.'

'No. I never said such a thing, no. Dear Sylvia. Where is she? She must be late . . .'

'Is she coming?' panted Wetmore.

'No, she's not,' snapped Minerva. 'I remember now, yes, she was meeting a man tonight, some man, more important than little old us obviously, and Mr Wetmore, I do not advise a reconciliation until you are feeling stronger.'

'She is my strength.'

'Boy can drive me over to your Mill next week and I'll invigorate you with sandwiches. Meat paste. Very nourishing. I'll put loads on.'

'Meeting what man?'

'Yes, I daresay she is, oh fie, have I let the pussy out of the baggy?'

There was a noise like the approach of an underground railway and Bob's shoulders went up and down.

'Oh, Mr Wetmore, don't cry! Forgive me!' Minerva put an arm and two breasts round Bob who sobbed against her for a while. They sank together onto a causeuse. It was a very elongating feeling, Minerva thought, and she was at first pleased to be of help, but when Bob's 'while' showed no sign of coming to an end, Minerva grew restless. It was her birthday party. She had to circulate. There were possibilities elsewhere. Indeed the time came when she felt it necessary to push him off and Bob rolled sideways under a console table with a 'schlurrup' sound where, among the table supports of gilt sea monsters, he lost consciousness. Minerva crossed to Ward Dashman and struck him playfully on the shoulder. 'Why are you staring at me like that, you naughty man?'

Ward was nonplussed. He'd been looking in the opposite direction. 'I hear you are a poetess,' he fumbled.

'I don't publish. I refuse to. The creatures from London come a-begging but I say no, not yet. My first volume will be entitled *Lockjaw*. Clever eh?' Minerva raised her glass and knocked back the remains of another cocktail. She'd quite got over her nerves.

Kevin bounded in and Glory Boy followed. He said 'No one else is coming now. Can I have a drink?'

'What do you mean no one else coming? Several more at least!'

'Who for example?'

'Pimm. And I don't recall inviting you. You're not eligible.'

'Aren't most of em married?'

Minerva rounded on Arbuthnot. 'Are *you* married?'

'Actually, yes.'

'You don't look it – which is the important thing. I want a child!' exclaimed Minerva to the ceiling, after which she looked round at them and covered her mouth with her hand.

Malcolm said to JJ 'I'm escaping, boss. Got an early start in the morning. By the way, the Upanishads have set up their tepee in the Aspen Paddock. Do I have your permission to shoo them off?'

'But do it nicely.'

Minerva followed Malcolm sulkily with her eyes and shouted 'Don't start leaving yet! You're spoiling it! . . . Good riddance then!' She was upset and searched for an anchor. 'Take another cocktail, Mr Dashman. I am now in a position to show you the Long Library.'

Crystal saw the two of them leaving the room and broke away from Paul Crimsoncourt. 'Where are you two going? Can I come?'

'No, you can't!' said her aunt.

'Oh, let her come,' said Ward.

'Do you want another smack, Mr Dashman? Follow me. I hear you are in software. I'm in need of some new underclothes so we shall have something to talk about.'

Ward shivered. They were walking briskly along a cold corridor painted with Pompeian arabesques and came to the library by a side entrance which was ajar. Holding on to Ward's sleeve, she peered cautiously in.

About two thirds of the way down its immense length, the gloom of the library was interrupted by a circle of lamplight. Within this circle a head was nodding over a text. Minerva launched herself at it.

'Why aren't you at my party?'

Pimm jumped in surprise. 'I got absorbed.'

'And we thought you were keeping to your room because of emotional trauma.'

Ward introduced himself and asked 'Aren't you that chap who delivered that baby?'

'Yes,' said Pimm. He closed the book he was reading with a flop of resignation.

'Mr Dashman and I were hoping to peruse in solitude.'

'I'll leave.'

'Please, don't,' said Ward. 'I don't want to disturb anyone.'

Minerva looked at Pimm from a number of angles. Lately he had touched mysteries which she never had. He had penetrated to the relentless, dispassionate core of life and death. But this had placed him beyond her, outside her capacity. 'It was a very sad occurrence of course, the girl dying up on the top there, but you did get yourself onto the front page of the *Gazette* and now you are missing an excellent party, isn't he, Mr Dashman.'

'I wouldn't have gone anyway,' said Pimm, 'because that awful Superior and his gang are there.'

'You've been spying! Emotional trauma my arse. There's nothing wrong with *you*.'

Sidney emerged from the adjacent dinge. 'M'lady, his lordship says can you come and blow out the candles because the cake is melting. And I'm afraid, m'lady, there is a gentleman to see Mr Pimm.'

A man with spruce ears and a suit of Bedford cord entered the library and came towards the circle of light.

'It's getting very crowded in here suddenly,' said Minerva. 'Mr Dashman and I – '

'Excuse me, Lady Minerva, but I need to ask Mr Pimm a few questions.'

'Who are you to barge in like a bus?'

'Detective Hoskins, madam.'

'May I touch your suit?' She did not await his consent. Her arm clicked at the elbow as she reached out and grazed the lapel with the back of her hand. The beauty of the policeman's bow-lipped mouth was painful to her. She wondered why she hadn't met him at least several hundred times before.

'Ward Dashman,' said Ward.

'Yes, I know,' said Hoskins. 'You're in consumerism.' He articulated the last word with particular care and Minerva very nearly swooned.

'Consumerism has had its day,' said Pimm and he somehow endowed the observation with an ethereal mystique.

'I thought Mr Dashman was in knickers,' said Minerva.

'It's all the same,' said Ward.

'It isn't all the same,' said Pimm.

Ward said 'Consumerism is humanity's playground. Look at this house. It is a temple to the consumerism of a bygone age.'

Hoskins said 'There is obviously high consumerism and low consumerism'. Minerva followed every flexure of the divine mouth and had quite forgotten Mr Dashman.

Ward replied 'I don't think the attempt of low consumerism to cheer up the lives of the less fortunate is an ignoble aim, do you?'

'Is God's work a litter bin?' remonstrated Pimm. 'Anyway you don't cheer up the lives of the less fortunate. People are less happy these days. That's been proven by research.'

Her ladyship looked hopefully towards the detective, keen for more articulation. She was soon rewarded.

'I fully understand the reason for your depressed spirits, Mr Pimm,' said Hoskins, 'but I'm afraid I need to ask you some more questions about the death of Melody Smith. Her father may accuse you of neglectful conduct.' Which didn't have the voomph of his earlier utterance on consumerism but Minerva was riveted nonetheless. The detective turned to her. 'Is Oliver Knott in the house, madam? I have reason to understand that he was involved in a fracas with the dead girl's father. And further-more is the Superior here? I wish to discuss his allegations against the Puck Valley Three, of whom Mr Pimm here is one, and in addition to raise the matter of the assault on Mrs Bladder-Williams of Church House. And lastly, may I ask is one Mr Tony Tucker present with whom I also wish to pursue my enquiries?'

Minerva wilted onto a spoonback chair and clutched at her necklace of cherubs. 'Oh, Detective Hoskins, what *are* you trying to do? C'est mon anniversaire. I'm not feeling well. If you will kindly help me upstairs to my apartment, you can afterwards do whatever you like . . . '

61.

Justice sat in the doctor's waiting-room, with a silent baby in his arms. He was wearing a new pair of spectacles and the slogans bore down on him from posters on the walls.

One in three men over 50 has difficulty passing water – do you?
No, he didn't. Always a gush.

Asthma? Do you need to talk? Must've been a misprint there.
Obviously they meant do you need to breathe? His own lungs
were magnificent.

Do you have M.E.? Wasn't that when you felt bad for no
reason? But he had a reason.

Huntington's Disease – information
How is your heart coping?
For local advice about AIDS and HIV, ring . . .
We're after your blood
Rubella? Ask your G.P.
Growing old is a family affair
Lifting the shadow of diabetes
Glaucoma?

The baby was quiet. It was always quiet. It was as quiet as Justice had become, for Justice had not uttered a single word since
his daughter's death. Since that event everything had grown so
much bigger that he was unable to get words around what he
wanted to say. He thought – I am bigger too and in fact I am so
big that I can no longer see the edges of myself. I was tryin to
remember when I came to this place, how I came to be here, but
my head has become so big that the sky flows through it and I
cannot remember, and where my Melody's face should be there
is only sky, cold flowing sky, so that I have to look at photographs
in order to remember what she looked like and when I look at
those photos they are not her but smudges of colour on paper and
I know she is not around any more and that she is dead and everythin about her is cold. People have been very good, very kind to
me, very gentle, but frightened to touch me, because how would
white people know how to cradle a big black man? They don't
know. I don't blame them. It doesn't interest me to blame them.
I don't care about blackness. I'm not interested in blackness. But
blackness is sure interested in me. Prejudice they call it. Every
man, woman and child on this earth experience prejudice unless
he have no identity at all. But one thing did worry me. In the
Sunday paper they published a list of the thousand top rich
people in England – every sort and colour of person in the list,

many Indians and many Chinese, but only one black man and he
a boxer. Everything in the world has become business but the
black man – the African man – he can't do business. I don't
understand why the black man can't do business. This is a very
interesting question for me, but nobody, black or white, will discuss it seriously. They only discuss this question stupidly, by
denying it exists or in a venom of insult, but never quietly and
seriously. If they keep on saying it's just prejudice that's stoppin
him we'll never find out why and therefore never be able to
change it because obviously it isn't prejudice stoppin him but
somethin else. I can repair cars but I don't go the next step and
employ people and have ten garages all over the place. In Africa,
where prejudice against the black man don't exist, it's even worse
– corruption, massacres, disease, debt. Horrible rulers there now.
Africa is off the map now. Everyone want to escape Africa now.
No people there soon. God intends that. Nature will take over
again in Africa and begin the healing of the Earth. For that the
black man will surrender his continent. So maybe the black man
does have something to offer you don't find anywhere else. Why
can't he do business? Because he is the opposite of this mad
modern mechanical business world. Business is cold and the
black man is warm and that makes the black man very valuable
indeed in a world dying from business. He still has the strange,
intimate, timeless, beautiful, dancing contact with the natural
thing which other people are losing. Which even the black man
will lose soon if he does what they want him to do which is join
the rich list. That's what the others want. They want the black
man to lose his special thing and join the rich list. They talk
about a black man one day for Prime Minister or they want the
African man to go worldwide with his music, dance, sport, and
love-making, so they can make more business business business
out of it, oh yes his love-making too because he do that better
than anyone else, he know all about that and he has the biggest
cock to do it with, which is no accident but evolution Darwin-
style, yes, the black man still has poetry in his cock which all the
other men lose, which means he still has the old poetry in his
heart and soul which is not the sentimental head poetry of books
but the old natural poetry straight from the gods which the other

men lose, the other women lose, and black man Prime Minister is
nothing in comparison to that, nothing at all. One thing I do
know – I'm sick of black man talk. Another thing I know – I don't
want ten garages and all that hassle, I want a peaceful life. But I
don't get it, no. I lose my daughter on a mountain. I lose my
memory. I lose my tongue. Another thing I do know – that Mrs
Bladder-Williams fancy me like crazy but she is ashamed of herself, not only because I am black but also because I am a working
man, and because I am big and black it makes her sex need even
more prominent and she is very ashamed of her sex need. She
thinks people say you dirty ol' girl at your age you just want his
huge one fillin yer hole and they would say that because it's
true, she does want that. She has a big hole and she needs a big
man. Most of all I want to rest my head on her universal bosom
and cry and let my heart go free in tears because she is the only
one round here big enough to cradle me, and then maybe I could
talk again.

   Daisy Lark came into the waiting-room with Tiny Colin. H
e'd fallen out of an apple tree into a bed of nettles and sprained
his ankle. Daisy asked 'Can I hold the baby?' and after Justice
had transferred the precious package, she said to her brother
'I used to hold you like this. You'd always stop crying for me.
Justice, yours is much gooder than Colin was. Yours don't cry at
all.'

   'Was I a little devil?' Colin asked her, snuggling up.

   A nurse gave the baby a thorough examination. The doctor,
filling in forms, glanced at it and said 'Seems very healthy and
contented but still not making any noises? Oh well, we'll give it
a bit more time. Still, the human baby is a queer kettle of fish,
you know. For example, it cannot distinguish between the edible
and the inedible. Such a distinction is absolutely fundamental to
existence and yet, strange to say, this has to be taught, and yet
swimming – much less fundamental to existence one would've
thought – is instinctive in babies. Nature is not a Darwinist. In
fact Nature is a bit of an oddball.'

   On the page of a notebook which he'd taken from his pocket,
Justice wrote: *I can't sleep.*

   'Not surprised, Justice. It was a terrible thing.'

Justice wrote again: *It's because the baby doesn't cry. I lie awake at night hoping to hear it cry but it doesn't. Total silence. Very frightening.*

'He's probably following your example.'

I do speak to him. But with other people I can't get the words out. I am worried because the Council want to take him away from me and that would be very bad.

'They know it is difficult for a single man, a working man.'

It is prejudice against men. He is my grandson. He is all I've got. But more important – I am all he's got. It's worth everything to him to have a bit of family. He must not be given to a stranger.

'I shall speak up for you, Justice, but they'd prefer it if you were able to speak for yourself. And if there were a female around.'

Justice wrote nothing.

'Do you want any sleeping-pills?'

Justice nodded no and took the long walk home, down by the river and up, to avoid the people in the High Street, singing a song to himself. It was called 'God' and his grandfather had taught it to him when he was a boy. He had forgotten it but it came back to him unbidden, out of the blue in his head.

> *Sky clean*
> *House old*
> *Food hot*
> *Beer cold*
>   *But You lousy to me*
>
> *Mermaid sing*
> *Sun shine*
> *Faun dance*
> *Money fine*
>   *But You lousy to me*

62.

Justice was not alone in the paralysis of despair. Since the funeral of Sir James, life had been a series of abruptly descending ladders for Lady Craddock and her son, one sudden jerk-down after another. Sorting through Sir James's papers, they had come across an envelope marked *To Whom It May Concern*. The contents stated: *On absolutely no account am I to be buried. I must be cremated and my ashes scattered off the cliffs near Puckermouth. Please understand that this is my final word on the matter.*

So there had been an exhumation, messy rather than macabre.

Followed by a cremation. Robin saw to it. Helen did not attend and neither did anyone else.

Followed by the scattering. Helen did go along for that. She wanted to be quite sure that her husband had finally blown out of existence. There was a half-cock ceremony and the weather was foul and when the ash was scattered by one Commander Malapert it blew backwards, spotting the mourners with wet filth. Robin had an erection which, thanks to the onshore gale, was obvious to a number of people. In the aftermath of his father's death, the son had experienced great sexual arousal (to add to the arousal he was experiencing before).

Back at the flat which they'd rented above the butcher's shop, Helen went on a sighing spree. She sighed this way, then she sighed another way. There was an enormous variety to her sighs. Some were quite like croaks, others more like gulps, and often they were accompanied by curiously slow blinks of the eyes and careening motions of the head. But they all had one thing in common: they absolutely infuriated Robin.

Hoggart the Butcher and his family were very considerate. They lived in the cottage next door to the shop and offered to sell her meat at a reduced price and she had reacquired the taste for it. Tonight's supper would be a veal sandwich, and tonight the butcher's friend, Selwyn Blagdon, said he'd call in to see her while visiting the Hoggarts. She didn't care. Let him call. It would be the second time. The shaggy thing made his own tea, gurgled on about the woods, paced the small sitting-room in a nervous way, and went off. That was all right. She liked woods. She liked gardens. She liked movement in others. And she was entertained by his discomposure in the confined space, for the flat was tiny.

When she and Robin had first moved in she couldn't stand it and had to go frequently outdoors to dispel the choke. But one by one her various horizons had curled up and rolled in towards her like carpets and she had grown accustomed to the reduced perspective, especially after they sold the car. Good heavens, she couldn't afford a car! Now she hardly went out at all and what's more, she didn't want to go out because she didn't like going out. When she went out she felt fuzzy. People with nasty faces ogled and pitied her. No, she wouldn't go out. Really there was no reason to.

Robin's mouth hung open, its lower lip slung forward. He was panting in short breaths. He was full of electrostatic which needed to be earthed by fucking Crystal, so he rang her but she wasn't there. She was having his baby but she was never there. He told his mother he was going to The Crag to check the falcon. The Dashmans had kindly allowed him to keep it there until he found another place. Lady Craddock was sitting in an unpleasant chair. She was turning the boards of a crested photograph album. 'That was you at four,' she said to her son. But he wasn't there.

63.

The lavish scent of hyacinths flowed to her uninterruptedly from the mossy pot on the table. Lucky hyacinths, for whom it is always a gala day, so dressy, fresh and unaware, whereas she was dowdy – no, she was worse – she was old – no – she tapped gently her own cheek – no backsliding please – stop negative self-indulgence – you are getting better, you know you are, I know I am – did she know? What did she know? Her upper parts pulsed with irritation. She sipped from her cup of coffee and pondered – yes, the room was wrong, that was something she knew obscurely, but *what* was wrong with it? Alice walked to the window and looked out. The crow was hopping on the grass with its damaged wing. Today she didn't sympathise, could easily have stamped on it in exasperation, except of course that she couldn't have, and took the last of a crusty bloomer out to the irksome thing but it fluttered in panic under the hedge and looked at her over yellow celandines with a beady eye twitching. 'Don't then,' she said and petulantly dumped the bread on the grass. Upon re-entry she recognised at once what was wrong with the room. No television.

The room was saying 'Can I have a television please? Please let me have a television.' Yes, she would acquire a television. An ultra-modern one to put in the corner. A big silver one with a letterbox-shaped screen.

64.

Clouds raced above the Beowulf Caravan Park and below, in the tin box which was home, Max jigged and rapped out one of the big numbers from a new musical called *King Lear*. With score in one hand, he jiggled his hips and, where narrow space permitted, threw up a leg. Max was going to audition next month for the title role at the Pier Theatre in Puckermouth!

> *With words splenetic*
> *And apoplectic*
> *I know that it's for the best*
> *To get it all off my chest*
> *Then wash my hands*
> *And change my vest.*
>
> *If I keep concealing*
> *The rage I'm feeling*
> *I'll probably drink a bar*
> *So though this ditty*
> *Is not so pretty*
> *At least it will tell you what crap you are.*
>
> *You're the pits*
> *You're a pre-flu shiver*
> *You're the shits*
> *A polluted river*
> *You're the endless fight of a sleepless night in hell*
> *You're a varicose vein, you're the rain in Spain,*
>   *you're a rotten smell!*
>
> *You're a quack*
> *You're a pain eternal*
> *You're a hack*
> *On a tabloid journal*

I'm a wino round the back door of the Ritz
But if, baby, I'm imperfect you're the pits!

Hey, sweet,
You're an utter bruiser
You're the feet
Of a Derby loser
You're the awful groan of a heavy loan from Lloyd's
You're a rabid puma, a malignant tumour,
   you're haemorrhoids!

You're not a kiss
You are laddered nylons
You're the hiss
From a row of pylons
Though I may be just a joke, a jerk, some bits,
But if, baby, I'm in pieces you're the pits!

At the end of it, Max shouted to the wall 'You're late! I knew you would be!' And he went through the song again for the umpteenth time.

In a mirror at the bungalow, Davis was fixing to her head a pepper & salt straw hat adorned with faded silk flowers. 'Hate it, hate it!' God, yes, she hated it. Not herself of course but more or less everything else. For example she hated that bloodless vegetarian cow who hadn't given her so much as a candlestick after all those years of service at The Crag. Serves her right she was stuck above the butcher's! Good job! And she hated that slimy incomer Ward Dashboard and his cheap foreign hussy of a wife who thinks she knows something about the supernatural – she'd *get* the supernatural all right! – what were they doing up at The Crag? No business being at The Crag! Nothing to do with The Crag! Varlets, vermin, pillagers! And I hate that other lot even more, that bag of rotten apples over at Heaven Park who never gave a spit after all that Mumsy went through. How she suffered! Call themselves nobility? Nothin but rats, parasites, pillagers! And I hate, I hate – Mumsy! Who's been a ruddy pain all my life, sitting there wetting er knickers year in year out. Why should I be punished? I never did nothing! But I'll do it now! I'll do em all! And I hate, hate – oh sod it, I'm late! Do I care? Nah! He's another creep. I hate him too but I'll use him, yes, oh I'll use him all right! Whassat noise? Don't want no interruptions!

There was a knock at the front door. Davis stubbed out her fag and went to it. 'What you doin ere?'

'I've come to see her.'

'You making it twice a year now then?'

'It was a year ago I was last here.'

'Liar.'

'I assure you it was. May I come in? My feet are hurting.'

'Chop em off! Give us all a break!'

Ignoring the slight, Sidney asked 'Where is she?'

'Where she always is.' Davis nodded over her shoulder. Sidney's arrival ladled fury onto fury. The silk flowers trembled on her hat. She snarled 'I'm late. I'm off. Make sure you close the front door when you leave.'

When all was quiet, Sidney changed from his boots into slippers which he'd carried in a brown bag and went into the parlour. 'Hullo, Daphne,' he said.

The Old Un raised eyes set in dead parchment. An expression which was more than recognition, was possibly even pleasure, tinctured them. She went 'Mmmmmmm . . . ', low and level. Sidney took her hand like a dry leaf and held it in silence.

Overcome by the delay to his four-thirty cuppa, Max's patience broke at four-forty when he put on the kettle. He inserted a cassette and pressed start and spooned five sugars into his tea. Davis turned up just as he was getting into the music and he wouldn't speak to her for a full minute during which time he took a packet of digestives from his wicker shopping basket and arranged them meticulously on a chipped plate, humming loudly, fending her off. Eventually he pushed a cup towards her.

Davis peered down at it as though down a well. 'It's tea. I never drinks tea. Everyone knows that.'

'I didn't.'

'Everyone knows it.'

He flung the tea into the sinkette. 'Would you like rat poison?'

'Coffee, ta, ever so.'

Max poured a line of Camp coffee syrup into a mug and put the kettle back on. The gas raged passionately beneath it.

'Did you get to er birthday party?' Davis managed to light her cigarette from the gas ring without singeing her hat.

'Um – whose party?'

'Lady M Pop's.' Nodding at the radio-cassette player Davis made a sucking-lemons face. A piano and orchestra were trilling out in fountains, splashing her with classical music. She hated it.

'No, I didn't go. I couldn't go.'

'You weren't invited. Thought she invited all the men. But she didn't invite you. You missed a right exhibition by all accounts.'

Max whipped off his dark glasses and flashed silver eyes. 'She thinks she's a poetess but she's crude! They're all pornographic up there! I hate em!' Max mimed an ornate pianoforte passage with his arms before bursting out anew. 'And I hate The Crag too!'

Davis jumped at him. 'What business is it of yourn to hate The Crag? I'll always be as loyal as loyal to The Crag! She's become all invalidated over the butcher's shop serves her right good job but to The Crag I'm loyal. The new un up there, she's ad continental experience.'

'Has she by Jove.'

'Mmmmm. I can tell. Funny voice, funny look. But to The Crag itself I'll always be loy –'

Max came up close and sniffed her whiskers. 'The problem with loyalty, dear witch, is that it inhibits growth, and it is time for us both to grow, you and I.'

Davis polished off the coffee and asked 'Got any whisky?'

'All right then, I don't hate The Crag, I hate the Dashmans!' Max stabbed the air in time to the music.

'Can't you stand still for five minutes? Why do *you* hate the Dashmans?'

'Because they're successful!'

'Who else d'ya hate?'

'That Alice!' he vipered.

'She's not successful.'

'I hate her anyway! She set the police on me just because she found a rubber toy at the end of her bed. She should be so lucky, frigid little fart! And I hate – look, having examined it objectively from all angles, I must accept the brute fact that I've been prevented from reaching my full potential by other people. I'd've been a great star if it weren't for – *other people.* So I hate em! And I hate the summer!' He was trembling and smartly readopted his specs. He sensed the approach of summer with a terror which flickered like cold serpents in his gut.

'Can't you turn it down?' asked Davis, nodding towards the music.

'If you don't like it, dearie, park yer hump somewhere else. Did you know that the silly little mouse of an Alice used to be the girlfriend of the Minister of Power? Was his secretary indeed. I looked it up at the internet café – no wonder she kept it quiet – coz we all hate him! That gangster will destroy everything!'

'Why as she come snooping round ere is what I want to know.'

'She's up to something. That's obvious,' said Max. 'Spying for the Minister of Power is my guess. I've informed J' – But there he halted. It wasn't for Davis to know about Joyce. Not for the time being.

'Did you say you didn't have whisky?'

'I have sandwiches. I've done it the wrong way round. Because you annoyed me. Because you were late. Punctuality I expect is beyond you but in future a telephone call would be kind.'

'You aren't on the phone.'

'I'll get a mobile. If we are to achieve anything we'll have to be communicado. Davis – a tip. Sodium bicarbonate, brushed vigorously on the teeth twice a week, is very effective at taking out *brown.*' And he took from the fridge a packet of sandwiches wrapped in clingfilm. 'Pork luncheon meat with chutney. Very tasty. And I hate – '

'I hate!' she echoed.

'I hate the people in this repulsive caravan park for being mindless, common dolts!'

'What about your precious Mrs Wetmore? Hate er yet?'

'Sylvia? Hate Sylvia? I never see her now she's living at the Park. Ever so grand aren't we. Ha, she talks about inheriting chocolate shops! All lies. Her mother sold sweets in Woolworth's and who her father was no one has been able to discover.'

'I want *revenge!*' said Davis in a hoarse whisper.

'Can't hear you.'

'Turn off that row then. I hates classical!'

'What an oik you are! It's *Africa* by Saint-Saëns.'

'I hate Africans! Nigger-nig-nogs! And I hate Muslims!'

With eyes blissfully shut, Max manhandled the air as the piece came to its close. 'Let's have it on again, dear moron, just for you and the niggy-noggies and the muzzy-wuzzies!'

'Revenge I say! And what are we going to do in that direction, may I ask?'

Max munched ruminatively on a sandwich. 'Have a look at this,' and he pulled a piece of paper from his breast pocket. It was the bill from the Monkshood Nursing Home.

'So what,' said Davis.

'I'm not going to tell you where I found this bill, not yet anyway. But the name, John Smith, does it mean anything to you?'

'John Smith, John Smith . . . ' Davis felt queer inside, as though the name should mean something to her, but she nodded in the negative.

'He's a vegetable. At that nursing home.'

'John Smith . . . Monkshood . . . '

'Ever been there?'

She pondered. 'Yes, I think I have. When I was little. Can't remember why. It's a big place. Lots of white.'

'It might've changed since you were small. Maybe it has lots of black now. I'll pay it a visit. When I have the time. When my work allows.'

'Your work? Don't make me laugh!'

'They want me to be in this new musical at Puckermouth.'

'Are you saying you won't have time to do the dirty?'

'Listen – I invited you up here didn't I? Because I thought you might be able to help me get to the bottom of this little Monks-hood mystery, in return for which I may be able to help you get even with those who have done you harm.'

'We in cahoots then?' she asked.

Suddenly airy and blasé, he twirled. 'Let's go for it, woman!'

Davis hadn't been called a woman in forty years and she war-whooped 'Whisky!'

'Have a wine gum.'

'I tell you what. There's letters. And that farmer's got em. In that box,' said Davis.

'What letters? What box? Which farmer?'

'Except that he don't know he's got em. That Dickon of course.'

'Ugh, the martyr, I hate him! It's the heart-rending expression he always puts on which makes me want to puke. Are these letters relevant?'

'They came from that old tree they burned up on Guy Fawkes. And when letters comes out of old trees, they're *always* relevant. It's no business of is to ave em, I'll get em back if it's the last thing I do!'

'Back, did I hear back? Do you mean they belong to you?'

Davis tapped the side of Max's nose and said pregnantly 'Uneasy frowns the head that wears a lie. I could say more – as how someone still pays Mumsy a visit every year – as how I over-heard him sayin things to her in the parlour one day – as how Mumsy's been mumbling a lot more of late and I been putting two and two together – yes, the box – that Meg's been blabbing and I know how to put two and two together – I bin putting two and two together round here all my life – and not so much as a candlestick in return! Yes, I could say more – a lot more – but I won't! . . . *Not yet anyway.*' Max snorted and Davis went sly. 'Enough is enough for now,' she said.

'Obstinate hag. Have it your own way. But here's how we'll play it for starters. I'll check the Monkshood Nursing Home, you check Lower Farm. Call on that Meg thing. Find out all you can. And cop that box of letters.'

'I hate em at Lower Farm!'

'I should hope so too! Why do you hate them particularly?' Max lifted another sandwich.

'Because . . . ' Actually there was no obvious reason which came to her mind, but from the depths of her soul a small grenade rose into consciousness and with a wild toss of the hatted head she burst out 'For the hell of it! Irrational violence!'

'I agree they're an appalling couple but kindly take your irrational violence elsewhere. We have to be clever and I have to get on with my day.'

After she'd gone, Max felt a fundamental thrill. He eased himself into the water-closet and sat down and began to sing *You're an utter bruiser* ... He'd certainly get the part, oh yes, of course he would. He would be Lear. He was made for Lear. He had Learitude to his fingertips! And when he'd got to the bottom of this funny business with the nursing home and Heaven Park and the letters and her Mumsy and all the rest of it, why – he'd tell Joyce! She'd be very happy to hear what he had to say and wouldn't consider him too old at all except in the sense of being clever, experienced, wise, and he would very likely become her favourite and would probably end up ruling quite a large portion of the world. Fulfilment at last. Fulfilment. A doddle really – when you knew how. After a degree of premonitory trembling, Max embarked on the evacuation of an absolute whopper almost two feet long. Everything was going so well. He was happy. To hate yet not be depressed, to hate and to act – that is life!

65.

Glory, who'd crashed for the night on a sofa somewhere within the labyrinth of Heaven Park, wandered towards the kitchen for a cup of tea, yawning and rubbing his eyes. Not enough sleep, which always made him feel raw and randy. Malcolm Gibbet was in there going through Cook's accounts and accordingly there was no evidence of Cook. Glory switched on a kettle. 'Where's JJ?'

'In a meeting with Alice,' said Malcolm. His ginger eyes remained firmly on the documents.

'Can I borrow a car?'

'No.'

'Go on.'

'Use your bicycle.'

Glory Boy meandered through the walled garden with its potting sheds and vegetable patches and climbing exotica. Of the

fourteen glasshouses, twelve were derelict with most of their panes shattered, the louvring apparatus rusted, and benches choked with nettles and bramble. Ben Thicknesse was trowelling in the end one.

'Got any weed?' Glory asked him.

'Run out. Ave to await the summer now.'

'Can I borrow your car, Ben?'

'Nope.'

Glory scuffed his way under a clocktower whose clock had no hands and into the outer stableyard. Sylvia saw him and came onto the gallery in a pink quilted house-coat. Pulling its lapels over her breasts in an uncharacteristic gesture of modesty, she leant on the railing and called down 'Looking for something, Glory?' One of her bare knees protruded between two iron palmettes.

'A car.'

As he walked through to the inner stableyard, she tracked him from above on clacking mules.

'That one,' he said, pointing to a dented little Ford. Though pimpled with rust, it was a cheerful yellow.

'You better ask JJ first,' she said.

'He's in a meeting with Alice.'

(This so-called meeting had been very brief and was now over. It had consisted of Alice saying 'So what's this terrible thing that's happened then?', and JJ saying 'I've lost a bill from the Monkshood Nursing Home – have you seen it?', and Alice saying 'No', and JJ saying 'Perhaps it's got mixed up with your papers', and Alice saying 'No, it hasn't. I know what's in my papers', and JJ saying 'I've looked everywhere', and Alice saying 'Why did you get a bill from a nursing home?', and JJ saying 'Please look again dammit!', and Alice giving him a funny look and saying 'Just ring them. They'll send another bill', and JJ saying 'That's not the point. I'm sorry, I've got to go now, I'm late for the train!').

Sylvia knew that Glory was JJ's favourite, and was uncertain of her tenure in the stables and since the car belonged to the estate she said 'Come up. I'll find the keys.'

Ten minutes later Glory was zipping down a green lane between flower-flecked hedges under a blue sky. He turned left at the abandoned marlpit, filled with a black and sinister treacle, and bowled on to Butterton. His destination was the car boot sale, held once a week in the playground of Butterton Junior School, where he hoped to purchase some recordable discs for his mini-player.

Helen Craddock was there for the first time, selling odds and sods: a lampshade, several paperbacks, cheap glassware, pairs of shoes, a board game. She'd rented a car for the day and probably wouldn't cover her costs but it was a valiant start. Next to her was Mrs Punch, the retired taxidermist's wife. She was an old hand at this sort of thing and had begun years ago with a collection of stuffed animals in glass cases arranged on a trestle table. Alas, her husband, a victim of palsy, was unable to supply further stock and so his wife had moved on to animals in other forms – china figures, cards, prints, etched glasses, ashtrays, brasses, tins. She did very well. One day Helen might do very well if she too could think of a gimmick.

In the far corner, a couple with matted hair presided over incomprehensible lumps of rag and bone. Behind them an infant, swaddled papoose-style, howled through the open door of a small van painted in psychedelic swirls. Glory nodded to the matted male and, when he was close enough to mumble, asked 'Got any weed?' The matted male disappeared round the back of the van while the female, sitting cross-legged in patterned hose, asked 'Wanna craft bag?' Glory politely pretended to survey various objects manufactured from re-cycled God-knows-what and noticed that among the rubbish there was a number of beautiful wooden-handled tools for sale, of large size, in good condition and obviously of quality. The male reappeared and slipped Glory a small polythene bag, in return for which Glory flourished a banknote which the female swiped at once with nimble marsupial hands and put away in the pouch at her waist.

Glory picked up a jam jar which gave every indication of having been painted by a distressed schizophrenic. 'What's this for?'

'For putting things in,' said the male.

'Herald, for fuck's sake, it's a nightlight,' said the female and turned to Glory. 'He's got no salesmanship. Could you ask your

Lord friend if we can stay on in the paddock? We don't know where else to go and that Gibbet cunt's been telling us to get off.'

Glory didn't respond directly but asked 'Where did you get them tools?'

'What tools?' huffed the female.

'Them ones.'

'Around . . . ' answered the male shiftily.

'I know where you bloody got em. Ben's big toolshed. I could shop you. So I think you better piss off out of JJ's paddock, don't you?'

Glory rotated casually from the waist, shading his eyes. He still couldn't spot what he was really looking for. He saw Selwyn Blagdon arrive, go to Helen Craddock's stall and buy a lampshade. Turning back to the Upanishads he added 'JJ don't appreciate thieving. So skedaddle. Vamoose. Pronto. Have I made myself clear?'

Leaf looked anxiously at Herald who looked anxiously at a far horizon.

A metallic turquoise car was parked obliquely to all the others. 'You're quiet today,' said Glory, shambling up.

'They told us to shut it off,' said the seller who was one of the Tewkesbury Boys. Normally pop music thudded from his car speakers, hitting passers-by in the chest, but the organisers had had complaints.

'You got any old recordable mini-discs?'

'Five for a quid.'

Glory purchased a quid's worth.

When he returned to the stables Sylvia said 'Malcolm's been giving me hell about letting you have the car keys.'

'I'll speak to JJ.'

'JJ's gone to London.'

'I thought he was having a meeting.'

'He was. Then he shot off to London.'

'That's not like him.'

'Perhaps he wanted a change. I often want a change. Don't you ever want a change?'

'He asn't been to London in years. How long's he gone for?'

'Haven't the foggiest.'

'Mean bastard. He could've taken me. He knows I've never been to London.'

'He'd be frightened you'd get charmed by the bright lights and he'd lose you.'

'I fancy Mayfair.'

'Fancy a cuppa?'

Glory ran up the steps to the flat. She poured him a glass of wine instead and closed a series of books on the table. 'I'm studying the Renaissance with the Open University,' she said. 'You see those round balls on the gate piers at the entrance to the yard – they're descended from human heads which once upon a time would've been stuck up there in triumph. That's one of the things I've learnt.'

'Really? I thought balls meant summint else.'

A shaft of sunlight from a Diocletian window fell onto an amount of bosom not covered by Sylvia's pink quilting.

'They've done this up nice,' said Glory, looking around.

'They're going to do a few more on the other side. Malcolm's idea. They're supposed to be holiday lets. I think Malcolm wants me out before the summer.' As she ran her hands through her red hair, the housecoat opened up seductively.

Glory swallowed half the wine and stretched his legs out from the chair and crossed his ankles, pushing up the dome of his buttoned fly. 'The Upanishads was at the car boot. Trying to flog a loada shit. Fancy a joint?'

She'd had him once before, ages ago, after the Trossachs' house-warming. Glory lit up and drew in the first puffs. As she leaned forward to take her turn, the housecoat gaped some more and Glory's eyes sparkled through the smoke. He said 'Them's a couple of big hitters. I'd forgotten.' Sylvia inhaled. Almost at once the thick coil of lust which encircled her tightened and she began to tremble, devouring him with her eyes and with quivers of her upper lip. Wordlessly she pulled the young man into the back bedroom. After which it happened very quickly. The violence of her nails in his back drew blood. She was soon on top, jacking herself wildly, tits thrashing the air, until the bed gave way at the climax and crashed to the floor. He fled without coming. But she'd come. My God, yes.

66.

Jocasta and Fortinbras returned from hospital, calmed and kitted out with Ventalin inhalers. The abrupt arrival of asthma in the Dashmans' lives had scrambled their priorities and Larissa decided to hold a séance at The Crag and call upon the spirit of Madame Blavatsky for advice. Alice was invited. She and Larissa had been on relatively easy terms ever since Alice had asked for her help with the Russian festival. Crystal invited herself to the séance. The girl had been turning up at The Crag in an unstructured way, even when Ward was in London. Larissa might enter a room and Crystal would be sitting there, reading a magazine or simply staring out of the window. As a Russian, Larissa was not surprised by eccentric intimacies, and as a woman she understood that pregnancy can do odd things to one's behaviour. Nonetheless Crystal was beginning to grate. Princess Lark, who cleaned at The Crag two days a week, was also to attend. Getting a man involved was not so easy. Little Lark finally agreed, then had to cover for Lois at The Zodiac instead. So Larissa would press-gang Bunjie as the filler. Bunjie would be reluctant – he'd had a nasty experience involving his mother at a previous séance – but that couldn't be helped. Asthma was no laughing matter.

On the appointed March evening, the four women assembled in the drawing-room of The Crag. It had been upholstered in terracotta silk with green polka dots. Soprano songs by Stanchinsky twittered glacially on the record player in the background as Bunjie entered, carrying celery, cheese and crackers on a tray.

'Nasty lump on the head, Bunjie.'

He'd been hit above the eye by a flying Ventalin inhaler but all he said as he set down the tray was 'If you're peckish afterwards'.

Princess Lark looked ill. She was a capable cleaner and not a very shy woman but sitting down in the drawing-room was something she'd never done before. The atmosphere and a glass of wine undermined her – not to mention the polka dots. 'Are you sure we're doing the right thing?' asked Princess. 'I'm all at sea.'

'Do you often go into magic states?' enquired Larissa.

'It's not easy with the kids.'

'And, Alice, this is a first one for you too?'

'Yup.'

'Drink up. It assists relaxing of consciousness.'

'Can I have a refill?' asked Crystal.

'No. This isn't a booze.' Larissa escorted them through to the morning-room, lately done up in dove grey velvet. It still smelt strongly of the glue used to fix the material to the walls. There was a circular table in the middle over which Bunjie threw a green baize cloth. They seated themselves portentously.

'Bunjie, you must stand in for Little Lark. Four peoples is too stable, too rectilinear, nothing happens.'

'Couldn't Jazz do it? '

'She's a woman. The spirits don't like solid oestrogen – and neither do I.'

'But, Larissa, what if my mother contacts me again?'

'You must learn to survive your mother, Bunjie. Put Hendrix out please. We don't want canine influence. *Anything* could strike from the other side.'

Crystal was bored already and vaguely headachy. Perhaps it was that ghastly glue smell. Alice had a tremor in her neck and hoped that the séance would convince her that séances were hooey, that life was life and death was death, it was as simple as that, and that one need be afraid of nothing. Larissa stroked a triangular amulet at her breast, worn for the occasion.

'Bunjie, the lights off please.'

All were turned off except a dull fringed lamp in the corner.

'Breathe easily, friends. Give the breath attention, but not interference.' Larissa sounded different suddenly.

They attempted to do as they were instructed.

A minute drained away.

Silence.

Not even a clock ticked.

More silence.

Alice realised that a heaviness suffused her limbs and wondered if she'd eaten something funny earlier.

'Hands on table,' intoned Larissa.

They obeyed.

'Thumbs together and little fingers touching those of your neighbours.'

'My little fingers aren't long enough,' worried Princess Lark who was feeling distinctly queasy.

'Move hands further to the centre and your fingers will get longer.'

Princess did this and the miracle occurred.

'Ring of energy. Breathe naturally. With attention but not – '

'Not with interference,' chimed Crystal.

Larissa gave her a tart smile. Crystal squared her shoulders and tried to breathe naturally.

Alice was feeling heavier and heavier. Or was it lighter and lighter?

Time became ductile. The taut awareness of time's passing now curved into a rounder sense of simultaneity. Time circled.

But Alice vaguely wanted to pee.

It was a distant irritation as when one needs to pee during sleep at four a.m. and one stirs beneath the sheets but cannot move out of bed.

'Any chance of a window open?' Alice whispered.

'No chance. Please concentrate. But without trying to concentrate.'

At last the walls of self-consciousness and interiorisation which customarily divide soul from soul began to dissolve. The paradoxical sensation of collective-force combined with effortlessness-of-being was felt by all as their breathing synchronised. A circle of personalities was transformed into a psychic radar bowl.

But nothing happened.

Silence.

And breathing.

And nothing happening.

One breath went out of synchronicity. It was Larissa's. 'Madame Blavatsky . . . are . . . you . . . there?'

Silence.

Only silence.

And breathing.

Which didn't mean that Madame Blavatsky wasn't there.

In fact the feeling that something was there – but staying mute – began to dawn upon them all. It was sensed as an outer pressure against the bubble of silence which enclosed them.

'Madame Blavatsky . . . '

'Are you there?' asked Crystal.

'Shut up.'

'It slipped out.'

'You'll upset them.'

Another silence went on for ages, five minutes perhaps, or maybe seven and a half since timelessness was a factor. Crystal wondered whether pregnancy was a factor, whether the child inside her were part of the séance or not, and the effect this might have on its mental development. Tricky one. But too late now. She was getting interested.

Meanwhile Alice felt her heaviness tighten. Or was it her lightness? Anyway a tension now mounted in her by inexorable degrees. She saw polka dots dancing before her eyes.

Urination was no longer a factor.

All Alice's extremities prickled while a thick wave welled up from the stomach.

Was vomiting to be a factor?

Really the stink of glue was overpowering.

The last thing she registered were her eyes and ears bursting, whereupon everything stopped for her, but viewed by the others from outside, this was exactly when things started to happen. A deep vibration was flowing through the room, accompanied by an ophidian hiss. The hair on the back of four necks became erect while Larissa noticed that the fifth neck – Alice's – had gone rigid at a curious angle. Moments later Alice's head began to jerk about in a manner which suggested it was not connected to her body in the normal way. The neck was at least twice its usual length and moving bonelessly while gibberish issued from the mouth. Mrs Lark raised a hand to her cheek in horror.

'Put that hand back at once!' commanded Larissa in a desperate undertone. 'It could be a matter of life and death!'

More rumbles from the beyond were heard. They flowed powerfully through the walls and into the room. Mrs Lark couldn't repress a scream. And again the dreadful hiss followed. Alice's bobbing head jerked over to its right and stopped there. Her gibberish became comprehensible.

'Killed on the bend. Killed on the bend.'

'Is that Madame Blavatsky?'

'No it bloody isn't.'

'Sorry. What bend?'

'Carrying paint bend.'

'Oooooo,' purred Mrs Lark.

Crystal said 'You thinking what I'm thinking?'

'That'll be Jack Thicknesse,' said Mrs Lark.

'Ben Thicknesse's brother was killed at sixteen,' said Crystal.

'On a motorbike carrying paint,' said Mrs Lark.

'Under his jacket,' said Crystal.

'A car came round the bend.'

'Knocked the tin into his chest.'

'Stopped his heart.'

'Killed instantly.'

'Who was driving the car?' Larissa asked Mrs Lark.

'They never discovered,' said Crystal.

'Let's ask him . . . Jack – is that you?'

Alice's head snapped up and began to talk. 'That's me!'

'How are you?'

'Fine. Apart from this tin of paint stuck in my chest.'

'Jack – tell us – who was driving the car that killed you?'

More rumbles below and above and about.

'I'm not supposed to say.'

'Why not?'

'Coz I'll go to hell.'

'Are you in heaven then?'

'No. But I'm in the queue.'

'How long is the queue?'

'It's not that sort of queue. Actually I shouldn't be speaking
to you.'

'Why not?'

'Heaven doesn't approve.'

'Does hell approve?'

'I guess it does. But I don't want to go there.'

'Is it so bad?'

'It's hot.'

'You prefer cold?'

'No.'

'But the nearer you are to heaven the colder it gets.'

'Why that's true. Hell does sound more attractive, doesn't it.'

'So you might as well tell us who was driving the car.'

'All right. It was Gibbon Tuft.'

Mrs Lark and Crystal drooled at each other. So that was it. Tuft. Did a bunk soon after. Incredible. But of course. Everything fitted.

'Wow,' said Crystal.

'Jack, is that all you want to say?' asked Larissa.

'No.'

'You want to say more?'

'Yes.'

Abominable hisses and bumps and rumbles.

The voice started up again as though Alice were a teleprinter.

'Beware.'

They waited, the breath clamped inside their chests.

Larissa, hoarse with excitement, croaked 'Beware what?'

'Beware.'

'Jack, that's not enough.'

'Beware.'

'He's got stuck. Let's just wait,' advised Larissa.

After about half a very pregnant minute the voice burst out again 'Beware the con . . . '

'Yes, yes,' urged Larissa. Her satin armpits were stained with sweat. It had never been this good.

'Beware the contents of . . . '

'What, what?'

'Of the fireproof box! Is Gibbon Tuft still alive?' enquired Jack.

'Probably,' said Crystal.

'Give him my love. To know all is to forgive all.'

'What fireproof box?'

'Don't be silly, there's only one fireproof box. I've got to go now. They're calling me forward.'

'What fireproof box for Christ's sake? You can't go!'

'You mustn't go!'

'Can't go? Mustn't go? Who are you to dictate these things?' And he was gone.

They stared at each other.

'Does anyone know what he meant?'

'What fireproof box?'

Alice slumped. Her chin glistened with saliva. Larissa said that was probably all, that they should wait quietly while Alice came round, and afterwards they could all enjoy the light supper which Bunjie had kindly brought in and did anyone have a preference for red or white wine?

Princess Lark stared at Crystal. 'So it was him.'

'Poor Ben's only relation.'

'Tuft driving the car.'

'Can we believe it?'

'Big always said it was Tuft.'

'How would he know anything about it?'

'Big knows a lot does Big.'

'I want to do more séances,' said Crystal. 'This is simply mind-blowing. And what fire-proof box?'

'Did you hear what I asked – red or white wine?'

Crystal was on the point of answering 'Any old plonk' when Alice's psychic teleprinter started up again. The movement was more violent than before and accompanied by a reptilian flicking of the tongue. Rumbles shook the room. It really was terrifying.

'What've we started! We shouldn't've interfered!' wailed Princess.

'Shouldn't we do something?' beseeched Crystal.

'Hands together immediately!' commanded Larissa.

When they reformed the circle, Alice's amentia quickened and multiple voices capered hectically from her. Out of the overall pandemonium the following might have been discerned.

'Is that you, Larissa, sweetheart? Madame Blavatsky here. Ouch!'

'Out of my way!'

'How can the English bear their loss of greatness?'

'Bunjie, are you cleaning your teeth sufficiently?'

'That's Mum!'

'Get lost, you stupid cow! This is my house!'

'Bunjie, are you staying out of the sun? You know very well that in India a pale skin is prized above everything.'

'I'm not in India, Mum!'

'Bump! Ouch!'

'Larissa sweetheart, there's an awful fracas going on here. I'm off for a spot of astroplaning.'

'Oh Madame Blavatsky, please don't go – I need to ask you about my babies' asthma.'

'Sorry, speak to you later, darling.'

Larissa moaned with frustration as Madame Blavatsky withdrew to an even higher plane.

'Bunjie, your underbockers, are you changing them repeatedly?'

'I won't tell you again,woman! This my house!'

This was the voice among the many which had most authority and, after various lateral squitters from Bunjie's mother and the rest, and much flicking of Alice's tongue, it was the voice which prevailed. It now transpired that the visitation from Jack Thicknesse was merely an overture. The main act was about to begin.

It was a deep manly voice and that it emerged from little Miss Alice was grisly indeed. The voice made a proclamation.

'Attend, all ye. I am the Spirit of Old England.'

Which is a very big thing to be but it turned out to have a more specific identity as well.

'I am Sir Timothy Craddock of The Crag. I have succeeded the previous Crag ghost who was getting past it. I by contrast am not getting past it in the least and intend to be very hands-on. The first thing I want to say is this. What a frightful shower you are. What a bunch of louts and blighters. These days people can do nothing properly. Everything is a mess. So attend to this. You will all get what you deserve. Some will get what they don't deserve. You will all get what you don't deserve. That's a riddle for you little Englanders. And here, by way of codicil, is a second riddle. The son of the princess, who is a fine lad, will witness something *extremely horrible*. Something horrible and *wet*.'

Mrs Lark squawked. How deeply she hoped it was all over with Sir Timothy and his bottom-pinching while she was doing a spot of cleaning at The Crag. He'd never left her alone and he, such a fine figure of a man, it wasn't fair, of course she'd strayed, just a little, just a little. But a little was enough. A little had consequences. But she thought it was all over. At his funeral she had

202 A History of Facelifting

experienced what she hadn't experienced since her girlhood: self-possession. He had gone to the hereafter and she had her self-possession back on this earth. Not that he would have said anything. Oh no. He would no more want a scandal than she would. The only difference would be he would be ashamed of *her*, whereas she would be ashamed of *it*. And now here he was – back – messing with her head. It wasn't fair. It just wasn't fair.

'What do you mean, O Spirit of Old England?' Larissa pursued.

'To which riddle do you refer, madam?'

'To both.'

'I think you mean to either. To both implies that the answer is the same in either case which is not so. There are two riddles with two different answers.'

'The second one then,' quailed Mrs Lark.

'No, first one first,' said Larissa.

'I feel sorry for you, madam. You should never have bought my house!'

'Don't threaten me, you nasty old man. We paid good money for your house.'

A loud rumble was heard, followed by several short bumps.

'And the second riddle?' pursued Princess Lark. 'Which of my boys are you talking about? Little or Colin?'

'The elder boy, dear. *My* boy. Our boy. But in another sense – the younger boy too. Big's boy. At least I assume Colin is Big's boy – one can't be sure of anything these days. That's all I'm going to say about that, so I wish you plenty of profitably sleepless nights working it out. I heard what you said to yourself about self-possession. My dear, what ever happened to love? Can people only think about self-possession these days? Believe me, from where I am right now, self-possession is the biggest joke going. Ah, I see I'm being called forward, but since I am the Spirit of Old England I should like to add four brief points before I go. Far be it from me to lecture anybody but do remember that *one* Democracy exists in time as well as in space, and *two* Young men need somewhere to put their excitement, and *three* The English instinct for fair play can degenerate into the decadence of decency in which we get shafted by the unscrupulous, and *four* A society which has lost the will to protect itself is doomed! Goodbye.'

'Wait, wait! Is there anything for me?' asked Crystal.

Silence.

'O Spirit of Old England, is there anything for Lady Crystal Popjoy?' ventured Larissa.

The Voice replied 'Hasn't that girl done enough harm as it is?'

'Spirits my arse! Alice, why are you being so rotten? Just because I didn't turn up for your bloody demo.' Crystal left the room in tears and soon her car was heard romping down the drive in phases (she was in the wrong gear).

Her departure broke the spell, Alice's head lolled to a stop, and the imp-laden atmosphere dissolved away . . . When after a few minutes Alice rallied, she asked 'How much longer do we have to wait?'

'It's all over.'

'Over? What do you mean over? It hasn't even started. Nothing's happened yet.'

'Oh yes it has. The spirits spoke through you, Alice. You were –' Larissa raked the air for the word – 'you were vouchsafed. It's all over for tonight. You were fantastic. You are gifted. Come to the drawing-room. Have some celery.'

'What did Tim mean my lovely Little will witness something horrible and wet?'

'Oh, I don't think he meant you, Mrs Lark. He will have meant a real princess.'

But Mrs Lark, pale and distraught, knew better.

Bunjie was subdued as he tinkered with the buffet but the women were in lively mood and disagreed heartily over interpretation. Alice wanted to know *everything* that had happened and responded with 'Amazing' or 'Unbelievable' or 'Are you having me on?'. It was as though she were hearing about a strange party in another house. Somehow none of it touched her emotionally. But as Alice drove up to her own front door a curious reaction set in. Snails' trails, climbing the front wall beside the door, glistened in the headlights and on seeing them she suddenly felt drained, and a large sadness like a moon rose above the empty terrace of her heart.

Meanwhile back in the vacated morning-room of The Crag, where only hours ago strange thoughts had precipitated into the external world, the dragon radiator began once again to rumble and bump, rump and bumble. It made extraordinary noises – like complaints from another world. Bunjie had forgotten to bleed it.

67.

JJ had a very important meeting with the Superior in Whitehall and beforehand, to centre himself, he swept from one de luxe emporium to another, annexing bags labelled 'Smythson', 'Charbonnel et Walker', 'Asprey', 'Clatworthy Jones', so that when at last he made his entrance into the Superior's office it resembled a camel-train halting in an oasis. The Superior surveyed the shopping among which his visitor was encamped and said in a drawling sneer 'So you want public assistance'.

'That's right.'

'To buy more chocolates?'

'The house is a national treasure but the Lottery Fund turned me down.'

The Superior pressed a button and a screen lit up. He vocalised 'Marquess of Heavenshire' and the screen blossomed into a mass of personal detail.

'They turned you down because you run it as a private home, no disabled access, that sort of thing.' The Superior tapped a number of keys. 'I see. Here we are. It looks as if you're loaded.'

'Well, I'm not. Keep reading. You'll discover I'm not.'

'Can you imagine the outcry if we subsidised you?'

'In that case I'm going to stop subsidising *you*. I'd like the Victoria & Albert Museum to return the articles they've borrowed.'

The Superior spoke again to the computer, tapped a couple of keys, and a further mass of detail spilled onto the screen.

'I don't think I can do that. The Popjoy Collection is a real crowd-puller. That Pan by Praxiteles – '

'I repeatedly tell them it's only Roman. And it's Silvanus.'

'Even so.'

'Grandpa lent these objects because he thought Granny would do something awful like gamble them away.'

'Very sensible of him.'

'Then why don't you buy them for the nation?'

'We don't have to because we have them for another . . . ' – he tapped a computer key – 'for another ninety-eight years.'

'I'll be dead by then.'

'So shall I. Console yourself with the thought that at least they'll remain in England.'

'Let me have back one of the Michelangelo bathroom sketches. A *little* one. Please. It'll buy me time to think.'

The Superior tapped again. 'Those sketches were in lieu of capital transfer tax. They are no longer yours.'

'For God's sake . . . '

'Look, why don't you give Heaven Park to the National Trust and go and live in the stables?'

'They won't accept it unless the estate is fully financed.'

'Do you have any London property?'

'No.'

Yesterday JJ had visited the site of his family's town house and found a huge hole in the ground. Not that it was the first hole there. After the house's sale and demolition, several generations ago, a jazzy office block had gone up. This in turn had been replaced by another office block, less jazzy, which had lately also been demolished and was soon to be replaced by an hotel. On the opposite side of the square had once stood Crimsoncourt House, where the famous D'Orsay hat first made its appearance. This too had been demolished many years ago. The site was currently occupied by a multi-storey car-park in cleverly wafered concrete. And a little further west, once upon a time, one would have come to Moon House where in her day Molly Moon entertained the rulers of the world in Robert Adam's 'four seasons' enfilade over-looking the Green Park. The site was now a telephone-exchange.

Why had every English nobleman sold his London palace to the developers for demolition, abandoned the life of the town, and retired to the country? This was JJ's thought at the site of the family hole in the ground and it was at once followed by another – why have I retired to the country? Is it because no one takes a lord seriously in the town? Because we have no power here? But I don't want to be taken seriously. I don't want power. Oh, well, yes, perhaps I do because seriousness and power are money, and money is why I came to town in the first place.

JJ dipped into one of his fancy bags and fished out a blue and silver box of chocolate-covered almonds. He peeled back the inte-rior flaps of silver foil and made offering to the Superior. 'Sir, you force me to sell my farmland to the developers of this new town.'

'We are not forcing you to do anything.'

'You allow me no alternative. It amounts to the same thing. You do realise that Heavenshire is the last bit of England which looks like England is supposed to look?'

'Sentimental twaddle. It's rather backward and a bit of a wilderness. I am sure you'll find a way to benefit from a large population on your doorstep. You know, Marquess, the sooner these shaggy spots are streamlined the better it is for everyone. See this as an opportunity.'

'But – '

'Marquess, please. You force *me* to be blunt. If, as you imply, everyone else's countryside has been wrecked, why shouldn't yours be? Unspoilt countryside is elitist!'

JJ sighed. 'Do you have Tony Tucker's private phone number by any chance?', but the Superior said he had no such thing.

On the way back to Brown's Hotel JJ called in at Waddington's and asked about selling the Twombly. At the hotel reception he collected a message, ordered an omelette Arnold Bennett in his room, and wondered how to kill the evening. Sitting morosely on a corner of the bed he opened the message which was from Lord and Lady Moon who'd heard from Sidney that JJ was in town and were inviting him to dinner at their flat in Observatory Gardens. No, he wouldn't accept their invitation. It wasn't sexy. In fact it was the opposite of sexy. He opened the *Evening Standard* and searched for the programme at Covent Garden – *L'Eremitaggio di Liverpool*. Nellie Gough was singing. He'd seen it in his youth. He'd see it again. Phoned up. Sold out.

'I'm the Marquess of Heavenshire – does that help?'

'Fraid not, love.'

After a bath he donned his new silk dressing-gown from Liberty and by the time the omelette was wheeled in, a rosebud nodding beside it in a silver flute, he'd decided simply to walk round town following his nose.

The night was cold and clear. A quarter-moon hung stylishly over Piccadilly Circus but the electrical illuminations killed off all stars. At first he was uneasy but, contrary to the cliché of the alienating metropolis, he found himself slipping into the urban fabric as into an overcoat. But nobody looked at him. Either they were looking elsewhere or talking to companions. Many were

hunched into their mobile phones outside cafés and pubs, spinning round on one foot as they talked, or with heads upraised
apparently talking to themselves. Only the beggars looked at him.
He gave one of them a £10 note and the beggar said 'Gawd bless
you, guv'.

In the Haymarket he noticed a tickle in his throat and began to
cough. One thing he'd certainly do when he returned to Heaven
would be to read his copy of John Evelyn's *Fumifugium*, the study
of London's air pollution published in 1661. It had been waiting
in JJ's bedside pile for twenty-three years, signed by the author.
He called into the cinema. An American film. After fifteen
minutes of men yelling 'Motherfucker!' at each other he walked
out, along a bit, and into the Sport's Café at the base of an elegant
steel and glass building. The adonis behind the bar said in an
Australian accent 'Hi, mate. What canna git ya?'

'Advise me,' replied JJ.

'Long Island Ice Tea.'

'Fine.'

It contained a shot of every white spirit in stock, topped up
with Pepsi-Cola, and JJ was soon jellied. 'Isn't White's somewhere near here, Jeff?' He'd never visited his father's club. The
barman, whose name was on a brooch pinned to his shirt, sucked
in his cheeks and said he did not know, so JJ finished the drink,
left a £5 note, and buttonholed a policeman outside. 'I know it's
somewhere round here – everybody knows where White's is – but
that Long er thing contained aaand I've not been in London for
absolutely ages and – '

'If you take your hand off my bottom, sir, I think I can put you
on the right track.'

JJ meandered some more. A group of black boys divided silkily
and passed either side of him. Were these the famous muggers and
druggers and shooters? My word, what luck, he'd got off scot free.
They'd gone their merry way. He thought the main reason negroes
were frightening at night was because you couldn't read their
expressions in the dark the way you could those of white people.
Their faces merged with the night. In daylight too their subtlety
of facial expression was not so easily visible which must explain
why their signalling was often exaggerated compared to whites.

He'd never fancied Justice Royal, not even secretly. But he longed to have a black boy now. He hadn't had one for donkey's years.

At White's he was refused admission. JJ explained his status but the porter said that not only was he not a member but also that he was improperly dressed and no, he didn't remember his father personally, though he'd heard about him from the previous porter, what had he heard, oh that he would regularly order the finest claret in the club and squirt soda into it for example and that he usually attracted attention to himself by wearing a brown suit and that he once won a Spanish forest at cards and really, sir, I must ask you to leave, you're blocking the entrance, at which JJ started to make a scene, declaring loudly that anyway he had no intention of getting stuck in this miserable shithole full of fascist farts, and what he was really looking for was a gay club, a fun spot with *boys boys boys*, d'you hear, whereupon the porter called out the under-porter who took the marquess aside, explaining with the candour of youth that there were many such places in the capital and could he be more specific in his requirement, to which JJ responded with maudlin thanks and the observation that there had to be sex clubs in cities because sex was the only way city folk could keep in touch with nature and that the last time he was in town he'd chanced upon a very helpful establishment called the Pink Swastika and where do the gorgeous black boys go? JJ stopped talking. He was feeling woozy and was about to dissolve into tears.

The under-porter put a kind hand on the fat man's arm and called out a number on his voice-activated mobile phone and eventually reached a bureau of some sort where he was informed that 'The Pink Swastika was closed down before any of us was born' but the under-porter said not to worry because there was a jolly place not far away, just off Regent Street, called Size Queens à Go Go, and it was in that direction that JJ dragged his unhappy bulk.

68.

Justice was desolate, his only child dead. But in that terrain of dust and flint, a few shoots quickened at last. For example, yes, he had begun to talk again. Mrs Bladder-Williams had bumped into him in the street and offered her services as a babysitter. In the shock of that sudden offer he had blurted 'Thank you for the consideration'. Daisy Lark next door also offered babysitting services over the back fence one afternoon but Justice was reluctant to leave his grandson with anyone, until one evening, when he was obliged to pick up spare parts from a dealer on the coast near Puckermouth, he cooked up a stratagem. He deliberately booked baby sitting services from them both.

Mrs Bladder-Williams turned up first and he said to her 'Forgive me. I completely forgot. I promised Daisy could do it. But would you like to come to Puckermouth with me instead? After my business, we could have a drink on the front.'

She'd never been publicly entertained by a black man. Her heartbeat quickened and with the instinct of her kind to extirpate any budding emotion, she said 'Oh don't bother Daisy. I'm just as happy here.'

What should he say next? It was slipping away, slipping away. How to turn it round? His brain had emptied entirely. His tongue was tied. He should never have gone out on that limb. He felt like a complete idiot. The doorbell rang. He answered it. When Daisy came into the room she said with surprise 'Oh, Mrs B-W!' but being a warm girl she went across to the cot and said 'I've been *so looking forward* to this. Hoozalittledarlingbabyden?' and beamed at all three with her saucy buck teeth and shining eyes.

Mrs Bladder-Williams was extremely surprised to hear herself say 'Well, in that case, Mr Royal, if it wouldn't be a problem for you, I think a touch of sea air would be wonderful.'

69.

His eyes cracked open.

Another one of those, he thought.

He always thought this on waking up in the morning, ever since his fortieth birthday. Another one of those. Several minutes passed while his mind, at the threshold of sentience, blancmanged between the impulses of indolence and guilt. On this day the latter won and he stretched his left hand towards the bell-pull which lay across the bedside table. It would ring in the butler's pantry where Sidney, engrossed in the *Daily Bark*, would irritably crunch the pages together and put on the kettle for his lordship's tea. On this occasion however, JJ's hand wandered fruitlessly about. The bell-pull eluded him. It wasn't there. And the bedside table likewise.

In his hut on the abandoned railway cutting, also without success, Glory attempted to record something onto one of those recordable mini-discs he'd bought at the car boot sale. It wouldn't work. 'Don't say the blasted thing's broken.' He bicycled over to Heaven Park and headed for the music machine in the cosy and saw JJ groggy on the sofa in a big pierrot costume with pompoms down the front. His lordship's thick lips were smeared with pink and so was his nose and chin.

'You all right?'

'Where's the bed?' asked JJ.

'Upstairs.'

'Come ere, beautiful . . . '

'Why are you dressed like that?'

JJ slowly looked down at himself and buzzed his tongue. 'It's coming back to me . . . Am I in the cosy?'

'Sip this.'

'Party in London . . . ' JJ took the glass of watered whisky.

'Whose?'

'Not *that* sort of party. What day is it?'

'I dunno, but it's six in the evening.'

'Oh . . . . . . ' JJ bent his head, squeezing out surplus chins. 'Ouch. There is in empty kisses some delight. Theocritus said that.'

'Good party?'

'Don't ask me to analyse it . . . '

'I'll come wiv you next time.'

JJ pulled a face.

'Can I use the music machine?'

'Certainly not. My head's killing me.'

So Glory bicycled over to Daisy's where no one was at home, but she saw him through Justice's window and rapped vigorously on the pane. 'I'm babysitting,' she said at the door. 'Wipe your feet.'

'Has Justice got a music machine? I want to record the Paedophilia concert. It's on in a minute.'

From his bag he took one of the used recordables but as he
pressed various buttons in exploring the controls of Justice's
music machine, a voice began to talk through the speakers.

'Who's that?' asked Daisy.

'Search me. It's what's already on the disc.'

'Bubble bubble bubble,' said Daisy to Baby John who returned
the compliment.

'We could make one of them,' winked Glory.

'I want a place of my own first. With nice things in it. You're
only interested in the making part, not what happens afterwards.
You're not listening to me.'

'Hang on. Hark at this geezer.'

The voice had distortion on it but the words could be made out
. . . *so we could bomb targets in the Midlands and the Home Counties
after sabotaging the power stations in the North. Ask Joyce about . . .*
The distortion became too great and the words were lost.

'Horrible noise,' frowned Daisy.

Glory zapped it forward. More words in crackle and haze, very
unclear, but they sounded interesting . . . *another good target
would be the Ministry of Rural Affairs at Canary Wharf. That ministry has done more than any other to destroy the national ecology and
it would be a symbolic as well as a . . . zzzzzzzxxxxrghhhhjjjjkkkl-
lzzzz . . .* He'd have a proper listen another time. Upon checking the other recordables, Glory discovered they had only crap
music on them and he used one to record the Paedophilia concert
while having a good session with Daisy.

70.

Yes, life is complicated. One thing just leads to another. There's
no stopping it.

71.

As slowly and methodically Meg prepared a soup, Dickon
watched her in depressed silence, drumming his fingers on the
black metal box. He didn't own the farm, he had no prospect of

children, and had lost all volition for anything which was not part of the automatic trudge. This metal box, for example. It had been brooding in the kitchen for months and still he hadn't bothered to find a way of opening it.

Meg did her best to put all her attention into the business of chopping up vegetables for broth, humming poignantly to herself. He hadn't even noticed the jonquils in the vase on the table. They were wild ones. She'd gone out earlier today and picked them where they grew under the far hedge. She'd gone out for the first time since last October and he hadn't noticed.

Dickon would soon have to go out himself, outside into the spring morning which scourged him by reminding him of his failure to flourish, and drive up and down, down and up the fields, head brimming with mental pus. A movement through the window caught his eye, alien activity beyond the orchard, and he was out of the door at once.

'Who the hell are you?'

'We're the Upanishads. Do you mind holding this a minute?' They were struggling to erect the poles of a tepee.

'You can't set up on my farm, sorry!'

'They said we could.'

'Who said?'

'That Malcolm bloke at Heaven Park.'

'He sent you down here?'

'Yeah.'

'If you don't clear off, I'll call the police.'

The papoose began to howl. It was the last straw. Dickon ran indoors and telephoned Malcolm and spoke to him in a hot rage, to which Malcolm coolly answered 'Your tenancy agreement reserves to us certain rights, including camping on any fallow field.'

Dickon slammed down the phone and rang Hoskins in Appleminster.

'Do you want the Upanishads done for trespass?'

'Of course.'

'But aren't you the *tenant*, Dickon?'

'So?'

'I'll have to ring the Heaven Park Estate Office. I'll call you back.'

Dickson tapped anxiously on the metal box, waiting for the return call which didn't come. Meg's mouth tightened more and more until she crashed the chopping knife onto the board and said 'I wish you'd get that bloody box out of the kitchen. It's been driving me mad all winter'.

Without speaking, Dickon picked up the box and went out of the back door.

When Hoskins called again, Dickon had gone riding and Meg answered it.

'Malcolm tells me there are camping rights, Meg,' said Hoskins.

'I don't know why Dickon's making such a fuss. I'd quite enjoy the company. They seemed quite nice. Is it this weekend that the clocks go back?'

Dickon hoped to calm himself on the skewbald but the animal picked up the bad vibes and the ride was a trial for both of them. On returning to the stables Dickon lifted a steel mallet and struck the black box with unmitigated force. Blow succeeded blow and each time his shoulders would shudder and his fury reduce by a degree. Exhausted, he at last slumped beside it. The box was shattered and its contents exposed: a few bundles of letters. Boring letters. He'd occasionally fantasised that it might contain money but knew in his heart of hearts that it would be something boring and so it proved. It wasn't until half an hour afterwards that he sought to examine them.

There were three bundles belted with purple ribbon. He dipped in. They were to a woman – *My dearest dear* – and unsigned. The writing-paper was thick and creamy but bore no address. The matching envelopes bore no mark of any kind. They were passionate letters. The author's heart was brimful. *My own darling, if only our happiness were . . .* An illicit relationship clearly. *My sweetest girl.* Dickon did not feel curiosity, he felt envy. And with the painful conviction that his own life was barely being lived, and that he certainly didn't wish to read about those for whom that was not the case, he put the letters aside for another occasion.

72.

The asthma attacks of his children came to have a radical effect on Ward Dashman's world view and after due introspection he cancelled his planning applications for the wind farm, the supermarket and the multi-screen cinema, and wholeheartedly threw his media skills into the campaign against the City of Cognitive Neuroscience. This evening, for example, he was to chair a meeting of the local core group. Outdoors, banks of wood anemones were shutting up for the night, while indoors Bunjie was arranging chairs round the dining-table and placing jugs of water on mats down its centre.

The guest of honour was Oliver Knott who, since it had become publicised that he'd been appointed an adviser to the Government on the new town, was construed as being the enemy and had agreed to subject himself to their questions. He arrived a little after eight p.m.

Ward opened the proceedings at an oblique angle: 'Detective Hoskins tells me that the Superior will drop his action against the Puck Valley Three if Mrs Bladder-Williams drops her action against him and she has most generously agreed to do this.'

There was applause which Mrs B-W acknowledged with dignity.

Dickon said 'As a gesture of appreciation, we have asked Tanners to deliver a case of pink champagne to Mrs Bladder-Williams next week'.

Further applause.

'Now,' said Ward, 'I think it will be useful to address some of the underlying ideas which condition our response to this proposed new town so that we can understand more clearly what we are doing and why. We have therefore invited Mr Knott tonight to assist us. He is not a member of our campaign – '

'Nor of any other campaign,' Knott reminded them. 'My advice is impartial. And I'm only one of many people the Government is talking to.'

'I've downloaded some useful statistics from the net.' Ward handed out the pages. 'I also had a quick zip round the project website. Pretty frightening, Oliver.'

'Maybe. Maybe not. Let us begin at the beginning and proceed by the Socratic method,' said Knott.

The twins were sitting on the Bokhara rug playing five stones. Fortinbras got off his knees and charged Knott's chair. 'Pinch punch first day of the month and no returns.'

'It's after midday,' said Knott, exposing his rectangle of dental plastic, 'so the joke's on you'.

'No, the joke's on you, sicko,' brayed Jocasta, 'coz it's April Fool's Day'.

A tut-tut escaped Mrs Bladder-Williams and Dickon said 'Shouldn't they be in bed? I thought this was a serious meeting.' A Ventalin inhaler flew past his ear.

Ward's thoughts floated between his children and Crystal, until it became clear to him that what he most wanted to do was make a baby with Crystal. On the other hand he was coming to the idea that having more than two kids in the modern world was a polluting act. The conflict jolted him back into the room where Knott was saying 'Life is evolution, not repetition. Where there is no sense of increase, no sense of prosperity, there is no life.'

'Hang on, Oliver,' protested Ward. 'Most of the country are living like rats in an overcrowded cage. After a certain point, increase equals suffocation.'

Alice, who had downed her wine too quickly, said 'And repetition is vital to our sense of well-being. The rhythm of the seasons for example, or of our breathing.'

Ward added 'The great challenge of the epoch is to devise a new economic model based on the idea of fewer people'.

'Oh yes please!' warbled Mrs B-W with her hands clasped to her collar-bone. 'We'll never solve anything with such hordes! Is this new city really necessary?'

'Very little is *necessary*,' replied Knott. 'Necessity is not the point. Enterprise is.'

'All I ask is that we behave intelligently,' she sighed.

'What's intelligence, cleverclogs?' demanded Fortinbras.

Ward put on his manly voice. 'You two. Shut it. Or bed.'

Knott rubbed the back of his neck and replied 'But it's a reasonable question. Something as simple as a puddle of oil can demonstrate one of the most intriguing aspects of the universe, self-organisation, which is when patterns in space and time emerge spontaneously from randomness. But when oil produces its beautiful swirl, is it alive, does it have intelligence?'

'No,' said Dickon, 'because it has no choice in the matter'.

'Does that tree outside have a choice in the matter? Yet it is still alive. So we have demonstrated – provisionally – that being alive and being intelligent are not the same thing.'

Mrs Bladder-Williams had lost the point and her mind rippled. She was offended by the richness of colour in the room – two green malachite lamps at either end of a Vorticist sideboard were particularly hard to accept – but was seduced by the affluence of her surroundings into a belief that all dangers were remote, that there was enough time to put things right in the world, and when she checked back into the debate Knott was saying 'But science *does* change, Dickon. This is because it is empirical. It was until recently entirely mechanical. It said that the universe is only the sum of its parts.'

'Actually,' piped Alice, 'it said that the universe is *less* than the sum of its parts'.

'I don't think it said precisely that.'

'Oh, it did!' Alice was feeling speedy this evening.

'She's trying to be a brainbox,' said Jocasta to Jazz who said 'No, she isn't. She's entitled to her opinion.'

Knott pounced on this at once. 'But truth isn't an opinion! It's a – '

'What does Socratic mean?' interrupted Fortinbras.

Knott fought against rising indignation and breathlessness. Both his physician and his psychiatrist had advised him not to get worked up. Life is imperfect – try to accept it – they said. But his disposition and all his training had urged a rigour of mind, and he loathed the idea that the price of contentment is surrender to the slipshod. 'If I may continue – I have become something of a liberal in scientific circles over the last few years. This is less from conviction, more from necessity. In other words I have allowed empiricism to undermine my habits of thought and am now able to grasp that science, once wholly reductionist, is beginning to entertain the notion that the total becomes *more* than the sum of its parts.'

'Here here,' said Dickon.

Knott lost his grimace with relief and added 'But we approach this notion entirely by rational means. With computers in fact.'

'But doesn't common sense quite often tell us things which science realises only subsequently?' proposed Mrs Bladder-Williams.

Mrs Bladder-Williams was to his mind a paragon of tact and kindness who had never once, by even so much as a hint, made reference to his loss of control in The Zodiac and the assault on Justice Royal, which had of course been a matter of much gossip in the village, and now when she put her question Knott got a soft feeling, a yearning to enlighten her. 'Indeed. But the value of science is that it works by calculation, not by instinct. Instinct may provide the idea but the science is in the proof. You will agree, Mrs Bladder-Williams, that people often believe passionately in total fantasies.'

'Some do. I don't,' she replied.

'I'd put it another way,' said Alice. 'Science is one way of organising information and imagining is another. I had a very strange experience at a séance not long ago in this very house. I hadn't the faintest idea what was going on but one thing it did illustrate is that the imagination is a very powerful force in creation.'

'I think that was a case of collective glue poisoning, Alice,' said Ward. 'I can still smell those walls from here.'

'But that wouldn't alter her fundamental point, Mr Dashman. The imagination is of course vital in the creation of the human world,' said Knott, 'but not in the creation of the natural world, and even in the human world the imagination is only the first step. There is a great difference between imagining someone on the moon and actually putting someone there. One is internal fantasy, the other is external reality. The importance of science as our guide through external reality is that we can all share it.'

'I'd question that, Oliver,' said Dickon. 'I can't share in quantum mechanics for example. I can't understand it. I must take it on trust.'

'That's only because you don't have time to study everything. It's not in the nature of the subject. And you don't have to take its consequences on trust. You may not understand electricity but that doesn't prevent you from using it for practical purposes.'

'I'm beginning to feel,' said Pimm, polishing the thick lenses of his glasses with a little rag, 'that even the empirical method itself is largely imaginative because, you see, although you can imagine a man on the moon without putting him there, you can't put him there without imagining it first'. He looked up and without his spectacles his face had something of the large-eyed charm of a bush baby's.

'Good point,' said Knott. 'But the imagination doesn't operate in a vacuum. It feeds on what we know, and what we know depends on what our senses apprehend, and science is the most efficient way of extending our senses in space-time. Cognitive neuroscience, to which the new city will be devoted, is the most advanced application of this. People can only handle so much knowledge in the form of data. They say we are already suffering from information overload. But computers don't suffer in this way. Let me tell you about one of the projects involved. The DNA-bearing chromosomes within the nucleus of one single human cell can store the thirty volumes of the *Encyclopaedia Britannica* three or four times over. An ex- colleague of mine is developing a DNA computer. Does that not excite you in any way? Just think of the power of such a machine!'

'Can it paint?' asked Jocasta.

'No. It's not a robot. It won't have an arm.'

'Computers are all based on numbers, right?' asked Dickon.

'They are all based on zero and one.'

'That's quantity. What about quality?'

'Quality involves the capacity for judgement. When the quantity of computations passes a certain point it takes on qualities.'

'If a computer understands qualities, doesn't it mean that it's alive?'

'Not if quality is an aspect of intelligence. Life is from the inside out, mechanics is from the outside in. That is why, in my humble opinion, computers can never live.' Knott was very paranoid about the concept of living computers; he loved computers, but he didn't want them loving him.

Bunjie tapped Ward on the shoulder and said 'I'll put some snacks in the microwave,' and when he came back in with steam-

ing plates of Indian tongue ticklers, the scientist was still in full
flow, explaining that 'Every body attracts every other body with a
force inversely proportional to the square of the distance between
them. Gravity is action at a distance.'

'In that case,' enquired Bunjie, as he offered round the snacks,
'how is it that science can believe in gravity but not in telepathy?'

'Um,' replied Knott, because for the moment he was stumped.
Gravity and telepathy? The first was real, the second not. Why?
His mind had briefly cabbaged.

'I'd go further,' said Mrs Bladder-Williams, 'and suggest that
gravity is like love. It's what holds everything together. My dear
departed Eustace always said that everything disappears into a
mystery and that you have to accept that and not be afraid of it
and I think he was right on that one. These snacks are delicious,
Mr Gunj.'

'Does science *not* believe in telepathy?' asked Dickon. 'I
thought it was beginning – '

'Yes, it's one of the new ideas. Not one that I personally consider very healthy.'

'So how would you define health, Mr Knott?'

'Health is harmony,' said Jazz.

'Too much harmony is the entropic soup,' said Knott. 'Discord
also has a role. The universe is dynamic and dynamism is only
possible where there is inequality. I should say that health is
growth.'

'So computers are unhealthy because they do not grow?' asked
Fortinbras.

'Computers do grow. But only with our help.'

'You mean like invalids,' said Jocasta.

Knott's grimace took on an extra rigidity. 'No, not like invalids.
All structure is binary and stable. All creation is singular and
unstable. People say – the computers will take over. People say –
the brain is no more than a sophisticated computer. Not true. The
computer at any one time is a closed system. But the brain is an
open system. It is dynamic, creative, unbalanced. Its chemical
composition alters not only from person to person but from
second to second. Every brain is individual. Every computer can
be copied. A human being can be open-minded, a computer
can't.'

'So what is it you are arguing for?' asked Alice.

'I'm arguing for open-mindedness, that's all. On the City of Cognitive Neuroscience as on everything else,' said Knott.

'I get the angle,' said Dickon. 'Look, Mr Knott, I can be open-minded at the level of ideas but when it comes to what is to be done, I must take decisons.'

'Then you are not talking science, art, the adventure of life. You are talking ethics.'

'No he wasn't!' protested Alice.

'There's nothing wrong with ethics, Alice,' said Mrs Bladder-Williams. 'That's the difference between us and those horrible terrorists of the Green Kingdom.'

'You'll never get anywhere, Mrs Bloody-Williams,' said Fortinbras, 'until you start to blow things up'.

73.

Good Friday arrived in a veil of rain. It set the tone for an Easter holday which was uneventful but apprehensive. On one side of the Puck Valley, Alice was smearing unsalted butter over her hot cross buns. She was alone. She was invisible. She was looking at her television set but hadn't switched it on. On the other side of the valley Sidney was polishing the presentation silver which was traditionally done on Good Friday to brighten up the glummest day of the year. He was hard at it in fine cotton gloves and a green baize apron and watched fixedly as Crystal and Sylvia lifted onto the newspaper-covered trestle the Armadillo Punch Bowl, a gift to the house from the Princess Montezuma. 'Hideous great thing,' said Sidney, 'and always was'.

At Saint Wendy's they paraded the Holy Maul, the club for killing off old parents which at one time used to hang in all English churches, and in the afternoon the Revd Sinus Simm called on JJ and they took tea in the cosy. 'I'm collecting contributions for a new roof on the scout hut, Marquess.'

'Of course, vicar. Here's fifty pounds. I was never a scout myself but I've made up for it since.'

'This is what the cloth has come to, Marquess, being a glorified repair man. Quite frankly I cannot forgive God for not existing.

Of course God exists in a general way. But the male God, the directing God, the God who had a choice in the Creation and chose to create, *this* God does not exist.'

'Oh dear, I am sorry. Would you like a spot of malmsey with your simnel cake?'

'Thank you but no. I should be getting back to toil in the glebe. Marguerite says I must do some weeding.'

'But what *does* exist, vicar?'

'What exists, Marquess, is the waiting, the endless waiting, for a sign, a clue, anything.'

'But life is – '

'A glittering fog, Marquess, that is all. A glittering fog. Can you come to the beetle drive on Thursday?'

'I'm afraid I'm watching television on Thursday.'

At the caravan park, the chestnut trees were out and dripping. Max, tucked into his capsule like a praying mantis in its lair, finished *Death by Pudding*'s final sentence. *The magnitude of her indignation was nonetheless fettered to an apparent equanimity by a tenacious and self-deprecating fear of seeming the termagant; therefore she detonated.*

Now that's what I call a good book, he thought.

But it was not a good day and he had only been trying to distract himself from yesterday which hadn't been good either. Yesterday he had received a letter thanking him for his interest but saying he would not be called to audition for any of the parts in *King Lear the Musical*. All my life I've had my wings spread in readiness but I've never flown, I have never had the break which would allow me to take to the air. So that's it, Max! From now on, no holds barred, don't even try to meet them half way! And he pressed the end of a pair of scissors into his palm until it bled.

Saturday was brighter. Blackthorn creaming the sodden hedgerows gave off, as it dried, a scent both goatish and sweet. JJ inhaled it with delight as he walked Kevin across the fields of the Home Farm. On reaching the muddy farmyard, sorry guitar chords and a young throaty voice from one of the barns betrayed the presence of his boy.

Hey baby
Something very strange
Is coming out of me
Is coming out of you

Hey baby
Is it our age?
Is it the sea?
Or is it the flu?

Hey baby
I'm growing hair
Everywhere
I'm a bustle
Of muscle

Hey baby
We must
Begin it
Coz we'll be dust
In a minute

Glory adjusted his bottom on a pile of mildewed encyclo-paedias.

'Go on,' said JJ.

'That's it,' said Glory.

'I love to hear you sing.'

On Easter Sunday the weather turned bad again by way of wel-come to the swallows who had streamed up from Africa. Crystal stared out of her bedroom window as the woods on the far side of the valley turned darker in the rain. She sat like that for over an hour in the knowledge that Gibbon Tuft had been driving the car which had killed Jack Thicknesse and aware that even when you know what the truth is, it is impossible to prove it, it is impossi-ble to prove anything, how Hoskins would laugh if she said the information came from a séance, how Ward had laughed, how all the men would laugh. At the last minute the Dashmans had flown off to the Caribbean for Easter, to palm strees and the shuffle of blue water on golden sand, and Crystal had never in her life felt so left behind by the world. In the evening she had a row with her father.

JJ: I'm not against free love.

CRYSTAL: You are.

JJ: Of course I'm not. But now a third party is involved.

CRYSTAL: Oh, I see. I should have an abortion.

JJ: Is it too late?

CRYSTAL: It's my life for God's sake!

JJ: Presumably you and the kid will want to live here!

CRYSTAL: You'd throw us out?

JJ: Don't be silly. But it's not unknown for a baby's father to provide a roof.

CRYSTAL: Anyway, it's not your house.

JJ: So does Robin figure *anywhere* in this equation?

CRYSTAL: It's the family house. You're only the looker-afterer. And you've sold Mum's Twombly, haven't you. It's gone from the library.

JJ: I, um, er . . .

CRYSTAL: You rotten beast, you've sold it! It was the last thing she left here!

JJ: We've got to live for Christ's sake. I haven't noticed you making much of a contribution.

CRYSTAL: That picture was for all of us!

JJ: Oh, I'm sick of the damn house and the damn family. There's no escape from it, not for a second. It's amazing I'm not a drug-addict.

CRYSTAL: I always assumed you were.

JJ: Crystal, a child needs a father.

CRYSTAL: You said last year 'Consanguinity's overrated'. I heard you at Sylvia's party.

JJ: My dear girl, do you think we're having party conversation? Is that what you think?

CRYSTAL: Daddy, you're bringing me down. It was the very last thing she left . . .

JJ: I'm glad it's gone. I have feelings too.

CRYSTAL: Why didn't you buy me an Easter egg?

JJ: I did. But I ate it.

Alice wanted to invite Dickon over. But after the gaol-bonding episode, instead of being closer, they had slipped into a curious kind of self-conscious clumsiness with each other. On Bank

Holiday Monday Alice motored over to Heaven Park to walk in
the grounds between showers. As the next downpour came on,
she withdrew to the great house which, as so often, gave the
impression of having been deserted by the human race. She
drifted aimlessly from wing to silent wing. Her footsteps rang in
lonely pillared halls. Enormous rainy windows chilled her. In
unused rooms, emptied of everything, the floors lay like dark
sheets. Eventually she heard voices and traced them to a small
chamber known as the Vicereine's Cabinet. When she entered,
Minerva and Pimm stopped talking and silently stared at her.

'Sorry,' said Alice.

'You can sit over there. I asked him why it's called Easter,' said
Minerva.

A bolt of lightning ripped across the Venetian window, followed by a long tumbling crash. Minerva moved to the window
seat and groped in a coloured carton which had been deposited
there. 'Leonardo da Vinci said that the face attains its subtlest
expression when seen by evening light in stormy weather. Does
either of you want a piece of egg?' They both accepted her offer.
As the lightning increased in frequency, Minerva's white face
flashed on and off like a lightbulb.

74.

Already swollen by snow-melt from the Mountains Beyond the
West, and with rain falling heavily for days, the Puck rose dan-
gerously. By lunchtime on Thursday the arches of the bridge had
disappeared and water was licking outwards onto the cobble-
stones at the bottom of the High Street. By teatime the Puck had
burst its banks along a fifty-mile stretch.

Although the village climbed sharply from the river, a number
of households in the parish had to be evacuated and many more
put on alert. Round the bend of the river the inundation slid rapidly towards the buildings of Lower Farm where the first victims
were the Upanishads who disappeared overnight no-one-knew-
where. Perhaps they had simply floated off on the stream like
dreamers. In the stonework on the side of the Great Tithe Barn
four horizontal marks were gouged where floods had reached

more than six feet above ground level in the past 600 years. The present flood was going for gold. So far Lower Farm had survived all, though not without damage. The Glade, higher up the side of the valley, had always escaped, and Alice said to Dickon 'You and Meg must come to me. I'll make up the other bedroom.'

'I'm not budging. Someone might loot the place or Malcolm could decide to change the locks and I'd not get back in, but I'll ask Meg.'

Dickon moved the livestock to High Field and valuables onto the first floor while from her upper window Meg watched water eat the fields acre by acre. Mute with terror, she was bundled into the pick-up and driven to The Glade where Alice made a mighty to-do of welcome with exaggerated smiles and flowers-in-bedroom.

She smells funny, thought Alice as she and Dickon helped the invalid up the narrow staircase.

'I'd prefer to lie in front of the fire a bit,' bleated Meg. She started to weep.

'You're overtired. You'll feel better after a sleep,' he said.

'But once I'm in bed it's very difficult for me to get out of it.'

Later Alice took a cup of soup to her guest. 'Do you want to come down and watch telly?'

'I think I'll read my book here if that's all right with you.'

'Of course.'

'Alice . . .'

'Yes?'

'When I'm gone . . .'

'You're not going.'

'I'll not make old bones.'

Alice couldn't help being pleased to hear this. Against all her nobler instincts, something about Meg's single plait dropping over the right shoulder had already begun to infuriate her. She marvelled, as she often did, at how anyone could work in a home for the disabled or the clapped-out. 'What do the doctors say?'

'Could be tonight. Could be ten years. Doctors know nothing. But when I'm gone, make sure he has enough to eat. He's inclined to worry and go off his food.'

75.

Church House wore a tight expression. It was standing in several feet of water. Mrs Bladder-Williams had descended the staircase at the customary eight thirty a.m., eyes barely open, and her fluffy slippers had gone splosh splosh half-a-dozen treads before the bottom. It was the biggest shock of her life since Eustace had come to her on their wedding night and begun to fondle her armpit. Justice at once invited her to stay at his house. To widespread amusement, she had accepted, packing into her suitcase several bottles of pink champagne. In Melody's bedroom he'd knocked up, especially for this guest, a four-poster bed hung with flowered polyester sheets.

76.

A hangover pounded in the slush behind his eyes. It shut the light out of his head. He pressed his temples and one thought ran between his fingertips – time is running out – that was all, again and again, time is running out. The corridor lengthened ahead of him and his vision was disturbed by flashes. His legs went soft. The walls pushed inwards. He ran, black velvet slippers slamming onto the marble flags, his mid-parts jolting. With dry grunts he clutched at nothing. The corridor turned upside down – there was a spear of hard light – and he was engulfed.

Coming to, after God knew how long, the poor creature was lead in all his limbs. He did not attempt to stand but lay in a heap against the floor, eyeing the skirting board sideways on.

> Who am I?
> Where am I?
> What has happened to the division between
>   the inner and the outer world?
> How do I awake from this nightmare?

He uttered the word 'help'. It didn't sound like that word or any other word and it ricocheted slushily down the corridor. Again the slush. No one answered. He was standing up. The wall of the corridor was cold. There was a noise. It was applause. Why were they applauding him? He hadn't done anything, so why were they applauding him? His eyes were hot. The applause was the sound of heavy rain outside. And it was dark too. It had been light and now the corridor was dark.

Again only one thought raced round the stadium of his mind and this time it was – I am merely memory – I don't otherwise exist – I am merely memory. He assumed it would exhaust itself and stop but it didn't, it went on, round and round – I am merely memory – I am a pile of memories – I am merely memory – I do not exist. He was moving again. Lights were on in the corridor and everything was dreamlike. He was sitting in the cosy with a glass of whisky in his hand, thinking – I better put another log on the fire. The fire swallowed the log with relish. The room glowed. The walls turned the colour of whisky.

I have had a heart attack
I have had a nervous breakdown
I have had a stroke
I have had a psychosis
I have had all of them
I have had none of them
Perhaps I have been murdered and this is what purgatory is

He found a pair of spectacles and searched slowly in a shallow drawer and took a blue tranquilliser from a half-empty strip lodged near the back, looking hard at the dear torpedo in his palm before swallowing it. Where is everybody? Where is solid ground? If you lose concentration for a second the universe collapses. I don't need solid ground any more. The soft blue tide of the tranquilliser had glided into him. In the last seconds an hour had gone by. A fat hand pressed some square buttons and turned the volume all the way up.

Out of silence, out of darkness, out of death, a sinister squelching noise crept forward, glanced about, and crashed forth. The whole building shuddered. The immense sound, dragonlike and voracious, heaved against walls and ceilings and climbed upwards in spasms onto the rooftops and outwards into the stunned night.

228 *A History of Facelifting*

Champagne rattled in dungeons where several bottles exploded. Bats and birds shrieked from the eaves. Tumults towered and plunged and towered again. And as the music jarred every vault, threatened every pillar, so he danced from saloon to saloon, swinging his bottom, waving his arms, tossing his hair, throwing open the doors one after another, lighting chandelier after chandelier which flung bouquets of rainbows to greet him.

It happened to be a little after two a.m. and since the sound system was wired into all the principal rooms of the house, no part of the building escaped. The noise could be heard in every bedroom in Milking Magna too, thanks to the amphitheatre of the hills. Even the rain had stopped with shock. But he danced on, until all the glory of the house was ablaze, until at last he swayed into the ballroom, laughing, out of breath, perilously purple of face, and pressed a button to the right of the main door before subsiding onto the floor. The music would not repeat again. It began to ebb and ebb and finally . . . slunk . . . away . . .

Starfishlike on his back, he lay looking up at Hope being Tortured by Chastity, amid the astounding crash of silence. The silence kissed his singing ears. All his body pumped with blood and this bathed him in nourishing consciousness. But after a respectful interval, there was a cough some distance away. There stood Sidney, Cook, Pimm, Kevin and Glory Boy. He could make out Crystal bobbing behind them, nervously pulling on a cigarette.

Nothing was said for a moment or two until Sidney made his little cough again. 'If you would excuse me, sir, the Heavenshire Camera Club have asked if they may take photographs in the Rotunda Hall on Saturday afternoon.'

This brought JJ round and he raised himself onto his knees.

'Ladies and gentlemen, I apologise if I've disturbed you but I've had a very strange day. It was like a horrible acid trip and I'm not sure that it's over yet. Not that my trips *were* horrible. Most of them were delightful. It's awful getting old, isn't it. They say you have the advantage of experience. All that experience has taught me is that there's no relief in sight. All things considered, I certainly wouldn't say that the orientation I now have towards life is in any way superior to the one I had as a young man. I didn't know you were staying the night, Glory.'

Glory replied that he couldn't get back to his hut because 'The Puck's flooded, sir.' JJ always had a secret thrill when Glory called him 'sir' which wasn't often. The way he said it wasn't at all obsequious. There was something in it that was tender and considerate. Glory added 'That was the grandest sound, sir. I never heard it before.'

'It was 'Voodoo Chile Slight Return' by Jimi Hendrix . . . Glory, will you sleep with me tonight?'

'Yes, sir.'

JJ's head fell back. No more hope. No more torture. No more chastity. Not tonight anyway.

'Procul recedent somnia et noctium phantasmata. And Sidney – '

'Yes, sir?'

'You are a dear.'

'Thank you, sir.'

77.

She rocked the baby against her comfortable bosom and looking out of the window decided that the lilac tree, which was all the front garden possessed, should be pruned in the autumn. Outside, Justice had washed and waxed the Riley's curvaceous black body and was turning his attention to its brown leather interior. Princess Lark, returning from her stint at The Crag, said to him 'Never ending, isn't it'. As she opened her front gate she looked in at the neighbouring window and Mrs Bladder-Williams turned away. They both knew they'd seen each other but there was only the inner recognition. Why had she turned away? Why am I worrying about what that wretched woman next door thinks? What am I doing here? It is not my sort of place. Once inside I feel secure but coming and going to this house embarrasses me terribly. And he is not my sort of person. I don't mean to be mean but it's true, he isn't. He says 'lounge' instead of living-room, sitting-room, drawing-room. Anything is better than lounge. Even parlour is better than lounge. In fact parlour is rather lovely. But lounge. Come in to the lounge. Every time I hear it I know it's impossible. I can't help it. It's silly but it's true – lounge screams common and that's the honest fact.

Justice never intruded into the bedroom he had prepared for her and yet his huge warm presence was all around. She walked into the kitchen as he entered through the back door. Slipping off his shoes, he took the baby from her. She was fascinated by his burly delicacy with it. Justice's own thoughts aroused by his grandson were more complex – love, hope, despair, curiosity, determination, cluelessness, all smeared over his insides like thick paint.

MRS B-W: I'll cook tonight.

JUSTICE: It's all in hand.

MRS B-W: What are you cooking?

JUSTICE: Slop-bucket. You put everythin in him.

MRS B-W: What the French call pot au feu. I'm quite interested in North African cuisine.

JUSTICE: I'm plagued by a question.

MRS B-W: If I can help.

JUSTICE: I think you can, but I'm afraid of askin.

MRS B-W: Now you're frightening me.

JUSTICE: The problem is – I don't know what to call you any longer.

MRS B-W: You mean –

JUSTICE: Yes, I want to know your Christian name. There – it's said.

MRS B-W: Oh.

JUSTICE: You see. I've caused offence.

MRS B-W: No, I . . .

JUSTICE: I have.

MRS B-W: Ever since I was a little girl I've been embarrassed by my name.

JUSTICE: No one uses it?

MRS B-W: My husband, Eustace, occasionally. Did you know it was Eustace who put a stop to the goat-flinging and revived the lambkin jamkin?

JUSTICE: You're very charmin in this confused state.

MRS B-W: Immacolata.

JUSTICE: Come again?

MRS B-W: Immacolata, that's my name. Immacolata.

JUSTICE: Phew!

MRS B-W: Yes, I know it's a silly -

JUSTICE: Silly? Why silly? I – mmac – o – la – ta. It's a byooooooootiful name.

MRS B-W: Ha!

JUSTICE: It's the most byootiful name I ever heard.

To celebrate the coming out of her Christian name, Immacolata suggested they accompany their slop-bucket with a bottle of pink champagne. That night in bed, pinkly vague and holding open *Green Coral* by Henry de Vere Stacpoole, she heard him sluicing in the bathroom. It was both peaceful and unsettling. Then he went quiet. She heard the bathroom door open and close. More quiet. There was the very tiniest tap on her bedroom door. 'Yes . . .' she said. There was a pause before he entered, a white towel round his waist. With pounding hearts and with great gentleness, they looked at each other for a while. All was acceptance and inevitability between them. The towel dropped from him and he advanced upon her.

78.

Alice sat on the end of JJ's bed and smoothed his quilted eiderdown with her hand.

'Are you better now?'

'Certainly not.'

'What did the doctor say?'

'He said it's stress.'

'They always say that.'

'And my weight.'

'If you could lose some pounds . . .'

'And my age. I don't think I can lose any years. What I said was "The point is, Doc, not any of that stuff, but that I've glimpsed the abyss, ontological terror, the godless universe". He just sat there, poor old thing, very out of his depth, and reminded me of my father in some way.'

'Was your father out of his depth with you?'

'Completely. He was appalling, my papa, with his awful unpre-
dictable outbursts. I should be more appalling too. Every morning when I wake up I say to myself *Be more appalling.* But as the
day gets going I find myself being sweet as pie to everyone who
crosses my path and it's hopeless. I hate being a wimp. Would you
be an angel and pour me a glass of that juice? I've got a terrific
thirst. Cook keeps giving me smoked haddock. You can't *imagine*
the dreams I'm having. One unpleasant thing – my head starts to
spin the moment I set foot outside the park. But the doc said it'll
pass. I must have some parties, get myself livened up, meet new
people.'

'Would you mind if I gave a party at The Glade? I was thinking I might some time.'

'You? Give a party?'

79.

While broadcasting several cups of pellets to the bantams out
back, Davis had a beastly idea. She'd seen that Popjoy bitch
flaunting her fat belly in the High Street, having the Craddock
child! Of course the pair of twerps hadn't married – oh but they
would. As the event approached, the splitting-open and the
oozing-forth of their brat, Lady Crystal Popjoy would surrender
to history and legitimise the child and the Craddock line would
be renewed just when we all thought we could forget about the
filth. Judging by the bitch's size she was obviously going to have
three sons. Well – no, she wasn't!

Davis ruffled through an ancient tome which customarily
resided on top of the kitchen cupboard where it had grown slimy
with cooking fat and dust, and halted at an account of raspberry
leaf tea which was *capable of inducing abortion.* Her face crabbed
with concentration, cigarette ash dropping twice into the central
valley between the pages. It was surprisingly easy to prepare –
only a couple of the ingredients were esoteric. Ground nail-clip-
pings from the toes of a woman destroyed by love – Mumsy could
supply those. The first beard shaved from the chin of an adoles-
cent boy. She'd lure Little Lark with a coin – he'd not yet scraped
off his sprouts. But how to get the bitch to drink it? Her new ally
of course. Lomax. He could slip it to the Wetmore cow as a tonic

for pregnant mothers and the Wetmore cow could pass it to its destination. And if she added burnt conker of Galadriel, Lady Toofullofherselfbyhalf would be rendered permanently infertile! The last of the Craddocks and the last of the Popjoys eliminated at a stroke! Such a brilliant idea to add to their plans! She must go at once to the caravan park to see *him*.

First she checked on the Old Un who was snoozing by the electric fire.

Better give er some gas.

She took a small gas canister from under the sink and blasted its nozzle several times up her mother's nose. The Old Un jolted and relapsed into slow breathing.

It was a black night and there wasn't a soul about. Hoggart's window was lit up but emptied of meat. Oven Ready Rabbits said a notice. Well-Rotted Horse Manure Already Bagged Can Deliver said another. She heard footsteps and nipped down an alley to avoid notice and found herself trudging in sludge. The way was dark as pitch but she was guided by the gurgle of waters to her right.

Soddin river.

'You are very rude, Brownteeth,' said a voice.

Davis stopped and sniffed the air. The hump on her back twitched.

'Where are you going?' asked the voice.

'No business of yourn!'

'You *are* pugnacious.'

'Talk English, damn you!' Davis slid cautiously forward on the mud. The sound of stampeding water grew very loud.

'You're a rough piece and no mistake,' said the voice.

'Varlet, declare yerself!'

'I'm Jenny Greenteeth,' answered the voice, 'and I think you're going up to Max Lomax with a beastly idea.'

'I aint too!'

'Don't be so combative, Brownteeth.'

'Talk normal else don't talk at all!'

'I want to tell you something important.'

Davis slithered a foot or so in the direction of the voice. 'It's black as hell.'

'Come closer,' urged the voice.

'I don't know no Jenny Greenteeth. Where are you?'

'I'm here, Brownteeth. I can help you.'

Davis stretched a little more towards the voice and smelt the
pounding current. 'I aint going no further see, coz the river's
all over.'

'That's fine. That'll do nicely.'

Davis's feet left the ground. She flailed her arms. Water rushed
in her ears. Her body spun. A maw of foam was before her, a
rowdy paleness, a furious threshing, and terrible knives of ice.
Then silence. The black muscular river sped on.

80.

Meg's presence at The Glade was suffocating. Alice blamed herself by saying that she'd been living alone too long but at the
weekend found herself staying out on her walk far longer than
usual. On this day, after putting all the teacups and mugs to
bleach in the sink (Meg lived on tea), Alice made for the woods
beyond Lower Farm via an upper path. At its edge rabbits
hopped through tangles of stitchwort while in the woodland itself
a flawless carpet of bluebells stretched ahead through a lattice of
birches. The soft vibrations of colour and scent were intoxicating.
A cuckoo called. There was no let-up in the bluish flood either
side her narrow path and a faint queasiness came over her. She
could hear the prattling of a brook but could identify nothing of
the kind and was pleased to discover that it was playful voices.
Some children were merrymaking. When near enough, she
implored 'Please don't tread them down'.

They laughed and cried out 'There's no end to the bluebells!
No end to them! Follow us!'

'Where are you going?'

'You'll see.'

She followed them as they skipped off. The path grew nar-
rower and eventually petered out and Alice fell behind but could
hear their bright voices echoing in the far glades. There were
bluebells everywhere, thicker than ever, with their giddying
scent. Then the children had gone. She couldn't hear them any
more. She could hear nothing except the swish of her steps

through bluebells. Now she was trampling them down. Now she didn't care. She wanted to get out of the sea of bluebells any old how and she started to run, crashing through the flowers, hoping to catch up with the children. But because the flowers spread uniformly in every direction it was as though she ran nowhere. Whenever she stopped and looked about, it was the same. Seamless bluebell wood. She continued to run, and was quite surprised that she had so much running in her. But the next time she stopped to catch her breath she heard – the sound of running. Someone else was running too. Someone was after her. Her previous panic had been such that she was rather pleased that someone was after her, at least it was company, and she stood on the spot to await their arrival. Daisy Lark and Glory Boy came pelting out of the trees. 'We're being chased!' wheezed Glory Boy.

'Why?' asked Alice.

'Because of the recordings!' blurted Daisy.

'Shut up, you! Gonna tell the whole world?' Now a deeper crashing sound came into earshot, as of a mammoth animal surging through undergrowth, boom swish boom swish boom swish boom. 'Quick!' urged Glory. Alice instinctively ran with them.

'I'm out of training,' she puffed.

'Fuck training, keep moving!'

The boom-swish-boom was gaining on them.

'Faster, faster!'

Abruptly the foliage slid off their shoulders and they were in a sunny field. On the far side of it was a tepee framed in the enormous arch of a rainbow. The Upanishads were about to have lunch.

Alice panted 'Someone's chasing us!'

'You've got to be nice,' said Herald, 'especially Glory'.

'We promise, we promise!' panted Glory.

'That's OK then. More bread and bowls, Leaf. Don't worry. The rainbow is creating a force field. I felt bad vibes. But it's all right now. Whatever it was that was chasing you has gone away now.'

And true enough, the boom-swish-boom must have turned round and was fading into the distance where the sound of it eventually merged with that of a remote tractor.

'Is it your rainbow?' asked Daisy.

'No. It belongs to nature. It's raining back there towards the mountains.'

Leaf emerged from the tepee with extra accoutrements.

'We thought you'd been swept away in the flood,' said Alice.

'Nature's not a problem for us,' replied Herald.

'Where are we?' she asked.

'Onward Butter,' said Leaf.

'Where's that?'

'Next one past Upper Butter.'

'And whose land is it?'

'Harry Pulp's. His chicken factory is over there. Acres of huts. You can't see it. That Robin Craddock came to see us. He works there. Do you know what he said? "We're having a headless chicken competition Sunday – the idea is how many headless chickens can you get running around at the same time using only your hands and teeth – would you like to come?" He said it right there in front of Sky. I think he's got a screw loose. Perhaps it was him what was chasing you.'

'No, he's not like that. I expect we panicked for no reason,' said Glory.

'We've all done that,' said Herald. 'But there's always a reason. Deep down there's always a reason.'

'I panicked in the middle of my pregnancy,' said Leaf. 'Fifth month. Two terrible weeks. Couldn't leave the tepee.'

Herald chanted 'Oh Mighty Lord or Lordess of Everything that is and was and will be – for what we are about to receive make us truly thankful. You may eat.'

Alice was pleased there was so much panic around. It made her less panicky.

'Come on, Sky. Eat up.' Leaf addressed the papoose in which a being of indeterminate age was wrestling with what looked like a wet flapjack.

81.

Brother and sister were in the Knockledandy Closet gnawing rabbit thighs to the accompaniment of Busoni's Chamber Fantasia on themes from Gilbert & Sullivan (in the four-hour uncut version performed by Ganglion Vapers) when Sidney announced 'Mr Boy, sir'.

Glory stood in the doorway on the edge of his shoes, feet tipped outwards, expression anxious.

'Is he going to join us?' queried Minerva.

'He can have some of mine, Minnie.'

JJ made a pattern of rings and half-rings on the white damask tablecloth with the moist foot of his claret glass while Glory wolfed down most of the food and Minerva gently dipped her tips in the finger-bowl and dried them on the napkin.

'I'm going to leave you two to it,' she said.

Glory closed the door behind her before he said 'I want you to help me'.

'Why should I? You were so mean the other day.'

'I wasn't in the mood. Sometimes I'm not in the mood with Daisy too. I'm not a machine, you know.'

'But there was no need to say I'm disgusting. I've been very sensitive since my attack.'

'You're not the only one aving attacks. I think the Green Kingdom are after me. I found this disc with voices on plannin outrages.'

'They wouldn't record their own conspiracy.'

'Who knows how it got on there. We was being chased in the woods and suddenly Alice was with us and Daisy blurted out about the recordings. I'm a bit suspicious of Alice suddenly.'

'I wish I were. She says she wants to hold a party. Here we all are dead broke and she wants a party.'

'Well, there you are then. Where's she getting the money for a party suddenly? You don't know nothing about Alice, do you. She's one of the Puck Valley Three and she could be in cahoots with the Green Kingdom.'

At this point Crystal came into the room and her father said 'Not now, love. I'm discussing something important with Glory'.

'You've never had any time for me!' she burst out, and withdrew, loudly slamming the door. A fine talcum of dust descended from the ceiling.

'Preggers,' said JJ.

'Do you want to listen to it now?'

'Listen to what?'

'That disc! It's in my bag over there.'

'I don't think you ought to implicate anyone else. Especially me. The Green Kingdom doubtless considers me an enemy. And you are wrong about Alice. I know quite a lot about her. She and I have our little chats.' JJ stubbed his cigarette out in a round ceramic ashtray, crested, chipped.

'But she never has anyone to stay, does she. No family or any-fing. No one from her past life.'

'She needed a break. I can understand that.' JJ was flushed and changed the subject. 'There's a hole in your trousers, Glory.' He moved across and, ripping the hole a little more, inserted his hand and stroked the hair of the boy's thigh, softly backwards and forwards with an hypnotic rhythm, calming him down, soothing him, until Glory's posture become suppple and the boy slowly turned on him lynxlike eyes . . .

During their sexual interlude, Glory said 'Ragamuffin's cat had kittens. You want one? I'll get you one. A present.'

'I don't want another cat. I've had cats. They always leave me for the kitchen. Give one to Cook.'

'But they're lovely. I'd like to give one to you.'

'I have this theory – the working class lives in the present, the middle class lives in the future and the upper class lives in the past. I'm upper class and I know from experience that cats don't like me.'

'Are you saying I'm not interested in the future?'

'You may be interested in it but you don't do anything about it.'

'You'll be sorry when I hit the road to better myself.'

'Are you intending to hit the road?'

'Shall I put the disc on then? See what you think?'

'I've told you I don't want to hear the bloody thing!'

Glory stood naked in the window, with sunlight on his bum, ferreting in his bag. 'Here it is.'

As he was about to put the disc in the player, JJ stayed his arm. 'Look, if you're really worried, hand it over to Hoskins. Let the experts deal with it. But I'll tell you for the last time, I do not wish to hear it myself.'

There the matter lapsed as JJ jammed his face into the heart of the boy's buttocks.

82.

Because of the floods Crystal had to drive the long way round. She took the yellow Ford from the stables and Sylvia asked to be dropped off at Puckford Mill where Bob was floundering in mud.

'He said he'd moved all the good stuff upstairs, but the little lamb doesn't know what good stuff is.'

'Don't you miss your own house?' asked Crystal.

'What sort of question is that?'

A bedraggled Bob in the drive lifted a limp hand of recognition as they pulled in . . . The second she left Sylvia at the Mill, Crystal's excitement redoubled. Her heart pounded. Her thoughts jumped at tangents in a balloon of warmth. She was going to her lover, the one she'd been looking for, the one who wasn't an embarrassment, the one she could develop a life with, given the chance. It had been unexpected, it was still awkward, but never before had she felt this versatile space with a man, and never before this awful urgency too. And it wasn't just the sex. Robin was sex. This was different. She was longing to meet *him*, be with *him*.

Crystal searched for a peppermint in the glove compartment with one hand while steering precariously with the other. Turning north off the Appleminster road at a field of black and tan pigs, she completed the last miles to her rendezvous in magnificent distress. The old RAF aerodrome was as eerie as ever, like chancing upon a Mayan settlement in the heart of the jungle. She swerved across rubble and broken glass and pulled up in front of a derelict hut. Of course he was late.

He loved driving. It was his meditation: dynamic stillness: you moved but you didn't move. Yet it also rendered the outside world less relevant and therefore less real. Which seems to be the way things are going, he thought. People are living more and more in their heads. They avoid public experiences in theatres and bars and streets. They shy away from interaction with strangers. It must have something to do with overpopulation. Everything was about overpopulation these days. Or computers. In the modern world the luxuries were time and space.

When she saw his car, Crystal stepped out of hers. 'Ah!' she gasped as one of her bare calves grazed a clump of nettles. Without looking at him she entered the hut where the mattresses were. They were wet and stinking. He followed.

'You've cut all your hair off.'

'Don't you like it?' she asked.

'I think I do.'

She was stroking him. Her dry mouth sluiced with saliva. They made love in tender contortions on their feet.

Afterwards he said 'I can hear Vera Lynn'.

'Who?'

'Someone who used to sing.'

'It's not nice to mention other women right now.'

'Is that what we're being? Nice?' He ran his hands over her swollen belly.

'It's not yours,' she said.

'Of course it's not mine.'

'I wish it were. I wish that. I love you, my sweet.'

'Tell me why you love me.'

'Because I don't have to think why. You don't remind me of anyone I know. You look at me properly.'

'That's because I love you too.'

'Why do you love me? I'm not the lovable type, I know that.'

'I don't know why. I really don't know. And it doesn't seem important to know.' He kept running his hands over her belly, staring at it thoughtfully. 'Will you marry him?' he asked.

'Not if I can live with you.'

He was silent.

She was silent.

He offered her a cigarette but she nodded no and said 'You love me, Ward. But that's all, isn't it? There's nothing else. Just love. Like a couple of teenagers.'

She made a funny noise and broke away, jumped into her car, reversed and sped off. It happened so quickly. It was twilight. He sat in the dewy grass and picked a few daisies, choked by the heavy air of misunderstanding she had left behind.

Crystal drove fast. She had proposed and been rejected. She understood now that she had no one in her life except this thing swelling inside and she didn't want it to be born into a fog of half situations. She must protect it and so, yes, she would accept Robin's murky, lingering offer of marriage. It was this she was going to tell her father when she walked in on him spooning with that damn boy. She took herself off to a distant wing of the house and found herself in the old nursery and sat on the drugget floor which was fixed round the edge with brass tacks. She ran her finger over their domed heads and sobbed.

Ward Dashman on the other hand was driving up to London. He was scraggy in the commotion of love. Half an hour into the journey he encountered something curious. The road curved to the right but ahead was a low hill. A mass of small lights shone back at him in his headlights. What on earth could they be? He was disorientated. In the time required to establish that they were a flock of sheep on the bank, their eyes reflecting his lights, he had misjudged the right turn and crashed. When the police arrived they found him hanging half out of the car, his cheek torn open and all the side-teeth and jawbone gleaming in the torchlight. But Ward was still alive.

83.

When Meg returned to Lower Farm she found a dead newt in one of her slippers which did nothing for her happiness. Alice on the other hand chose to give a soirée to celebrate the recovery of her own space. Of course Meg and Dickon were both invited but Alice knew that only Dickon would come, unless of course he didn't come either, in which case the event would fall very flat. Over the other guests she deliberated. Living in a small community meant that everyone would know about her bash and since it was her first bash it would be a statement of her social position. She couldn't invite everyone but anyone who wasn't invited would be offended. She couldn't invite only close friends because she didn't have enough close friends and, besides, she wasn't sure who her close friends were. In the end she decided that since it was impossible to avoid causing offence, she'd simply invite those whom she liked. Or didn't actively dislike. Or with whom she was more or less involved on a regular basis. Or whatever.

The first to arrive was the Revd Sinus Simm who said 'My, you *have* done wonders with this place. It was an absolute disgrace when Gibbon Tuft had it.' In surveying the interior his head struck a beam.

'Be careful, vicar. A sandwich?' She was serving cucumber and sweet cecily sandwiches, meringues glued together with clotted cream, and white champagne.

Simm began 'In this season of prolix garden and mellifluous river . . . ' but the door-knocker went again. It was Oliver Knott. 'I expect I'm the first,' he said.

'No. The vicar's here.'

'Vicars don't count.'

'Good evening, Mr Knott. Are we going to discuss astral projection at last?' enquired Simm with a slip of his dentures. Perhaps the concussion had loosened them.

'Have you any whisky, my dear?' asked Knott, his dentures defiantly fixed. 'The doctor said I mustn't have wine in my state.'

'Are you in a state, Oliver?'

'I'm always in a state.'

'Where would he be without his state?' chirped Simm.

'I think the Church could do more for human anguish,' said Knott.

Alice jumped as the knocker sounded, wondering if it were *he*, but it was Robin Craddock. 'Is it all men?' he asked – and hit his head on a beam. 'Sod it!'

'Crystal's coming later,' encouraged Alice.

'Oh dear.'

'Aren't you two getting on?'

'She's awfully upset about something,' said Robin.

'Ward Dashman's accident I think.'

'Really? She didn't say that. No, I think you're wrong. I think it's the baby.'

Lady Craddock followed directly with a potted azalea.

'Oh, you shouldn't've. Robin, could you open a couple more bottles?'

Robin was relieved to have something to do among these painful people. Crystal and Minerva arrived. For God's sake, where was Dickon? Crystal waddled through the front door in a sack looking dreadful. Minerva exclaimed 'Lipstick at last, Alice!'

In her personal appearance Alice had indeed made an effort. The past year had been a struggle with loneliness, confusion, an influx of strangers into her life, and overall twitchy yuk, OK, so it was the flux universal. But how to ride it? In reality, people do walk in and out of one's days and nights trailing glimpses of their lives. How does one make it all add up to something? By knowing where one's going of course. Did she know where she was going? Not really, no – but she could at least make herself *appear* as though she did. This personal crisis in her life had been conducted, most of the time, in jeans and jumper, with hair tied back and face obscured by spectacles or hood or scarves, thereby announcing to the world that she was emaciated within. But this evening the hair was free, cut and waved. It tempted her to throw it about a bit so that a curl might flop seductively over one eye and she would push it back, mouth half open and throat exposed. Make-up enhanced the resuscitating facial features. Drop earrings. Shoes with heels. Fingernails painted the same colour as her lips. Her black dress was almost daring but not as daring as the white one of Sylvia who said, when she arrived, 'I could eat you, Alice'.

'I unpacked the suitcase with my evening clothes in it.'

'You've been here eight months without unpacking your evening clothes? I could cry. I've bought you a potted azalea.'

'So sweet of you, Sylvia, and you're looking fabulous – makes me feel quite – '

'I'll let you into a secret – I found an old tube of Bob's haemorrhoid cream and smeared it under my eyes. Bags vanished in seconds.'

'Am I allowed more than three glasses of champagne in my condition?' asked Crystal. Her eyes were puffy. She'd only come to get out of the house. Heaven Park had never been so tiny as in the last few days – barely a shed.

'Hullo, Mrs Bladder-Williams.' Why didn't he come? Why was he putting her through this? Surely he knew? Immacolata was looking extra large and out of character in a red and blue check frock.

'Why did you cut your hair off, Crystal?'

'It's more convenient when you're pregnant.'

'Alice, how did you get your hair so soft and shiny?'

'The secret is – shampoo it – rinse it with juice of boiled nettles – rinse with vinegar – rinse with water.'

'I envy that flyaway look,' said Minerva, 'but it wouldn't work on me. My hair needs to be *roped*.'

'Alice looks like a fifteenth-century Florentine rent boy,' said Sylvia.

'Is that good?'

'For her, yes. Not for everyone. Guess what, only in European art is there such a variety of hairstyles.'

Oh God, Alice didn't want to discuss hair all night! Where *was* he?

'Hair tip,' offered Pimm. 'Don't wash your hair with a perfumed shampoo if you're going for a walk. Flies love it and buzz about something awful.'

'Hi, Pimm,' said Alice. 'I didn't hear you arrive. Have you seen Dickon?'

'Is he coming? I saw him today. He didn't mention it.'

Alice died on the spot. All the heart went right out of her. Speaking to her guests instantly became a job she hadn't the strength for, and so she sat down and a whole glass of champagne slipped down her throat all-of-a-piece and everything else seemed to be going down as well, the light, the temperature, the very building. The only thing which went up was the noise. The clatter of conversation suddenly rankled terribly.

'Any news of Davis?' asked Mrs B-W.

'Not a squeak. It's a total mystery,' replied Lady Craddock. 'Robin thinks she drowned herself. Davis was as upset as we were by the end of life at The Crag. But I've a feeling she's gone to South America. She sometimes spoke of it and never spent a penny of her wages. We're having to visit the Old Un daily and do things. It's a complete turnaround from how everything used to be.'

'I'll call in on the Old Un when I've got a minute but getting Church House to rights after the flood is a monumental job.'

'I'm sure Mr Royal is a godsend. He's got such a wonderful back.'

Looking drawn but splendid, Larissa entered with – it was another potted azalea. Alice wondered where she was going to put all the buggers and whether a job lot had fallen off a lorry somewhere. Before doing anything else Larissa issued a bulletin to the effect that Ward was going to be all right and would be convalescing at the Monkshood Nursing Home where he would welcome visitors but please ring first and let's not talk about it any more this evening. 'In Russia we say food must follow tears.'

'Would you like a cucumber sandwich?' asked Alice. Of course it was sad about Ward but Alice resented the way Larissa took over the room and dictated the terms at *her* party, her bloody awful shitty party – why on earth had she bothered to spend good money on these total bores? And now she was on such tenterhooks that she didn't *want* him to come, it would freak her *out* if he came, she wanted the party to be *over*, she wanted to be *alone* and to go to *bed*.

Crystal sagged up to Mrs Dashman like a lachrymose kangaroo, her eyes spots of grey in pools of red, and said 'It's brilliant of you to come'. Larissa scowled through her grooming at Crystal's belly, knowing intuitively that the girl carried Ward's child.

The knocker went. Alice was afraid to look. Pimm held a cucumber sandwich between his teeth in order to open the door with both hands. Jason and Hopkins shot across the threshold wielding a bottle of champagne apiece. 'We wanna bop! We wanna boogie!' Both their heads struck the beam at the same time.

'Oh God,' wailed Alice. She couldn't take any more of this.

'Somebody should do something about those beams,' said Robin.

'What can you do about beams?' moaned Jason. 'You can't take them out.'

'They wanna boogie,' echoed the vicar who rather fancied a bit of a rhumba himself.

Dickon turned up shyly, crouchingly, evading all beams, and pecked her on either cheek. 'It's not your birthday, is it?'

A bicycle pump went off inside Alice. In a trice she was *all there*. Even too much there – bursting. 'Hi, Dickon. Would you like to open this bottle of shampoo? I mean champagne.' And she quickly turned away.

Knott said 'I'm a little hurt, Mrs Bladder-Williams'.

'I don't live with him, Oliver. And call me Immacolata. People are doing that now.'

Alice's laughter glittered all over the room like golden rain. But stupidly she couldn't look at Dickon. She was quite terrified of looking at Dickon.

Justice arrived carrying a cake piped with loops and frills of vanilla and coffee cream. He bent low as he crossed the threshold. 'Happy birthday!'

'Everybody thinks it's my birthday!' tinkled Alice.

Robin approached Crystal in the kitchen. 'Hi – as the *Titanic* said to the iceberg.'

'I've got something important to ask you.'

Robin sat down and put his face very close to hers.

'Robin, don't laugh, but will you marry me?'

'Will I marry you?'

'You were always asking me. Now I'm asking you.'

'Let me think about it. Yes, I'll marry you.'

'Oh God, it sounds so awful. Have you got a cigarette?'

Justice to Oliver: 'Let's be friends.'

'We've nothing in common.'

'All the more reason.'

'It's all right for *you*.'

Oliver was made very uncomfortable by the presence of Justice and said to Immacolata 'I hope you haven't found happiness. It is a misfortune to find happiness at the end of one's life, because that would make one feel cheated of all the period before, when one was unhappy. Much better to remain unhappy and be grateful for death. Where did you get that funny dress from? That's not your sort of dress.'

'Oh Oliver, I'm so sorry. Gin rummy doesn't do it for me any more.'

Crystal and Robin emerged from the kitchen like a couple of cod.

'Alice, guess what, Robin and I are getting married.'

'Oh, Crystal!'

'You don't look very pleased.'

'It's a surprise, that's all.'

'Hardly a surprise. He's been going on about it long enough.'

'But I thought you'd decided, you know – '

'Well, you thought wrong.' Crystal lightly tapped her belly. 'And as soon as possible.'

Alice clapped her hands together and the hubbub dropped like champagne foam. 'Ladies and gentlemen, a little announcement. The Lady Crystal Popjoy and Mister Robin Craddock are betrothed!'

Crystal said 'For God's sake, I didn't say tell everyone!'

Robin said 'What the hell!'

Dickon slipped into the kitchen and opened the back door for some air. Alice had virtually ignored him and indeed appeared happy to welcome everyone *except* him. Hardly a friendly glance, let alone a word. What was the matter with her? What had he done wrong? Had something happened while Meg was staying here? Had Meg put her foot in it?

Lady Craddock stuck a finger in a sandwich and Bob Wetmore came drunkenly through the front door and hit his head on a beam but didn't notice. He lumbered over to his wife and pawed her bare shoulder. Alice rang JJ and asked why he and Glory hadn't come. JJ replied that Crystal had informed him she would be marrying Robin Craddock and it had set back his recovery by several weeks.

'How can she've told you? They only decided here. Now. In my kitchen.'

'You know Crystal. She decides on something, then informs the relevant parties.'

'Perhaps it'll be the making of her.'

'And the breaking of me. How am I supposed to pay for it?'

'Does she want a big one?'

'If she does she's out of luck. I'll sell the Lucrezia Borgia ring. That'll have to do. I only propose a bring-a-bottle party in the ballroom. I hope you're looking after Minnie.'

'Come on down, JJ. It won't be the same if you don't. Jason and Hosky are here.'

'Oh, all right. Glory can drive.'

Lady Craddock looked up at her son. 'You'd never have married that girl if your father'd been alive.'

'Can you accept it, Mum?'

'Of course. But I don't feel good about it.'

Sylvia asked Alice 'Who are you sleeping with?'

'With whom am I sleeping?' Alice sipped from her flute. 'No one.'

'After one's own party one has to sleep with someone. Jason agrees, don't you, darling. It's horrible to be left alone at the end of one's own party. Minerva thinks Hoskins should sleep with you – doesn't that stupid creature know *anything* about men? Why don't you chivvy up Dickon? He's skulking in the kitchen. He needs a cuddle.'

So Alice went off to try and flirt with Dickon; she tried to throw her head back in a laugh of nonchalant sophistication which would expose her throat; but try as she might, it all became intense and serious and faintly shameful between them. Fortunately before she seized up altogether Glory Boy came into the kitchen and said 'Better late than never. E was in one of his moods. This is for you.' It was a kitten. Alice thought she was going to cry. Her chin trembled. 'You're touched,' said Glory. He rubbed her upper arm. If Alice were indeed an agent, he wanted to stay on the right side of her. 'We called him Bernie and discovered it was a girl, so she's Bernice.'

Sylvia bustled in and asked 'Is Dickon being a bore, darling?'

84.

A hooded figure tiptoed out of the village, a thin silhouette in the dusk lifting his knees high. How well he recalled playing cowboys and Indians in the parks and wastelands of his boyhood, creeping through undergrowth, all senses alert, entirely alive. He was always an Indian. And how well he recalled the spree of cops and robbers in the side streets of the northern city, looking to left and right, hopping from corner to corner, face sooty and inspired. He was always a robber. Oh, the thrill of subterfuge, the exhilaration of battle, the beauty of stalking!

And these days? Wrestling with tax forms, bank managers, household bills, only to ascertain that you still owed them more, always more, never free of debt. Were men to live and die this way? Must men's souls turn to slurry in an endless round of crap in the shops, poison in the air, junk on television? No man wants the shrivelled do-nothing life; all men want adventure; a man is forged by challenge.

The hooded figure shook its fist at the church as it tiptoed by in the knee-lifting style. A full moon shone yellowly behind fragmented cloud, making an effect like cracked glaze. After three-quarters of a mile he halted at a group of oaks, looked stealthily about, and high-stepped up the track. There was a cottage ahead but a mass of cars in the turning-space blocked his view, so he crept along the hedgerow and parted the ancient twists of branch and leaf. Two silver eyes gleamed out from the hood and through the window into Alice's soirée.

'So it's true! She is having a party and the bitch didn't invite me!'

Max looked a long time at the alien revel, chewing wine-gum after wine-gum, attempting to feel a wrathful disdain but achieving only despondency. There was that buxom sow, Sylvia Wetmore, barging into all and sundry, pissed as a newt. She'd dropped him after all these years. Found him embarrassing now she was at the stables. Right place for her. She looked like a drunken Shetland pony flinging her tits round the room, the fat little thing. All she needed were some bows in her and a rider with a whip! And now Davis, his new accomplice, had disappeared. She'd been a hateful hag of course but it was someone to plot with. If one's own hate were flagging one could always be fired up by the other's hate. There was a rustle in the hedge and Max started violently. He saw a crow with damaged wing attempting to render itself invisible among the exposed roots. 'How dare you frighten me like that! You should've been put out of your misery long ago!' And Max pressed his foot slowly down upon the bird until he heard a satisfying crunch.

Yet another car drew up and two people got out, one diffuse, the other compact, Lord Heavenshire and his catamite! Max's eyes glinted among the twigs.

Then it dawned on him.

'Of course. Why didn't I realise it before? It is so obvious. It all makes sense now. The sudden arrival in the village of the Alice creature, her going to work for Lord Heavenshire, previously having worked for the Minister of Power, and then pretending to get in with the ecology crowd, even going to prison for it, getting pally with the martyr, that Dickon, that was a masterstroke. But you don't fool me, Miss Alice. You're a double agent! You are pretending to be on the side of the protesters but you are all the time reporting back to the Minister of Power and his cronies! Wait until I pass this on to Joyce! Joyce will listen to me now. No more talk of my being too old now. And as for you, Alice, little miss party girl, we're going to dream up a big surprise for you, dearie!'

His cream leather shoes made a popping schlup-schlup as he disengaged them from the mire and on the way home he sang to keep himself going.

> *You're the pits*
> *You're a pre-flu shiver*
> *You're the shits*
> *A polluted river*

How he dreaded setting foot inside that caravan again and, when he came to it, it had never looked more wretched, the lowliest hovel, the merest sink, the sum total of his lifelong endeavours. Only his anger enabled him to open its tin front door.

85.

This is the Nine O'Clock News from the BBC in London. We have unconfirmed reports of the kidnap earlier today of the Minister of Power from his home in London. The police are saying only that he has gone missing after evidence of a struggle in the early hours of the morning and that as yet no organisation has contacted them. The Minister was alone in the house while his wife and children were on holiday in Portugal. Here is our political correspondent Ricky del Mar.

86.

May the first. Beltane. At the hairdresser's. The wedding of Crystal and Robin was on the morrow but few of the customers who sat under a row of hairdryers, solidifying their hair-does into the usual frightful frizz, would be going.

Mrs Bladder-Williams entered and was placed in the chair beside Princess Lark's. She nodded her greeting into the mirror. Muriel moved on to her and an assistant took over the completion of Princess.

'Same as usual?' asked Muriel.

'Less so,' said Immacolata.

'Not the marcel curls?'

'A bit looser and softer I think.'

'I've had something drastic,' said Princess. 'You should have something drastic.'

Immacolata looked at the woman's violent yellow mop and replied 'No, nothing drastic, Muriel'.

She had briefly been the Larks' neighbour and though Church House was almost back to rights and Princess once again came to clean, the old certainty of their relationship – gentlewoman employs peasant – had been lost. Indeed, ever since Justice had entered her bed and given her the most ecstatic time she'd ever had in her life, Immacolata no longer knew where she stood in the scheme of things.

'We're going to Puckermouth as usual,' chattered Princess. 'Every year Big says can't we be more adventurous and try somewhere else and I say good idea why not and then we go off to Puckermouth again. It's like ruts. Still, they know us there and the kids love it but Little said he didn't want to go this year which isn't like him, still he's at that age, and I said you got to, don't spoil it for everybody. We always stay at the Miramar on the front. They can see us coming, that's what they say. We all fit nicely into one bedroom and the beach is opposite, if you want the beach. Big likes the beach. I prefer the lido. Because of the tar. There's tar all along from the ships. Are you having your hair done for the wedding then?'

'I'm otherwise engaged.'

'You weren't invited? I am surprised. We're all helping out. It'll be good fun.'

'Don't cut any more off, Muriel.' And Mrs Bladder-Williams shut up tighter than a budgie's arse.

87.

Strange to say, the wedding went off without mishap. It wasn't even eccentric, unless you would conclude eccentricity from the fact that Robin had not one but five best men, having been unable to choose between his Scottish quintuplet cousins, Rory, Rollo, Redvers, Reynard and Rufus who, all singing merrily, drove down from Yester Lulu in a small charabanc.

JJ had woken up in a terrible state, or rather had roused himself from the night-long failure to go to sleep. In the cosy he'd come over super-prickly and had taken a tranquilliser which did nothing for him, so he took a stimulant which also did nothing only more so. Well, then, he'd have to see the gruesome day through on what remained of his own resources.

In fact the main risk was from the estate church, Saint Nectan's, which was opened for the occasion. It was classified not only as a Grade I listed monument but also as a dangerous structure and anyone wishing to attend the ceremony signed a piece of paper absolving JJ in the event of accident. Afterwards over 200 guests from far and wide staggered down the turfy hummock to the house where they were splendidly fed in the ballroom. The only disappointment was that Minerva was so overcome that she was unable to read her *Nuptial Ode in Cellophane*. It would have been magnificent, especially as Cook had stitched her into an outfit of raven feathers.

Crystal wore an ivory silk mini-dress to emphasise her pregnancy, a wide hat of cream organza, and a cape of polar mink which had been discovered in a broken wardrobe in a forgotten bedroom in an abandoned wing. Having spent her life avoiding official occasions, Crystal was very nervous beforehand and clung to her father who had adopted morning dress featuring grey jogging bottoms tight against his corpulence and black patent leather pumps. Once the ceremony was over she became very sentimental and clung to everyone else.

Towards the end of the reception Sylvia slumped down next to Alice, knocking her coolie hat in navy blue silk, and said 'Crystal says you've been brilliant and she couldn't've done it without you and you've got to have a puff of this, Crystal said, like I just had but it's done nothing for me and I always think this homegrown's never what it's cracked up to be but it's there, you stretch out your hand and it's there and that's life, I mean, the grass may bell we greener on the other side of the hill but you can't be forever trudging over hills and if you've plenty of grass on this side anyway, green or otherwise, well you tend to stick out your hand and it's there and you have a life without endless trudgery and so have a go, here you are.'

Alice took a modest puff and coughed. She hadn't often smoked marijuana. She thought to herself I can't detect any effect at all, but when it came to the final wedding toasts she found herself in a corner of the ballroom where Dickon was leaning against a wall and she was glad she'd been whacking on haemorrhoid cream under the eyes because lots of her bags had simply shrivelled away which had given her that extra little bit of carefree confidence and she sort of accidentally but subconsciously probably not really *lolled* against him and fell right into him as though he were a wonderfully plush sofa with a mouth and all in one slow, rolling, velvety movement it turned into the most glorious snog which went on and on and was all moistened with tears and laughter and the amazing fabulousness of life and still the kiss went on like a compelling ride through a theme park.

As the last guests dribbled away or were absorbed into obscure rooms of the house, JJ and Pimm, Sylvia and Alice found themselves in the cosy, their minds high and clear and warm. Following all the hurdles of the day, this was amplitude indeed, the reward for having come through.

But after that long, bold, enflaming kiss, Dickon had broken away from Alice, saying 'I've got to get back', and he'd fled in terror.

Alice asked 'Is it me, JJ?'

'No, my love. He was always like that. Never knew what he wanted. Only what he didn't want.'

'You're saying he doesn't want me.'

'Who knows what Dickon wants? When he was a boy, the factor let him swim in the lake. He'd go in naked in the evenings when it was quiet and no one around except me peeping through the bushes. Next thing we know, that Meg's got im. All very odd.'

'He doesn't have a sex-life with his wife any more.'

'He told you?'

'More or less.'

A shadow passed over JJ. His only child had gone off on her honeymoon with a man he could never relate to. Not only did he feel horribly left behind but the wedding scene itself disgusted him. He had hardly been out of the house since his attack. And now he couldn't stay in.

'Let's drive somewhere. Hit the open road. Pimm, you're sober.'

The Rolls had been tuned and polished and filled with petrol for the day's events. The Popjoy crest on the doors – monkey azure rampant, coronet or with lilies orange akimbo – shone forth as new. Yet all the car had done was bump up the turf to Saint Nectan's and bump down again. It seemed a shame not to use it.

At around seven p.m. therefore the dented wagon passed out through the gates of Heaven Park and an hour or so later out of Heavenshire altogether. Pimm, who was by temperament very single-minded, drove sleekly fast while those in the back laughed and gossiped about the wedding. Every so often, as the fancy took him, JJ called through the partition 'Left here' or 'Right at the next one' or 'Turn off the motorway' and, had there been nothing but water in the rear cabinet, all might have remained relatively straightforward. But there were cannabis, vodka, and some red powder said to simulate the effects of paragliding over Kew Gardens – and a significant blank period which even Pimm, driving through regions unknown to him, was later unable to explain. The where, the who, the how and the why flew into the air like a pack of cards and fell to earth incomprehensibly.

It was a little after ten-thirty in the morning of the following day when the four of them 'came round'. Probably the red powder was the principal culprit. It was Paul Crimsoncourt's wedding present to Crystal but she'd stupidly asked her father to look after it.

Pimm, to his consternation, awoke beside JJ in a four-poster bed facing a trefoiled casement. In a similar bed next door, Sylvia opened her eyes. She was lying beside Alice. Outside the day was astir with birds. Pimm worked out that he was naked and inched nervously away when he began to suspect that JJ was naked too. How on earth could he reach his clothes, neatly arranged on a coathanger hooked to the outside of a wardrobe, without exposing himself to JJ's rapacious eye? For the marquess too was stretching himself awake. A sliver of memory shifted in Pimm. He seemed to remember someone saying there were only two bedrooms prepared and boys must kip with boys and girls with girls.

'Where are we?' JJ's voice was hoarse and dry. He groped on the bedside table for a water jug and saw that he still wore his grey wedding-gloves.

'I don't know who they were and it was very dark but you said "Drive in here, they know me", and so they did.'

'Oh, don't put those frightful spectacles on – I haven't combed my hair yet. Pimm . . . '

'Yes?'

'You have a rather appealing smell.'

Pimm leapt from the bed with the fleetness of a wood nymph, holding a pillow to his mid-parts. 'Nothing happened, it's not what I do, you went out like a light!'

'If nothing happened, why are we naked?'

Pimm thought for a moment and replied 'Because we left our pyjamas at home'.

'You've got very big hairy feet for a midget and your ponytail is all loose. You look like a god of the underworld.'

'Stop it!' He was rapidly hoisting his trousers.

'Come back to bed and I'll forgive you for raping me.'

'Ugh, rape!' Pimm patted himself rapidly about the body as though looking for mislaid money.

'I thought Melody's death had improved you, but you're behaving like an uptight prude. Oh, come on.' JJ was suprised to find himself attracted to Pimm after all these years and threw back the sheets to display himself.

'No!'

'You're so ungame. You spend your life uncovering dead things but when it comes to the living . . . '

'I want to pee.'

At that moment there was a tap at the door which did not wait for a reply before coming in. JJ yanked up the bedclothes. A fair head appeared and said calmly 'My brother and I are going to serve you breakfast in the small dining-room opposite. There's a bathroom down the corridor. Epsom Salts are on the window-sill in there. Billy couldn't get your gloves off. Sorry.' And withdrew.

JJ was thunderstruck and said to Pimm 'Slap me'.

'He seemed very nice.'

'Did you hear what I said?'

'Slap yourself, you fat pervert.'

'Don't you know who he is?'

At last, peed and evacuated, washed and dressed, they crossed the corridor to the dining-room where Sylvia and Alice were already seated.

'Got any ciggies, JJ?' asked Sylvia. She looked ill at ease.

Alice said 'A delightful young man said he's going to bring us breakfast. No sign of it so far. I'm dying for a cuppa.'

'This is some kind of creepy hotel you've landed us in, JJ. Am I going to be presented with an appalling bill? I don't have a bean on me. Are you sure you haven't a cigarette?'

At that moment two fair heads came round the door. The upper head said 'Ready?'

'Yes,' nodded Alice.

'Then here we come!'

The lower head emerged carrying that day's newspaper. The upper emerged wheeling a trolley with a large teapot on it and various edibles and they both set the table with cereals, milk, marmalade, butter, and boiled eggs in silver cups.

'Back soon with the toast,' said the shorter.

'Could I have a packet of cigarettes?' ventured Sylvia.

'Fraid not. We're not eighteen yet,' said the shorter.

'The world's in awful shape,' said the taller, indicating the newspaper with a nod of his head.

When they'd gone, Alice said 'What nice boys. But they didn't seem very professional.'

'The tall one looks familiar,' said Sylvia, spooning cereal into her mouth.

'I slept like a top,' said Alice. 'What a pretty room this is.' The view was over a garden, lush but simple and battlemented along one side, and led to where a group of mature elms survived with their high lift and incomparable elegance of massing.

The crunch of cereal and toast occupied the ensuing quiet until noise of a different order froze their jaws mid-chew. It was a distant fanfare of trumpets. They looked at each other. The fanfare sounded again.

'What on earth was that?' asked Pimm.

'Oh hell, here it comes,' sighed JJ, forlornly flicking back his hair. He threw his napkin upon the table, rose to his feet and adopted a demeanour of apprehensive detachment.

The fanfare sounded a third time and soon after there came a sharp rap on the door. Two figures in black costume entered and stood either side of it. They bowed deeply from the waist as a very tall, very slim woman about forty-five years of age made her entrance. She wore a closely fitting floor-length dress of pale stuff embroidered with green ivy leaves, and a three-strand pearl choker, pearl bracelets, and drop-pearl earrings. A small pearl tiara perched in her short feathered hair. JJ bowed low and said 'Your servant, Ma'am'. Pimm followed his example while Alice and Sylvia made movements which may be described as deeply confused curtseys.

'What a nice surprise this is, JJ,' said the woman.

JJ introduced Alice, Sylvia and Pimm to the strong and gracious creature who stood before them, none other than the King-Mother herself, one of the great personalities of the age, some said the greatest. Wife, mother, virgin, betrayed lover, betraying lover, goddess of eternal youth, fertility symbol, symbol of vapidity, single woman, tragic woman, great innocent, great witch, rich bitch, nymphomaniac, collector of pictures and shopaholic, royal highness and woman of the people, predator and victim, mortal and immortal, these and many other archetypes had been attributed to her. But quite who or what she really was remained indecipherable and it was this which was the source of her charisma. She who had enjoyed all, suffered all and survived all, without losing her compassion or sense of mischief or lightness of touch, she it was who stared them softly out and down and who now turned to Alice and said 'But he might've warned me. He was always so impetuous when we were young. He hasn't changed. But I have – unfortunately.' The King-Mother was smiling sadly and they were bathed in her radiance. Suddenly all was effortless delight. 'Have the boys been looking after you?'

'Exquisitely, Ma'am.'

'They love to be useful.'

'Your elder son seems well, considering . . . '

'His burden is considerable. I discovered something the other day, that already when Victoria was on the throne, the English monarchy was second only to the Papacy in antiquity among the political institutions of Europe.' A number of appreciative 'really's were batted about. The King-Mother became abstracted in reflections and no one dared move.

The taller boy rushed in. He was breathless. 'Here's the toast. Sorry it was late.'

'Sire.'

The guests bowed down before the King-Emperor who said 'Er, please, enjoy the marmalade coz I made it myself,' and vanished bashfully.

His mother sighed and said 'Billy still misses his father dreadfully. They both do.'

'It must be ten years since the – '

'Six. Billy's been reading Plato. So of course, not to be outdone, Hal's simply *devouring* Aristotle. JJ, why don't you invite us all to Heaven in the autumn? You could discuss the ancient world with them.'

JJ shivered at the prospect and said 'Certainly, Ma'am'.

'Because the King-Emperor is upset by this city they're planning to slap down near you.'

'Oh, tell him not to worry, Ma'am. We'll sort it out.'

'No, he's keen to help but you know one mustn't interfere too obviously. My, the trouble I've had because I dared to stand up once in a blue moon. And what about that Polpotto, JJ?'

'Alas, Ma'am, by the terms of the trust . . . '

'We can break trusts.'

'If only.'

'One simply has to know which little hammer to apply in what little spot.'

'In this case nothing less than an Act of Parliament.'

'Oh, Parliament, yes . . . ' She crossed to the window. 'Why don't you walk at Virginia Water after breakfast? The rhododendrons won't last much longer. I can't ask you to lunch I'm afraid.'

'We wouldn't dream of imposing . . . '

The King-Mother looked more closely at Alice. 'Haven't we met before? Did you perhaps work for the Minister of Power?' Small clouds appeared behind Alice's eyes. The great lady was at once sensitive to this and continued 'But I must leave you to your breakfast. Do you really want that newspaper, JJ?'

'I never read before lunchtime, Ma'am.'

'Good, because I want to read it. There's a long article about me in the lifestyle section. Congratulations on Crystal's marriage by the way. Jaynellen Mellon rang me last night and said she'd had a wonderful time. I'd've come if you'd asked.'

'You destroy me, Ma'am.'

'Don't exaggerate. You didn't want the fuss. I understand. See you at the Garter thing.'

She nodded an adieu to the others who bowed and bobbed again as she exited. The two black costumed figures withdrew and shut the door behind them with a click, muting a fanfare of trumpets. The four regarded each other blankly. In a while another distant fanfare was heard. Then nothing.

On the return journey, JJ was very quiet and looked out of the window. Sylvia and Alice conversed thus:

SYLVIA: So we finally made it.

ALICE: We certainly did. I never thought I'd ever be waited on by the King-Emperor! He had incredible eyes, did you notice? So deep, so sad, so alive, all at once.

SYLVIA: I meant you and me. Last night. We finally made it.

ALICE: You may've made it, Sylvia, but I certainly didn't.

SYLVIA: You just can't remember.

ALICE: I'd've remembered that. Is that all you can think about? We crash out at Windsor Castle and –

SYLVIA: Sorry, that's me.

ALICE: It's not me, Sylvia.

SYLVIA: Pimm, stop at the next shop. I need some fags. Have you got any money, JJ?

JJ: No, I left it all under the lamp for the chambermaid.

ALICE: I know you and JJ have this theory that everyone's bisexual really but I'm not theoretical about this sort of thing. The relevant lights don't switch on unless I'm with a certain sort of man.

SYLVIA: What sort is that?

ALICE: A man I want to be close to.

SYLVIA: Dickon. We all saw it. The snog of snogs. That must be what turned you on last night.

ALICE: What a terrible thing to say. We all saw it. So bloody what?

JJ leaned forward and said through the partition 'Didn't you hear what Sylvia said? We're dying for a fag.'

'Can't you be a bit more civil?' rebuked Pimm. 'One minute you want to shag me, the next you're treating me like shit.'

'You rejected me, remember? That always stings.'

'Well, you should've tried harder.'

'What are you saying, Pimm?'

'It was a very new idea for me. Of course I was nervous. If you'd made an attempt to reassure me more, stroked me a little, then I might, I mean, who knows?'

'Oh for shit's sake, man, it's too late now, I've gone off you. I'm over fifty years old and I don't have time for this farting about. It was one of those flashes, Pimm. They must be seized as they occur. Life moves on. So drop dead.'

Pimm philosophised that even very nice people can be nasty for no reason.

88.

Ragamuffin was sitting on a hilltop with his dog Scrumpy in the May sunshine. All was now out, even the oak leaves, those last arrivals of spring, and the Puck Valley spread its lush detail below them. This was one of Ragamuffin's favourite spots. He could see everything but was above it and away from it and not oppressed by it. Occasionally he was drawn into the doings of the village but his impulse was always to escape as soon as possible into the comforting woods or the aerial freedom of the hills.

In the centre of the view were Milking Magna's unruly rooftops rising to the pinkish stone of Saint Wendy's. Over to the left bristled The Crag and, to the right, the council houses of Gypsy Castle with the pale rectangles of the Beowulf Caravan Park beyond. Further right but closer to the river, whose serpentine course made visible glints here and there through the alders and willows which knitted its banks, were the buildings of Lower Farm. Two pasture fields up from the farm was The Glade, barely discernible among shrubbery and trees.

Continuing on round to the right and crossing over to the side of the river on which Ragamuffin was perched, the first landmark to be noticed was the apex of Heaven Park's chief portico breaking above the puffs of foliage. But nothing more of the pile could be seen. Neither the Obelisk nor the Hermitage nor the Propylaeum were visible, nor the Temple of the Inexpressible nor the lake with its Hanging Bridge and Boathouse, nor the Mausoleum nor Saint Nectan's: the angles of the landscape and fullness of the planting protected all.

To Heaven Park's rear was the deer park. Beyond that, climbing the hillsides, were the fretted fields and copses of the Home Farm and Upper Farm. The farmhouse at the Home Farm had been closed for many years and the two were run as one from Upper Farm by Malcolm Gibbet, assisted by the woman who was almost his wife (Winnie or Dulcie or whatever she was called), and by a number of contract drivers and by Ragamuffin. The shepherd boy occupied an ancient two-room cottage at Upper Farm's furthest perimeter where the known world dissolved into mist.

Ragamuffin was by nature mild, even moronic, but repulsive to Malcolm on account of his filthiness. Everything about the farm buildings at Upper Farm was neat, clean, plucked, scrubbed, but Ragamuffin was none of these things and neither was his cottage. Indeed it stank. Curious to say, Ragamuffin did not. Maybe after a while the unwashed body attains an inoffensive equilibrium. Maybe he took secret dips in the Puck; if so, he never combed his hair, because it was always a thick, silky tangle. His clothes too were unwashed and resembled bark; and like bark they were periodically discarded. Though he had not stench, he did smell – a pre-industrial smell akin to that of seventeenth-century hymnals or of cut grass in muddy weather or of cherry crumble drawn freshly from the oven.

Ragamuffin's gaze, calm and complete, continued moving and came to that area of exhumatory activity known as the Temple of Mercury; while at the top, on the rough beer belly of the heath, stood the Ring of the Moon, still the possession of the Earls of Moon. Lord Moon's main estate at Bloodwood was an hour's drive further north and its principal house, though very quaint and very old, was in fact just that, a house, whereas Heaven Park would be better described as a milieu. And beyond everything to the right, beyond even the mist and therefore presently invisible, were the worn teeth of the Mountains Beyond the West; whereas beyond everything to the left, hidden behind diminishing swells, were the fat and fruity lowlands which stretched eastwards from Appleminster. It was intended by mediaeval theologians that the central spire of Appleminster Cathedral should be visible from the altar stone of the Ring of the Moon. But the spire was never built.

Ragamuffin hugged his knees contentedly as he attempted to tot up the number of smoke-plumes rising from the village chimneys and reached a different total every time. Glory Boy approached across the springy grass. Scrumpy turned a doggy head and thumped his tail a few times but did not otherwise move.

'Chilly up ere,' said Glory, squatting down beside his friend.

'Thought you was at the wedding.' Ragamuffin's eyes were far apart, excellent for focusing on distant places. But they gave him a poetic and impractical look, an air of bemusement, when viewing people or things close to.

'Left early.'

'Weren't it good?'

'Not bad. Toffs guzzling champagne.'

'What's that shit in your hair?'

'It's not shit. It's pudding.'

'What's it doing there?'

'Daisy got hyper. What you bin doin?'

'Nothing much. Combing clouts.'

They both watched a skylark ratcheting itself up the sky.

'You're an anan . . chornism,' said Glory.

'What do you mean?'

'Clouts is an anchorism.'

'You got that word from im.'

'He said he's one too. I get lots from him.'

'We knows that.'

'What of it?'

'Nothing.'

'Don't give me that look. You've done it wiv im.'

'Not all night.'

The conversation lapsed, as it always did at a certain point on this subject. A squadron of golden-eye ducks whistled by at eye-level. Glory followed their flight until they dissolved into another dimension. He said 'I'm thinking of going away'.

'Yeah?'

'Yeah.'

'Where?'

'Anywhere. There's nothing round ere. Aren't you fed up with nothing happening?'

'I won the hairy bum competition at the pub. By miles.'

'I'll comb your clouts too.'

Behind them sheep munched, shuffled, tinkled and shat.

'Ere, what's that?' asked Glory Boy.

'What's what?'

'That.'

Ragamuffin trained his wide eyes in the direction of Glory's finger.

89.

The boys saw an ambulance belting away from Lower Farm, its claxon braying and its lights flashing. What had happened was this. The letters in the fireproof box had been lodged at the top of the house to protect them from the flood and, while Dickon was enjoying himself at the wedding, Meg had struggled up the attic steps and begun to browse through them. She was soon drawn into the passionate and tormented relationship they revealed . . . *but without you somewhere under the same roof, my existence is intolerable. It's all my fault I know. Forgive me . . . My life here is a tragic burlesque. Only you are real . . . Angel, you are stronger than I who am weak and cowardly, so do not reject me in so harsh a tone. Of course you are right but I am dying within . . .*

Max, fervent with misanthropy on the day of the Craddock-Popjoy wedding, decided to make a grab for the letters which Davis had spoken of, and as he hunched his way along hedgerows to Lower Farm, discovered that he was really beginning to relish this creeping about the village, the sense of secret power it gave him. The farmer's car wasn't there – the martyr had abandoned his wife to join the party – good – he deserved to be done. Max high-stepped up to the back door where he donned a carnival mask hidden in his pocket and pulled a crowbar from beneath his mackintosh. Meg up in the attic, reading of love's luscious pains, stopped mid-sentence. She heard something. Her heart contracted as the efforts of the crowbar filtered upwards.

The sick slag won't put up any fight, thought Max, so why don't I ring the front doorbell, knock her out, and shanghai the letters? Probably she wouldn't answer the door when alone. Very wise. Blast this – back doors aren't supposed to be tough. In the good old days it would've been open anyway and I could've walked in and stunned her with a single blow. She's probably shitting herself stupid by now. Coming, dearie. Shan't be long. Then you're going to tell me where those letters are, like a nice little invalid. Ah, I think I heard the wood crunch. We'll be open any second now, dearie – '

'What the hell do you think you're doing?' demanded a voice at Max's back.

It was the turn of Max's heart to contract. 'Don't shoot, don't shoot,' he babbled and turned slowly round while his right foot went into an involuntary tap routine.

It was Herald, naïvely coming to ask Dickon if they might repitch their tepee now that the waters had receded (though their move to rainbow valley had its plus-points, the reek from Harry Pulp's chicken farm when the wind turned was nauseating). Max lashed out with the crowbar. Herald dodged it, leaping sideways, and gasped 'Fuck me! What's going on?', while Meg, aware of the kerfuffle, wailed in the attic. Max lunged and lashed again. Herald was too nimble for him and Max began to think – I'm wearing the wrong clothes for this – the mac's too flappy. Herald squared up with his fists, legs apart and on his toes, slender calf muscles pumping alternately. 'C'mon, ya bastard, c'mon!' Max spat at his adversary thrice in succession but the spittle wouldn't go through the lip-hole and remained unpleasantly trapped behind the mask.

Max thought, I've buggered this up good and proper.

'C'mon, ya bastard!' challenged Herald again, but Max flung aside the crowbar and, lifting the skirt of his mac, took flight with vigorous movements of his cranelike legs.

Herald chanted a calming mantra before calling aloft 'Are you all right, Meg?'

She crawled on trembling knees to a dormer window and unlatched it. 'Is that you Herald?'

'Yes. He's gone. Don't be afraid.'

'Thank the Lord. I'll throw down the keys.'

Once inside he ran upstairs. Meg was lying on her bed racked by short dry breaths. 'I'll get you a brandy.' He rummaged about in the parlour until he found a bottle, took a slug for himself, and poured one for her. Setting another pillow behind her head, Herald rhythmically stroked her cold hand.

'Be calm. You're safe now.'

'Who – was – it?'

'Don't know.'

'Malcolm Gibbet?'

'No, it wasn't im. This one was tall. Funny clothes. In a horrible mask like Little Bo Peep with yellow bunches of hair at the sides.'

'Don't. The very thought of it. Shall we call the police?'

Herald frowned. 'Not me.'

'But what if he comes back?'

'You've got enough locks on that door!'

'Dickon put them on. He's frightened we'll be evicted.'

'Maybe that's who it was. Evicters.'

'But you said it wasn't Malcolm.'

'He wouldn't do it 'is self.'

'We'll be homeless!' He made her sip more brandy. 'If you hadn't come I daren't think what would've happened.'

'Where is your husband?'

'Up at the wedding.'

Herald telephoned Heaven Park but no one answered and so he telephoned for an ambulance. Meg fell into exhaustion. A watery fog bedevilled her eyes but she was nervous of closing them because masked bogeymen, enraptured love letters, cruel landlords, red Indians, and Little Bo Peep came flying at her out of the blue. Her breast was jerking. She raised herself with difficulty on the pillows. How heavy felt the single plait of hair over her shoulder. Her hands, seeming to move of their own accord, untied the plait and spread it lock by lock in a silken fan about her head. Still her breast jerked. Still her hands moved. She was comforted by this spreading of her hair and at last an unusual tranquillity expanded from the region of her navel and the jerking in her breast came to an end and a great sleepiness infused her, which was not fatigue but energy of a different order, as though she were being unfolded, as though plates of armour were being gently unlaced, as though a million knots were untying themselves, and after a while her various components and elements, all loosened and restful, began to shift apart and move outwards, effortlessly, on a warm rocking tide, and the late afternoon glowed beneath her resting eyelids with a reddish gold of softness, of slowness, of warmth, and Meg thought – I have never been so comfortable in my whole life. And the warm soft reddish gold took her deeper and deeper. And the filaments of her being continued to relax and unravel and she thought . . . there never was such profound ease . . . such effortless well-being . . . such bliss . . .

By the time they reached the County Hospital, Meg was dead.

90.

'Come on, Kevin. Get shot of it,' cajoled his master.

Once more Kevin went into a quivering squat. His hind-quarters vibrated and his head turned away with a curl of the lip, an expression both of embarrassment and concentration, but still nothing happened. Kevin lifted his bottom a little, crept forward and again squatted, but to no avail.

'Jesus!' JJ threw up his arms. He wanted to get back to the lane, the car, home. He was feeling exposed walking about in this open area for all to see. He'd only come this way because Kevin had implored him.

Dickon, eating a packet of crisps, was hedge-trimming down the side of a field when JJ plodded into view. Dickon thought – What's he after? – he never comes this way – and drew to a halt and opened the cabin door. 'Want a trim, sir?' he bantered. The engine stopped. Silence swamped them and neither knew what to say next.

JJ was struck by Dickon's handsomeness. The man looked airy and light, as though a crushing weight had been lifted off his shoulders. In fact one thought above all others plagued Dickon as he went up and down in the tractor, and the thought was that Meg had probably died at the very moment he was kissing another woman. The foil crisp packet floated gently to earth and JJ was delighted to have something to do. He retrieved it with great dignity, as the Emperor Charles V once stooped and retrieved a dropped paintbrush for Titian (and reading a biography of the painter twenty-five years hence, and coming to that gesture of the Emperor's, JJ unexpectedly recalled this moment in the field with Dickon). JJ put the packet in his pocket but could not resist saying 'Must keep the place tidy'. Dickon flushed with irritation at his own carelessness. All of which is to touch upon the complexity which had always existed between them.

'So you're carrying on as normal,' said JJ.

Dickon climbed down. 'Not as normal, no.'

'But keeping up the routine, yes, that's important.'

'What else is there to do?'

'There's always something else, Dickon.'

'I know you want me out.'

'When you're ready to talk, we can talk. But not now. You look well.'

The farmer said 'Better finish the hedges'.

'I'm always telling Malcolm to let ours be, so that we can enjoy the wild flowers.'

Dickon felt a heat at the sides of his neck and might have said something unwise had not Alice, waving her arms in the air and shrieking like a stuck pig, sped down the field towards them.

'Help! Help!'

She skidded on a cowpat but righted herself.

'It's happened again!'

Trying to recover her breath, she bent over with her hands on her knees. Her arched back was heaving.

'Take it easy a second,' said Dickon holding her gently by the shoulders.

'In the bed. The most awful thing in my bed.'

'What?'

'A pair of trousers.'

'But that's rather nice, rather friendly.' JJ attempted to pacify her.

'No. Disgusting old grey flannel ones. Like dead man's things. Will one of you please tell me what the hell's going on!'

Part Four
SUMMER

91.

Insofar as he was able, John Smith felt very unwell. The venetian blinds were lowered in his room at the Monkshood Nursing Home and tilted against the burgeoning seasonal light, and a number of additional contraptions were wheeled in to keep him under even closer observation. He remembered a nurse called Melody and wondered why she didn't come and see him any more.

92.

Sylvia turned up at ten a.m. in the yellow rusty Ford and said 'There's a hamper in the back'.

'I'm getting Bernice's food. Where are we going?' The kitten coiled affectionately round Alice's bare ankles.

'Surprise.'

When Bernice had been catered for, they hit the road. Through the windows gusted the scent of the cow parsley. A bird zipped over the hedge. Dipping and rising at switchback angles, it flew ahead of them down the corridor of hedgerows. Brilliant sunshine made a looped shadowline of telegraph wires on the tarmac.

'Be a darling and light me a fag.'

Alice lit the cigarette, took a puff and passed it across. 'Lighting up's the best bit. Then it's downhill all the way.'

They bowled past a signpost which indicated Puckermouth to the left.

So it's not the seaside, divined Alice.

'Where *are* we going?'

'We're just going.'

'Is that the surprise? Going nowhere?'

'Get lost!'

Sylvia was addressing a farm dog which had propelled itself out through an open gate and was chasing the car. For a mile or so afterwards the pong of artificial fertiliser loaded the nostrils.

'It smells like rotting flesh,' said Alice.

'So you know how rotting flesh smells?' asked Sylvia.

They were now well out of that district where one would wave automatically to most of the drivers of oncoming cars. The landscape was losing its lushness. Secret copses among the outcrops of rock were threaded by tumbling streams. As the little Ford bombed round a curve in the road, the blue peaks of the Mountains Beyond the West loomed suddenly close.

A petrol station appeared and Sylvia pulled in. Two thin boys in blue dungarees approached and scrutinised the small panting car.

She smiled up at them through the driver's window. 'Fill it up please.'

'I'll do it,' said one of the boys.

'No, it's OK, I'll do it,' said the other boy.

'Sure?' queried the first

'Well, you can do it if you want.'

'Why don't you make it self-service?' suggested Sylvia, 'then I could do it'.

'Which would you prefer, me or him?' asked one.

Sylvia got out of the car and rested her arms on the car-roof, examining the two boys. Two friendly young faces kindled by the sunshine. They were not twins – one was blonder than the other – but there was little to choose between them.

'Can I have a pee?' asked Alice.

'We don't have a place for a lady,' said the blonder one colouring. Males who blushed were one of Sylvia's favourite things. 'I'd go on to Smackie Force, miss. There's a caff there with all the, you know – '

'Trimmings,' completed the darker.

'What about my petrol, boys?' They were so thin and sweet –

it made Sylvia feel fat. She stood beside the car, in her creased linen shorts, feeling rounder and rounder.

'I'll put it in,' said the blonder one, 'and he'll take your money'.

Sylvia followed the darker one into the shop, if shop it was, more of a hut really, constructed from wooden slats painted green. The boy stared at her breasts unselfconsciously. Sylvia felt her breathing quicken and her mouth fell open. The boy's mouth fell open too, his ears reddened, and Sylvia noticed his dungarees bulge at the crotch. Alice called out from the forecourt 'Hurry up, I'm bursting!' Sylvia brushed the boy's hand as she took her change. His lips were wet. She dithered and left.

They drove on. Unable to chance upon a bush which came up to Alice's standards, they stopped at Smackie Force, so called because a tributary of the Puck was here forced into a narrow channel by rocks and shot its water in a leap that plunged sixty feet. The sound of the gush made Alice want to pee even more. Torrent ducks palavered on the café lawn. Faces, chewing, stared out at them from windows and Alice braced herself for the latrine. When she returned to the car she was all ease and gratitude and said to Sylvia 'What a shithole'.

Ten minutes later they spotted a meadow of grass and flowers below sheltering rock, the perfect suntrap concealed from the road if you went round the side, and they settled their picnic there. Sylvia said 'Hoggart makes the best pork pie I've ever tasted. Here, you open the wine. Oh, Alice, I'm so fat! And look at all the food I've brought.'

'But you always look so wonderful, Sylvia. That shape is you.'

'It isn't me. I don't want fat to be me.'

'Then eat and drink less.'

'I can't exist on air. Pass me one of those smoked salmon baps, darling.'

'Men find you very attractive.'

'They find me sexy. It's different. I don't want to be *fleshy*. I want to be angular. Like you.' Sylvia tore at the bap with petulant teeth.

'I'm not angular. I go in and out, that's all.'

'And I hate being short. Not that I want to be tall, not like

Minerva Popjoy, not like some mutant Amazon. I want to be medium. I want to be normal. Don't you want to be normal?'

'In what way am I not normal?' protested Alice.

'You can't be normal working for JJ.'

'I sometimes feel I hit normal but I can never keep it there. It swings off again. Sylvia, face it, you're not an angular person. You're a warm round emotional person and I think that's lovely.'

'Do you really?'

'Yes.'

'But fat isn't healthy, especially if you smoke.'

'Then stop smoking.'

'Are you trying to destroy me? My husband likes me fat – which is one of the reasons I married him and one of the reasons I left him. I was fed up with being this fat doughy thing for him to pull about, not that he can do much he's so pissed, so it's never over with, he goes round and round and I don't even get started, it's just being pulled about and pawed, bloody awful. Anyway I'm getting to like living alone. One thing I never could stand is other people's pubes on the soap. Oh Alice, I want to project past the fat, above the shortness – I always did want that – so I became an actress which was no good because I only got character parts when they realised I wasn't going to grow any more. The French maid with feather duster and dimpled knees. There are lots of short actresses. Actually most of them are short. But short *and* fat gives a director problems. Pour me another glass, darling. Isn't this heat bliss? Thank God I had my own money, otherwise I'd've had to become a secretary or something ghastly.'

'I was a secretary. I still am.'

'We know that and look what that awful Minister of Power did to you. It can't be fun being a secretary, always at the beck and call of some prat.'

'It's not perfect but one has to survive. It's like that question they always ask prostitutes – are you happy doing this? And if the girl says not particularly they pounce with their self-righteousness. But she is obviously a lot happier than working in some crappy sweatshop or factory for peanuts – otherwise that's what she would do.'

'How did we get on to tarts? I grant you I was lucky. I inherited. Daddy had a string of chocolate shops in the north of England. It may be a bit common but I couldn't care less because it enabled me to – to – what did it enable me to? Perhaps it prevented me from – from – do you think it could've prevented me from realising myself?'

'You seem fairly real.'

'It's so hot. Let's strip off.'

'Aren't there people about?'

'Not a soul.' Sylvia began to shed the remainder of her clothing.

Alice responded with 'Oliver Knott said that if you stand near rocky mountains, especially with sheer drops, in high winds, you become positively ionised and this can produce dangerous electric shocks. Someone once died that way apparently.'

'Why are you telling me this? We're not near any drops. We're not in high winds. Just take some of your clothes off.' Sylvia slithered out of her panties and looked about nakedly under the hot blue sky. A blue merlin scouted her and flew away.

'I've already taken some off,' said Alice.

'Take off more.'

'No.'

'Why not?'

'Because you've got a funny look in your eye.'

'Don't be mean.'

'I'm not being mean.'

'You are. You know I'm fond of you.'

'We're friends.'

'A little more than that, Alice. We slept together. And I'm a teensy weensy bit in love with you.'

'Love?' Alice twitched.

'You were very good in bed.'

'Nonsense. This is crazy. How do you know it's love?'

'Because I feel like a city descending into the sea. That's how it feels when I begin to fall in love. Thrilling and not very nice. I didn't really mean that about pubes on the soap, in fact I like it.'

'It was you who put the trousers in my bed! Those horrid grey flannel trousers!'

'It wasn't! How could you. I'm not madly in love, just a teensy. Superfond.'

Alice looked at Sylvia's unclothed body as charitably as she could. 'Sylvia, I couldn't fall in love with you in return, I'm sorry.'

'You don't have to fall in love in return.'

'I know what happened at Windsor was – maybe it was romantic for you but for me it was – well, being at Windsor Castle at all was like being on another planet. Funnily enough I could probably get excited with anybody right now because I am so wound up and frustrated and confused by Dickon but I think that would be an unfair reason, don't you?'

'I think it would be a lovely reason. Sometimes the reason doesn't count. It's the contact that counts. I wish you'd stop putting up these barriers.'

'They're not barriers – it's my identity! It's not meant to be nasty.'

'You have a qualm.'

'Yes, I have a qualm.'

'What sort of qualm?'

'A great big one trembling somewhere between my breast and my stomach and it means no.'

'I must have a pee.'

Upon returning from round the other side of the rock, Sylvia snappily put her panties back on but left her breasts unfettered and lit a cigarette. Alice asked 'Won't you go back to Bob?'

'Oh, shut up. I once tried to murder him by pushing a fibre-tip pen up his nose. Dickon's much more real now his wife's dead. I suppose you'll be in like Flynn.'

'After the incident with the trousers, he asked me to go and live with him.'

'Really?'

'Yes.'

'Will you?'

'Yes.'

That shut Sylvia up all right.

'What's the time?' asked Alice.

93.

The Justin Fashanu Leisure Centre in Appleminster was quiet on Thursday evenings. No one knew why. It was just one of those things. A round-shouldered arrangement of blue and grey steel girders, the centre had been put up with a development grant from Brussels, or lottery money, or was it national-regional aid? In the foyer with the full explanation was a brass plaque which had been unveiled at the opening by Dame Monica Winstanley-Stanley, Chairman of the County Council. So on Thursday evenings Dickon had lately chosen to work out in the gym there. As he passed through the turnstile with his usual surly expression, Helen Craddock came out.

'Don't worry. It may never happen,' she teased.

'Hullo, Helen. You're looking well.'

'Just had my third shiatsu.'

They had both lost their partners that year and on that account neither wished to linger with the other.

The gym was empty except for one girl who soon left. After forty minutes Dickon became bored and returned to the men's changing-room, stripped off and went into the steam-room. He loved to be naked, free and clean. There was no one else in there today and soon he was swooning in images of the gymnasium girl and her breasts bouncing as she jogged on the running-machine. Letters floated across her body, letters from the fireproof box, those letters which had come out of lives trapped in impossible conflicts and obligations yet still managing to dream and soar and hope, those damn letters which still seemed to be causing so much trouble – he'd found them spilled all over the attic after Meg's death. A few hot tears stung his eyes, mingling with the steam and the sweat. Meg hadn't had a life. He could've done more, taken her out more, they should've moved to the town, there would've been more for her in the town. And now she was gone and he discovered he hated living alone. It felt unnatural to be alone. It frightened him in fact.

A burst of steam gushed up from the floor. He always assumed steam to be grey in colour but now, giving the matter his attention, he saw that it had blue and lavender in it and something of whiteness and something too of blackness. As he looked the steam appeared speckled with tiny black dots, or maybe they were dark brown or even dark red. Dickon became fascinated by the complexity of colour. The contrapuntal overlay of his mind quietened down, enabling its deeper deposits to rise, and thus it was, with a rupture of improbability, that something quite extraordinary occurred to him.

Dickon found himself subjected to a revelation. Something he never knew before, or didn't know he knew, matter of factly became self-evident. The letters in the fireproof box: he actually knew who it was who had written them so many years ago. No. It couldn't be. But, yes, of course, it couldn't be anyone else. This revelation was followed by another even more outrageous, which was the identity of the person to whom the letters had been written, which was amazing, unbelievable, grotesque, but it had to be, it couldn't be anyone else, it had to be her, and yes, it had to be he who'd written them, and as the prodigious secret continued to explain itself in his mind, he had another notion which was, that is to say, could it be that their child was, no, of course not, that was mere absurdity, his imagination was running away down impossible paths, because if that were true, nothing would ever be the same again, and as it was it was dynamite without the addition of their child being – the steam sat on him like a dead weight and he had to escape the steaming, airless box and recover under a cold shower.

Shshshshs . . .

What should he do? How could he assume the responsibility for these new and alarming facts? How could he presume to redesign so many other lives? Should he put the letters in the bank? Or would it not be all for the best to burn them and say nothing?

94.

Oliver Knott sat in the doctor's waiting-room looking round the walls in order to avoid looking at the seven other people also waiting.

Chlamydia!

National Bed-Wetting Day

If your tinnitus is too much for you

Mental illness – what does it mean? It means you can't sit in a waiting-room with seven other people without getting alarmed by posters on the walls and pamphlets on the table. No, Oliver, you aren't mad. Take your hand away from your heart. Stop staring at the pulse in your wrist. You are here simply to ask for different sleeping-pills because your customary ones don't work as a result of your crisis of conscience over the Puck Valley Development Scheme. Are you for it? Are you against it? You are torn.

Visiting Africa, Asia, South America? Think malaria

Folic Acid. What all women should know

How to use your inhaler properly

Contraceptive advice. It doesn't matter how old you are. Now here was proof that *they* were mad.

What should you know about head lice?

Passive smoking

Reduce the risk of cot death

All these reasons for feeling bad, all these scientific rationales of illness, a pill at the end of every symptom. The way his precious reductionist science had decomposed everything into tiny mechanical bits, he saw it as precisely analogous to mental depression, saw it for the first time in this waiting-room staring at the posters, the way both science and depression squeezed the life out of everything, the endless breaking down, the getting stuck in localised cul-de-sacs, when what was needed was building up, the big picture, the greater perspective. These pills, which had begun as a safety-net, weren't making him better, they were now obstructing his recovery of the big picture.

'To recover the big picture I must throw out the pills, but in order to do that, I must view the universe differently from the way I was trained because pills are the creation of scientists and I am a scientist.' This obvious fact hit him like a bucket of cold water. A pill for this mechanical bit, a pill for that mechanical bit, no end to the bits and the pills. He'd never be free of pills until he took a different view. But he was a scientist nonetheless. Non-computable mathematics – maybe that was the door which would resolve his dichotomy. He would say goodbye to pills by saying goodbye to computers, and he'd say goodbye to computers by saying hullo to non-computable mathematics. Yes, a science beyond computers, a science where computers could not follow, that was it! And Oliver picked up his jacket, told the receptionist he was cancelling his appointment, and walked out of the surgery.

95.

Bees bubbling in the blossom. The distant racket of tractors and harvesters gathering in the silage. Red campion and dog-roses mottled the hedgerows.

Justice, carrying the baby in a rucksack on his back, took Immacolata's hand as they entered the wood. A weak breeze shifted in the upper leaves. The baby gurgled contentedly. Baby John was making plenty of noises now. 'That's a badger's set,' said Justice where reddish earth had spilled. He halted beside half a trunk of fallen tree and unrolled a groundsheet. Immacolata ran the back of her hand lightly against the baby's cheek. 'Poor little mite,' she said.

'He'll not want for anythin,' said Justice.

'I didn't mean . . . ' She pulled at a tuft of grass but quickly drew back her hand. A blade had sliced the finger. Justice took her hand and sucked the fine line of blood and she felt again that swelling fullness in her breast. He buried his face in her bosom and she kissed the top of his head. He sprinkled her body with kisses and delicate nips. He smelled of sandalwood and cloves and woodsmoke. She smelled of fruit and talcum powder. She heaved against him.

In another part of the wood Helen Craddock was walking along a path with Selwyn Blagdon. A line of balsam poplars sweated a heavenly scent. 'The one thing I miss is James's songs,' she said. 'Do you know any, Selwyn?' Whereupon he sang in a bad barking voice –

Oh sweetheart
How lovely
The fruit of the vine

> *The virgin*
> *Is dancing*
> *Her head full of wine*
>
> *Oh sweetheart*
> *How funny*
> *That pattern of red*
>
> *A woman*
> *Is falling*
> *Her heart full of lead*

'It's sad,' said Helen.

'Just a song,' he replied, looking upwards. A warbler was trilling somewhere.

'Does it have to be like that? Growing up, I mean. Experience being merely a journey to disillusionment?'

'Nothing has to be anything. No rules. It's what you make of it.'

'I don't think so. I think life is mostly accidents and maturity is coming to terms with the failure of one's dreams.'

'That's a miserable way to put it. What I'd say is – maturity is not being inhibited by failure.' He laughed and stroked her back as they walked along.

In a third part of the wood Ragamuffin had removed all the clothes from his faunlike body which was black with hair from the navel downwards. Kissed by long grass, parded by sunlight, in a transport which gleamed from his half-closed eyes, and blowing short bursts of air from his pursed lips, he was slowly wanking.

After they'd made love, Justice held her tightly and asked 'You know who I am? Who am I?' And tighter. 'Who am I?'

'Justice.'

'That's right.' He relaxed his hold and exhaled with relief. 'That's right . . . Justice. Yes.'

'And who is he?' Immacolata was looking at the baby who had observed the whole sexual procedure with alternating curiosity and indifference.

'That's John.'

'But who is John?'

'She promised to tell me after the birth . . . I don't know who the father is.'

'Isn't that unusual?'

'Is it? These days . . . '

'Melody wasn't like that. She was a good girl. Something else must've been involved.'

'Yes.'

'You can talk about her with me, Justice.'

'I know.'

But he didn't say anything else. Immacolata said 'I must put my clothes back on. If anyone saw me like this I'd die.'

96.

It was Alice's birthday but she hadn't told anyone and didn't want to celebrate it. Driving back from work, she turned on that other pillar of BBC security, *The Six O'Clock News* . . . *The terrorist group the Green Kingdom in a surprise move has today claimed responsibility for the unsolved kidnapping of the Minister of Power and has demanded a tripling of the price of petrol at the pump as the condition for his release. The Prime Minister has stated that government policy on petrol prices is not made in this way. The Minister's wife and children renewed their appeals for his safe return* . . . Alice, having pulled over to listen to the item, drove on. Back at The Glade she opened a bottle of champagne left over from her soirée and wished herself happy birthday. Serves the old fart right. Hope the kidnappers are roughing him up. No I didn't mean that. No really I didn't. She did mean it of course but not so very passionately. As she sipped in the back garden under the apple tree she was relieved to note that the fate of the Minister of Power was at last moving from a particular to a general interest.

97.

'Ooooooooowwwwwwchchch!'

'Stop being silly.'

'It urt.'

'We've got to get the core out.'

'Gently!'

Princess Lark was squeezing a boil on the neck of her husband while watching a soap opera on television.

'The core aint ready,' she said. 'I'll do you a kaolin poultice later.'

Tiny Colin, who was holding Dettol and a large chunk of cotton wool for his mother, asked 'What's it about?'

'What it's always about. Give us that.'

'I don't get it,' complained her son.

'Time to give im a talking to, Big.'

'When ee's older!'

Despite his ignorance of life, Tiny Colin was captivated by the on-screen canoodles. 'They're snogging now,' he said in a dreamy voice.

'He *is* older, Big.'

Princess slammed a swab of Dettol on her husband's open sore.

'Ow! OK, oi'll ave a chat wiv im.'

'I know what a willy does,' said Tiny.

Daisy and Little sniggered on the polyester sofa.

'Finished the washing-up then?'

'Of course,' said Daisy, glued to the screen. 'When are those two going to have it off ?'

'Ave you both packed yer cases?' asked Princess. 'We're going first thing.'

'*First fing*,' emphasised Big. He winced as Princess dried the boil, applied Germolene on cotton wool, and fixed it with a band of plaster.

'I'm packed,' said Little, rearranging his long limbs over the arm of the sofa. The Larks were off for a week's holiday at Puckermouth during the Whitsun half-term.

'What did she mean ave it off?' asked Tiny. 'I know about making babies, but thems were two mens.'

Daisy said 'Sometimes men go with men and women with women.'

'Get me another bit o' that flan, girl,' said Big but his tone was relatively mild. The aroma of Germolene had soothed him, had reminded him of Mum, of tenderness, of safety, of kissing it better.

'I understand now,' said Tiny and, happy of heart, he went off to pack his case.

'I need this break,' said Princess. 'I've been avin right rotten nightmares ever since that séance.' She shuddered at the very word.

'That'll learn you to go messin wiv funny folk.'

'How was I to know?'

'What's a séance?' asked Little.

'Flan!' bellowed his father.

'You asked Daisy to get it.'

'Don't get fresh wiv me, boy.'

'It's where the dead speak to the living,' explained Daisy.

'You mown that lawn yet, Little?'

'I like it how it is,' said Daisy. 'With all those dandelions and daisies, it's a lawn of suns and moons.'

'It's gottabemownaforewego, Miss Poetry. Too stuck up fer yer own good, the pair of you. Kiss it better for me, Princess.'

Princess pecked him lightly.

'You knows what oi mean. Let's go upstairs,' he said.

'You're disgusting,' sneered Daisy.

Big laughed and said 'At least we's married!' Little went red again. The kids soon heard rocking from their parents' bedroom.

98.

They were reclining on ottomans in the Turkish Kiosk after dinner, having a 'What's your favourite word?' conversation and smoking an undemanding mixture of tobacco and marijuana through a hookah. It was dusk above the glass vault of the kiosk. It had been dusk for ages.

'What's *your* favourite word, Robin?'

'My favourite word is *son*.' The drug had made him morose. Or more likely marriage had, that is, having to come back after the honeymoon and live at Heaven Park until he showed himself capable of coming up with an alternative.

'With a "u"?' enquired Minerva.

Crystal stroked her pregnancy and looked candidly at Robin but what her candour expressed no one could tell. Crystal's candour was always mysterious. In fact she was trying to come to grips with the notion that this boy was her husband. She couldn't come to grips with it – he was just Robin of The Crag – and she stroked her belly some more and said 'I'm hot'.

'Alice, be an angel, and open the door into the garden,' requested JJ.

'We don't want Crystal catching a chill,' said Robin.

'I never catch chills,' said Crystal.

Alice lingered on the threshold overlooking the dewy lawn. The last light stained the western sky. A stone fountain nearby splashed in the moonlight and a lunar rainbow hovered in its spray. JJ dreamed of the *Astronomical Poems*, the lost manuscript of Leonardo da Vinci. Crystal dreamed of Ward Dashman. Pimm dreamed of Veronica. Robin dreamed of his son. Alice dreamed of Dickon.

Minerva tried to dream and couldn't and moved off her ottoman with a creak. She wore a green silk blouse and pantaloons with gold slippers. Her hair was bound in a tangerine tarbouche fixed at the front with a diadem and aigrette. Against an iron column she intoned –

> *Faint with disgust I totter*
> *Then rouse myself and scream abuse –*
> *Slug! Wouldst thou decant me into a thimble?*
> *I whereupon impel the beakered pus!*

She cackled and opened a seedless satsuma.

'Auntie's got the giggles. Can I have a piece?' asked Crystal.

'Ooo, she'd love a segment,' said Minerva and guffawed but almost at once subdued herself with a hand over her mouth.

'What I'd love is a thick slice of bread still warm from the oven, with lashings of butter and medlar jelly on it,' said JJ.

'I'm fed up with all this waiting,' said Robin.

'*You're* fed up!' glared Crystal and she shuffled across and took a puff from the hookah and returned to the divan where almost at once she acquired the calmness, the certainty of mountains.

'What is your favourite word, JJ?' asked Alice, turning towards the room from the glass doors.

'*Hypoxia.*'

'He has a double first in Classics from Oxford,' said Minerva. For some reason she found that hilarious.

'And he didn't do a stroke of work,' said Pimm.

'I was born fluent in Latin and Greek and I read everything like it was Enid Blyton and I had a memory in those days.'

Sidney entered, mopping his brow. 'Any chance of a puff, sir?'

'By all means, Sidney.'

Sidney drew matter-of-factly from the hookah before asking 'Will there be anything else, sir? I should like to retire now and watch the Disabled Olympics on television.'

'Doesn't it make you want to throw up, all those geeks jerking about?' wondered JJ.

'On the contrary, it makes me chuckle, sir. I find a good chuckle last thing at night helps me to sleep better.'

'Sidney, why doesn't Cook make medlar jelly any more? There are masses of the things in the walled garden.'

'I'll mention it to her, sir.'

'We always used to have medlar jelly. What's your favourite word?'

'*Bed*, sir.'

'Oh, very good, yes, awfully clever, you old tart, go on then.'

'I'm always surprised by how early midsummer is. It's midsummer night tonight,' said Robin. A glossy magazine lay unopened in his lap. 'Alice, are you going out or coming in?'

'I'm quivering on the threshold,' she said.

'You've got a weird look. I hope you're not going to do your séance thing. Wobbleneck wobbleneck.'

Minerva clutched her silken breast and howled with laughter at this remark of Robin's. Her aigrette feather went positively berserk. When she showed no sign of stopping JJ began to laugh. The spectacle of her aunt and father baring their teeth and shrieking uncontrollably struck Crystal – surveying them from her mountain top – as a malady from which they would soon recover, but they didn't recover and she found their predicament pretty laughable and so started laughing too. Alice came back from the threshold, drawing a violet mist with her from the garden and pulling a bemused face at the three of them – tight mouth with eyebrows raised – which only made them laugh more. A horizontal whistle shot out of both sides of Pimm's face – this was his laughter – which started Alice off as well. Which left only Robin not laughing. Robin wasn't one of life's laughs. But he was the father-to-be and it would be a poor show if he couldn't raise at least a smile. So he forced it by stretching his lips at either end, but when he took off the pressure they contracted back to misery shape. After a number of goes this struck him as ridiculous. In fact the whole thing – marriage, babies, houses – struck him as ridiculous. And he began to laugh. Within moments he had been swept away by a typhoon of hilarity. Like a brand-new convert to a cause, like so many people who rarely do a thing, who when they do do it therefore overdo it, Robin's laughter took on a vehement, demonic, self-slapping quality not altogether pleasant, his eyes dry and piercing. As the devils of laughter trampled him with sharp shoes, he glanced across at his wife who seemed similarly afflicted, howling and rocking like a drunken goose. But the comparison was inaccurate. She was convulsing. Through the welter of mirth it became apparent that Crystal was going into the convulsions of labour and that this labour had been brought on by laughter. Which struck her husband as so horribly funny, so scorchingly preposterous, that he collapsed to the floor, legs kicking the air, wailing and gasping for breath. During his apoplexy the others fell silent while the incongruity of his own laughter made Robin laugh even more, if that were possible. And it was possible. Crystal's odd expression of face was sheer cosmic comedy for her husband, and when she was assisted from the room by Minerva, JJ, and Alice, nothing more hilarious had ever happened in all human history.

'Let it be in the Best Bedroom,' said JJ. 'It's on the ground floor not too far away.'

But Crystal didn't make it to the Best Bedroom. Parturition began in the Rotunda Hall where a heap of cushions was hastily assembled on the hard mosaic floor. Plonking herself down, the Lady Crystal Popjoy embarked upon the argosy of birth with uninhibited yells.

'Look,' said Alice almost at once, 'something's happening'.

Crystal's perineum tore and gaped and a bloody scalp asserted itself in the aperture.

I've been here before, thought Pimm.

'Yuk,' said Alice. At which point the waters burst – slipush! – and Alice said 'Superyucky! Gosh, I'm the only one talking.'

Cook arrived with hot water in a lobster cooking-pot, and towels.

Minerva, betrayed only by the bobbing aigrette, had retreated behind a pillar at the first rip of flesh and now called out 'What's happening? Describe it.'

Sidney, halfway to his bedroom, summoned back by a rapid relay of bells, was close to a religious encounter: another Popjoy on its way. Craddockisation hadn't occurred to him. Where there were Popjoy genes, all was Popjoy. Alice tried to regard it with the appropriate awe and respect for the miracle of life and so forth but had to admit she found it quite the most revolting event she'd ever witnessed. She thought – if I'd been God I'd've designed all this much better. God obviously isn't a woman. What a mean, dirty, sadistic bastard God is to design it this way. A great clock in another part of the pile struck midnight as the creature finally slithered out. A boy. Sidney was celestialised.

JJ considered his grandchild with mixed feelings. Craddockisation had definitely occurred to him. If the law of male primogeniture were to be observed, all would pass to Archie Popjoy. JJ approved of male primogeniture. His reasoning went like this. It had produced the middle-class in the Middle Ages, by displacing younger sons downwards, and this had produced the House of Commons and our system of constitutional monarchy within parliamentary democracy, from which the greatness and stability of England had derived. On the other hand Archie Popjoy was a nightmare and this grandson might well be better suited to the job. He had to admit he didn't know what to do for the best. He decided not to voice these thoughts at the present time. However some resonant statement was definitely called for and he was moved to declare that 'When we are born we know everything. As we grow older we know less and less. We die in complete ignorance, face to face with the astounding mystery of it all.'

'Don't be pompous, Daddy,' panted Crystal from the floor.

'But it's true.'

'It may be true but don't be pompous.'

The aigrette bobbed behind its pillar and a harried voice implored 'Tell me, is the worst over?'

Well, the birth was over. But the worst was yet to come.

Pushing through the circle of observers, Robin knelt penitently beside his wife and bit through the umbilical cord with determined teeth, severing son from mother. He kissed his Crystal's salty brow and, lifting the infant, stood triumphantly above his wife. Crystal looked up at him and fell in love with Robin for the very first time. 'Let me lick our son's face,' she breathed.

'It's a mess,' smiled Robin and he passed the baby to Cook who slapped its bottom. The thing started to cry as Cook began to clean it up. Sidney slipped away to prepare the birth breakfast in the kitchen.

'I want him christened – baptised – whatever the word is – with godparents – I never had those things,' announced the mother as she received from Cook the swaddled babe.

JJ was staring – he couldn't put his finger on it but there was something odd about the new arrival.

Robin's too was staring at the child – at his child – while Crystal beamed epiphanically at nothing in particular. Robin suddenly stiffened and began to shake and said to his wife in a low, sulphurous tone 'You slut, you fucking slut'. Next – and it was simply awful – he spat at her. Everyone reeled as though the earth had given way. 'Don't tell me you didn't know,' continued Robin. An elemental fire consumed him. 'This brat has yellow skin. And a streak of jet black hair. And slitty black eyes. It's half Chinese. I don't know what you've been up to but the fucking mongrel isn't mine and it's not going to have my name.'

Robin's face, as he walked out, was tragic, epic, Homeric.

When Sidney re-entered a few minutes later he must have passed the cuckold in one of the corridors because he said 'What's the matter with Mr Craddock?' Sidney was carrying his largest tray, laden with the birth breakfast of cucumber sandwiches, ginger cake with blackberry jam and cream, and a first flush Darjeeling. He placed the tray on a side-table and looked round at them nonplussed. All were mute. It was Minerva who broke the nightmarish spell by running unexpectedly forward in a rush of pantaloons and exclaiming over the new born 'Well, I think he's terrific!'

99.

It was a hot morning in Puckermouth. The sea was colourless, the sky was colourless, and the kittiwakes looked out from their ledges and gables wondering what to do. On the pier, strapped to ornate railings, was a banner which announced *Stormy Weather in King Lear the Musical.*

The Larks had bivouacked on a bank of pebbles above the sand and Tiny Colin was waiting for the waves to come in and assault his sandcastle, pricked all over with Union Jack flags. He'd have a long wait because the tide had gone out extraordinarily far and the vast flat expanse of beach made a hissing, crackling sound.

Daisy, pale and shapely in a bikini, was covered in lotion. 'Pass the Tizer, Dad.'

'Wouldn't mind a maisonette ere when oi retires,' said Big.

'You can't retire coz you aint got a job,' said Little.

'You wanna thick ear?'

Princess ran her hand over her husband's greasy white shoulders and thought – pig fat. 'I'd like to retire from cleanin,' she said.

Little stood up sourly and loosened his bathing shorts from the crack between his buttocks and walked down the beach, slowing his pace as he passed two girls on towels. One girl said to the other (and she obviously intended him to hear) 'What a skinflint'. A shaft of nausea stabbed him. He wasn't skinny, he was lean and wiry and fit, and he turned his head and said 'Fat slug'. Little scooped a hank of bladderwrack and walked on with more resolve, popping the hard dry bubbles.

The sand became wetter and firmer and ridged, but the sea appeared ever to recede from his approach. It was still bloody miles away! Several people walked dogs; children pottered with spades, placing items into painted buckets; and between these figures there extended long glossy levels of emptiness. A smattering of yachts chased each other on the horizon but the going was slight and to the eye they never moved. As for Puckermouth, it had shrunk behind him to a quaint jostle, with a seedy square block to the left, disproportionately large. This was the Grand Hotel Royal. The original building, where Queen Victoria had once spent almost the entire week-end, had burnt down a generation ago and been replaced by this lump.

At last Little's feet were splashing. The tide, after its mighty withdrawal to the horizon, was once again on the advance. The tiniest wave raced over the strand towards the shore. He was soon elated by the chill rush of foam and swam out with a slow crawl of contained strength. No one else was swimming. After a good stretch Little trod water with his great paddle feet and surveyed the coast. From here nothing was identifiable. What should he do with his life? Perhaps the Royal Navy, perhaps back-packing round the world working his passage, perhaps art college. None of the options seemed real. He flopped over into a backstroke and winched himself through the rocking sea at a leisurely pace. Perhaps he'd be one of life's swimmers, some of this, some of that, never anything shattering, but staying lean, wiry and fit, paying his way, staying afloat. Splosh – splosh – first one arm then the other wheeled elegantly over and sliced down into the water behind his head. He was sploshing contentedly along when his arm struck something as it came down into the water. He wriggled round to look. It was a shock at first and he thought himself involved with a giant fish, but was relieved to discover it was only another swimmer. In all that empty liquid space they had of course to collide. 'Sorry, mate,' he said, treading water again. The other swimmer did not reply. It was with a sensation which involved a rapid shrinkage of his mind and body, immediately followed by a cancellation of all feeling except the intellectual perception, that Little understood that the swimmer was dead, was a bloated floating corpse. The sun's glare on the water became unbearably bright.

'What shall we do tonight?' wondered Big as he dipped his hand into a brown paper bag of orange pippins.

Princess said 'I'm happy just taking a turn on the front'. She noticed Little when he was still far away. He was walking towards them with an oddly stilted gait.

'People-watching I like. In a café,' said Daisy.

'Where's you then, the Riviera?'

When Little reached his family he said 'There's a dead body in the water. It's coming in on the tide. I'm going to the police.'

He continued up the pebbles to the esplanade, leaving the rest of them to make of it what they would. They would all discover soon enough that it was the corpse of poor Robin Craddock.

100.

Beneath a tricorn hat of green and orange parrot feathers, Stormy Weather sipped wine as she watched the tennis from Wimbledon on the television. She was in her room at the Grand Hotel Royal and life at present seemed good. The pier show was going well; the weather was fine; she'd had an excellent night's sleep; this morning she'd purchased a new frock at Hussey's, Puckermouth's maison de couture; and this afternoon Stormy was going to test drive a new Jaguar which she had no intention of buying. Yesterday, measuring out for her a pint of shrimps in an enamel mug, the seafood-seller on the prom had said 'My girl an I as seed you twice in the show an we gonna go a third'. The telephone rang.

'There's an outside call for you, Miss Weather. Will you take it?'

'No ploblem.'

'Cly me a liver,' said a voice on the other end.

'Clystal! Fab fab!'

'How are you?'

'Epileptic! Gland Hotel Loyal ever so comfy! How are you?'

'Oh, Stormy . . . '

'What matter?'

Crystal began to cry.

'Tell Stormy, Clystal.'

'Oh, oh . . . '

There was a sniffling interval at the other end and when Crystal came back on the line she was more composed, even down-to-earth. 'I had my baby last week.'

'Conglats.'

'That's not all.'

'Go on, lubbly bum . . . ' Stormy took a thoughtful sip.

'Well – I hate to say this Stormy dearest but – it's yours. You're the only person I've slept with from the East and that one night did it. We have a son. What shall we call him?"

Stormy went all funny and dropped the receiver.

'Are you all right., Stormy? Where are you? Answer me,' pleaded Crystal's voice from the carpet.

Stormy had built her whole life on being a woman. Not that she kidded herself, and not that she intended to change sex, because from all she'd read on the subject the operation was a terrifying ordeal she could do without. Besides, she quite liked her willy – and so did her friends. For Stormy, transvestism had been more of a career move. Back home in Hong Kong it was easier for girl singers to find employment and she'd been good at it and it sort of stuck. Except when she went to bed with someone when it sort of unstuck. But never until now had she gone as far as becoming a dad.

Stormy picked up the phone and cleared her throat professionally. 'I dropped de terrorphone. I fought you were on pill.'

'I discontinued. Because of Robin, I suppose, or maybe – oh I don't know! You took me by surprise, Stormy, and I never thought – '

'Who knows about this?'

'Everyone knows.'

Stormy dropped the receiver again but this time retrieved it before it hit the floor. 'Who knows what?'

'They know I've had a child of quasi-oriental appearance for God's sake. Of course they don't know it's yours.'

'Don't tell. Let me fink.'

'I'm going to have to say who the father is soon. That's the way we do it in our family.'

'If they know I'm transvestite they cancel show and Stormy flat bloke, flat bloke.'

'Robin's walked out on me. His reaction was the worst thing I ever went through in my entire life. He cursed me. It was so . . . primordial. I don't know where he's gone and I'm frightened in case he comes back one night and kills me.'

'Are you alone?'

'No, no. Minerva's being absolutely wonderful. She adores the little thing.'

'What about you, Clystal?'

'I don't know yet. I feel funny about it.'

'Minerva nice. Smashing nice lady. Does it look like me?'

'He doesn't look like anybody. What shall we do?'

'Can't fink. Very sudden by terrorphone. I speak wiv you to-

morrow. Don't worry. We sort out.' Stormy rang off. She was
frantic for a pee and performed the task, as usual, standing up.

101

They were on their way back from the Pick Your Own farm at
Upper Butter, had pulled over to release a bee caught in the rear
window and decided to walk awhile. The air and sky merged in a
humid grey sludge which dulled the mind but the meadows were
flooded yellow with buttercups. 'Look,' said Dickon. His large
hand touched the red nipplelike fruit of wild strawberries. He
caressed them gently with the pads of his fingertips. They
crossed a field stippled blue with Crane's-bill and eventually
came to a pool whose surface was another flood of yellow, this
time of marsh marigolds. Alice ducked. A dragonfly with translucent azure wings skimmed her head. It was the day after Robin
Craddock's funeral.

'There were a couple of pools like this at Lower Farm but
Malcolm had em drained before I took over. He said he wanted
all the secret places removed. I used to work for the estate as a
lad.'

'Yes, JJ told me.'

Alice bent down to examine a flower she hadn't come across
before and when she looked up Dickon had taken off his singlet.
The shape of it remained printed on his torso by the suntan of his
arms and shoulders, neck and face. Her sensations were curious:
something of drunkenness, of malaise, of excitement.

'Thanks for coming to the funeral with me. I know you didn't
want to,' she said.

'Poor bugger.'

'I couldn't throw myself off a cliff into the sea no matter how
bad I felt. But I understand why Crystal didn't go.'

'I don't understand that. None of the Popjoys went. I think it
was disgraceful.'

'I thought JJ might have gone.'

Although Dickon had asked Alice to move into Lower Farm,
she hadn't done so, explaining that she felt they didn't know each
other well enough yet. What she meant was they hadn't had sex

yet, they weren't natural in each other's space, they hadn't discussed it through. Was he asking her in as a lodger or a lover? And looking at him now, she thought – How could a beautiful man like Dickon fall in love with a mouse like me? He wants to be kind to me and he needs companionship and no doubt the occasional screw but would he open himself to me in a proper relationship? No, it will never happen. He'd always be aloof. Anyway I don't want it to happen. What would I do with a wretched farm?

Dickon surveyed an adjacent field where calves, their hind legs disproportionately long, buttocks pert in the air, moved restlessly about the cows. He was thinking, she's a woman of the world. She's lived and worked in London and mixed with important people. What could she ever see in a bumpkin like me? There will always be some kind of wall I can't get past, some space I'll never be admitted to.

'JJ's a funniosity,' he said. 'His father was more of the old school. Gave my father a fine pair of Purdeys. I was out shooting crows with one of them this morning. Did you notice the east field?'

'The poppies and cornflowers.'

'Yes, it's our first organic wheatfield. You'll see a dozen dead crows stuck along the fence to discourage the others.'

'I used to know a crow. Its wing was broken. I don't know what happened to it. I expect it got better and flew away.'

'It might be on my fence now.'

'Oh, Dickon, don't say that.'

They started to kiss, and kissed for ages
and finally
after months of circling about
they had it off
like grown-ups.

Amazing how walls which seem eternal can vanish in seconds.

102.

Robin's will was a suicide note put in the post to his bank manager. Crystal said she wouldn't challenge its terms. 'For God's sake keep me out of it!' were her precise words. He left everything, such as it was, to his mother, but added *To Little Lark, my half-brother, enough money for a motorbike.* Little Lark's paternity Helen Craddock had always known and the way her own son had chosen to make it public was only a minor shock compared to the enormity of the main event, his suicide. She disappeared from the village.

After the subtraction of motorbike money from Robin's estate, £14 would be left. But Little Lark refused to accept the money and said he'd buy his own bike in his own time. It turned out that Big too had always known about Little's biological origins and when it came out he behaved with impeccable grace. He and Little grew closer as a result and family life at the Larks improved enormously, as though an unspoken, festering splinter had been extracted from it.

103.

Tucker came to stay with Hoskins one hot week-end while Jason was doing DJ Meat work in the next county. Hoskins said to Tucker 'Let's go somewhere different this evening. I don't want to be seen too much with you because people would think I was taking sides in this new town controversy.'

'Really? I thought it was because you didn't want it to get back to your boyfriend,' said Tucker.

Hoskins looked bashful. 'People round here are, I mean, my Aunt Immacolata occasionally sees a black man and the gossip is dreadful. I thought I'd take you to the Village of Recluses. There's a decent pub there where we can eat.'

As they drove out of Appleminster, Hoskins quoted 'God made the country and men made the town. Cowper said that and Byron repeated it.'

'But it's not true.'

'It's roughly true.'

'This landscape is manmade.'

'Man-controlled, not manmade.'

'What about crop circles?'

'You've got me there. They say you don't get them in organic fields.'

'There's a new one over Puckford way. I wouldn't mind having a look.'

The car got stuck behind a flock of sheep being chivvied along the lane by dogs and a ullulating farmer. Flies entered the car off the flock and Hoskins raised the windows. They drove on quietly. 'Find some woods then,' said Tucker. They found a thicket of young disease-resistant elms, removed all their clothes, shagged, and visited a ruined abbey. Twenty more minutes on the road and the outlying buildings of the Village of Recluses showed up among trees.

It was typical that Hoskins had an ulterior motive in coming hither, for he'd had a tip-off that there was some as yet obscure connection between this place and the Green Kingdom and he wanted to take an informal look round. The village, a few streets leading off a dainty square, was built in red brick which had become marked by yellowish lichens, and the paintwork was pale blue. All the garden flowers were red or yellow. In the window of the only shop a notice in large black copperplate read 'Can Deliver'. The shop was closed. Hoskins hoped there might be a list of personal ads hanging behind the glass but there was nothing. And not a soul, not a sound, not even a bird. It was uncanny, and still very warm, but since they were both in shorts the light breeze stroked their bare legs deliciously. Tucker tried the door of the village church and pulled a face. It was locked.

Although they saw no one, everywhere they wandered they were tracked from behind curtains, from remote black recesses, from top-floor windows, by pairs of frightened eyes, housebound eyes, the eyes of people who could no longer mix freely in the open air but paced anxiously within, behind bolted doors. One particular pair of eyes bore down on them from an overhanging gable window and this pair of eyes, exceptionally in the Village of Recluses, was without fear. It was without any expression at all except that of a concentration of intelligence so complete that it bordered on death. Fringed by pale albino lashes, the eyes were colourless except for a sharp black pinhead at each centre. They were also abnormally large and this abnormality was exaggerated by the smallness of the head in which they were housed. Her thin hair was drawn tightly against the bony skull and fixed at the back with a clip. The entrance to the house where the eyes lived was not on the square but round a secret corner. In fact the entrance was impossible to find unless you were informed, and very, very few people *were* informed. As Hoskins and Tucker poked about the village, the eyes from the overhanging gable took in everything. These eyes belonged to Joyce and just as they were very large eyes, so the ears of Joyce were very large ears. With her eyes and her ears, Joyce scooped up the whole world.

'Let's go to that pub,' said Hoskins.

At The Basilisk Tavern in the square the landlord said 'The dinner tonight is nettle soup, pig's trotters, cabbage with juniper berries and new potatoes, followed by chocolate omelette'.

'Isn't it a bit hot for that?'

'Never too hot for pig's trotters.'

'Can we eat in the garden?'

'Wherever you like. We're quiet on Saturdays.'

The landlord of The Basilisk was memorable for his unremarkability. Everything about him was fawn, including his eyes and teeth. He wasn't unfriendly – that would've been too positive a characteristic – but there was nothing about him on which you could hang a statement. The garden was full of red roses and geraniums but its scent was overwhelmingly that of honeysuckle. Tucker and Hoskins patiently sipped their beer on iron benches.

When the landlord came out with their dinner Tucker asked him 'Why are the people in this village so reclusive?'

'Coz they don't like to go out. Some of em take their cars out or jump around in the fields when no one's looking.'

'You're not a recluse,' said Hoskins.

'No. But I'm lazy. So it suits me. Couple of years ago a group came from Cambridge University to study the village.'

'What was their verdict?'

'Can't rightly remember. Something about eco-terror-angst.'

'Are you saying the village has an exaggerated fear of ecological or terrorist catastrophe and that this keeps everyone indoors?'

The landlord narrowed his eyes and said 'I'll get the potatoes'.

A hundred-mile chasm had soundlessly opened between the landlord and his two customers and, though Hoskins asked several more questions, the man now answered only in non

sequiturs. Eventually they ate their dinner in silence as the setting sun inflamed the brickwork around them. After the pudding,
which had made his thick red lips very chocolaty, Tucker said 'I
don't think they've been struck by eco-angst. They are happily
sitting at home doing nothing. Don't you feel that? That you
could sit here for ever with a gentle smile on your face and closed
eyelids and do nothing?'

'I prefer a bit more action, me.'

From her invisible redoubt Joyce muttered 'Silly little boy
scouts in their shorts! That twerp Hoskins thinks he can find me?
Bah! He doesn't even know I exist.'

With a click, clatter and lurch, she turned back into what once
upon a time had been a bedroom but there was no bedroom furniture in it these days. Instead it was packed with communica-
tions technology, bank upon bank of screens and buttons and
digital panels, forever winking and bleeping for attention. There
were no printers and no conventional files. Nothing was ever
written down or printed out. And how one of her conversations
had been hacked into and recorded on a mini-disc was a source of
great consternation to Joyce.

She walked on crutches to a keyboard and with difficulty
seated herself. Crippled by a car accident in early childhood, she
had nonetheless still been able to walk unaided until, during an
adventure holiday in Guatemala at the age of ten, she had trodden on a landmine which had blown one foot and all her growth-
hormones to kingdom come. Joyce was scarcely four feet tall, and
just as her eyes appeared enormous by virtue of the smallness of
the head, so the head appeared enormous by virtue of the minute
dimensions of the body. To tell the truth, if you removed her eyes
and ears, there was very little indeed of Joyce except brain and
with that brain she had invented a computer virus innoculation
which had been purchased by every significant operator in the
world and made her a fortune and this, unknown to anyone except
herself, had embodied a code which allowed her access to the
planet's memory banks. There was nowhere she couldn't go with
the dexterity of those bony keyboard fingers.

Taking a thin watercress sandwich from a plateful prepared by
the faithful servant Lucy Girl, Joyce inserted it into the narrow

slit of her mouth, where it was absorbed like a diskette, without any apparent motion of the jaws. Afterwards she typed several instructions into a computer as though in response to instructions from the sandwich. On the monitor appeared the face of the Minister of Power. Tapping more keys threw up information on everything the wicked man had done – what a sorry tale it was. Not a continent undefiled by his crass and devastating decisions. The Government of course had refused all the kidnap demands but one couldn't release the Minister of Power just like that, one simply couldn't, it would make a mockery of all one's work, an admission of failure, oh no, one wasn't going to do that.

However one of Joyce's contacts had radioed in with a message a few weeks back. It had mentioned some oddity who lived in a caravan and who longed to be useful to the cause, who kept on pestering them for something to do, who'd already been informed that he was over the age limit, who was obviously a sad old crank, the sort of man who might indeed be useful on account of his absolute expendability . . .

104.

'Bernice, you are a darling but please don't play with the zapper – I'm trying to watch the Men's Final.'

Bernice was gaily batting a succession of television channels.

Mrs Bladder-Williams rang. 'Alice dear, any chance you might take over from me and look after the Old Un for a bit? Helen's rather bowed out and what with the fête coming up I'm snowed under. It's merely a question of looking in once a day and helping her poo-poo. Meals on Wheels and the Council visitor do the rest.'

'Can't the Council visitor help her poo-poo?'

'There was some sort of fracas and the visitor has refused that particular service.'

'What time does she like to poo-poo?'

'Any time. She wears a nappy. You have to change it, that's all. There's a stack of face-masks on the sideboard. Thank you so much. Good match, isn't it. I want the Hungarian to win.'

Bernice was being exceptionally frisky and batted across to another channel from which Alice was about to switch back again to the Men's Final when she realised she'd been batted into a newsflash -

... Thirteen people have been killed. Police say that but for the late hour the toll would have been much greater. Because it was on the site of next week's Oecumenical Conference the atrocity was thought to have been the work of Islamic fundamentalists. But in a lunchtime announcement the Green Kingdom has claimed responsibility and apologised to the Archbishop of Canterbury, saying that their bomber made a mistake and that their target was the Ministry of Rural Affairs which is next door to the Conference Centre. The Ministry of Rural Affairs was relatively undamaged due to its bomb-proof construction. In a statement to the Commons the Prime Minister said the country would not be held to ransom by terrorists and asked for the safe return of the Minister of Power. Canary Wharf has been sealed off and motorists are advised to avoid the area.

The broadcast switched to the Archbishop of Canterbury interviewed in the library of Lambeth Palace (a woman could be seen polishing in the background). He said: *We had delegates arriving from all over the world to discuss understanding and co-operation between faiths. And now this! We are working hard to re-schedule but it isn't easy finding somewhere else at a moment's notice. Besides people are suspicious of us now and believe we're trouble.*

Alice was thinking. Not about the Minister of Power. Though she was very curious as to what might happen to that man, she was ashamed of her curiosity because in every other sense he had been superseded. Yes, he'd been superseded, hadn't he, of course he had. New life now. New life. Please let there be new life.

She went outside to water the terracotta pots by the back door with their clouds of blue and mauve lobelia and afterwards took a glass of white wine from the bottle in the fridge, thinking. By the time she'd switched off the box, brushed her teeth and gone to bed, she was still thinking. She didn't stop thinking until after three a.m., but by eight a.m. she was awake and lucid again and thinkingly came downstairs. She made her tea and, nibbling a corner of toast, switched on the radio for a Canary Wharf bombing-update. The Green Kingdom had issued another statement.

They vowed to protect the Oecumenical Conference wherever it took place by threatening the severest imaginable reprisals – removal of body parts was only the start – against any religious terrorists who sought to sabotage it.

Alice stopped thinking and called directory enquiries and requested the number of Lambeth Palace which she rang.

This is Lambeth Palace. If you have a touchtone telephone please press the star button twice now. You have eleven options. For the shop, press one. For information on open days of the Palace Garden, press two. For information on the sale of church property, press three. For information on religion, press four. For the press office, press five . . . You are held in a queue. Please be patient. You will be answered as soon as possible.

She held on and on but couldn't get through. Later from the office at Heaven Park she tried again. Same message. Different queue. This went on all morning. Until she had a shock. A human being answered.

SWITCHBOARD: Lambeth Palace.

ALICE: Really?

SWITCHBOARD: Please tell me what you want. A queue is forming behind you.

ALICE: I'd like to speak to the organiser of the Oecumenical Conference please.

SWITCHBOARD: That's the Archbishop himself.

ALICE: Can you put me through?

SWITCHBOARD: What aspect of the Conference are you concerned with?

ALICE: Just put me through. A queue is forming behind me.

SWITCHBOARD: He's in a meeting.

ALICE: I'll hold.

SWITCHBOARD: Who's calling?

ALICE: The secretary of the Marquess of Heavenshire.

SWITCHBOARD: Hang on a second . . . (*the operator was gone a full minute*) . . . I'm connecting you.

ARCHBISHOP: Hullo?

ALICE: Is that the Archbishop?

ARCHBISHOP: Yes. How is JJ?

ALICE: He's very well, Archbishop, and he sends you his best wishes and would like you to know that we have conference facilities at Heaven Park and when we saw your problems on the television we thought we could be of help. After being bombed out of the city, why not try the country?

ARCHBISHOP: Isn't it a bit far away?

ALICE: Less far than you think.

ARCHBISHOP: What about security?

ALICE: JJ's Colonel-in-chief of the local regiment.

ARCHBISHOP: Food? Bathrooms?

ALICE: Loads. I mean, we can't do it for next week. But we could do it for next month. Besides, well, Heaven Park, it's a great publicity gimmick.

ARCHBISHOP: We don't need any more publicity. Some of the delegates won't be able to make August so it will be a bit raggle-taggle but, what the hell, let's do it. I'm determined to show the public we aren't easily deterred. Thank you for your call. Tell JJ I'll ring him this evening.

105.

The Ultimate Attention roamed through undifferentiated time and space. It sang as it went, trapezing the multiple spectra of all conceivable realities, playfully looking for someone. By spiralling degrees it approached a certain universe, a certain galaxy, a certain solar system. It skidded tra-la along the atmosphere of a certain planet and with a shrug fell through a hole more mind than matter and glided suavely down a ray of sunshine to hover above a venerable Elizabethan mansion set among ornamental trees of unpleasant hue.

After a moment (or was it a month?) of subtle pulsations, the Ultimate Attention snickered down a chimneypot and burst out through the fireplace into a white hall with white vases of sweet peas on the window-sills. It travelled down a corridor in soft peristaltic jerks and its passing was evident only in the slightest crinkle of the air. It ignored a door with 'Marilyn Dashman' on it, and another door with 'Ward Dashman' on it. Not yet the occasion for either of these. But when it came to a door bearing the name 'John

Smith', it corkscrewed in through the keyhole and drew itself up in translucent shapelessness at the end of the bed to contemplate the supine figure.

The whole being of John Smith was racked by anguish. His white hair was damp with sweat and sticking out in unkempt tufts. His brow was painfully clenched. His eyes were not so much closed as pulled shut. The mouth was dry and the breath sounded like sandpaper on stone. The Ultimate Attention drifted up to the ceiling and waited there, looking down.

After a month (or was it a moment?) of inaudible throbs, it made a movement which in a mortal creature would be called a lunge or perhaps an exhalation. Yes, it exhaled itself all over the anguished creature in the bed, in consequence of which John Smith's breathing embarked on a slow even inhalation and his body became the plaything of coruscating rainbows. This was followed by the Ultimate Attention's inhalation, which exacted a corresponding exhalation from John Smith. He did not exhale rainbows however. His being precipitated out showers of thorns and tin-tacks and nail-pairings and splinters of glass. These fell as dust to the floor, and left behind on the bed was a man whose features had become disposed in a natural pleasantness, whose face bore the hint of a smile, whose limbs rested on the sheet in a condition that was entirely tension-free, in short a man who was absolutely dead.

106.

It was the hottest day of the year so far. The temperature under the great ash tree on the south-west lawn reached 100 degrees Fahrenheit for the first time since records began in the reign of Charles II (when the house was known as Heavenynge Hall). The humidity of early summer had gone and they were into a period of dry heat, supposedly easier to bear, but JJ loathed it all the same. His bulk oozed at the slightest exertion. His lovely ankles, his only slimness, were swelling to the point of no return. As youngsters everywhere shed their clothes and became more beautiful, JJ hid in cotton and knew that he was ugly and fat and old. How well now he understood Lomax's terror of light, the

unyielding brilliance, the callousness of a sheer blue sky, everything stripped naked and exposed and subject to the destructive
power of the sun. How he longed for wind and rain. The word
'sleet' had never sounded more luxurious. As for his mind, it
squelched vapidly in a torrid no-man's-land. Relief came only
with the dusk and even then was marred by a dread of tomorrow's
sunrise.

Usually he would hang about the cooler rooms of the house
feeling enervated and trapped but on this 100 degree day he
decided to go deeper and told Sidney that he wished to wander
the cellars beneath the rustic basement. The butler drew a long
key from his waistcoat pocket. It was new and steely, for the locks
had been changed only last year in an attempt to foil Cook, and
when the butler opened a deft slice of trompe-l'oeil wall, a chill
blast of air hit them, more reviving than anything in weeks.
Sidney leant forward, switched on a light, and stood back, while
JJ, in striped pyjamas of cotton fabric so thin that it glued itself to
his sweating flesh, descended the long flight of steps at an acute
angle. The cellars swallowed him, a mere morsel, at a single bite.
Cellars? These were dungeons, subterrranean halls, an entire
nether world with its own laws of space and time and significance.

The lightbulb at the entrance did not penetrate very far and JJ
picked up a torch on a ledge – surprisingly it worked. He recalled
his father's voice from boyhood: 'If you get lost in the cellars,
keep turning right and you'll escape.' He sprayed the beam. A
wide vault, like the crypt of a great church, leapt to right and left
on the massive underpinning of the foundations and he took the
right-hand side, keeping to the main passage off which, every so
often, smaller passages opened. Down here the whole weight of
the house pressed on him but there was nothing to indicate what
rooms might be overhead, no markings of any kind on the walls.
As he advanced the passage grew more damp, its sepulchral coolness clearing the head, its greenish slime home to creepy-crawlies
without eyes.

The main passage led to a t-junction and he turned right into
a smaller passage and, on arriving at another t-junction, he
turned right again and came into a large space, circular, brick-
domed, with many tunnels off it, but by the time he'd examined

the succession of mouths he'd forgotten which one he'd emerged from. JJ experienced that panic which is the loss of one's external reference points and called out instinctively to the ancestor who had created the colossal labyrinth below as well as the one above. This was Sir Radiant Popjoy, traveller and libertine, both of whose wives were sugar heiresses. When Sir Radiant inherited the estate and titles from a cousin, he promptly set about transforming charming Heavenynge Hall into a palace for titans.

JJ's voice ran away from him like frightened rats down the tunnels. Whereupon the torch beam faltered. A lesser man than JJ would have quaked at this coincidence, but JJ was too aware of the past to believe in ghosts. Immediately he switched off the torch to conserve energy while he appraised the situation. Well, he was lost beneath his own house. There were not many men in the world who could say that. But his eyes and ears slowly expanded in the solvent darkness. It was thus that a faint light at the end of one of the tunnels was permitted to reach him. As he walked towards it, the air grew warmer. Another minute and he had the distinct impression of daylight.

JJ exited beside the old icehouse into an explosion of heat and sunshine and he heard voices. Peering carefully round a wall he looked across a brick parterre, hot as an oven and beflagged with columbine, and saw his sister talking to Bob Wetmore. They were sitting under the porch of the old fountain-keeper's cottage, a redundant and roofless building which afforded them little shade but Minnie had at least dressed for the weather in a batik sarong. Bob had merely taken off his jacket, displaying shirt and braces. His face was noticeably moist.

Minnie was saying 'You mean you know *nothing* of Chinese culture?'

'Only what everyone knows, bound feet, opium, chicken with cashew nuts.'

'There's a great deal more to it than that, Mr Wetmore. Pagodas for example.'

'And minge.'

'Do you mean Ming?'

'Vases.'

'It's pronounced Ming. Crystal wants the boy baptised because she never was and always regretted it, which is the first I've heard of it, her regret, that is.'

'Baptise it what?' enquired Bob.

JJ cocked his ear. Crystal had never discussed names with him.

'I proposed Pinkerton,' said Minerva excitedly, 'because we haven't yet had a Pinkerton in the family and it's what I would call my own son. But as you are not aware of, Mr Wetmore, so this is a confidence, please respect it, I myself can no longer conceive. My tubes are in knots. The doctor told me.'

Bob mumbled without saying anything precisely. His mouth had gone loose and he squirmed painfully, for the heat had brought up his anal pruritis.

'Thank you, but do not feel sorry for me,' she replied. 'Procreation is merely one of the by-products of human love, and not the most interesting by-product either.'

'So what is the purpose of love, Lady Minerva?'

'That we should be close, Mr Wetmore. Attraction between people is not primarily about reproduction at all but about sanity. It is like a gravitational force which binds the species together and prevents us from being lost, random particles.'

'That's a beautiful thing to say.'

Her skin was electrified. 'You find me comely, do you?'

'Lady Minerva, I should like your feet to treat me as a pilgrimage!'

'Oh, Mr Wetmore, I've been so lonely!'

JJ could endure no more. He felt as though a lorry had parked in his stomach. But in the knowledge of the secret tunnel which ran from the icehouse to the grotto he could continue his journey unseen and have a swim at the end of it.

The marquess emerged into the grotto via its rectum. Reflections of water shimmered on the shell-encrusted interior. The grotto's mouth was fringed with ferns which coolly filtered the sun and looked out towards the lake. Reed-clogged and reduced, the lake itself needed a thorough clean but this could not dissuade JJ who, leaving his clothes on the grass, flopped thankfully in and embarked upon a stately breaststroke. Only his head and occasionally his buttocks rose above the surface as he swam beneath the hanging bridge and past the derelict boathouse where the *Golden Hind* had sunk against the left side and was far gone in rot. Three coots trailed him, quarrelling among themselves, while the verdant glories of the park revolved majestically, and it was only when he was nudged by one of the lake sturgeon and had an atavistic fear for his private parts that he came ashore. JJ strode up the bank through hemlock plants, disturbing several toads and a plover, sweeping back his wet hair with broad motions of his hands and quite frankly, after a great deal of self-criticism in recent weeks, feeling rather beautiful. But oh, no, really it was too much – there they were again. Where he had left his pyjamas, Minerva was having one of her laughing fits, the blubbery beau dutifully adjacent, and JJ realised the pair had come a considerable way in intimacy since his last eavesdrop.

'Dear Mr Wetmore, please describe more of the life of the Turf for me. It sounds so wonderfully giddy-up.'

'I can do better than describe, my lady. I can demonstrate.' And with that Bob pressed her down onto the grassy bank with his lips against her cheek. She squawked and sat up at once. He was going to do it again but this time she turned her head so that his lips pressed against her lips. One of Minerva's arms shot out at the side and, with its two leading fingers rapidly rubbing against each, the arm slowly erected until, lip suction to lip suction, her index finger pointed directly to the sky. They separated with a pop.

'You've got that bobbly green stuff all over your shirt,' announced Minerva. 'You've been snouting in the undergrowth, haven't you. Yes, you have, you have!'

'Naughty naught naughts!' honked Bob.

'Bobbly Bob!'

'Can we go in and watch the Test match now?'

'No!'

'Cruella!'

'Cochon!' She shrieked with delight.

Covering himself with a bunch of dock-leaves, JJ interrupted them. 'Sorry, I need my clothes.'

'There you are! We knew they were yours.'

'You might've spared me the embarrassment, Minnie.'

'Oh, Julius, what a stuff-pot you are. We've been waiting for you because we want you to be the first to know.'

'I don't want to know.' JJ fixed his eyes on her narrow hairy shinbones.

'Bob and I are to be married.'

'Steady on, old girl,' said Bob with a twitchy eye.

'Well, you can't, Minnie. He's married already.'

Bob concurred with a vigorous nod.

'Oh, Julius, don't be such a kill-joy. Haven't you heard of divorce?'

107.

The stones of the bridge, charged by the day, gave off a perceptible heat, while out of darkness came the churrup of a nightjar. Sidney, caught on the horns of a poignant dilemma, had paused at the bridge to reflect on whether to do something or whether to do nothing. But arriving at no definite conclusion he returned to the Rover, and motored the remaining two hundred yards to the off-licence for his monthly bottle of Calvados. On the pavement outside, he encountered Bunjie Gunj who had come for his fortnightly bottle of Bombay Gin.

'Mr Sidney, how do you do. How is everything at the Park?'

'Fine, thank you. And The Crag?'

'Likewise.'

'And Mr Dashman?'

'Improving slowly. Yes, we saw you.' Bunjie's lisp seemed to thicken

'You did?'

'At the Monkshood Nursing Home. Larissa and I were visiting Mr Dashman and a man had died, some kind of lunatic. From Mr Dashman's window we saw his body being wheeled across the gravel and you were there walking behind it.'

'Oh,' said Sidney.

'We didn't want to rush out and surprise you at that moment. Was he a relation of yours?'

'No.'

'Condolences anyway.'

'Thank you.'

On the way home Sidney thought – Yes, I was there. The only one. JJ said he wanted nothing to do with it and that the whole business could be forgotten now. Little chance of that, your lordship, because they handed over to me a marriage certificate, and I shall soon have to do something. Yes, I shall soon have to do something.

108.

Across a tract of nettle and neglected orchard she came to a brick wall about twice her height and followed it to where a section had flopped into the grass. Senile fig trees writhed in the space and scrambling through she found herself for the first time among the abandoned greenhouses at one end of the walled garden. In a corner favourable to the sun a gazebo had been built from flints and thatched with reeds. Its door was open in the boiling heat and Ben Thicknesse, the head gardener, indeed the only gardener, was sitting inside.

'My tea,' he said with a smile which did not interrupt the movement of his jaws. 'Hang on. I'll clear some of this stuff off and you can sit down.' He shifted a pile of decomposing notebooks. She picked one up and fanned its pages. 'Sketchbooks and bridge ledgers,' he said. 'Belonged to his lordship's grandmother. She died long before our time.'

'But why are they here, Ben?'

'She left em here.'

'I'm looking for JJ.'

'I haven't seen im this week.'

'If you see him, would you ask him to ring me at home? I've got a list as long as your arm. We've got the holy men arriving soon. He wouldn't allow contract cleaners. He said they do too much damage.'

'The village girls know that cleaning the house is basically leaving it alone.'

'Don't worry, we're buying in the veg.'

'I can help out with the fruit.'

When she got back to The Glade, Bernice was playing in the porch, prancing about some object she'd found, batting it this way and that. 'What've you got there, my adorable one?' Alice threw off her sweaty clothes and went upstairs to run a bath.

It was horrible. She stood in the doorway of the bathroom, unable to move forward, her heart banging. 'It's another trick, that's what it is. And I don't care,' she said in a scratchy voice. Her mouth was dry, her throat tight. It was facing away from her in the empty tub.

Then the paralysing glaze dissolved off her and she jumped forward and picked it up by a tuft of hair. Dark jam dripped from the neck. She dropped it immediately. It fell back into the bath and rolled to a halt, smearing the white enamel sides with the red jam. It looked up at her. The skin of the face was taut and pale and smeared with the jam. He looked up at her. She saw that this time, after all the jokes, it was real. Which made all the other times real too, as she knew they were, real in their malign intent, that is, in their horror. It was a real head and the head was that of the Minister of Power. He looked at her with a single penetrating eye. Something messy, indecipherable had happened to the other one. Alice – blank, autonomic, almost peaceful – went downstairs, collected her keys and locked the front door.

'Come along, Bernice,' she said and went to pick up the cat. It was then that she noticed what it was that Bernice was dabbling with. An eyeball. Alice drew back and made a noise which was not a groan, not a scream, not a gasp, but something more primitive and guttural. She walked briskly across the field.

He was mixing creosote as she came unannounced through a tangle of burdock and cow parsley. 'I'm coming to live with you, Dickon.'

'About time,' he said with a crooked countenance.

The smell of creosote rising into her face was clean and safe and male. She remembered that years later.

'Please telephone the police,' she said quietly.

'What?'

'Dickon, just do it please.'

'What are you on about?'

'For God's sake, phone the fucking police!'

109.

Lammastide, the season of shooting stars above and foxgloves below, of agoraphobia and claustrophobia both, when the soul is unravelled, helpless, fretful. Oliver Knott had stopped taking all his pills – justlikethat – stopped all of them – and after some frightening and sleepless weeks, he found himself in a land where everything was unfamiliar. It was as though a screen had fallen away and exposed him to the void. He had once believed, and stated in an article, that 'It is impossible to envisage the universe without also envisaging its limitations.' But those limitations had gone. He was open on all sides. He was uncertain. Most of all he was open to the future. In the past few years he had skirted madness but now felt that he could outrun madness simply by carrying on, day after day, regardless, somehow, and this had given him the confidence to throw away those pills and override the abstract trains of thought which so often ran through him like hot wires.

> Cyclophrenic is the opposite of schizophrenic.
> Yet subjectivity is the direction of madness.
> Therefore objectivity is the direction of sanity.
> Yet centripetal is integration.
> Therefore centrifugal is schizophrenic.
> However since cognition versus perception
> Is cause-and-effect versus revelation . . .

These sequences had once been his mind's life-blood, until it got out of hand, but lately, when the conceptual vertigo started up, he had begun to hear the voice of his father calling from beyond the grave. 'Stop acting soft,' said the old man. Or 'Stop making such a meal of it and eat yer dinner.' And this common-sensical, caring voice of his father sustained him so that he had been able to reach a point where rebirth, freedom, peace of mind, whatever it was which enabled you to walk down the street without needing a pill, to reflect on life without fearing for your mind, this state which, after a period of growth and destabilisation, was the recovery of self-possession, but a slightly different self, a more generous possession – Oliver stopped there, brought the knife down there, severed the chain of thoughts there. He was getting quite good at doing that.

Hot weather never bothered him. It was the winter he couldn't bear. The hills were blocked in green and gold. The cows stood or lay in the heat like toys. Whenever he stopped on the track a subtle symphony of insect sound took over, Linnets flashed from hedges. Not another human being did he see all afternoon. He walked for many hours and when in the evening he sat on a stile and finished off his water and sandwiches, he knew he was lost and relished it. To be lost – and content – what joy. In the distance he heard a drover moving a herd from one field to another. It was far off, nostalgic. He walked on as the sun began to go down, pinking the few lines of cloud on the horizon, enriching the colours. All the details of the landscape were wondrously clear in the levelling golden light. As he teetered across the stones of a slovenly brook he realised how weary he was, and as luck would have it, on the rise ahead a small cottage had a lamp in its window. Perhaps he could ring from there for a taxi home. A dog barked eagerly as he approached the front door.

'Who's there?' demanded a female voice within.

'My name is Knott. I'm a walker. I'm lost. Can you tell me where I am?'

A light went on in the porch. Masses of wisteria lanterns dangled overhead.

'Is that you, Oliver?'

He didn't recognise the voice and when she opened the door he hardly recognised the person. She'd put on weight and was smiling. It was Helen Craddock. A Clumber spaniel flew out and hopped up at him affectionately.

'Suzie, down.'

'I didn't recognise your voice, Helen.'

'It hasn't changed.'

'Yes, it has.'

She laughed. He was astonished to see her laugh. 'It's lovely to see you,' she said. 'You'll have to spend the night.'

'I thought I might ring for a taxi.'

'You'll have a job, Oliver, we're not on the phone. Do stay, it'll be fun. You surely didn't walk all the way from Milking Magna. It's absolutely miles.'

'I've had the most marvellous day, Helen.'

She drew him in by the hand. The interior was simple but demonstrated her elegant touch. A garish cock pheasant lay on the table, surrounded by apples and vegetables as in a still life.

'You can tell me all the news, Oliver. I bet you'd love a glass of cold cider.'

'Do you live here alone?'

'Not bloody likely. I live with Selwyn Blagdon. He's away for a few nights on a forestry course.'

He took the cider. She had one too and said 'Cheers'.

'You look well, Helen.'

'After Robin's suicide – '

'I understand –'

'Listen. I want to tell you. That was the turning point. I decided I couldn't take any more sorrow and began to see life in a different way.'

'Sadder and wiser.'

'No. Easier and lighter. It took time of course but, you see, I couldn't keep playing the tragedy card. It was a kind of deep . . . boredom with it. Tragedy became a monumental bore. Does that sound heartless? Maybe I'm heartless.'

He ran the soft flap of one of Suzie's ears through his fingers.

'I still cry for Robin of course. But not for Tim. Tim was not a man to make one tearful. Forgive me – would you like some bread and cheese? We can take it into the garden. The cheese is very good. Our neighbour makes it. She lives two miles in that direction and is our *nearest* neighbour.'

Wild roses bathed them with scent as the long summer twilight faded sensuously in the west.

'Is that the Plough?'

'Or is it Orion?'

'You should know, Oliver.'

'I seem to've forgotten everything.'

'Nobody knows the names of stars any more. Or of anything else, come to that. Should I take up the study of astronomy, living out here?'

'In which case you'll keep coming up against the imponderables of cosmology.'

'That's an added incentive, isn't it?'

'Helen, I've decided something on the walk today.'

'What's that then?'

'It's that I can't be a government adviser on this new town any more.'

'Jolly good.'

'In fact I'm going to oppose it. Putting a town here would be pure evil.'

Helen chuckled. 'My goodness, you *have* enjoyed your walk. Oh, look! Above the trees.'

Oliver strained forward. 'What on earth is it?'

'It's a UFO,' said Helen. 'Pretty, isn't it. We saw one last month. A bunch of coloured lights in the air. And Selwyn saw one last year. They're getting more frequent.'

'Of course it isn't a UFO.'

'What is it then, clever Dick?'

'The Northern Lights, I expect.'

'Oliver dear, we're facing south. Of course it's a UFO. It's lovely. Oh, look, it's rotating!'

'So it is. Helen, are you suggesting that it's an interplanetary device from an alien world?'

'Presumably.'

'Well, I'm suggesting that it is a collective hallucination brought on by the heat.'

'There are only two of us, Oliver. That's hardly collective. But have it your own way.'

110.

To find a head in one's bath is one thing; for it to belong to a member of the Cabinet is quite another. So it was not Hoskins this time but police from Scotland Yard who arrived. They turned Milking Magna, and especially The Glade, upside down.

And then they went away.

It was very odd – they simply returned to London, saying nothing of what they'd found or thought. The whole episode struck Alice as a gap in reality through which a lot of foul, stale air gushed out, and it became fully apparent to her how shallow and unpleasant her involvement with that man had been. She took away no memory of any sweet incident between them, no small saving grace, only a sense of horror, embarrassment, fatuity. She'd been a fool and she'd been used. She snuggled up to Dickon's back, wondering if he were the reality now.

III.

JJ was late and made later by wagons en route. The loads of gold hay, lemon hay, green hay rumbled on with unflagging disregard, and he sweated behind them in Sidney's blue Rover until a straight stretch appeared and it was safe to overtake. Crystal and Minerva were in Appleminster shopping for baby and Crystal insisted that her father join them for lunch at The Green Dragon because she had something important to say. Surely the cosy was the proper place for that sort of thing instead of putting him to all this trouble.

'Halloo, Daddykins,' greeted Crystal. She was sitting with Minerva at a table against the far wall, breast-feeding young Blaze. That was the name she'd chosen.

She's always had dreadful table manners, thought JJ. He was disconcerted by the immensity of the exposed breast. So much for Daddy's little girl.

WAITER: Would you care to order, my lord?

JJ: I'll have Stilton soup to begin with, followed by a slice of game pie and a green salad.

WAITER: We don't have game pie or Stilton soup.

JJ: You had it when last I was here.

MINERVA: That was ten years ago, Julius.

JJ: What's today's special?

WAITER: Fish and chips, my lord.

CRYSTAL: That's what we're having.

JJ: Did you tell him I was a lord, Minnie? You know it's not done except for opera tickets.

MINERVA: I wouldn't dream of describing you in public, Julius.

WAITER: We've met before, my lord. At White's. I was the under-porter. They sacked me for insubordination.

JJ: That club you directed me to, do you still have the address? I couldn't remember anything –

MINERVA: Are you two going to talk all day?

JJ: Bring me a chilled Chassagne-Montrachet, my friend, and I'll have fish and chips too.

CRYSTAL: Daddy, would you like to hold Blaze for a while?

MINERVA: Julius, I've enrolled as a mature student at the School of Oriental and African Studies in London.

JJ: Minnie, you haven't.

MINERVA: I have.

JJ: How could you be so disloyal?

MINERVA: I won't go if I marry Mr Wetmore.

JJ: That's blackmail. He's after your money, Minnie.

MINERVA: I don't have money.

JJ: That wouldn't stop him.

WAITER: Would you like to try the wine, my lord?

JJ: I'd be thankful if you'd not use that form of address. Those people over there keep looking round.

MINERVA: Mr Wetmore read the newspaper to me this morning. Do you know how they did it? They forced glue down his throat. Evo-Stik Adhesive.

CRYSTAL: Can I have some wine too? Here, give me back Blaze. (*She lugs out the other tit.*)

WAITER: (*crimson*) I'll get your fish and chips, sir.

CRYSTAL: You embarrassed him, Daddy.

JJ: Nothing to do with you of course. Minnie, would you tell her.

MINERVA: Tell her?

JJ: Tell her that one is supposed to pack away the first breast before pulling out the second. Both out at once gives the wrong impression entirely.

CRYSTAL: I've had a baby, fruit of my womb, I am earth, I am sky, I am mother, I am sea –

MINERVA: And they've found the rest of the body. The remainder. Guess where? In the old marlpit near Butterton.

JJ: Minnie, what are you gabbling about?

MINERVA: What everyone's gabbling about. The Minister of Power. They murdered him by forcing glue down his throat. The walls of his windpipe stuck together.

JJ: Who did?

MINERVA: That's what they're investigating.

JJ: So they chopped his head off afterwards?

MINERVA: Correct.

CRYSTAL: Alice has been brilliant, going to live with Dickon and not being a snob and saying what she said and being so brave.

MINERVA: What did she say?

CRYSTAL: She said she felt like Salome.

JJ: She said that to me too.

MINERVA: Bloodthirsty piece underneath, isn't she.

JJ: I'm rather grateful for this murder of her old boss. Alice has thrown herself into organising the conference as a kind of therapy. In fact the murder has been the making of her.

WAITER: (*with fish and chips*) Tartare sauce, sir?

JJ: How could anyone refuse an offer like that?

WAITER: Will there be anything else, sir?

JJ: Here's my telephone number.

WAITER: Thank you, sir. (*Exit waiter in high colour*)

CRYSTAL: He couldn't take his eyes off my tits.

JJ: Something he has in common with the rest of the dining-room. Anyway I've said my piece. If you want to lunch topless . . .

MINERVA: You mustn't be afraid of boobs, Julius. I noticed that at my birthday party –

JJ: What did you mean about Alice not being a snob?

CRYSTAL: You know, Dickon being a yo –

JJ: Don't you dare call him a yokel.

CRYSTAL: If you'd let me finish – I was going to say being a yeoman.

JJ: You're the biggest snob in the book, Crystal. You think life is going slumming.

CRYSTAL: You're the one who likes a bit of rough.

JJ: You see? That's your attitude. It's not mine.

CRYSTAL: What is your attitude, Daddy?

JJ: That people who are limited to their own kind are little people.

MINERVA: You're a snob, Julius, for objecting to Mr Wetmore because he is a nice, straightforward, middle-class man.

JJ: Ha! I object because he's an alcoholic.

MINERVA: He enjoys a drink like the rest of us, that's all.

JJ: Oh, marry the sod then. But you'll have to move into the stables. I'm not having him lying about my house sozzled for the next thirty years. Think of little Blaze here with such an example in his formative period. Booder, booder, booder. I don't think he looks very Chinese at all, Crystal. I think Robin overreacted.

CRYSTAL: That's right. It was Robin's illness which killed him. His personality disorder.

JJ: Is Bob religious, Minnie? He might as well start earning his keep now. We need someone to be hall porter at our conference.

CRYSTAL: Daddy, you're such a pig sometimes.

JJ: Is that what you got me out here for, to tell me that I'm a pig, when you know how busy we are right now?

CRYSTAL: Yes, I wanted you to understand that Aunt Minnie should be allowed to have someone special of her own and you mustn't put obstacles in her way just because you're jealous because you don't have a proper relationship but only that awful part-time thing with Glory.

JJ fell silent and quaffed from his glass. Minerva's resolve – to get married or go to London – unnerved him almost more than anything this year and now his own daughter had gone for the jugular. He was indeed distressed by the prospect of being left alone in the midst of *couples*. Heaven Park, citadel of singledom, was being overrun by the blasted things! Where had they all come from suddenly? Minerva and Bob. Pimm and Veronica. Alice and Dickon. Helen and Selwyn. Justice and Mrs Bladder-Wiliams. Even Crystal had her Blaze. He hated couples. If he went to a party and saw that it was dominated by couples he knew it was going to be dreariness incarnate. Self-completing, self-cancelling, non-dynamic, couples killed off all hope, never doing anything except together, never going anywhere without dragging the partner along, never having a thought or committing an act without watering it down to accommodate the other. One could have love, sex, companionship without being locked into the living death of the couple, couldn't one?

112.

The Old Un was trembling. Trembling unusually, that is. Mrs Bladder-Williams noticed it when she called. It was as though the Old Un were travelling on a high-speed train. Despite the hot weather, her first thought was that the Old Un must be cold or in a draught, so she closed all the windows and bent close to the walnut face. 'Would you like me to switch on the fire?' The Old Un angled up an opalescent gaze, grunted 'Innit romantic,' and looked through her to infinity. Was she looking for a drowned daughter? If so, she gave no hint of it. She muttered only 'Innit romantic, innit romantic.' A bee buzzed in the closed window. Mrs Bladder-Williams plugged in the electric fire which sat in the fireplace and went into the kitchen to wash up and make a cup of tea.

The bee in the window was joined by a second. They made quite a racket buzzing confusedly up and down the panes, unable to understand the nature of glass and why they were not out of doors. Then a third bee – and a fourth and fifth – joined them. Before long there were many bees, not only buzzing in the window but whirring round the room. The eyes of the Old Un, like two gristle suckers, became unstuck from the windows of infinity for the first time in years and began to pay proper attention to the immediate surroundings: the Old Un knew she was in danger.

The electric fire had disturbed a swarm of bees resident in the chimney. Instead of being sensible bees and flying up and away, they were silly bees who decided to move downwards in search of another place to swarm. Whirring round the room they discovered there was no more charming spot than the Old Un's hair. As Mrs Bladder-Williams marched back in with the promised tea she was knocked back by a sound like that of an aeroplane engine. The swarm covered the Old Un's head entirely. Her two little hands like withered leaves were fluttering. By the time the ambulance arrived she was dead from the shock of a thousand stings and her head resembled a giant blackberry.

It fell to Mrs Bladder-Williams to go through the Old Un's effects. A tin of sets of false teeth, a tin of obsolete banknotes, a tin of brass curtain rings and so on – and an envelope. It was yellow with age. On its outside was written *To be opened in the event of my death*. The sealed flap loosened very easily.

113.

'I want you to read the letters,' Dickon told Alice.

After they'd eaten he took her into the sitting-room and opened a tongue-and-groove cupboard beside the fireplace.

'I got em out of the bank yesterday. Take your time. I'm going to repair a door in the big barn. Then you can help me decide what to do.'

114.

The day before the start of the Heaven Park Oecumenical Conference, one task remained. Not since the Coronation had the Great Gate on the main road been opened, and getting it open now wasn't easy. The overarching ironwork involved, among curlicues, a family of monkeys holding aloft the Popjoy motto SEMPER, but the letters 'MP' had fallen off years ago and the local farrier was recruited to solder them back on. In the process part of a gate pier crashed into the grass, taking one of the large stone coronets with it, but by lunchtime all was reasonably secure and Glory was able to attach a hand-daubed sign, The Gates of Heaven, and the Tewkesbury Boys roared through on motorbikes. They had been co-opted for extra security, although the property itself was staked out by a detachment of the King's Own Heavenshires, and armed policemen with walkie-talkies occupied key sites. From two o'clock onwards the delegates themselves began to arrive, a very mixed bunch.

Alice was in charge, because the days when Sidney could take on a house-party of this size had long gone, and she sought to prepare herself by walking round the grounds with a glossary of heteroclite terminology. Merely the names of these people would test the patience of a saint! At one end of the walled garden, she came upon Ben Thicknesse drowning grey squirrels in a rain butt.

'No end to the buggers,' he said affably.

'Rather what I was thinking,' she replied, flourishing her list.

'Take them jargonelle pears. You'll need em.'

She sauntered on to the soldiers who had planted their cream bell tents in the Aspen Paddock. Tanned by the summer, the young men resembled sepoys up-country.

'Everything all right, chaps?' she asked.

'Yes thanks, lady,' they replied, under the impression that she was a duchess at the very least.

Alice's first crisis was to sort out Pravinda Govinda Perambulata, held in a ruffianly grip on the front steps by one of the Tewkesbury Boys who was repeating 'Tinty car, tinty car!'

She said 'Be nice, Dan. He's traipsed all the way from Saint Pancras Station,' and to Pravinda she said 'He's checking identity cards. Show him yours, please.'

'But I have no identity,' said Pravinda.

Alice tried to be less off-hand. 'We sent everyone an identity card. The Home Office said we had to. They fear a nuclear device.' Pravinda fumbled cluelessly at his dhoti and shrugged. 'Oh very well,' she said, 'your room, sir, is number 18 in the south-west pavilion'.

'But 18 is a very bad number.'

'Pretend it's 81 and you're seeing back to front.'

A crocodile of males, stripped to the waist, were carrying chairs across the Great Hall to the Ballroom and Alice started to follow them but was waylaid by the Abbot of Downboys, nervously turning his ring. 'I came with Cardinal du Lally Berzerque and his accommodation, he wouldn't mention it himself but I know it isn't suitable. His Eminence is praying in the billiard room but really he deserves *more*.'

'Abbot, do you know by any chance what's happened to the Archbishop of Canterbury?' Alice thought the Archbishop really should have been here by now to help her calm these people.

Cardinal du Lally Berzerque, no less concerned for a colleague's sleeping quarters, had trapped Minerva against a pillar, with his condescending eyes and flanges of crimson silk, because she didn't make him feel overdressed (she was got up for the occasion as an eighteenth-century shepherdess and her sunburnt face was peeling in rebellious curls of skin).

'My room is wonderful, madame. How did you know a lumpy mattress is my secret joy? But the Abbot of Downboys – above the kitchen – in this weather – it's too hot for him. And we gather that the Abbot of Amplemouth has a bedroom in the Cameron Suite with violet glass pillars and a bronze bath.'

'Leave me alone, you big red bully!' she said. It was sheer nerves.

Alice crossed the hall to receive the Bishop of Lubumbashi accompanied by Mr Mustafa, the Hyperwhirling Dervish, whom the bishop had encountered rotating outside Appleminster Railway Station. 'Is the Archbishop of Canterbury with you?' she enquired. 'I can't sleep facing north,' responded the dervish. Then a bus turned up on the gravel with a load more of them. The Lutheran mystic Claus von Schimmering blustered in late and the very last to arrive that evening, wearing a Burberry mackintosh and a bone through his nose, was the Observer from the Highlands of New Guinea representing the Corrugated Animists.

At eight p.m. JJ addressed them in the Great Hall. 'Welcome, ladies and gentlemen. I'd like first to mention the park itself. It is very dry, so please be careful not to drop your dog-ends outside and perhaps you might implore your various deities to give us some rain. I should also warn you that this is a house of devious mazes. But if you get lost, remember that it doesn't matter. You are safe. You are all in one place. Which I feel is an apt symbol for your oecumenical objective. Now we may eat. A buffet has been set in the Turkish Kiosk where you should take the opportunity to enjoy the scagliola panels salvaged from Nonesuch Palace. Please follow Mr Boy.'

As they ambled away, Minerva's peeling face emerged from behind her pillar. So many religious men all at once had hit her terribly on her shy bone. 'Do we have to eat there too?' she asked her beau who was resting his pruritis on a hall chair.

'Fraid so,' said Bob Wetmore.

'I'm glad you're not religious, Mr Wetmore.'

In clacking high-heels Alice walked smartly to the main door where Sidney was having a surreptitious fag and said 'Sidney, please, to the Turkish Kiosk. The food's your territory. The Larks can't cope by themselves.'

'Oh gawd, miss, steady on, it doesn't come easy being bossed in me own house and Cook's complaining like hell.'

'I know the catering's a nightmare. They all want to eat different things. I tell you there's nothing like trying to feed this bunch to remind you how bloody *stupid* people can be. And, Bob, there's still some luggage to take upstairs.'

When all seemed set and beginning to flow, there was a further scuffle under the great portico where the Tewkesbury Boy was still doing his duty. The interloper hopped up and down, shouting 'Let *go of me,* you clod!'

'It's all right, Dan,' announced Alice imperiously.

Dan was getting to like Alice's tone and asked 'Fancy a shag arter?'

She gave him her cute headmistress look before turning to the newcomer. 'Sorry, Sylvia, we have to be careful. There have been atrocities.'

Sylvia, whose keen instinct detected a glass of something on a ledge, gulped from it with her left hand and waved rapidly with her right to indicate that no one should take over the conversation while she polished off the wine. Having drunk, she harried them with bulging eyes.

'What is it, Sylvia?'

'They've arrested Max Lomax.'

'My God, what for?' asked Bob.

'For the murder of the Minister of Power.'

'That's incredible!' enthused Alice.

'Hoskins arrested him an hour ago up at the caravan. They've taken him into Appleminster.'

'Did he do it?' asked Lady Minerva.

'Don't talk rot!' spat Sylvia. 'My God. What happened to your face? Were you in a bomb outrage?' But before the unfortunate woman could reply, Sylvia reeled against a wall, sobbing 'Max was my friend!'

'Is your friend,' corrected Bob. 'Anyway he wasn't really your friend.'

'Bastard, I adored Max!'

'Adore, Sylvia. Present tense.'

'And I'm going through the menopause for Christ's sake!'

Minerva rallied and screeched 'Who are you trying to kid?'

'I am, I am, I know I am!'

'Shut up, you three!' bawled Alice. 'There's a religious conference going on, so just fuck off, will you!'

And amazingly they did.

Left alone in the hall with the butler, Alice adjusted her shirt-waister and pushed back her hair. Never before had she spoken like that in this house and it was shocking even to herself. 'Forgive me, Sidney. I think the heat's getting to us all. And JJ had a call from MI5 asking us to watch out for bio-terrorism. Lobbing germs over the wall. Pick up some extra newspapers tomorrow so we can read about Lomax. You don't know what's happened to the Archbishop, do you?'

'I'm afraid I don't, miss.'

'He'd better show because my duties don't extend to chairing his conference as well. Lomax a murderer. Fancy that. To me he was some oddball one would try to avoid at the grocer's. Murder seems too grand a charge for such a ridiculous person. I never thought of him in that way.'

'I did, miss. Or a child-molester. Or a shop-lifter. He always looked as though he needed to do something dreadful in order to fulfil himself.'

'You knew him better than I did.'

'On the contrary. I didn't know him at all.'

'It's been quite a day, Sidney.'

'Indeed it has. And take it from me, miss, there'll be another one tomorrow.'

115.

The Archbishop did not let them down. He arrived the next morning, accompanied by the Archimandrite of Zosklivosk, and hurried directly to the ballroom where the gilt chairs with raspberry velvet upholstery and pads on the arms had been arranged into a horseshoe. There were no placements. People seated themselves spontaneously. That was one of the ideas, to be spontaneous. The Archbishop, after making play with a propelling pencil on a notepad, rose to his feet and surveyed the fifty or so delegates over his half-moon spectacles.

'Ladies and gentlemen, we are here to loosen a little the bonds of dogma so that we may glimpse the features common to us all. The purpose of the world oecumenical movement is not to eliminate difference but to reduce hostility between religions, and therefore the subject on our first day is Peter Abelard's great injunction: diversa non adversa.'

The Archbishop paused to press a Milk of Magnesia tablet out of a cardboard square and Devon Shocklatch, the post-electronic theologian from Yale, took advantage of the interval to dive in with 'I would like to start by asking the Imam Aziz Azwaz why it is that Muslim men hate women so much'. Before the Imam could respond to this vigorous opener, Mrs Glottle-Ganges, the Hindu intellectual, followed up with 'Religious opposition to birth control and sexual pleasure is the male terror of the empowerment of women!' It looked as though a feminist hi-jack were underway.

ABBOT OF DOWNBOYS: But I like overpopulation. It's cosy.

SHOCKLATCH: Well, I don't want smelly old men with beards telling me I'm unclean thank you.

MR PHEW, A ZEN ADEPT OF THE ETHERIC GARDEN: It is difficult –

CANTERBURY: Before you go any further, Mr Phew, I want to say sorry we dropped those nuclear bombs on you.

MR PHEW: Don't worry. If we'd had them we'd've dropped them on you. I was going to say that it is difficult for us in the Etheric Garden to view your cult of the Virgin Mary as other than a perversion.

CARDINAL DU LALLY BERZERQUE: What about your lot hitting each other with tea-trays?

SHOCKLATCH: No, Cardinal, there *is* something fetid about virginity when it persists into adulthood. A kind of infantilism. The notion that the denial of life produces a higher spiritual type is absurd. Chastity definitely produces a lower type. All stunting does.

SHADNI LAL, SPIRITUAL ADVISER TO THE FAL LAL OF KONK: Higher type, lower type – illusions! Because there is no such thing as progress.

CANTERBURY: Well, we crawled from the slime to explore the stars. That's progress of a sort.

CLAUS VON SCHIMMERING, THE LUTHERAN MYSTIC: Evolution can be progress for a specific case, if not for the general one.

For example, the perception of colour is a late development in human evolution and continues still. In the future there may be colours which are completely new and the auras of things, occurring beyond the violet end of the spectrum, may become generally visible.

ARCHIMANDRITE OF ZOSKLIVOSK: And very disgusting things *used* to happen which don't happen now. For example, during the feast of Apollo at Philae a prize was awarded to the youth with the deftest kiss.

BISHOP OF LUBUMBASHI: Ugh, pshaw, spit! It is definitely progress that *that* sort of thing doesn't occur any more.

IMAM AZIZ AZWAZ: But it does occur! It is the shame of Islam!

SHOCKLATCH: I'm a lesbian and homosexuality is a very natural activity.

MRS GLOTTLE-GANGES: Of course it's natural. That's why the churches want to stamp on it. Churches are pledged to the unnatural – to fasting, virgin births, beds of nails, miracles, shrouded women, and so forth.

CANTERBURY: Don't be too hard on us, ladies. What the Dark and Middle Ages did do was foster the growth of the ordinary man's inner life. The gothic, the northern, the tender, the compassionate – without all that, humanity would have remained too brash. Yes, Archimandrite, even the Greeks were too brash, too external. The southern needs the northern to achieve depth, just as the northern needs the southern to become visible.

WRINGNECK WOGAN OF THE MORAVIAN RAVERS: And what will the Present Age do?

THE UNPRIEST OF THE UNCHURCH: The Present Age is all about breaking down barriers.

IMAM: A mind in which there are no barriers is random and must be classified insane. The same is true of society.

CANTERBURY: In other words both correspondences *and* distinctions are essential.

CLAUS VON SCHIMMERING: This was the fundamental law of alchemy.

REVD. SINUS SIMM: Pelagius, a Briton of the fifth century, said that men do not need a church for salvation.

MRS GLOTTLE-GANGES: So what is the correspondence between salvation and society?

ABBOT OF AMPLEMOUTH: Does not Ambrosiaster tells us as early as the fourth century that God makes all men free?

PRAVINDA GOVINDA PERAMBULATA: Churches are gangs and clubs. Gangs and clubs reassure people. The theology is almost irrelevant – any old colourful rubbish will do so long as it fits local climatic conditions. Being in the club is the important thing.

SHOCKLATCH: That's right. Organised religion is not about ultimate reality but about social control.

RABBI DE GOLDSTEIN: Don't underestimate the importance of social control. Without it everything falls apart. On this the Imam and I would surely agree.

CLAUS VON SCHIMMERING: Jung said that churches arise spontaneously to protect us from the religious experience, from the overwhelming power of God.

REVD. SIMM: But this overwhelming power, are you sure it still exists? I don't think men any longer walk in that fear.

SHOCKLATCH: Yeah, dead magic. Traditional religion is all dead magic now.

IMAM: Oh no. I assure you Islam is hitting the headlines everywhere.

CARDINAL: It's floating on oil money, that's all.

IMAM: At least it's floating, Cardinal. Christianity is sinking.

SHADNI LAL: Floating. Sinking. Illusions!

CANTERBURY: Right, we seem to have disposed of churches and God. What about the soul? Does the soul exist?

MRS GLOTTLE-GANGES: Of course! Because the universe could be purely material only on condition that it did not move. With movement you have things coming into being. Potentiality is spiritual because it is about what doesn't exist yet.

LAMA OF LAMAS: Soul is what comes into being when the whole is greater than the sum of the parts.

VICAR OF SAINT ANDREW UNDERSHAFT: But must the parts come first?

CANTERBURY: That is the question. And on the subject of parts, if I may be permitted to quote from my recent autobiography

Words Are Not My Only Tool, copies of which are available for purchase in the Great Hall . . .

Thus they deliberated, continuing through a cold buffet lunch-eon served in the hot Temple of the Inexpressible, and through a hot buffet dinner served in the comparative coolness of the Great Hall. Alice had decided to make it all buffets. It was simpler. People could pick up those bits their religions permitted them to eat. A secondment from the catering corps of the King's Own Heavenshire's turned up in time to take the pressure off Cook and Sidney. This was fortunate because that very evening Sidney had an engagement elsewhere.

116.

Earlier in the day the ancient butler received a telephone call.
'This is Immacolata Bladder-Williams.'
'Hullo, Mrs Bladder-Williams.' He sucked in his teeth and waited.
'Do you think we could meet? As you may know I cleared out the Old Un's things after she died and she left an envelope marked *To be opened in the event of my death.* So I opened it.'
'Yes. I see. Quite. In that case, Mrs Bladder-Williams, I feel we should meet at Mr Royal's house. Yes, in the circumstances, I think that would be the proper thing to do.'
The whole of Heavenshire flushed red in the setting sun. As the Observer from the Highlands of New Guinea performed a hip-writhing rain-making ritual on one of JJ's brown lawns, Sidney drove resolutely up to Gypsy Castle and the house of Justice Royal. Mrs Bladder-Williams opened the front door before he had a chance to ring the bell and, and squaring her shoulders with something of the old belligerence, said 'Please come in'.
'Thank you.'
'What a business.'
'Indeed.'
Justice was in the front room standing in a gonging pool of gamelan music, patting his grandson's back as he gently rocked him. Mrs Bladder-Williams turned the music down.

'Forgive me, Mr Royal,' began Sidney, hand to his forehead. 'I should've come before. But I didn't know what to do for the best.'

'I'm not interferin, sir. It was Immacolata who found the letter. Nothing to do with me.'

'But you don't understand. There are things the Old Un could not have known. It is very much something to do with you. That's why I suggested we meet here.'

Sidney mopped his brow with a hanky before continuing. 'Can we all sit down? I have to explain about your little boy,' he said.

117.

The Second Day of the Oecumencial Conference. The Archbishop of Canterbury, submitting to the weather, wore a crushed linen suit, and sandals which disclosed his hammer toes.

'Today our subject is Badness,' he announced, 'and I'd like to open by asking if anyone here has had experience of cosmic desolation?'

'Do you mean universal godlesssness?' whirled Mr Mustafa.

'You tell me,' responded Canterbury. 'Cosmic desolation. Knock it about among yourselves.'

WRINGNECK WOGAN OF THE MORAVIAN RAVERS: We blame Darwinism for this because it claims the universe is accidental and has no intelligence.

DEVON SHOCKLATCH, THE POST-ELECTRONIC THEOLOGIAN: But it was necessary for mankind to *pass through* Darwin as it was necessary to pass through Freud. Darwin helped us to navigate time and Freud to navigate inner space.

MRS GLOTTLE-GANGES, THE HINDU INTELLECTUAL: Otherwise you Christians would still be stuck in that drivel about how God created the world in 4004 BC.

BISHOP OF LUBUMBASHI: Don't be so tart, you. Writing was invented around 4000 BC. Since the Bible says 'In the beginning was the Word and the Word was God,' we can infer that the scriptures date the beginning of creation from the beginning of writing. It is a tenable position.

CARDINAL DU LALLY BERZERQUE: And of course we have to *pass through* Einstein also.

RABBI DE GOLDSTEIN: Einstein and Freud were Jews, and since the Jews have suffered more than any other race –

MRS GLOTTLE-GANGES: Here we go again. The chosen race has got to be top of the pops in suffering too. Other peoples have also suffered dreadfully, Rabbi. It's not a competition.

ARCHIMANDRITE OF ZOSKLIVOSK: Jews constantly calculate and compare their holocaust. And that is correct. Horrors must be identified and described. We Russians had to endure *two* holocausts – fighting Hitler and suffering Stalin. And it was 20 million souls *each time*. What was yours, Rabbi? Six million once. So we win.

MRS GLOTTLE-GANGES: For me the tragedy of life is that God has a destiny too. He was incapable of making a world that is happy for us.

MR PHEW OF THE ETHERIC GARDEN: God's struggle to be subjective produces Man. Man's struggle to be objective produces God. Since the universe includes both subjective and objective, it is clear that God needs Man quite as much as Man needs God.

THE UNPRIEST OF THE UNCHURCH: Or to put it another way – neither is required.

ABBOT OF DOWNBOYS: And what about the Devil? Is he required?

Boom!

REVD. SINUS SIMM: What was that noise?

MRS GLOTTLE-GANGES: Was there a noise?

SHADNI LAL, SPIRITUAL ADVISER TO THE FAL LAL OF KONK: Illusions, illusions!

REVD. SIMM: No, there was a booming noise. Like an explosion.

CARDINAL, DOWNBOYS, AMPLEMOUTH: We didn't hear anything.

PRAVINDA GOVINDA PERAMBULATA: I did. Distant thunder?

CANTERBURY: There's not a cloud in the sky.

WRINGNECK WOGAN: Perhaps it was the Second Coming.

VICAR OF SAINT ANDREW UNDERSHAFT: I have a story about that. Jesus has come back again. But looking round the world and seeing the dreadful things done in the name of religion, he thought it would be better if this time he lived quietly and didn't open his mouth too much. So he takes a flat near Fenchurch Street Station and walks about the city keeping his head down but giving off an erratic light. I noticed this light one day and approached and said 'My goodness, it's Jesus, I don't believe it!' And He said 'Shush, go away, keep it under your hat.' But I couldn't keep it under my hat and went round telling everybody. By the end of the week I had been sectioned as a lunatic and prescribed strong drugs. Jesus discovered this and came out of hiding and said to them 'You must let him go. It's true. I am Jesus.' So they did the same to him.

118.

Responding to a tip-off, which came from the Green Kingdom itself though that wasn't known at the time, Hoskins was ordered by Scotland yard to arrest Max Lomax and charge him with complicity in the murder of the Minister of Power, specifically with hacking off the head and planting it in someone else's bathtub, although after consideration the police did not feel that Lomax was the one who actually forced the superglue down the victim's throat, to which were added the additional charges of harassment and trespass and shop-lifting. Bail was not granted and Lomax was to be sent to gaol on remand. Accompanied by Hoskins and three armed policemen from the anti-terrorist squad, Lomax came back to the caravan to collect his things. His erstwhile neighbours turned out to hurl insults. Hoskins said 'Remember that in England a man is innocent until proven guilty. Please go about your normal business.' But few of the residents had normal business.

'I'd like to change into some fresh clothes, officer.'

'I'll have to position a man at the rear in case you nip out the back window.'

'By all means.'

Once inside the caravan, Max pulled himself upright and looked in the mirror. 'No, by Jove, they'll never get you, Max.' He turned the gas taps of his cooking rings full on. The gas hissed furiously. 'Stupid little poof won't get me . . . Shan't be long, officer!' He flicked some dust from his lapel and tried not to swoon or cough in the thickening fume. When he thought he could delay no longer, he took the box of Swan Vestas off the cooker and, with an indomitable whinny, struck a match.

The explosion was heard all over Milking Magna. Many of Max's gawping neighbours had their faces permanently disfigured by flying bits of caravan. Mrs Punch had to have one of Max's fingers surgically removed from her forearm. A rocketing saucepan killed outright the policeman at the rear and Hoskins himself was thrown right out of the caravan park into the adjacent field, landing conveniently in the branches of a chestnut tree.

119.

The afternoon of the third and final day of the conference found JJ in a reflective mood in the old nursery. If the murder of the Minister of Power had done him a favour in the form of Alice's efficiency, it was to be followed by a disfavour: a financial scandal of enormous ramifications. The Prime Minister had promised an official enquiry into all aspects of the matter but already environmentalists had decided to exploit the Government's vulnerability by staging a major protest against the City of Cognitive Neuroscience. This would centre on the Ring of the Moon and would go down in history as the Great Demo. The chances of JJ being able to turn his fortunes around by selling off Lower Farm for development were diminishing rapidly by the hour.

Something more personal troubled him too. It was decided to end the conference in a spirit of good cheer with a Grand Oecumenical Ball. Fabulous. Terrific. He'd been limbering up in the cosy with the duets of Dinah Washington and Brook Benton. But Detective Hoskins had put the mockers on that as far as JJ was concerned by demanding an urgent meeting with the marquess during the ball at midnight, and when JJ protested that this was hardly the most appropriate time, Hoskins had replied 'On the contrary, all relevant parties are likely to be at the house then'. The detective said he was intending to announce something of great import in connection with his investigations.

In addition to all this, Sidney was behaving oddly, not looking JJ in the eye. Alice had been behaving oddly too. Well, she often did but this was a different sort of oddly. Something was up and JJ didn't like the feel of it.

He contemplated a dusty trainset, plugged in the controls and pressed some buttons but the system was dead. A harlequin doll of faded costume was propped in a chair. He recalled winning the doll in a raffle at The Crag fête when he was a boy, and how furious his father had been that he'd gone to The Crag fête at all. The harlequin's mysterious smile had always touched him, as though he and JJ shared a secret joke. It had been donated to the raffle by Sir Timothy Craddock's father and had before that been in one of the lumber rooms at The Crag for generations. It was in fact of the late eighteenth century but in the old days people didn't attach a great deal of importance to such things and it had ended up on the raffle table.

As he returned the doll to its place he thought of his nurse whose favourite chair this was. She had a touching smile too but it wasn't mysterious in the least. When he was unwell she would give him soaky – bread in warm milk sprinkled with sugar – and if he had been especially good she would ask Cook for a pink blancmange with strawberry jam on top. Looking out of the window, he saw that yet more food was being delivered to the back of the house for those gluttonous holy men. There'd be no profit from this outing, that was clear. It was time to have another word with Alice.

She was sitting in the shade of a great ash tree whose leaves were printed sharply against the blue sky. The delegates were conducting their intercourse out of doors and she was listening to them. Tea-cups dotted the grass. Today's subject was Goodness.

MR PHEW OF THE ETHERIC GARDEN: Yes, let's have a laugh!

WRINGNECK WOGAN OF THE MORAVIAN RAVERS: Christ never laughed.

CARDINAL DU LALLY BERZERQUE: Correction. There is no *mention* of Christ having laughed, but nor is there *mention* of him doing ca-ca.

WRINGNECK: Perhaps he never did ca-ca either. If you can have a virgin birth you can have a shitless messiah.

ARCHIMANDRITE OF ZOSKLIVOSK: Antiochus wrote in Pandectes that it is generally forbidden to Christians to laugh. However, to my knowledge, evacuation was always permissible, certainly in the Eastern Church.

SHADNI LAL SPIRITUAL ADVISER TO THE FAL LAL OF KONK: Before the smile of the Mona Lisa there was the smile of the Buddha and he came out of Hinduism which talks often of the cosmic joke.

WRINGNECK WOGAN: So the cosmic joke isn't an illusion then?

SHADNI LAL: Yes, I'm sure it is. That's what makes it so amusing.

ARCHIMANDRITE: Hecataeus of Miletus, who lived around 500 BC, is the first recorded person to have thought the gods funny. Homer almost did but not quite.

ABBOT OF AMPLEMOUTH: Aren't we being led down the cul-de-sac of laughter? Happiness and goodness are not the same thing.

THE OBSERVER FOR THE CORRUGATED ANIMISTS: They are the same in New Guinea.

ARCHBISHOP OF CANTERBURY: Welcome to the Observer over there. A first from him. It always bucks one up to see a man pass from observation to participation.

ABBOT OF DOWNBOYS: May I suggest that goodness is compassion?

IMAM AZIZ AZWAZ: Compassion makes one dither.

MRS GLOTTLE-GANGES: That's a very male statement.

DEVON SHOCKLATCH: What did you expect from him? Islam is rampant testosterone.

IMAM: You are forgetting a billion floral tiles.

RABBI DE GOLDSTEIN: Testosterone and floral tiles. That's about it. When did someone from a Muslim state last win a Nobel prize? Islam has shut down the life of the mind in its own countries and is now trying to do the same worldwide. If you didn't sell your oil to the west you'd be worse off than the bloody negroes!

BISHOP OF LUBUMBASHI: Oh shove a pork sandwich up yer arse!

CANTERBURY: Now, now. I think I can take the heat out of this by saying that we're all against fanatics. Don't you agree, Imam?

IMAM: I'd like to keep a bit of a low profile on this one, because this morning I received a death threat from one of my own.

CARDINAL: Well, I didn't, and I disagree with Monsieur Canterbury. One needs the éclat of fanaticism now and again to wake
people up.

VICAR OF SAINT ANDREW UNDERSHAFT: Have you noticed –
fanatics can't play football. The winners of the World Cup are
always from nice countries.

CLAUS VON SCHIMMERING: Fanaticism is the opposite of play.
Play is beyond the absolute. Play renders the absolute relative.
The absolute is merely more material for play.

CANTERBURY: Can you be more specific, Herr von Schimmering?

CLAUS VON SCHIMMERING: For example, in a totalitarian society
the writer must be a democrat. In a democratic society the
writer must be an elitist. In a religious society he is an atheist.
And in an atheistic society he is holy.

Alice, who had been in several minds as to whether she might
make a contribution, was emboldened by learning from the Imam
that compassion makes one dither. So she decided not to worry
about what other people thought and felt, and stood up to say her
bit.

'Ladies and gentlemen, putting on a funny hat and adopting a
list of rules, isn't any kind of answer to what we really face day
after day in our hearts. Watching all you religious people, I've
come to realise that it's no use running to any of the religions. You
can do religion afterwards. Put on the funny hat which fits, yes,
but afterwards. In the first place, if you want to be a dignified
human being and not some zombie, you must be strong enough
to grasp the idea that there is nowhere to run, that there is no
person or thing to run to, that deep down nobody knows any more
than you do, that nobody knows what the hell it's all about, that
we're all in the same bloody boat, and that anyone who says he
knows what God is, or what truth is, or what life is ultimately all
about, is a bloody liar and a dangerous idiot. Goodness and badness have nothing to do with wearing a particular hat. Good and
evil are above religion.'

The Archbishop of Canterbury put on his 'Very interesting,
my dear' face but did not speak. From the others too there was a

polite silence but Glory Boy applauded enthusiastically from a nearby bough and beckoned to her. He swung down from the ash tree and she followed him into a part of the house where she'd never gone before. 'That told em,' he said as they climbed a bare staircase, stirring dust which shone in the shafts of sunshine.

'I think I only made one more contribution to the general clap-trap.'

'No, no. Calling religion a heap of shit is a very good beginning.'

'What does JJ want me for?'

'He didn't say.'

She hoped it wasn't going to be an interrogation.

Along a butter-coloured corridor with collapsed plaster at their feet and exposed ceiling joists above. Along a second. At the end of which JJ awaited them. He opened a wicket into the nursery wing. There was a faint smell of graphite and chalk.

'This was the schoolroom. Mine and Minerva's.'

'Not Crystal's?'

'She went to the village school to start with.'

'It's baking in here. Can we open one of the windows?'

'Unfortunately not. They were all sealed for security. Come through.'

They entered the nursery sitting-room where JJ ran his hand along the window-sill dislodging flakes of yellow paint. Alice picked up the harlequin doll and sat down on the chair.

'I wanted to ask you, Alice, if you'd like to renew your contract with me for another year. It looks as though major development in the Puck Valley is under a cloud and this first conference has gone all right and we should continue. Do you think we've made a profit?'

Alice coughed. 'No. But you don't expect to on the first one. It's a learning experience. As for another year, that depends . . . '

'I thought you could turn the nursery here into a proper office. Even fix up a bedroom, so that you could crash out if necessary. Which brings me to the second point. Now that you are sort of living with Dickon at Lower Farm, do you think Crystal could have The Glade? She needs her own place and after your unpleasant experiences there – '

'Fine, I'll move out, no problem.'

'Really? Oh. I was expecting more of a tussle. You're allowed to stand up for yourself, you know.'

'Is there anything else? I have to check the ballroom.'

'Not at the moment.'

'I'll see you at the ball then and at the meeting in the Long Library afterwards of course.'

'What? Are you coming to that meeting too? I thought it was strictly a family affair.'

'Didn't he tell you?' Alice became very uncomfortable and twisted the doll recklessly in her hands.

'No, he didn't.'

'He said it was something about your brother, JJ.'

'My brother?'

'I didn't know you had a brother.'

'What about my brother?'

JJ had gone dreadfully pale and Alice realised she was out of her depth and became more anxious still. 'I'm sorry if I've spoken out of turn.'

'What *has* Hoskins been saying to you?'

'Tonight, JJ. Not now . . . '

'He wasn't the usual sort of brother.'

Glory was smoking quietly in the window.

'Oh, JJ . . . ' Alice became emotional.

She knows something, he thought, but said 'Be careful. Don't hurt him. He's my lovely harlequin.'

In Alice's overwrought hands the fragile fabric of the doll tore open across its back and tufts of horsehair protruded.

'Oh gawd.'

'I'm so sorry, silly me, but I'm sure it can be repaired. If we do this – and this – '

'My lovely harlequin! Alice, stop it, you're making it worse! Now look what you've done. It's falling to bits.'

'JJ, there's something funny inside it.'

'Leave it alone. You're horrible.'

'A little book of some sort.'

'Let me get my spectacles. You're still horrible. My poor lovely harlequin.'

JJ froze. The seconds ticked by as he turned green.

'You don't look very well.'

'I'm not very well.'

'What is it?'

'Unbelievable!'

'Tell us, JJ' insisted Glory, stepping forward.

'Only the fucking *Astronomical Poems* by fucking Leonardo da Vinci, that's all. Excuse me, but I think I'm going to faint.'

120.

Henceforth it all happened very quickly, as a pan of milk, after a gradual accumulation of heat, will suddenly foam up and boil over.

In preparation for the Grand Oecumenical Ball all the state rooms were opened up and freshened with trees in tubs and flowers in pots. Cook passed out drunk, extra food was bussed in from the fish & chip shop and there was a paying bar. Many came up from the village for the occasion, and faces familiar and unfamiliar thronged the glittering saloons. The night was hot, overcast, oppressive but eventually everyone of whatever hat was dancing in the ballroom, all the religions of the world swept up into one gyrating movement, their ambition of coming together realised briefly on the wings of melody and the helter-skelter of rhythm.

At the last stroke of midnight there was a flash of lightning and a clap of thunder. Since DJ Meat was producing at the time a driving mix of Irving Berlin's 'Dancing Cheek to Cheek', the thunder could barely be heard. But it came again and DJ Meat noticed that everyone had stopped dancing and he took off his headphones and switched off the music. The silence ran over them like hissing snakes. The breaking storm flashed and banged again and a great cheer went up. Through the open glass doors they all charged out to the terrace and down the steps to the lawns where the trees were strung with coloured lanterns. Two hundred happy upturned faces awaited the deluge as the hot stones of the enormous Palladian house steamed in the first drops of rain.

Minerva and Sidney however were not among the revellers, for Sidney felt obliged to take JJ's sister up to her bedroom, sit her down and tell her things about her family she had never even suspected. Minerva sat motionlessly in a pink chenille chair, smoothing from time to time the skirt of her gown of pimpernel red embroidered with seed-pearls, and when she came down the Staircase to Eternity one hour later she moved as though in a trance and her face was vacant, as of whiteness subtracted from whiteness.

Nor was Crystal among the revellers, since Hoskins had earlier explained everything to her and she'd taken herself off to the quiet of The Crag.

And nor was JJ among the revellers. He of course was in a state of nervous excitement in the Long Library, awaiting the arrival of everyone else.

Hoskins came up to Alice on the grass as the rain drenched them and said 'JJ's waiting. Let's get this over with.'

'Yes,' she said quietly.

'Can you help me round up the others?'

As DJ Meat started up a ravishing version of 'Isn't This a Lovely Day to be Caught in the Rain', Alice tapped a number of bopping shoulders and when the group entered the library, JJ faced them at the far end in a large armchair covered in a tapestry woven with varieties of English songbirds. The dog Kevin lay at his feet, Tiny Colin Lark sat on an arm of the chair, and Glory stood behind, resting a hand on JJ's shoulder.

Hoskins and Alice walked towards him with Sidney, Minerva, Bob, Dickon, Pimm, Mrs Bladder-Williams and Justice Royal trailing after in varying degrees of dampness. Outside the elements raged.

'You look like Tiberius,' said Pimm.

'I daren't think what *you* look like.'

'Veronica cut off my ponytail.'

'Castration already. What did she use, a chain saw?'

'Secateurs . . .'

Minerva whimpered and Bob put a supportive arm round her.

'I wish you wouldn't do that, Hosky.'

'Do what, JJ?'

'Look people up and down as if they were items of furniture.'

'I didn't realise.'

'It's not very nice being made to feel like an object that's being judged genuine or repro.'

'That's sort of why we've come. I've been steeling myself.'

'Well, you can unsteel yourself. I'll save you the embarrassment, Mr Hoskins. You were going to tell me that when I succeeded to the title I was not the rightful marquess.'

'That is so.'

Ripples of unease or astonishment all round. The lamplight from the table emphasised the violet of JJ's eyes.

'Where's my daughter?'

'She's gone over to The Crag,' said Alice. 'She said she couldn't face it.'

'She should be with me at a time like this. For those of you who don't know all the painful details – and of course you've got to know everything, haven't you – I really don't know why you're all here – including you, Mr Royal – have you been having a nice dance? Let me see now, Detective Hoskins was going to explain that I had an elder brother and that he was the rightful marquess. We were switched as babies because it turned out that he had a damaged brain. I was born less than a year after he was, so the switch was not difficult to conceal. A semi-vegetable, he spent virtually all his life under the name of John Smith in a nursing home in the next county. Sidney, if you don't sit in a chair at once, I'll call a halt to the proceedings.'

'Forgive me, your lordship. Now the time's come to bring it out, I feel all winded.'

'It's not very pleasant, I agree. Well, ladies and gentlemen, I was not aware of this switch while I was growing up. As you know my father died when I was twelve years old and the title came to me then. The truth of the situation was divulged to me only on my majority at eighteen Divulged to me by you, Sidney, who'd been in on it from the start. Apparently my parents were genetically incompatible so my normality was a bit of a fluke. It was a deception but it was done with the best intentions, for the good of the family, the house, and all that sort of thing. Sidney and I have for some time been the only living souls who knew about it, all other relevant parties having kicked the bucket.'

Sidney rocked backwards and forwards with his hand to his brow and forced himself to say 'Not quite all the relevant parties, my lord'.

'Doesn't any official body check up on these things?' wondered Mrs Bladder-Williams.

JJ was rattled. 'What would you like, madam, a visitation of the heralds? Bob, please help Minnie to a chair.'

'Julius, I was a fluke too, how could you forget!'

'Sorry, yes, you were a fluke too. The first fluke actually. The oldest of the three siblings by some years.'

'Stop it, Julius, don't tell them that!'

'I'm sick of forever skirting round the question of your age . . . '

'Julius, you still haven't grasped the situation.'

'Minnie, you too would be up here with me if you had anything about you!'

'Oh, Sid, I can't take any more,' and Minerva clambered from the library, holding on to the grilles as she went. Not even the mesmeric movements of Hoskins's mouth could detain her.

Bob however was not intending to follow, for he was riveted by the prospect of more revelations, but JJ jumped to his feet, almost knocking Colin off the arm of the chair, and shouted 'For God's sake, man, go and comfort her!'

Bob dutifully slunk out and JJ frowned deeply with closed eyes, pinching the top of the bridge of his nose. He ran a hand slowly through his long hair and with an awkward twist of his bulk he turned to Glory. 'Be an angel and pour me a glass of red wine. Please, everybody, sit down. All this standing about is ridiculous.' He sat down again himself, kissing the top of Tiny Colin's head as he did so. 'It's past your bedtime, Colin.'

'Can't I stay?'

'All right. There's nothing you can't hear. Thanks, love.'

The last two words were addressed to Glory as he passed across the wine. Glory Boy's fingers were stained purple from blackberrying. Something of the delicious aroma clung to them too which, mingling with the whiff of the wine, imparted a small solace to JJ.

Hoskins said 'If you've finished, JJ, there's something I must – '

'I haven't finished. I'd like to say that I feel I should've confessed the truth of the situation years ago, but it seemed such a huge thing and with no benefit to anyone and now my elder brother has died. He died last month at the nursing home as of course you know, Hosky. Sidney organised the funeral. I didn't go myself. Guilt of course. Terrible guilt. But if I was an imposter then, I am not now. His death meant that the title rightfully passes to me and that I have at last become what I always seemed to be. It is unsavoury, I grant you. But the whole business was not of my making. Sidney, I am not blaming you in saying that, so you can take your hands away from your face.'

'Oh, your lordship, oh, oh.'

'Give the old boy a drink, Alice. Please, everybody, take something from the drinks tray. I also have some wonderful news to announce on a completely different subject – '

Hoskins cut in. 'Can we clear this subject up first?'

'It is cleared up.'

'I'm afraid it isn't.'

JJ ran his hands through his hair again with exasperation and asked thickly 'All right, why is everybody looking at me in such a peculiar way?'

'Sidney, is there any chance you could take over from here?' asked Hoskins. The detective was suddenly sensitive and weary.

'Of course . . . ' said the butler. 'Mr Boy, would you kindly help me with this chair?' He directed Glory to place it beside JJ and when he had settled himself into it, Sidney took JJ's hand and gently rubbed the back of it. 'Now, young master, it's going to be all right. I promise you, it's going to be all right.'

'Sidney . . . ' JJ's voice cracked with feeling.

'Really, young master, I promise, it's going to be all right. But what you need to know is that Mr John, when he was in that nursing home place, he fell in love. She was a beautiful young nurse. And they were married.'

'Sidney . . . '

'It was a bit of a surprise to me too, young master, I can tell you. But they were married rightfully and properly and they had a baby together, a son together, and – ' Sidney's voice cracked here too – 'the beautiful young nurse was Melody, Justice's daughter, and the baby . . . the baby . . . the baby . . . '

Sidney's needle was stuck. Justice Royal stepped forward with the bundle he was holding. He didn't like any of this and so far as he was concerned, he was losing his grandson, but he obligingly proffered the infant to JJ's baggy gaze. A string of saliva descended to the carpet from JJ's open jaw and he wiped it away with his hand.

The silence was dire.

Pimm broke it with 'I delivered him . . . '

JJ swivelled bloodshot eyes onto his old college mate and said with a ghastly magisterial detachment 'We all know that'.

'So . . . ' Hoskins tried to carry on from here but petered out again.

Mrs Bladder-Williams came to the assistance of her nephew. 'So – Justice's grandson is the rightful Marquess of Heavenshire.' Her pleasure was visceral but, being by and large a decent soul, she hoped it didn't show.

JJ took a slow-motion sip from his wineglass and crossed his legs. A monogrammed toe stuck out at a sharp angle. Great blocks of granite were rearranging themselves in his head and merely continuing to sit upright was extremely arduous work.

'There's something else, my lord,' said Sidney in a voice as soft as cornflour between the fingertips.

JJ gave a laugh that squeaked oddly. His mouth had gone from very dry to very wet to very dry again and then dried up altogether.

'Is JJ still a lord, Sidney?' asked Dickon. He too was enjoying the noble collapse. Alice moved across to the window and looked into the night. The tempest had slackened but lightning was still aflicker among storm clouds.

'As a younger son he is Lord Julius Popjoy,' said Pimm. He meant to be kind but all he'd done was cue the next blow.

'Mr Hoskins, if you'd be so kind as to continue . . . ' Sidney extended a quavering hand towards the detective. Glory recharged Sidney's glass. 'Much appreciated, Mr Boy.'

It is always painful for a detective to break bad news, particularly to a friend, but it does come with the job and Hoskins rallied by virtue of that professional cynicism which is no more than a peremptory need to get the case wrapped up. Poor JJ looked

from Sidney to Hoskins and back again, wondering what on earth
could be coming next.

'How can I put this? All right. The reason you were secretly
switched as babies, JJ, wasn't only because of brain damage to the
other one. If you think about it, the estate could have been
entailed on you, or whatever they call it, as a true and competent
brother capable of safeguarding the inheritance. It would be
embarrassing of course to have the title borne by a mental defective but a number of distinguished families regularly survive such
embarrassment. No, the switch was made *in secret* on account of
the simple fact that – you weren't a true brother.'

An almighty blankness descended on JJ. He did however hear
a distant thud thud thud as of a discothèque several miles away.
It was his heart beating.

'It seems', continued Hoskins, 'that the first son's brain
damage was caused not by any fundamental genetic incapability
as you have said, but by a problematic birth. The Marchioness
was unable to conceive again and marital relations with the Marquess ceased. By that time they were no longer in love. Your
father, JJ, had for many years used the services of other women to
satisfy his surplus needs. In due course he'd fallen in love with
one of the maids at the Park. She'd been widowed in the war and
had a young daughter. It was a serious relationship. It was also an
impossible one. He and his love exchanged many frank letters.
His letters to her have survived. But the pressure grew intolerable and the maid left Heaven Park in the interests of her own
sanity and went to work at The Crag. But her letters from him
were all she had and she could not bring herself to destroy them.
Instead they were placed for safe-keeping in the hollow heart of
that old oak tree on The Crag lawn. They were discovered only
last year when the tree came down. By the time the maid went to
The Crag she was already pregnant and told the Craddocks she
had to go away but that her daughter could fill her position which
is what happened. She gave birth to a healthy son. She informed
the child's father who persuaded her to relinquish it, to her
undying regret. The family wanted an heir who was fit and who
would be able to continue the family line. Ironically, as we have
discovered, JJ had only a daughter whereas the heir was eventu-

ally produced by the original, brain-damaged son. The maid in question, as you've probably guessed, was the Old Un. Davis's mother. Strange to think that the Old Un was once beautiful and alluring, so much so that your own sister, marquess, who is old enough to remember, used to call her Marilyn Monroe. And the whole business eventually unhinged her mind. Yet, unable to retrieve the letters, and fearing that the truth might never be known, she put much of this in a document which came to light after her death when Mrs Bladder-Williams sorted out her things.'

'Only I knew her true story,' said Sidney, 'and I'd've gone to the grave with it. They were different days. I was sworn to secrecy on the big black Bible down there at the end under the window. And after the birth of the damaged boy and no hope of another child, Lord and Lady Heavenshire were so sad. Many's the dinner Daphne and I served them in total silence. Not a single word spoken through seven courses. That was your mother's name, young master. Daphne. Then Daphne left here and went away from The Crag too. And the Marchioness went away at the same time and when the Marchioness came back she had a beautiful baby boy. And the house became light and happy again. Young master, you brought so much happiness here. So much happiness.'

JJ looked at Sidney but was unable to speak. Each knew what was behind the other's eyes but could have no more put it into words than they could reverse the planets.

The silence lasted and lasted.

Eventually it was Mrs Bladder-Williams who dared to break it. 'I nursed your mother through her last days.'

'Do you want a medal?' wondered JJ. He palmed his eyes and breathed deeply several times. 'Forgive me, Mrs Bladder-Williams. It isn't very easy.'

Hoskins said 'I think that is all for today. We'll leave you now.'

'It isn't all for today,' said JJ, and he threw back his head in a hollow, soundless laugh. He was aware of a rage boiling up from below, a rage at a system which preferred lies to truths, a rage at being stripped in public, a rage at everything, above all a rage at his parents for bringing him to this parlous state, but the rage would take time to identify itself clearly, and he was for the moment blotted out by disbelief. And so he was able to continue with a little of his own agenda.

'I think you might all like to know that in addition to these rather grotty revelations, something marvellous has also happened. Our wonderful conference organiser, Alice, has done us the ultimate good deed. She found the *Astronomical Poems* by Leonardo da Vinci. The manuscript was stolen by one of the Craddocks in Napoleonic times and hidden in a doll which later came back into this house thanks to a raffle ticket. I have been reading the poems, Alice. They are without any emotion and yet very tender and curious, and very delicately illustrated too by the master's sublime left hand. An incomparable treasure which the family is able to sell. So you see, Mr Royal, your beautiful grandson will have a beautifully restored house to grow up in.'

121.

One last horror awaited JJ that night. With Glory's assistance he was about to embark on the spatial adventure which is the Staircase to Eternity when a commotion burst through to the Middle Hall. It was Crystal who flew towards her father like a harpy, shouting 'Surprise, surprise, surprise!' Yes indeed, for she was pushing Ward Dashman ahead of her in a wheelchair. Parts of him were still immobilised in plaster while his head jumped wildly about as though it might at any second drop off and roll against the skirting board. It wore a cretinous grin. 'We thought we'd cheer you up! We've got great news!' exclaimed Crystal.

JJ stared at them in a parlous state.

'Go on, tell him, Ward!'

Ward looked up at JJ with goggle eyes and slobbered 'I've found God, I've found God!'

'And what's really great,' panted Crystal, 'is that I have too!'

For a moment JJ thought he was going to vomit or pass out but steadied himself against Glory and said 'Have you really? Well, next time you see God would you do me a favour and punch him in the mouth?'

122.

The following Sunday Alice drove with Dickon to London. An orange moon rose in a mauve sky across England. The suburbs drew her into thickening streams of traffic and they pulled up outside the white stucco house with its pillared porch. A car alarm was screaming on the corner where a group of young people drank from tins. Tomorrow would be the main day of the Notting Hill Carnival. She opened the front door, checked for mail on the hall table, and they went upstairs to her flat and threw open the windows. Dance music pumped in through the trees. 'We won't get much sleep.'

'Were we going to sleep?' asked Dickon. He was very aroused by being in the city with his loved one.

She looked around. 'Good tenants. No disasters. Forwarded all the post. When were you last in London?'

'When I was a kid.'

'It's worth quite a lot this flat,' she said.

'Good.' And he started to remove her clothes.

The next day hordes of bodies swarmed into the surrounding streets. It was exciting but the sense of pleasure came later, in the evening when the pressure relaxed; and the sense of peace came later still when they lolled on the sofa with the sultry night air shifting through wide-open windows and the whole world with them, buoyant and mellow. After the Bank Holiday Alice visited the estate agent and put the flat on the market. She and Dickon returned to Lower Farm to embark on their new life.

123.

The plan for the Great Demo Against the City of Cognitive Neuroscience was drawn up by the Heavenshire Heritage Group who envisaged a day-long march from Appleminster Cathedral to Milking Magna, with a sit-in and speeches at the Ring of the Moon. The local constabulary predicted a heavy turnout, possibly 25,000 people. In the run-up to the event however, a number of tougher minded protest groups became involved. Then all sorts of people. Press, television and radio caught the fever.

'It must have touched a chord,' said the Chief Constable of Heavenshire.

A couple of days beforehand the routes approaching Appleminster were filled with travellers. Every bus or train arriving in the city was packed solid. The whole area went into gridlock, vehicles were abandoned and their occupants proceeded on foot. By Friday evening the multitudes made the Notting Hill Carnival seem a modest affair and police helicopters calculated that more than 5 million people were drifitng through a landscape of honeysuckle and buttercup, forget-me-not and meadowsweet, towards Milking Magna.

The village to which all journeying was bent had long been full, but now a numb panic reigned. The protesters brought with them a good-natured camaraderie but few were of rural origins and most of the villagers boarded up their windows and prepared for the worst. The Government, roused at the eleventh hour, ordered the police of surrounding counties to block the roads into Heavenshire, but it was too late. Urgent appeals secured several battalions of the King's Own Heavenshires to protect the Temple of Mercury, Heaven Park, and the Ring itself, while a bulletin from the Green Kingdom asked demonstrators to respect these sites as well as private property, livestock and fields with crops, with the implication that the penalties for not doing so didn't bear thinking about. By lunchtime on Saturday the Chief Constable ordered the helicopters to be grounded to avoid aerial accidents as dozens of hot-air balloons sailed across the scene, parachuting food parcels and mini-loos from their baskets.

Daisy and Glory Boy tramped up the hillside but the Heath, unreachable now, was solid humanity, the bracken flattened by patient bottoms waiting for the speeches to begin. They stood awhile, surveying the infestation of the hills: tents, musicians, cooking pots, flags as far as the eye could see.

'By the way I've got a job,' said Daisy.

'You ad a job.'

'I've got a proper job.'

'Where?'

'Boots the chemist. In Appleminster.'

'Lot of travelling.'

'I answered a flatshare ad. I'm moving in next week.'

'Yeah?'

'Pretty spot behind the cathedral.'

'Oh,' said Glory.

'Is that all you can say?'

'Spose you think you're middle-class now.'

'That's a rotten thing to say.'

'Let's go,' said Glory. 'I've ad enough of this.'

The Great Demo continued for several days. The speeches were interminable. But at last this great amoeba of popular feeling, embracing all ages and walks of life, withdrew and dispersed, taking every single piece of litter with it, returning to the cities and suburbs and towns, and to the dreams and hopes for a more beautiful world. Or at least a world in which the gods of greed and despoliation could be kept in their place. Where millions had trodden, the grass and flowers sprang up again and birdsong, bees and the ripple of water were once more heard, and Ragamuffin, who had burst into tears at first glimpse of the gathering alien mass and taken himself far off into the wilderness, now returned to his favourite hillside and, after checking that everything in the view was as it should be, his tear-smudged face broke into an adorable smile. But nothing in the corridors of power was ever the same again.

123.

Directly after the scrapping of the new city in the Puck Valley it was proposed that the county west of Appleminster should become a national park contiguous to that which embraced the Mountains Beyond the West. Many local people objected on the grounds that it rendered them inauthentic but it was the only way to protect Heavenshire from repeated assaults. As for the Brussels allocation of funds, it was diverted to a scheme called Tronitron City in a run-down district of Birmingham.

Being embedded in a protected zone served Heaven Park very well but did not solve the immediate problem of its repair, nor at first did the recovery of the Leonardo book. The manuscript was indeed a treasure and therefore there was an immediate dispute as to ownership, principally between the old trustees of Heaven

Park and the new representatives of the child-marquess, while the British Museum and the Victoria & Albert Museum also advanced claims. Negotiations threatened to stall. Here the King-Mother stepped in. She described Heaven Park as 'one of the forgotten wonders of Europe'. She gave dinners, lobbied MPs and charmed highly placed tycoons. The outcome was the passing of the Heaven Park Resettlement Act which broke the original trust and reformed it, enabling the Leonardo manuscript to be sold and the record-breaking proceeds used to establish the estate on a sound economic footing.

The King-Mother's 'fee' was that the Crown should be permitted to purchase Polpotto's *Massacre of the Innocents*. So after its vagrant history (looted from the Doge's private chapel by corsairs in the seventeenth century, confiscated from the Gangi princes by the Vatican in the eighteenth, sold to the Popjoys in the nineteenth), the great canvas was winched down from the wall between the windows in the cosy, crated up and despatched to Windsor where it was at last reunited in the St George's Hall with its companion piece, *Massacre of the Guilty*.

Once over the initial shocks, JJ took these developments remarkably well. In fact he throve on them. Unchained from his opulent prison, he spent a number of years travelling the world with Glory Boy, having offbeat adventures which he jotted into a journal, and he returned home a slimmer man. Glory stayed on in the middle of the Pacific Ocean to run a bar. They remained friends but JJ was to find a more stabilising love elsewhere.

By the terms of the Resettlement Act virtually nothing of the estate remained in private hands. But the new trust granted JJ, Minerva, Crystal, Sidney, Cook, Ben Thicknesse, sundry others and of course the new marquess, Baby John Popjoy-Royal, incomes and accommodation at the Park. Immacolata quietly married Justice at the Appleminster Register Office. To be the stepmother of a marquess gave her the final social courage she needed. They too lived at the Park, receiving incomes by virtue of their work on the committee constituted to run its affairs until Baby John came of age.

Ward Dashman became a trustee, at Crystal's suggestion, on account of his business acumen. Having recovered the use of his legs, he rented a cottage in the village for a while but when Crystal took off for Santa Fe in Arizona to live with the drummer from Toxic Genitalia (she hadn't found God after all), Ward returned to his wife Larissa who accepted him with thorough contempt. God told Ward to found the Institute for Population Reduction whose desks and files duly occupied The Crag's attic floor. In this task he was greatly assisted by the ghost of Sir Timothy Craddock. For reasons which a psychologist might be able to explain, the twins developed delightful personalities during their father's absence and this development survived his return. Jocasta became a barrister and Fortinbras a green terrorist in what remained of the jungles of South East Asia.

When Pimm had completed the piecing together of the Temple of Mercury, he went off and did the same again to something very similar near Montpellier. He and Veronica lived together but did not marry and showed no interest in adding children to the many entertainments of their life. Stormy Weather's career, once the truth of his transvestism was out, went from strength to strength, and he even sang for the Loyal Family at the Loyal Albert Hall. Blaze Weather Popjoy was raised largely in New Mexico and in adult life became the manager of a department store there and made Stormy a glandfarver several times over.

The new marquess, Baby John, grew up full of love for his country, his county, his estate and his house. During his long reign, not as grand possessor but as guardian, Heaven Park was fully restored to a meticulous standard, with the able assistance of Bunjie Gunj who succeeded Sidney. Justice predicted that Baby John would probably get hitched to some blonde Henrietta with big knockers – and Justice was correct. Baby John's son did likewise – and so did *his* son – and *his* – so that after several generations the Popjoy boys were very fair and started anew to cast their eyes at girls of dark complexion with soft brown eyes. And thus the full spectrum of colours passed backwards and forwards over the House of Popjoy, enriching its beauty and talents. Actually this was only possible, given the overwhelming number of brown and black people in the world, because parents had their embryos genetically modified to produce blonds.

Lady Minerva and Bob Wetmore were married, and being abandoned by his sister – albeit half sister – upset JJ as much as anything. But he wasn't left alone for long. At the age of sixteen, Colin Lark went to live with him and gave him all the love and companionship and worry that anyone could desire. Colin read business studies at university and returned to Heaven Park as Baby John's financial manager. After the sale of the Mill and the divorce settlement, Sylvia Wetmore went off to live in more stables, this time in Gloucestershire. They were attached to another great house, though not of course a house so great as Heaven Park. It belonged to some amusing people called the Madder-Pitters whom she'd first met at Crystal's wedding. They were devotees of trepanning and under their influence Sylvia had a hole bored in her head too. Letting out whatever it was that was let out didn't reduce her weight, which was the original hope, but it did give her the greenest fingers in the West and in the fullness of time she became a successful television personality with a series called *The Fat Gardener.*

Is there anything else to mention? Oh yes. Detective Hoskins, for his achievements in uncovering whatever it was he uncovered, was promoted to Scotland Yard and he and Jason went to live in a large flat overlooking Clapham Common. And dear little big-eared, bug-eyed Joyce, undiscovered, continued her apocalyptic work upstairs in the Village of Recluses, the hub of her global network.

And Alice and Dickon? They were able to buy Lower Farm on the proceeds of the sale of Alice's London flat, Meg's life assurance, the cashing-in of Dickon's pension plan, and a surprising kindness from JJ. The letters from JJ's father to the Old Un, JJ inherited from his mother. The Resettlement Act also granted him copyright which still had many years to run. They were increasingly valuable as the story became known and of interest to the media. JJ eventually bequeathed them to the Heaven Park Trust but he split the copyright with Dickon who had rediscovered and protected them.

Lower Farm went organic and glowed with an inner satisfaction which was only threatened when the polytunnels which increasingly covered its fields were deemed offensive and became the object of a campaign. Hoskins called on Alice and Dickon the day before he moved to London to take up his new position at Scotland Yard.

'Come in, Hosky. Have some tea,' said Dickon.

'Wanted to say goodbye.'

'You've taken out your ear-ring,' observed Alice.

He neatly flexed his bow-lips. 'That's what promotion does.' A sparkle shone in his eyes.

She said 'You know, with all the goings-on, you seem to have forgotten something.'

'What's that then?'

'Those nasty things someone put in my cottage.'

'I told you, we're almost certain Robin Craddock did the first one and Lomax did the last one and I assumed that one or other of em did the ones in between. I think you can rest easy.'

'But you don't really know, do you?'

'Some things in life, Alice, we can never know utterly and completely and you have to accept that or you go round the bend.'

'Do you know what I think, Hosky?' said Dickon. 'I think that ninety-nine point nine per cent of life is done on faith.'

'That's just about it, Dickon, that's just about it. Well, good luck, you two. I best be making tracks.'

They waved his car off down the muddy drive and Dickon took the Land-Rover up to High Field to mend a fence. Alice turned back into the house, poured another cup of tea, and sat by the window as a blackberry and apple pie browned in the oven. Of course she was pregnant, though did not know it yet. A fly buzzed in the window. An earwig walked across the sill.

END